Praise for the Charmed Pie Shoppe Mysteries

Peach Pies and Alibis

"An original, intriguing story line that celebrates women, family, friendship, and loyalty within an enchanted world, with a hint of romance, an engaging cast of characters, and the promise of a continued saga of magical good confronting evil."
—*Kirkus Reviews*

"Adams permeates this unusual novel—and Ella [Mae's] pies—with a generous helping of appeal." —*Richmond Times Dispatch*

"I love the world of Havenwood that Ellery Adams has created and every single one of her characters is fantastic. She fills each book with warmth and humor, and still manages to ground the magical elements within satisfying human conflicts."
—*Badass Book Reviews*

"A great book . . . The mystery kept me guessing but it was the relationship between Ella Mae and her relatives in this character-driven whodunit that made me feel like I was right there as they sought out a killer with an unexpected result." —*Dru's Book Musings*

"A magical story, closer to urban fantasy or magical realism than mystery, although it still has murders and mystery . . . It's absolutely perfect, and left me eager to read the next book when it comes out. It's deep, and dark in spots, with references to Arthurian legends." —*Lesa's Book Critiques*

Pies and Prejudice

"Will leave readers longing for seconds."
—Jenn McKinlay, *New York Times* bestselling author of the Cupcake Bakery Mysteries

"Enchanting! . . . Ellery Adams brings the South to life with the LeFaye women of Havenwood. This new series is as sweet and tangy as a warm Georgia peach pie."
—Krista Davis, national bestselling author of the Domestic Diva Mysteries

"[A] savory blend of suspense, pies, and engaging characters. Foodie mystery fans will enjoy this." —*Booklist*

"A little play of Jane Austen with a nod to Arthurian legend gets this new series from veteran author Adams . . . off to an enchanted start. A sensory delight for those who like a little magic with their culinary cozies." —*Library Journal*

"Charming characters and a cozy setting make this mystery, the first in the series, warm and inviting, like a slice of Ella Mae's pie fresh from the oven." —*The Mystery Reader*

Praise for the Books by the Bay Mysteries

"Not only a great read, but a visceral experience. Olivia Limoges's investigation into a friend's murder will have you hearing the waves crash on the North Carolina shore. You might even feel the ocean winds stinging your cheeks. Visit Oyster Bay and you'll long to return again and again."
—Lorna Barrett, *New York Times* bestselling author of the Booktown Mysteries

"Adams's plot is indeed killer, her writing would make her the star of any support group, and her characters . . . are a diverse, intelligent bunch . . . *A Killer Plot* is a perfect excuse to go coastal." —*Richmond Times Dispatch*

"I could actually feel the wind on my face, taste the salt of the ocean on my lips, and hear the waves crash upon the beach. *The Last Word* made me laugh, made me think, made me smile, and made me cry. *The Last Word*—in one word—AMAZING!"
—*The Best Reviews*

"A very well-written mystery with interesting and surprising characters and a great setting. Readers will feel as if they are in Oyster Bay." —*The Mystery Reader*

"This series is one I hope to follow for a long time, full of fast-paced mysteries, budding romances, and good friends. An excellent combination!" —*The Romance Readers Connection*

Pecan Pies and Homicides

Ellery Adams

BERKLEY PRIME CRIME, NEW YORK

THE BERKLEY PUBLISHING GROUP
Published by the Penguin Group
Penguin Group (USA) LLC
375 Hudson Street, New York, New York 10014

USA • Canada • UK • Ireland • Australia • New Zealand • India • South Africa • China

penguin.com

A Penguin Random House Company

PECAN PIES AND HOMICIDES

A Berkley Prime Crime Book / published by arrangement with the author

Berkley Prime Crime Books are published by The Berkley Publishing Group.
BERKLEY® PRIME CRIME and the PRIME CRIME logo are
trademarks of Penguin Group (USA) LLC.

For information, address: The Berkley Publishing Group,
a division of Penguin Group (USA) LLC,
375 Hudson Street, New York, New York 10014.

ISBN: 978-0-425-25241-3

PUBLISHING HISTORY
Berkley Prime Crime mass-market edition / January 2014

PRINTED IN THE UNITED STATES OF AMERICA

10 9 8 7 6 5 4 3 2

Cover illustration by Julia Green.
Cover design by Diana Kolsky.
Interior design by Laura K. Corless.

For my friend Judy Beatty.
Thank you for working your special magic.

Promise me no promises,
So will I not promise you:
Keep we both our liberties,
Never false and never true:
Let us hold the die uncast,
Free to come as free to go:
For I cannot know your past,
And of mine what can you know?

—"Promises Like Pie-Crust" by Christina Rossetti

Chapter 1

"Do I have icicles hanging from my beard?" asked a small elderly man as Ella Mae LeFaye ushered him into her pie shop. She tried to shut the door quickly against the cold, but a breath of winter stole inside. The other customers hunched their shoulders and shivered as the brisk air snaked under the collars of their heaviest sweaters. Cradling their coffee cups, they launched into a fresh round of complaints about the record lows northwest Georgia had been experiencing for the past three weeks.

"Don't get your scarves in a knot, folks. I'm comin' around with coffee as fast as I can!" announced a middle-aged woman with nut-brown hair and the sharp chin and high cheekbones of a pixie. She filled half a dozen mugs and then intercepted Ella Mae on her way to the kitchen. "You've gotta warm these people up. And you know I'm not referrin' to the thermostat. What's in the oven? Somethin' real special, I hope."

Ella Mae gestured at the chalkboard menu mounted behind the counter. "Lots of health-conscious dishes. It's

the beginning of January, Reba. The whole town is on a diet.
Except for you. You're in perfect shape, as always."

"Don't try to butter me up. And I know what the specials
are. I'm a waitress, for cryin' out loud. You've got a fine list
of hot dishes written on that blackboard. Cheesy quiches and
meat and potato pies. Warm berry cobblers and molten
chocolate tarts. But where's the *heat*?" Reba put her hands
on her hips. "I know you've been feelin' wrung out lately,
but these folks need somethin' *more*." She shot a quick glance
around the room and then lowered her voice to a conspirato-
rial whisper. "It'll do you good to give them a dose of magic.
You haven't used any in weeks."

Ella Mae pivoted to look at her customers. As a whole,
their faces were pale and wan. The Charmed Pie Shoppe
was normally an animated place, full of conversation and
laughter, but today it felt lifeless and dull. Ella Mae's gaze
swept over the room, and she couldn't help but notice the
empty tables. A few months ago, there wouldn't have been
a vacant seat in the place.

Frowning, Ella Mae was about to turn away when her
eyes fell on the elderly gentleman she'd let into the pie shop.
He was clutching the lapels of his wool coat with the thin
fingers of one hand and reaching for his coffee cup with the
other. His lips had a bluish cast and his scraggly beard did
nothing to hide the gauntness of his cheeks. At that moment,
he looked up and caught Ella Mae staring. In his pale blue
eyes she imagined too many long and lonely winter nights
and wondered if he spent most of his evenings sitting in
front of a fire, dreaming of springtime and warm memories.
Though she couldn't recall his name, Ella Mae knew that
the old man lived a solitary life in a crude cabin off the
mountain road. The fact that he'd driven to town in this
weather made Ella Mae realize that he must be desperate
for a homemade meal and a little companionship.

The old man lowered his face so that it hovered above
his mug. He closed his eyes as the steam flooded over his

wrinkled skin, and Ella Mae could see the slightest loosening of his shoulders. Ella Mae turned back to Reba. "Okay, I'll do it. I'll bring him a summer day. I'll give him heat and the drone of insects and the sound of fish splashing in the lake. I'll remind him that he belongs to this community—that he matters. I'll make him smile from the inside out," she promised and pushed through the swing doors into the kitchen.

Ella Mae had just begun to comb the shelves of dry goods in search of a particular ingredient when Reba entered the room. She perched on a stool and pulled a red licorice stick from her apron pocket. "What do you have up your sleeve? A little cayenne pepper? Some dried jalapeños? Curry?"

"Red Hots," Ella Mae said, dragging a stepstool in front of the shelves. She climbed to the top step and reached for a plastic tub of bright red candy. "There you are."

"That old man's dentures don't stand a chance," Reba muttered.

"Don't worry about his or anyone else's dental work. I'm going to bake them into a pie. An apple pie," Ella Mae said, jumping off the stepstool. "Trust me."

Reba put a hand over her heart. "With my life. Always." She popped the rest of her licorice stick into her mouth, plated two orders of spinach and mushroom quiche with a side of field greens, and left the kitchen, humming as she walked.

Ella Mae peeled, cored, and sliced apples. While she worked, her mind began to wander.

"Hot," she murmured as her knife flashed side to side and up and down, chopping the apples into bite-sized pieces. The word automatically called forth an image of Hugh Dylan, the man she'd been in love with since high school. She could practically feel his muscular arms sliding around her back, pulling her in for a deep kiss. "No. That is not the kind of heat I need to generate. I need something with a PG rating."

Adding the cinnamon Red Hots and a tablespoon of lemon juice to a saucepan, Ella Mae cooked the mixture on low heat. As the candies melted, her thoughts drifted back to her childhood, to a steamy July afternoon on the banks of Lake Havenwood. She remembered how her mother and her three aunts, Verena, Sissy, and Dee, had stretched out on picnic blankets. The four beautiful sisters sipped Tab soda and gossiped while they sunbathed. Ella Mae's mother, who wore a red and white polka dot bikini and a black straw sunhat, looked every inch the movie star to her gangly, freckled daughter.

"Mom," Ella Mae whispered, jerking the wooden spoon out of the saucepan. "I can't think about her. If I do, all of my customers will be sad. I need to find a memory that can't be tainted by my present problems. Something innocent and sweet."

Removing the pan from the heat, Ella Mae poured honey and a pinch of cinnamon into the mixture and began to stir it with slow, deliberate strokes. The aroma of the honey made her think of the bees that gathered around the raspberry bushes along Skipper Drive during the peak of summer. Suddenly, she was a teenager again. It was another humid day. This one was in August, and Ella Mae was older than she'd been in the memory involving her mother and aunts, though she was still gangly and freckled.

In this memory, she was fifteen. School would be starting soon. Determined to savor every last moment of freedom, Ella Mae had ridden to the swimming hole with a towel and a transistor radio in her bike basket. She wore a cherry-red swimsuit under a Bee Gees T-shirt and her favorite pair of cutoffs and felt completely carefree.

Because a street fair was being held downtown, the other kids of Havenwood were unlikely to be at the swimming hole that day. And when Ella Mae dumped her bike at the top of the dirt path and raced down through the dense trees to the water, she saw that she had the popular hangout spot all to herself. Shucking her clothes, she climbed to an outcrop of rock and dove off, a blur of long limbs and a tangle of whiskey-colored hair rocketing toward the cool water.

Once the dust and sweat had been washed away and she'd grown tired of floating on her back and gazing up at the circle of trees, Ella Mae climbed out of the swimming hole and found a flat boulder to sit on. Dragonflies flitted through the air and she could feel the heat from the warm stone soaking into her skin. She lay back against its smooth surface, feeling every muscle in her body relax. She rested like this until the sun had dried the last drops of water from her skin and she felt the stirrings of hunger.

Ella Mae got up to gather wild raspberries from the nearby bushes. When her hands were brimming with berries, she brought them back to the flat stone and ate them one by one, relishing each sweet and slightly tart bite. When she couldn't eat any more, she leaned back on the stone again and sang "How Deep Is Your Love" at the top of her lungs. She didn't care that she was off-key or that the echoes of her song startled a pair of whip-poor-wills from their nest in a pile of leaves. She shouted an apology to them as they rose into the clear sky, flying higher and higher until they were tiny pencil dots on a canvas of endless blue.

Years later, Ella Mae now stood in her pie shop's kitchen and remembered every moment of that perfect summer afternoon. Holding on to that feeling of warmth and utter contentment, she scooped up a handful of apple pieces and loosely arranged them in a pan lined with her homemade piecrust.

Smiling, she poured the melted candy mixture on top of the apples and then dropped tiny squares of butter over the fruit filling. After weaving a lattice top crust, Ella Mae brushed the dough with a beaten egg yolk and then sprinkled it with finishing sugar and put it in the oven.

She was cutting a ham, wild rice, and caramelized onion tart into generous wedges when Reba reappeared. "Perfect.

I've got six folks waitin' on that tart." She raised her nose and gave the air a sniff. "You did it! I don't even have to taste the pie to know that it'll light a fire inside your customers— like they've gone and swallowed a pack of sparklers. The magic is thick as a cloud all around you. You're gettin' real strong, Ella Mae."

"What good has magic ever brought me?" Ella Mae demanded. "Being enchanted has robbed me of my mother and forced me to keep secrets from the man I love."

Reba made a strangled sound in the back of her throat. "Regardless of your thoughts on magic, we still need an extra pair of hands. The two of us can't run this place from dawn to dusk. I could ask around. See if any of our kind are lookin' for a part-time job."

Ella Mae shook her head. "Hiring someone to take the position as a way of paying homage to my family won't work. It was my mother who sacrificed herself to keep all of us safe, not me. I don't want people doing me favors because she was brave and selfless." She finished adding garnishes to the tart orders. "No, I need to hire a waitress from outside Havenwood, though finding someone interested in moving to an isolated mountain town in the middle of winter to serve pie isn't going to be easy. If I'd held interviews when this place was packed, when it was hip and fun, then it would have been more of a draw. But now? I hear people whispering that The Charmed Pie Shoppe won't see its first anniversary. Maybe they're right. We have smaller and smaller crowds every week."

"My tips have been mighty lousy too," Reba complained. "I keep tellin' you that it's time to snap out of it. I know Christmas was awful rough without your mama, but you're not alone. You've got me and your aunts and your best friend, Suzy. And you've got sweet Chewy and that beautiful fire-man. Your louse of a husband is now officially an ex-husband, so you and Hugh are free to do all sorts of things together." She fanned herself with her order pad. "Lord help me, but I'd better think about somethin' else or I may just spontaneously combust."

Grinning, Ella Mae grabbed a handful of flour and tossed it at Reba. "Don't you have customers to serve? What about that old man?"

"His name's Mr. Crump," Reba said. "And he's takin' his sweet time over lunch. I don't think he has much to go home to."

Glancing at her watch, Ella Mae inhaled a breath of cinnamon, baking apples, and buttery dough. "Whatever you do, don't let him leave. I made this pie specifically for him. Just keep topping off his coffee."

"The poor guy's gonna float away," Reba mumbled. After placing the ham and onion tarts on a tray, she made room for a slice of cranberry and almond pie and a pear crumble drizzled in warm cardamom vanilla custard and left the kitchen.

Ella Mae stared at the empty cooling racks next to the oven and thought that not so long ago they'd been loaded with pies and tarts. A few months ago, Ella Mae had barely been able to keep up with the in-house and takeout orders. She'd had to turn down catering requests because she was too busy baking and serving half the town on a daily basis. She drove around Havenwood in her retired U.S. mail Jeep, waving at friends and neighbors like a homecoming queen. Everyone recognized her pink raspberry truck. One of Aunt Dee's artist friends had transformed the white Jeep. A luscious cherry pie glistened on the driver's-side door while a peach pie with a lattice crust sparkled on the passenger side. Silver stars shot across the hood, and the name, location, and phone number of the pie shop had been painted in a butter yellow font across both side panels.

"This is the most beautiful car I've ever seen!" Ella Mae had exclaimed when Dee revealed the transformed mail truck. But now the Jeep was encrusted with dirt and needed an oil change. Like everything else in Ella Mae's life, the lovely truck was showing signs of neglect.

Until I can find a way to free my mother, nothing else matters, Ella Mae thought. For the thousandth time, her mind returned to the moment in which her mother had sacrificed herself to renew the magic of Havenwood's sacred grove. Adelaide LeFaye had spread her arms and leaned against the rough bark of the shriveled and dying ash tree. In the space of a few horrible and spellbinding seconds, the tree and Ella Mae's mother had merged. Instantly, the grove's power had been restored and everyone had celebrated. Everyone but those close to Adelaide. In the beginning, Ella Mae had been able to communicate with her mother, but with each passing day, she became less and less human. Eventually, she would forget that she had a daughter.

The oven timer beeped, jarring Ella Mae from her maudlin reverie. The Red Hot Apple Pie was done baking. Grabbing a pair of potholders, Ella Mae opened the oven door and a blast of cinnamon-spiced air rushed out to greet her. Unlike the sharp, wintry wind that had snuck inside the shop with Mr. Crump, this was a warm and gentle caress.

Without waiting for the pie to cool, Ella Mae cut a large wedge and plated it. Pushing through the kitchen's swing door, she carried the dessert to Mr. Crump and set it before him. "This is on the house," she said, smiling. "When you mentioned having icicles hanging from your beard, I felt inspired to bake you something special. I promise that it'll only take one bite to transport you to a place of sunshine and birdsong." With that, Ella Mae moved behind the counter and began to assemble takeout boxes that she didn't need. From the corner of her eye, she watched Mr. Crump study the pie warily. Eventually, he lifted a forkful to his mouth.

Ella Mae held her breath.

Reba came around the counter to refill the coffee carafe. "Don't worry, hon. You were born to inject food with magic. To influence how folks feel. That, and so much more. Watch Mr. Crump there. Watch how he changes for the better. If you'd just believe in the good your gifts can do, then you'll realize that you're capable of anythin'. You can rescue your mama, unite your kind, and bake a helluva pie. Watch and believe."

Reluctantly, Ella Mae complied. She saw Mr. Crump chew, swallow, and hesitate. He stared down at the food on his plate as if he couldn't comprehend what he'd just tasted. Clearly surprised, he took another bite. A glint of light surfaced in his eyes and as he continued to devour the pie, his entire face started to glow. His sallow cheeks turned pink and his mouth curved into a wide, boyish smile. After one more bite, he was shrugging off his coat and unwinding the threadbare scarf wrapped like a noose around his thin neck.

"What's in this pie?" he shouted. His voice was no longer weak and reedy. It resonated with strength and virility.

The other patrons stopped talking and turned to see what Mr. Crump was eating.

"It's a Red Hot Apple Pie," Ella Mae said, stepping out from behind the counter. "I was hoping it would warm you up."

"It's done more than that, my girl!" Mr. Crump sat back in his chair and grinned at her. The joyful expression transformed him, erasing years from his skin and making his eyes shine like sunlight on the lake. He stood up, tossing back the dregs of his coffee as if it were a shot of whiskey, and turned to face the other customers. After clearing his throat, he began to sing.

Ella Mae didn't recognize the melody or the lyrics about woods and fertile meadows, but the song painted a picture of the mountains surrounding Havenwood. She could visualize the blue hills as they looked in springtime, dressed in green leaves and sunshine.

At first, the pie shop's customers gaped at Mr. Crump, but by the time he'd reached the third stanza, their gazes had turned wistful and several of them swayed in their chairs.

And then, a woman who'd been sitting alone near the rotating display case slowly rose to her feet and added her soft, sweet soprano to Mr. Crump's rich baritone. Together, they sang. The words soared through the pie shop like graceful birds, casting a spell over everyone in the room.

Hail to the blue green grassy hills;
Hail to the great peaked hummocky mountains;
Hail to the forests, hail to all there,
Content I would live there forever.

When the song was finished, Ella Mae and her patrons clapped heartily and someone cried, "I'd like what he had for dessert!"

The request was taken up by all of her customers.

"You'd best get back in the kitchen, girl," Reba said with a sly wink. "Keep on singin' folks," she announced gaily. "A slice of Red Hot Apple Pie in exchange for a song."

As Ella Mae hurried through the swing door, she heard the organist from the Methodist church sing the opening line of the hymn "Another Year Is Dawning."

Surrounded by music and warmth, Ella Mae began rolling out dough.

Two hours later, she peeked into the dining room and was surprised to see that none of her customers had left. Some had changed seats to chat with other diners, and the organist and the town florist were playing cards with Mr. Crump, but every person was still there. The room had grown loud. Gone was the subdued lunchtime murmur, replaced by story swapping and raucous laughter.

"Has a nice ring to it, don't you think?" Reba asked, looking smug.

Nodding, Ella Mae reached for the tray of dirty dishes Reba had set on the counter. "Okay, you're right. I've been moping far too long. My mother wouldn't want that. She'd want to see what I'm seeing: the people of her community coming together to share a meal, a song, and a laugh."

"Like I said before, anythin' is possible," Reba said gently as the two women returned to the kitchen. "Break your mama's spell. Yes. But don't forget to weave a few of your own. Speakin' of that subject, Suzy Bacchus just came in. She looks like a kid waitin' to ride the Ferris wheel. She's so antsy that I couldn't even get her to sit down. Want me to send her back?"

Ella Mae, who'd been busy loading cutlery into the dishwasher, froze. "Please. And can you ask her to bring me a cup of coffee? The day feels like it's lasting forever. Not that I mind. I'm thrilled with what's happening in that dining room. I just need a jolt of caffeine before I clean the kitchen."

"Sure, I'll let Suzy play waitress. But I'm not sharin' my tips," Reba teased and then vanished through the swing door.

Suzy Bacchus owned Havenwood's book and gift store, an eclectic shop called the Cubbyhole. Like Ella Mae, she had special abilities. Suzy had a photographic memory. Despite the fact that her mind was a storehouse of knowledge, she was humble, bubbly, and fun. Whenever she entered a room, she immediately filled it with positive energy. When she breezed into The Charmed Pie Shoppe's kitchen, Ella Mae felt as if the lights shone a little brighter.

"I have big news!" Suzy said, setting a coffee mug on the wooden worktable. She yanked off her fuchsia hat and a pair of hand-knitted mittens and tossed the accessories on top of a crate of potatoes.

"I'm all ears."

After pushing back a lock of light brown hair from her cheek, Suzy took a deep breath and said, "I know we've spent the past few months poring over any and all references to the Flower of Life in hopes that it would free your mom. We started at the beginning by researching the Gilgamesh legend. That story described the original Flower of Life."

"Suzy, we've read everything under the sun about Gilgamesh. I'm sick to death of the guy. He got his flower. We need to find another one. Preferably, within driving distance."

Suzy grabbed Ella Mae's hands. "That's what I'm here to tell you! According to the Gaelic scroll I found in your family's library, these magical blooms can be found near our sacred groves. In other words, if a sacred grove is located near a body of water, then there's a Flower of Life growing in the deepest part of that water."

"Like a lake? As in Lake Havenwood?"

Suzy's eyes glimmered with triumph. "I think so, yes." Her exultant expression dimmed a little. "There's just one teeny tiny complication."

"Naturally," Ella Mae grumbled and then quickly squeezed her friend's hand. "I'm sorry. You've been such an amazing friend. I have no right to take my frustration out on you."

"*I* should be mad at *you*. Do you realize that I've gained ten pounds since we started hanging out?" She gave Ella Mae a wolfish grin. "Speaking of which, what's got your customers feeling so merry? It's like Christmas in that dining room."

Ella Mae cut a wedge of Red Hot Apple Pie for Suzy. "You can have the whole pie if you'll finish telling me what you learned."

"You've got yourself a deal!" Suzy popped a bite into her mouth and nodded enthusiastically. "Hmmm. This is *good*." Licking her lips, she said, "To make a long and complicated story short and complicated, I'll begin by saying that over two hundred years ago, a local man wrote a book called *Lake Lore of the Americas*. I can only find references to this book in other authors' bibliographies. But apparently, this nifty little tome was all about lake magic. Elemental spirits. Sea foam women appearing to the colonists. That sort of thing. There's also a whole chapter devoted to the rare and powerful objects *within* certain lakes. And while I can't track down an actual copy of *Lake Lore of the Americas*, I believe I know someone who can. Are you ready to hear the awesome part?"

"I am." Suzy's optimism was contagious. Ella Mae could feel it singing through her blood, more beautiful and sweet than any of the tunes she'd heard today.

"Because the author was from Havenwood, his family might have a copy of his book. I bet the print run was quite small, and since the subject matter was obscure, the title's virtually disappeared off the face of the earth. Still, I like to think that at least one copy would have been kept by his children and his children's children."

"Let's hope so." Ella Mae touched the burn scar on her palm. It was shaped like a four-leaf clover and she often rubbed the smooth, puckered skin when she was anxious. She'd gotten the burn several months ago when a glass pie dish had slipped from a potholder and made contact with her skin. According to legend, the mark indicated that she might be the Clover Queen, a woman born of two magical parents who would one day unite the descendants of Morgan le Fay and Guinevere and forever break the curse placed upon their kind by the warlock, Myrddin.

Suzy shot a quick, fascinated glance at the burn before meeting Ella Mae's gaze. "The only drawback is that you don't exactly get along with his descendants."

"Let me guess," Ella Mae said miserably. "He's a Gaynor."

Suzy nodded. "And I know exactly when to broach the subject of the book with your old pal, Loralyn."

Saying nothing, Ella Mae only raised her brows.

"I've been invited to a party at their place tonight," Suzy continued airily. "Guess who's going to be my plus one?"

Ella Mae groaned.

"That's the spirit! Now why don't you go home, take a long, hot bath, and put on your nicest dress? We can have a cocktail before we head over to . . . what's the name of their estate?"

"Rolling View," Ella Mae said. "Listen, Suzy. I know that you're on good terms with the Gaynors, and really, I'm happy about that. The feud between our families is just that. A feud between our families. But they won't be pleased when I show up tonight. I haven't been to their house since Loralyn's seventh birthday party."

"What happened at that party?"

Smiling, Ella Mae said, "I hit Loralyn with a Wiffle ball bat."

Suzy's jaw dropped. "You went Babe Ruth on the birthday girl?"

"I was aiming for the piñata, I swear, but I was blindfolded and Loralyn's friends had spun me around so many times that I didn't know which way was up, so I just stumbled forward as fast as I could and swung away." Ella Mae smiled wickedly. "You should have heard the *smack* the bat made when it connected with Loralyn's cheek. I hightailed it out of there without even bothering to pick up my loot bag."

Suzy started laughing. She threw back her head and let the laughter bubble out of her. She couldn't seem to stop. Before long, Ella Mae was laughing too.

Reba entered the kitchen a moment later and glanced at the two friends. "I don't know why the two of you are hootin' and hollerin' like hyenas on crack, but I came back to say that I've started kickin' folks out. It's time to close and I've made enough cash to enjoy myself at the bowling alley tonight." She gave her apron pocket a satisfied pat. "All thanks to your special pie, Ella Mae."

"And Mr. Crump?" Ella Mae asked. "Is he still feeling good?"

Reba snorted. "I haven't seen a happier man in ages. Well, other than the ones who wake up next to me, of course. Mr. Crump's been invited to play bingo tonight and bunco next Monday. And if he wasn't a churchgoer before, he's gonna become one real fast. That organist is sweet on him. Cal Evans wants to go ice fishin' with him. That man's calendar is fillin' up." Reba studied Ella Mae. "What about yours? You have any special plans for tonight?"

"Yes," Ella Mae said. "I'm going to fortify myself with a few shots of whiskey, pack my Colt in an evening bag, and crash the Gaynors' party."

"That's my girl," Reba said, beaming.

Chapter 2

That night, Ella Mae grew restless waiting for Suzy to show up so they could drive to the Gaynors' party together. Pulling on a heavy coat, she grabbed a bottle of wine and two glasses, and whistled for Chewy. Together, she and her terrier strolled through her mother's garden. There was a hush over all the dormant plants, and the only light came from the reflection of the stars off the windows of Partridge Hill, Ella Mae's childhood home. The main house was empty now, and though Ella Mae's aunts had urged her to move in, she refused to leave the cozy guest cottage tucked in a secluded nook in the rear of the property. Partridge Hill was her mother's domain and Ella Mae refused to give up on the idea that her mother would soon return to take care of it.

Finally, she heard Suzy's car and sent Chewy to fetch her friend. Her faithful dog returned a minute later, Suzy following on his heels. "In case you haven't noticed, it's the dead of winter." She pointed at the wineglass in Ella Mae's hand. "And where's mine?"

"I didn't mean to start without you," Ella Mae said with a wry smile. "I was just letting it breathe."

"Sure, you were. I can see it breathing all the way to your lips." She looked around. "What are you doing out here anyway? It's freezing!"

Ella Mae smiled. "I wanted to see if the New Year's roses had bloomed yet. When January 1 came and went and the buds hadn't opened, I was certain that the bush had died. Noel has a green thumb, but he doesn't have my mother's gift."

"No," Suzy agreed. "But I'm glad he and Kelly are taking care of her house and yard. I wish you'd invite one of your aunts to move in until your mom comes back. I don't like you being here alone."

"I have Chewy," Ella Mae reminded her. "Though my sweet boy isn't a puppy anymore. And I think he needs a friend. Even when I'm around, I'm not giving him enough attention. He wants to play every second of the day. See?"

Suzy glanced to where the Jack Russell, whose formal name was Charleston Chew, sat on his haunches on the garden path. He had a stick in his mouth and his short tail was thumping against the ground in a feverish rhythm.

"Come here, Chewy!" Ella Mae clapped her hands and the terrier ran to her. When he was close enough to be touched, he paused for half a heartbeat and then zipped by the two women without giving them a chance to grab the stick.

"You're such a tease," Suzy chided, laughing. "I'll bring Jasmine over on Sunday afternoon. She can chase Chewy all over the yard while we're hopefully perusing the pages of *Lake Lore of the Americas*."

Ella Mae led Suzy to the garden bench where she'd left a carafe of red wine alongside an empty glass. "We can go back inside now."

"Not until you show me this rose. I've never seen one before."

Suzy poured herself half a glass of wine and followed Ella Mae around a statue of Pan to where a semicircle of rose-bushes sat huddled against the side of the house. Like most of the plants, the bushes were brown and leggy. Yet here and there, tiny white roses bloomed amid the tangle of twigs and thorns. The petals were paper-thin and fragile and were streaked with pale blue veins.

"They're not that pretty," Ella Mae said. "It's the scent that makes them so special. Go on, give them a sniff."

Suzy leaned over one of the roses, closed her eyes, and inhaled deeply. "I smell grass covered with a layer of frost. And pine trees." She paused and smelled the roses again. "And a trace of peppermint." Straightening, she smiled at Ella Mae. "Your mother's magic is still here."

"I have to bring her back. She'll need to bring this place to life when winter's over. I just don't know how I'm going to convince the Gaynors to help. Our families called an uneasy truce at the harvest, but I've barely seen them since. I'm sure Loralyn's been hatching all kinds of diabolical plots and has probably seduced another rich old fool with a heart condition. She'll get him to marry her and then do her best to cause his next heart attack."

"Is she really that bad?" Suzy asked.

Ella Mae paused and tried to put her feelings for her nemesis into words. "She's a bully. Always has been and always will be. And she uses people. Takes what she wants from them and then tosses them away like garbage. With her looks, money, and talent, she could do so much good, but making the world a better place has never been her goal." Ella Mae put her arm through Suzy's and led her out of the garden. "But I'm glad to hear that she's nice to you. I'd like to think there's another side to her than the one I know."

Suzy shrugged. "She buys almost every health and beauty book and magazine I get in. It keeps Jasmine in organic dog treats for months." She nudged Ella Mae in the side. "Just keep your eye on the prize tonight. Besides, you're the daughter of the Lady of the Ash. Everyone has to treat you with respect and you should have been invited to this party anyway, considering it's for a bunch of our kind from Tennessee. Loralyn told me that their grove was destroyed a few days after Christmas."

Ella Mae gasped. "How awful!" The loss of a grove meant the end of magic for the people living nearby. If they didn't relocate to a new town with a source of power, they'd eventually lose their gifts. "Maybe the Gaynors are actually going to help others for a change. I'd love to see that." She let Chewy back into her house and then jiggled her car keys. "I'll drive, though you might regret it later when the bouncers toss me out. When Loralyn and I get together, there's always some drama."

"You're on a quest," Suzy said. "There's supposed to be drama. The dull stories never make it into the books."

"The stories are all wrong anyway," Ella Mae said. "The real versions are locked away in secret libraries like the one in my mother's house. I can only imagine what tales the Gaynors have hidden inside theirs."

"Oh, what I'd give to find out!" Suzy cried. "Just be on your best behavior. We really need to see their copy of *Lake Lore of the Americas*. If they have one, that is."

"They must," Ella Mae said firmly. And under her breath, she added, "And I'll do anything to get it from them."

Dozens of cars blocked Rolling View's circular driveway so Ella Mae parked her Jeep on the side of Sulphur Springs Road. At the entrance of the Gaynors' Georgian mansion, a woman clad in black pants, a white blouse, and a burgundy vest took their coats while a man in matching uniform offered them a glass of champagne.

"I like the way this party is starting," Suzy said and took a sip. "Hmm, nice bubbly."

Ella Mae glanced at the enormous portrait of Opal

Gaynor hanging over a mahogany hall table. Opal must have been about sixteen when she sat for the painting. She was dressed in a debutante's gown of shimmering white, and though her waves of golden hair and regal features were lovely, her eyes were cold and calculating, lending her a hardness that didn't suit her tender age or demure posture.

"An example of what good breeding looks like," said a haughty voice from behind Ella Mae. "You should take notes."

Ella Mae turned and gave Loralyn Gaynor a polite smile. "I apologize for being here without an invitation. Suzy asked me to accompany her and I couldn't say no." She forced herself to smile even wider. "The parties at Rolling View are always the most talked-about events of the season, and since Suzy didn't want to come alone, I didn't want her to miss out."

"How generous of you," Loralyn said with icy courtesy. She smoothed her strapless black gown and pivoted to welcome Suzy as if they were the best of friends. Hugging her, she exclaimed, "You're gorgeous! I told you that moisturizing facial would make you radiant."

Suzy gave Ella Mae a helpless shrug. "Loralyn keeps trying to make me glamorous." She gestured at the luxurious surroundings. "Speaking of glamour, you must give me the grand tour. This place is divine. I'd also like to thank your mother for putting me on the guest list. Is she around?"

"She's in the kitchen instructing the caterers," Loralyn said. She glanced behind her to make sure that none of the hired help was within earshot. A waiter saw her looking and moved forward with a tray of hors d'oeuvres, but Loralyn waved him off with an impatient flick of the wrist and whispered, "We're entertaining the upper crust from a small town west of Chattanooga. Their grove is gone. Forever." She tried to sound sympathetic but failed. Ella Mae wondered if the Gaynors were working on a way to profit from others' misfortunate.

"Suzy's grove was destroyed by developers," Ella Mae said, uncertain whether Loralyn was aware of this fact. "That's how she ended up in Havenwood." She didn't want Loralyn to say anything insensitive about the displaced Tennesseans. It had been horribly upsetting for Suzy to have to leave her home on the North Carolina coast. "What happened to the grove in Tennessee?"

"Someone set fire to it." Loralyn was unable to conceal the gleam in her eyes. Even as a child, she'd relished tales of devastation and tragedy. "The whole thing burned to the ground. Even the Lady of the Ash is gone. She's nothing more than a pile of black cinders." She covered her mouth with her hand. "I'm sorry, Ella Mae. I didn't mean for you to imagine your own mother meeting a similar fate."

Ella Mae pushed down the rage welling inside her. "I'm not. But perhaps this is a good time to remind you that your powers are intact because my mother committed a brave and selfless act? She sacrificed her life for our kind. All of us—not just the rich and influential. I see you and your family have only invited the highborn tonight. What will happen to the rest of the people from Tennessee?"

Loralyn gave an eloquent shrug of her bare shoulders. "I don't know. Why don't you hire a few of them? Or has business fallen off too much for you to need any extra help?"

Suzy cleared her throat. "Come on, ladies. Isn't this supposed to be a party?" She took Loralyn's arm in hers. "I heard that the Gaynors are one of Georgia's first families. You must have some amazing books. Could I see your library? Pretty please?"

"Forgive my rudeness, Suzy." Loralyn's voice was a soft purr. "Ella Mae and I have known each other for so long that we sometimes act like kids and need a third party to act as referee. Thanks for blowing the whistle." She smiled. "Come on. I'll show you our entire collection. I'm sure Ella Mae would prefer to mingle. Perhaps she'll even drum up a new customer or two."

"Actually, I need to speak with your mother," Ella Mae said crisply. "As the Lady's daughter, I should be involved in any decisions about relocating these Tennesseans to Havenwood."

At this, Loralyn widened her eyes. "No one wanted to burden you. Ever since the harvest, you've seemed too fragile to be burdened with our affairs."

As much as it stung, Ella Mae couldn't deny the truth of that remark. She suddenly realized how her obsession with freeing her mother had caused her to neglect her duties. It was her responsibility to keep abreast of the major issues concerning her kind. Yet, she'd been so wrapped up in her personal quest that she had no idea what those issues were. "You're right, Loralyn. I haven't been playing the part my mother fought so hard to win me, but that's going to change as of this moment."

Suzy gave her a thumbs-up and then tugged on Loralyn's arm. "Enough of the serious stuff. Loralyn, please tell me that some of these wealthy and powerful men from Tennessee are also young, hot, and single. I have a feeling it's going to be a long winter and I need someone to keep me warm."

Loralyn laughed and pulled Suzy after her into the next room. Ella Mae watched them disappear in a crowd of elegant men and women and then headed for the kitchen. The catering staff swarmed around the cavernous space like an army of ants—chopping, sautéing, frying, garnishing, and plating one delicious dish after another. When she asked after Opal Gaynor, a woman holding a tray of bacon-wrapped scallops jerked her head in the direction of the sunroom.

Ella Mae found Opal conversing with a middle-aged man in a wheelchair. A beautiful young woman with creamy skin and long silvery blond hair stood behind the wheelchair. She didn't appear to be listening to what was being said and her gaze was fixed on the French doors leading to the back terrace.

Seeing Ella Mae, Opal didn't bother to hide her surprise. "Ms. LeFaye. I wasn't expecting you this evening."

Ella Mae smiled at the strangers and introduced herself. "I know, and I'm sorry to interrupt. I just need a moment of your time."

"Can't it wait, dear?" Opal asked with disarming sweetness. "Mr. Morgan and I were just discussing the relocation of his successful computer software firm to Havenwood."

The man looked Ella Mae over with an air of detachment. She felt like a racehorse being examined for sale. "A LeFaye? Any relation to Adelaide LeFaye?"

"She's my mother."

"In that case, yours is another important Havenwood family and I believe you should be made aware of our circumstances. Please"—he waved at the vacant chair next to Opal—"I'm Robert Morgan and this is my wife, Eira."

The lovely young woman smiled shyly. Ella Mae caught a quick glance of pale gray eyes before Eira averted her gaze once more. She was as slender as a ballerina and wore a slip of a dress made of ice blue satin. "Your name is beautiful," Ella Mae said. "What does it mean?"

"Snow," Robert answered before Eira could even open her mouth. "My wife was a dancer when we met. I went to see *The Nutcracker* in Atlanta and she was in the 'Waltz of the Snowflakes.' She outshone every woman on the stage. The Sugar Plum Fairy couldn't hold a candle to her."

"You look so graceful just standing in place that I can't imagine how wonderful it would be to see you dance," Ella Mae told Eira. "Are you still performing?"

Robert rapped his knuckles against the arms of his wheelchair. "Unfortunately, she spends most of her time taking care of me. Speaking of which, my darling girl, would you get me another helping of Thai shrimp? They're irresistibly delicious."

When Eira hesitated, Robert's tone turned brisk. "Go on,

you don't care for this business talk. Actually, forget the
shrimp. Why don't you have a little fun? After what we've
been through, you should enjoy the party."

"Of course," Eira said. Head bent, she excused herself
and made for the door.

Ella Mae touched Eira on the elbow as she passed. "I'll
make sure to find you later on. My aunt runs the Havenwood
School of the Arts and I'd love for the two of you to meet
once you're settled."

Eira's face lit up like the sun. "Oh, I'd like that," she said
in a voice filled with longing, and then left the room.

"You'll have to forgive my wife," Robert said. "She hasn't
been herself since the fire. It's not easy to be shackled to an
older man in a wheelchair either, but I couldn't do without
her. She's an angel."

Robert Morgan's words didn't sound sincere to Ella Mae,
and she tried to hide the instant dislike she'd taken to the
man. After all, he and his community were in need of a
fresh start, and since Ella Mae had so recently been given
one of her own, she decided to be as friendly as possible to
the people from Tennessee.

"Would you tell me about the fire?" she asked.

He nodded gravely. "It was set deliberately. There was no
camper forgetting to stamp out his fire or a careless smoker
leaving a lit butt on a pile of dry leaves. This was arson. And
it caught us all by surprise. Our grove has never been threatened and we've flourished in our little mountain town for
over two hundred years. Of course, our numbers have grown
smaller and smaller over time, but we've remained strong."

"My friend's grove in North Carolina was bulldozed last
year," Ella Mae said. "She told me that the most influential
Elders had passed away and the next generation didn't secure
local government seats or other positions of power, so there
was no one to stop the sale of their land. They tried to get
an environmental coalition involved, but their efforts were
too little, too late." Ella Mae sighed. "The loss of two groves

in one year is tragic. We must find a way to bring all of your people here. Do you employ many of our kind?"

Robert smirked. "I hire only the best and the brightest. That's how I turn a profit. For Eira's sake, I decided to live near a grove, but there are other reasons I chose Havenwood. I'm a businessman first and foremost. Everything else in my life comes second. Opal has found a suitable site for my offices and I believe my top executives will fit in nicely here. However, with our Lady burned to a crisp, there's no one to take responsibility for the blue-collar types of our community." He picked a fleck of lint off his suit jacket. "I'm afraid they'll have to fend for themselves."

Ella Mae's hands curled into fists. He spoke of his dead leader with such disrespect that it was obvious her loss didn't affect him at all. As long as he could keep making money and have his, or at least his wife's, magic renewed during Havenwood's spring equinox ritual, he didn't care what would happen to the rest of his kind. Keeping her voice calm and her expression pleasant, Ella Mae said, "Perhaps I could be of some assistance with the 'blue-collar types.'" She turned to Opal. "I'll tell the Lady about this. I'm sure she'll have an opinion on what should be done for the *entire* community."

For a brief moment, she thought Opal might argue, but she surprised Ella Mae by nodding in agreement. "That's an excellent idea. And you might be in need of help in the pie shop very soon. As co-chair of the winter carnival, I was planning to have you supply the food for the event. We'll still have the chili cook-off and the Junior League will handle the hot cocoa stand, but the steering committee thought a selection of potpies and warm cobblers would be a nice addition to our usual fare."

Robert Morgan yawned. "I think I'll leave you ladies to discuss your charming little event. My wife and I look forward to attending it, of course. Eira will be lonely being in a new place, and I hope she makes friends with the right sort of people. Like your lovely daughter," he told Opal. And then, so as not to appear rude, he turned to Ella Mae and added, "And you as well, Ms. LeFaye."

He pushed a button near his right palm and his wheelchair shot forward. The moment he was gone, Opal narrowed her eyes and hissed, "*This* is when you decide to finally act the part of the Lady's voice? We were finalizing a major land deal!"

"I'm sorry. I admit that I've been completely self-absorbed since the harvest, but the displacement of these people has snapped me out of my stupor. I won't sit by and let you and those of Robert Morgan's ilk choose who can and cannot move to Havenwood. Our kind has been shrinking in numbers with each passing generation. We need to offer sanctuary to all who need it. We have to protect these people from harm."

Opal frowned. "An interesting choice of words considering one of *them* started the fire."

"What?" Ella Mae was aghast.

"That's right. The blaze began *inside* the grove. Where only we can enter. That means the arsonist was neither human nor Shadow Child. No assassin started a fire at the base of the Lady's trunk. One of our kind is a killer."

Ella Mae was astounded. "Why would someone do that? Not only did they commit murder, but they ruined their ability to recharge their own magic."

"As I'm sure you've noticed, being enchanted isn't always sunshine and buttercups. It's a challenging life." Opal took a dainty sip of champagne. "The arsonist wouldn't be the first of our kind to grow tired of being different. Perhaps his or her gift wasn't useful. Perhaps it was a burden or a hindrance instead. Perhaps . . ." She trailed off, her gaze drifting to the dark sky.

"They fell for someone they could never share a future with," Ella Mae said very softly.

Opal, who'd carried a torch for Ella Mae's father long before Ella Mae was born, nodded. "That's a possibility.

Sometimes we end up loving the most unsuitable people."
She made a dismissive gesture with her hand. "Either way,
the Tennesseans will boost our local economy and increase
our strength as a grove, but they will also bring a threat into
our midst. Being that the Gaynors are one of Havenwood's
prominent families, I felt it was my responsibility to get to
know their Elders and the other important individuals from
their town."

"Absolutely," Ella Mae said. "However, we can't stop there.
What about the regular Janes and Joes? We can't ignore them.
Not only do they need shelter, but someone has to get close
to these people—to find out if the arsonist is among them."

"All right," Opal grudgingly conceded. "Why don't you
and your aunts handle the lower echelons? Find them gainful
employment and places to live. Become their friends and
mentors. Someone knows more than they're letting on about
the destruction of their grove."

Ella Mae moved toward Opal and lifted her champagne
glass. "Then it's decided. We'll protect the residents of
Havenwood—both the old and the new—together."

After a moment's hesitation, Opal raised her own glass
and touched it against Ella Mae's. "Together," she agreed.
"Now if you'll excuse me, I should return to my guests."

Opal departed in a wave of hairspray and expensive perfume. Ella Mae retraced her steps to the front hall and began
to search for Suzy. She passed through the dining room and,
after casting a curious glance at what looked to be a sumptu-
ous buffet, continued on to the ballroom.

Some of the guests were dancing, but most stood around
the perimeter of the room watching as one couple swept
across the floor. Ella Mae gently shouldered her way through
a knot of people in time to catch Eira performing an effortless
pirouette before returning to the waiting arms of a good-
looking young man in an ill-fitting tux. His cheap suit didn't
hamper his grace, however, and as he spun and dipped Eira,
it was obvious that he was smitten with his partner.

As for Eira, she shone like moonlight on snow. Her pale skin glowed beneath the soft light of the chandeliers and her hair floated around her face in a silvery blond cloud. With every move of her body, her icy blue dress sparkled like morning frost.

"She was a professional ballerina before Morgan got hold of her," a man next to Ella Mae informed the woman on his arm.

"What a waste of talent," the woman said, clicking her tongue in disapproval. "I heard he's paralyzed from the waist down. And he must be fifteen years her senior! Why on earth did she marry him?"

The man snorted. "For his money. Why else?"

Ella Mae forced herself not to scowl at the man. Eira didn't strike her as a gold digger and she knew the type well enough. Loralyn fit the description to a tee, but Eira was nothing like Loralyn. Eira seemed sweet and reserved.

"Look at her," the woman said. "She belongs onstage. Instead, she'll spend the next fifty years waiting on him. It's really quite sad, isn't it?"

"Come on, Madge. There's a tray filled with cream puffs calling my name."

The song came to an end and the guests clapped heartily for Eira and her partner. The string quartet at the far end of the ballroom played a waltz next and half a dozen couples took the floor. Ella Mae couldn't stop staring at Eira. She moved like water—fluid and effortless, her arms wrapped around her partner's neck, her gaze locked on his face.

"She's in love with him," Ella Mae murmured, completely entranced by the pair's synchronized movements. Every time their hands met or the man pulled Eira against him, a shimmering light seemed to wash over them. It was a beautiful but bittersweet sight, for Eira belonged to another man. A man who could never dance with her and probably had never gazed upon her the way her handsome partner did—as if she were the most exquisite woman in the world.

When the waltz was over, Eira's partner gave her a tender kiss on her palm and then led her off the floor. The crowd parted and Robert Morgan rolled forward, his eyes glittering coals of anger as he watched his wife reluctantly drop her partner's hand. Robert stared at her with a look that promised repercussions in the near future and then turned to respond to a waiter's query.

Eira was flushed from dancing, but her joyful expression quickly evaporated. Her partner had vanished and she darted anxious glances around the room, pivoting this way and that, like a lost child searching for her mother.

"Hi again!" Ella Mae waved to her from the edge of the dance floor. "I was hoping to run into you."

Eira's grateful smile tugged at Ella Mae's heart. "You were?"

"Yes. But I was so spellbound watching you that I almost forgot what I was going to say." She led Eira to a quiet corner. "I wanted to tell you about my aunt's school. One of her dance instructors is retiring at the end of the term, and I know she'd love to have someone with a rare talent such as yours working with her students. Have you ever thought about teaching?"

Clasping her hands over her heart, Eira cried, "Oh, yes! Ever since I stopped dancing professionally, I've dreamt of opening my own little studio and of having the chance to work with children. But this would be the next best thing!" She reached out and grabbed Ella Mae's forearm. "There are others who need jobs. Places to live. Hope for the future. People like Barric Young, the man I was dancing with. He's a farmer. And Jenny Upton, who works at our coffee shop. And Aiden. That's Jenny's brother. He's an electrician. *Those* people." She lowered her voice to a whisper. "No one's looking out for them. No one here cares. Except for me."

"I care, and I have an idea," Ella Mae said. "I have a big house that's totally empty right now. We can move Barric, Jenny, and Aiden into the house and help them find jobs. Once they get back on their feet, they can lend a hand to others. We can use Havenwood's upcoming winter carnival as an impromptu job fair. I'll be the main food vendor, so I can hire a few people to assist me with the event and they can get the word out that those folks are looking for work."

"That sounds great." Eira released a heavy sigh. "I've been so worried about them, and Robert . . ." She glanced over her shoulder. "Well, he has his own agenda."

Ella Mae took a business card from her evening bag and wrote her home and cell phone numbers on the back. "Call me tomorrow. We'll meet at my house and hammer out the details."

Nodding, Eira tightened her grip on Ella Mae's arm. "I don't know if I'll be able to get away. If I can get someone else to look after Robert for a bit, could we meet at your grove? I could use a safe haven for a little while. A place to think."

Ella Mae could feel the younger woman trembling. "Of course. But can't I do something for you now?" She thought of the hostile glare Robert Morgan had given his wife as she'd left the dance floor. "Do you feel threatened?"

"Everyone here faces the same threat," Eira said grimly. "My people and yours too. We're all in terrible, terrible danger."

Chapter 3

After uttering this chilling statement, Eira saw her husband beckoning and hurried away to join him.

Ella Mae watched as Robert Morgan took his wife's hand in his own and gave her a reptilian smile. His eyes were still dark with fury and Ella Mae could tell that he was squeezing Eira's hand too hard. His knuckles had gone white with the effort and her pretty mouth twisted in pain.

"That bastard." Ella Mae pushed her way toward the couple, intent on rescuing Eira from another second of abuse, but Opal suddenly appeared in front of Robert, a waiter on her heels.

"I tracked down a platter of Thai shrimp just for you," she said and shot a quick glance at Eira. "Mrs. Morgan, your husband will probably need something to drink. I believe the caterers made these even spicier than the previous batch."

Releasing Eira, Robert said, "A member of your household generously offered me whiskey from Mr. Gaynor's personal supply. I was told to help myself from the decanter in his office." He gave his wife a tight, cold grin. "Do you think you could find it for me, dear?"

Eira nodded rapidly and hurried off.

"Am I taking liberties?" Robert asked Opal, whose hostess smile had slipped at the mention of her husband's whiskey.

She recovered quickly, however. "Of course not. You're welcome to anything you find within these walls."

Clearly appeased by her solicitousness, Robert eyes roamed up and down Opal's formfitting dress. "A man does long for the best." His gaze lingered on her décolletage. "Your husband is a very lucky man."

"He is. And he knows it," Opal said, an unusual hint of playfulness in her voice.

"Traveling for three weeks," Robert went on. "Quite a lengthy business trip. He trusts you to look after everything while he's away?"

Ella Mae saw a flash of annoyance cross Opal's face. Either Robert Morgan didn't realize that Opal ran the family business or he preferred to pretend that her husband was in charge. "We're quite accustomed to being apart," Opal said airily. "I've heard it said that a marriage works better when one spends time away from one's spouse. For Jarvis and I, that's certainly proven to be the case. We have our personal ventures and those activities often prevent us from spending a great deal of time together, but when we do, we have a great deal to talk about."

Robert raised his brows. "Then you subscribe to the 'absence makes the heart grow fonder' adage? Perhaps it's true, but in my experience, distance encourages . . . indiscretion. I like to know where Eira is and what she's doing at all times. Who could blame me? She's a beautiful woman. I see the way men look at her. They'd kill to be leaving this party with her tonight. But she belongs to me." He popped a shrimp in his mouth.

Smiling politely, Opal excused herself, saying she had to

check on her other guests. Robert Morgan murmured something and continued to gorge on shrimp. He then pivoted his wheelchair to better focus on the dancers, and since Eira had yet to return, Ella Mae decided to resume her search for Suzy.

She found her friend in the dining room, filling a plate with slices of beef tenderloin, roast turkey, smoked salmon, and roasted vegetables.

"You've worked up a healthy appetite, I see," Ella Mae teased.

Suzy paused in the middle of digging into the center of a vat of garlic mashed potatoes. "I used my gift to memorize all of the titles of the books in the Gaynors' library. That always makes me hungry. Grab some chow and then I'll fill you in while we're eating. And before you say another word, I got the book. So let's relax and pretend that we're at a party, okay?"

"You're awesome," Ella Mae said, feeling a thrill of relief mixed with excitement. "Now that I know you have the book, I'm suddenly starving."

Minutes later, she sat across from Suzy with her own laden plate. Taking a bite of the beef tenderloin, Ella Mae gasped. "Wow, this Cognac sauce is good."

Suzy speared a piece of turkey. "This has a delicious cider glaze. I'm loading up on the main course because there's no way the desserts are worth the calories. After all, you didn't make them."

Ella Mae glanced at the dessert table. "I don't know. Those red velvet cupcakes and the warm chocolate bread pudding don't look too shabby. But I don't want to stick around long enough to sample either. I want to read that book. How did you get Loralyn to part with it?"

"I just asked to borrow a few volumes from her library. Specifically, I told her that I'd like to read books written by her relatives because I wanted to get to know her family better. It's the truth," she added, loading her fork with mashed potatoes. "I'm very intrigued by both the LeFayes and the Gaynors. Talk about your colorful histories. No work of fiction could compare to a war dating back to Arthurian times."

At that moment, Eira's dance partner entered the room. He paused, looked around, and left again. There was such misery in his glance that Ella Mae's eyes followed him as he strode from the room, his hands clenched.

Suzy noticed him too. "He must be really upset. And yet he was so happy a little while ago. Did you see the way he and that pretty blonde danced together?"

Ella Mae nodded. "I did, and though the man who just stormed out of here might have been having the time of his life, I don't think the blonde's husband was pleased." She went on to share her observations of both Eira and Robert. "The man's a bully," she said after she was finished. "I'm worried about Eira."

"After we eat, I'll introduce myself to her. It sounds like she could use a friend or two, especially since she's joining our community."

"She's not the only one who needs a friend." Ella Mae explained her plan to open up Partridge Hill to the displaced Tennesseans.

Suzy smiled in approval. "Hey, I've got a spare bedroom. Count me in. Who knows? Maybe Eira's handsome dance partner has a brother."

Once they were done eating, the two women didn't linger for long. Ella Mae couldn't find Eira and she was impatient to get home and spend the rest of the night reading *Lake Lore of the Americas*. Loralyn was on the dance floor when she and Suzy decided to leave, so they thanked Opal for her hospitality and drove back to Partridge Hill. The moment Ella Mae put the Jeep in park, Suzy handed her a thin book with a dark blue cover. "Call me tomorrow, okay? I'll be on tenterhooks waiting to hear about what you discover in these pages."

Ella Mae gave Suzy a quick hug and promised to talk to her first thing in the morning. She then rushed inside, gave Chewy half a dozen kisses and twice as many treats, and changed into pajamas. She'd just hung her dress in the closet when the phone rang.

"Well, Cinderella. How was the ball?" Reba asked.

"I didn't meet a prince, but Suzy got the book we were after. And Reba, I learned some awful news about another grove." She told Reba everything she'd learned at the party. "I need you to get in touch with my aunts tonight. I know it's late, but I'm calling an emergency meeting tomorrow. I'm done letting grief rule my life. It's time I stepped up and fulfilled my role as the Lady's voice. We'll visit my mother and then present the Elders with a course of action. Until then, here's my plan. I'm going to bring new life to the pie shop, free my mother, and take care of our people—both the new and the old."

Reba gave a joyful holler that reverberated through Ella Mae's phone speaker. "Praise the Lord! My girl is back! I knew you'd rally. You always do."

"Thanks for believing in me," Ella Mae said and wished Reba good night.

It didn't take long for her to become engrossed in *Lake Lore of the Americas*. Rupert Gaynor wasn't a skilled wordsmith, but his subject matter was fascinating. She read about water spirits and sprites, devils and demons, and elementals. According to the tales, many of the water spirits were playful, fun-loving creatures. They were primarily nocturnal and avoided contact with humans, but there were instances in which they'd saved a drowning child by turning into a large turtle and carrying the child to shore.

Gaynor didn't waste much ink on these innocuous spirits, instead choosing to focus on demons and monsters. Ella Mae's eyes grew round as she read about horned water serpents. These mammoth snakes, which had thick scales and daggerlike teeth, lurked in lakes and rivers. According to legend, the horned serpents possessed powerful magic and could control the weather. Other monsters, like the water panther, were even more dangerous. A cross between a dragon and a cougar, the water panther lured men and women to the deep water and then proceeded to drown them.

"Okay, but what does this have to do with Lake Haven-wood?" Ella Mae rubbed her eyes and sighed. It was getting late. The wind was whistling outside and Chewy was sound asleep at the foot of her bed, encouraging Ella Mae to snuggle under her comforter. She felt warm and drowsy and it was tempting to turn off the lamp and surrender to sleep, but she couldn't give in to the feeling.

Throwing aside the blankets, she moved to the window and stood there, uncomfortable in her thin cotton nightgown, and stared out into the dark garden. Even in the dead of night, it was easy to picture her mother moving among the plants, a pair of pruning shears in one hand and a basket in the other. Ella Mae could see her dressed in her favorite straw hat and waterproof clogs, murmuring to the flowers as bees and butterflies hovered above the magnificent blooms.

On impulse, Ella Mae threw open her window. Chewy raised his head and growled in alarm, but she whispered softly, telling him to go back to sleep. The cold air rushed into the room but Ella Mae ignored the discomfort it caused. Hugging herself, she closed her eyes and breathed deeply. All she could smell was wet grass and wood smoke. And then, she caught the faintest hint of roses. It was subtle, but the perfumed air served to drive the drowsiness away. Shutting the window, Ella Mae climbed back into bed and continued reading.

"Here it is!" she declared thirty minutes later and tried to slow her pace as she read Gaynor's introduction to Lake Havenwood. He didn't identify the lake by name, but Ella Mae knew it by the way he described its size, shape, and the island in its center. She knew it was the lake she'd dipped her feet into, swam in, and rowed boats on for most of her life.

"Listen to this, Chewy," Ella Mae said to her snoring terrier. "Gaynor writes that this beautiful lake surrounded by blue green hills is quite unique. He says that it is a place of great power and greater peril. I don't like that second bit. He claims that a magical object resides at the bottom of the deepest part of the lake. This object is guarded by a fearsome . . ." She turned the page, eager to read the next sentence, and frowned. Flipping back to the previous page, she shook her head. "No, no, no. This can't be. The pages jump from one-twelve to one-seventeen. Someone's torn out two pages!"

Sliding the book under her lamp, she gently pressed the open pages as flat as they'd go and peered into the gutter. A pair of ridges was still embedded in the gauze glued to the spine, proof that two pages had been meticulously cut from the book.

"Damn it!" Ella Mae swore and Chewy groaned in his sleep as if in sympathy.

Fighting a wave of despair, Ella Mae kept reading, but whatever secrets Rupert Gaynor had been about to share concerning Lake Havenwood's enchanted object and its guardian were gone. In his concluding paragraph, however, Gaynor confirmed Ella Mae's theory that obtaining a Flower of Life was the key to freeing her mother and renewing the magical powers of her people.

" 'Seeds from the original Flower (as described in the Gilgamesh legend) were entrusted to a select group of water nymphs.' " Ella Mae read the words aloud, absorbing each and every one. " 'The seeds were planted in oceans and lakes across the world and were cared for by the nymphs. These lovely and lethal women were also tasked with helping or hindering those seeking the Flower. A Flower of Life was only given to the pure of heart during times of dire need and could be used to restore their health, magic, and vigor.'"

Closing the book and switching off the lamp, Ella Mae lay back against her pillows and gazed out at the night sky. She wondered what Gaynor had written about the dangers lurking beneath the surface of Lake Havenwood.

"I must find the Flower," she whispered to the bright, high stars. "And figure out what monster I'll face when I do." She reached down and stroked Chewy's fur. "I'd better work on purifying my heart, because all I want to do at this moment is strangle the person who cut out those two pages."

The next morning, Ella Mae called Suzy from the pie shop to report her findings. Suzy gave a little shriek when she heard about the damage the book had suffered.

"All book vandals should be struck by lightning," she said heatedly. "It sounds like someone took a straight edge to those pages. But why?"

"To make sure that no one could get the magic flower in Lake Havenwood. Think about it. The Gaynors' powers have always been connected to water. What if they're the nymphs bound to guard the Flower of Life?"

Suzy made an unintelligible noise. "Neither Opal nor Loralyn strike me as being very nymph-like. Nymphs are willowy and ethereal—more like Eira. They love nature and are playful and capricious. Opal and Loralyn are slim and gorgeous, yes, but they're bossy, ambitious, and direct."

"Have you ever met a nymph?"

"No. I'm just regurgitating facts," Suzy said. "But I'll swing by to pick up *Lake Lore of the Americas* during my lunch break. I want to take a look at the section where the pages were removed. Maybe Loralyn knows what happened to them."

Ella Mae snorted. "If she does, you're my only hope of

finding out. She's not likely to lift a finger if it means helping me."

"I'll give it my best shot," Suzy promised. "Speaking of lunch, what are you serving today?"

"A huge helping of happiness, warmth, and satisfaction," Ella Mae said. "If I'm going to pack my café, reel in a bunch of catering jobs, and hire some of the folks from the Tennessee grove, then I need to turn my business around. Fast."

"Well, I'll be there at high noon. There's no way I'm going to pass up one of your enchanted pies." After a moment's hesitation, she added, "Unless it's going to give me the urge to take my clothes off. It is way too cold to go streaking through the town square."

Ella Mae laughed. "Don't worry; I won't be injecting any feelings of lust into my pies." At the mention of lust, her merriment vanished. "My dates with Hugh haven't exactly been hot and heavy."

"Do you want them to be?"

"You have no idea how much," Ella Mae said, turning on lights in the kitchen and dining room. She paused for a moment to consider how long she'd waited to be with Hugh Dylan. She had fallen in love with him in junior high, but he'd been too captivated by Loralyn to notice her. Following her college graduation, Ella Mae had married Sloane Kitteridge and moved to Manhattan. Seven years later, after leaving her cheating husband and returning to Havenwood, she soon realized that her feelings for Hugh were unchanged. She was just as hopelessly in love him as she'd been as a gawky teenager. And now Hugh was courting her in an old-fashioned and rather chaste manner. Ella Mae would have preferred things to be a little less chaste. "On one hand," she continued to answer Suzy's question, "it's been nice to have gotten to know each other all over again. I didn't think it was possible to love him more than before, but I do."

"And on the other hand?"

Ella Mae touched the framed four-leaf clover hanging

over the cash register. "Loving him shouldn't make me miserable, but how do I do this, Suzy? How can I be with Hugh, knowing I'll always keep secrets from him, knowing I'll have to lie to him again and again, knowing I can never show him who I really am?"

"You get used to it," Suzy said gently. "Secrets are the only way to protect those who aren't like us. Do you know what happens to people who suddenly start believing in magic? They end up in psych wards."

"I understand that, and I know keeping these kinds of secrets have worked for other couples, like Aunt Verena and Uncle Buddy, but what if things get really serious with Hugh? What if we get married? He'll have no idea what he's gotten himself into and I won't be able to tell him."

Suzy hesitated. "You can solve that riddle after you get your hands on a Flower of Life. You don't need to stress about that now."

Ella Mae smiled. "One miracle at a time, right? I should get started on today's culinary miracles. See you at noon."

By the time Reba arrived, Ella Mae had a dozen breakfast pies in the oven and had begun to mix graham crackers and butter to make crusts for some of the dessert pies.

"No country music this mornin'?" Reba asked as she slipped her apron over her head. Like Ella Mae's, it was peach and had been embroidered with a rolling pin and the phrase, "That's How I Roll."

"Nope, this kind of magic requires Elvis. We're going to fill every chair today," Ella Mae said.

Reba grinned. "I like the sound of that. What are today's specials?"

"A pork and apple pie with a cheddar cheese crust, a winter vegetable tart, and a hearty beef and ale pie. For dessert, we have warm chocolate tarts, caramelized pear and hazelnut turnovers, apple and pomegranate cobbler, and dulce de leche pie. Everything will make our customers feel cozy and cheerful."

"Talk of yesterday's impromptu concert is all over town, so I expect us to be real busy. I hope you're plannin' on givin' a few of these pies that extra sparkle."

Ella Mae nodded. "Not just a few, Reba. All of them."

Reba's eyes went wide. "Then I'd better get the coffee brewin'. You and I had better drink a whole pot before I hang the open sign."

Ella Mae hadn't felt so good in months. There hadn't been an empty seat in the dining room for either the breakfast or lunch services. All day long, the murmur of conversation and merry laughter had drifted around The Charmed Pie Shoppe, mingling with the aroma of buttery dough, melted cheese, warm chocolate, and baking fruit. By the time Ella Mae's aunts arrived, Reba's apron pocket was stuffed with cash.

"Best tips I've had in ages!" she declared, carrying the last of the dirty dishes into the kitchen.

Verena was close on her heels. "What did you put in those pies, Ella Mae?"

"Memories. The snowflake mittens Reba knit for me, a handful of plump marshmallows bobbing in a cup of hot chocolate, the feeling of sinking into a steaming tub of water at the end of a long day, winding a soft scarf around my neck, holding my hands in front of a roaring fire. Warm, happy thoughts."

Reba waved a licorice twist at Ella Mae. "Well, your memories sure did the trick. We filled a dozen takeout orders too. Another few weeks like this and you'll need another waitress and a delivery driver. And then there's the winter carnival."

Sissy performed a graceful twirl as she entered the kitchen. "It is such a *delight* to see your gifts in action, my talented niece. People are walking down the street, arm in arm, smiling as if they can't even feel the cold."

Dee hooked her thumbs under the straps of her overalls. "Since we're all here, I wanted to tell you that we've decided to open our homes to those in need of shelter, but most will end up at Partridge Hill." She studied Ella Mae. "How will you organize living arrangements and job placement for these people while running your pie shop?"

"You need a manager!" Verena announced. "Someone from their grove who's well liked and can act as a liaison between our two communities."

Ella Mae nodded. "I'll ask Eira. She has a friend who works at the local coffee shop. This woman, Jenny Upton, probably knows everyone."

"Eira's the dancer, right? I cannot *wait* to meet her." Sissy folded her hands over her heart. "Suzy told me all about her before she left clutching some book to her chest for dear life."

After placing a beef and ale pie and three pear and hazel-nut turnovers in a picnic basket, Ella Mae checked her watch. "It's time. Dee, can we all pile in your car?"

"Sure. I'm assuming you'd like to get Charleston Chew from Canine to Five first?"

Reba answered for Ella Mae. "Do you know how many squirrels that dog can chase up there on the mountain? Of course we're takin' him."

"Better bring your man a treat too!" Verena advised.

"I'm way ahead of you." Ella Mae pointed to the white bakery box on the counter. "I made that one especially for Hugh."

Verena threw her hands into the air. "I do not want to know what memories went into that pie. To me, you'll always be a little girl with pigtails. Let's move it, ladies!"

When Ella Mae entered Canine to Five, she was met by the usual cacophony of barks, yips, bays, and a growl or two.

The woman behind the front desk smiled, gave Ella Mae a detailed report of Chewy's activities for the day, and went off to collect him.

Ella Mae headed for Hugh's office and found her boyfriend standing in the threshold with his back to the hall, talking on the phone. As owner of Canine to Five and one of Havenwood's volunteer firefighters, Hugh was as busy as she was. Ella Mae tried to bring him homemade food whenever she could. Placing the pie on the floor, she studied her handsome man for a moment and then stepped up behind him and slid her arms around his waist.

He faltered midsentence and then covered her left hand with his. "Hey, Dan, something's come up. Can I call you in the morning?"

Hugh tossed the phone onto the desk and turned around. "Hello, beautiful." He smiled and traced the line of her jaw with his fingertip. "I missed you last night. I can't remember what I used to do on Friday nights before you came along. How was the party?"

"It was okay. Loralyn and I managed not to pull each other's hair out and Suzy enjoyed herself, which is all that matters."

"It was nice of you to go so Suzy didn't have to be there by herself," Hugh said. "You're a good friend."

Ella Mae wanted to confess that it was Suzy who deserved his praise, but she couldn't tell him about the book, what happened to her mother, or the Flower of Life. Instead, she kept another secret from him. Added another lie to a growing list of lies. "I would have liked to have danced with you," she said, gazing into his brilliant blue eyes. "Tonight, I'm all yours."

He kissed her lightly on the lips. "I like the sound of that."

Ella Mae pulled away before his kiss became more demanding. She'd been avoiding his embrace too much lately, but whenever their lips met for any length of time, she felt a burning sensation. It wasn't just the heat of desire she felt, but an actual, physical pain. It always started slowly, like a spark igniting against her skin, but the more she and Hugh kissed, the more the fiery feeling intensified. At first, Ella Mae had assumed that the bizarre reaction had something to do with magic, but Hugh hadn't come to the grove for the harvest festival, and that meant that he was human.

Or something else, Ella Mae silently thought. *If there are nymphs and assassins called Shadow Children in the world, who knows what other creatures live among us?*

"I brought you a pie." Ella Mae took the box off the floor and put it on Hugh's desk.

He frowned. "That's not fair. You won't let me give you a discount for Chewy's care and yet you're constantly bringing me food."

"This is dessert," Ella Mae said, grabbing his hand. "You can make me dinner."

Hugh grinned. "Deal. Meet me here at seven and bring a swimsuit."

Ella Mae wasn't sure she'd heard him correctly. "What?"

He ran his thumb over the back of her hand. "Trust me, I've been thinking about this for a long time. A hundred times a day. I want to be with you, Ella Mae. In every way. Is that all right? Are you ready?"

She knew exactly what he was saying. Her throat turned dry and her heart began hammering. "Yes," she whispered and thought back to the only time they'd ever come close to making love. It had been late November and they'd been caught in a thunderstorm running from a restaurant to Hugh's truck. Once inside, they started kissing. Ella Mae had peeled off Hugh's soaked shirt and he'd unbuttoned her drenched blouse. For some reason, the water had acted as a buffer and there'd been no pain when they kissed.

"Are you thinking of that rainy night?" Hugh asked now,

pulling her from the memory. "Because I've thought of little else since then. I don't know why we react to each other the way we do, but there has to be a way to deal with it. Let me show you what I have in mind."

"Yes," she said again. "Yes."

And then they heard the scrabble of Chewy's paws on the tile floor, and together they moved into the hall.

"Hey, boy!" Ella Mae bent down to greet her terrier. Taking Chewy's leash from Hugh's assistant, she gave Hugh a smile filled with promise and then left.

"What took so long?" Reba demanded after Ella Mae and Chewy got into the car.

Sissy giggled like a schoolgirl. "Look at her face! What do you *think* took so long?" She sighed theatrically. "Oh, to be young and beautiful and in love."

Reba and Ella Mae's aunts reminisced about the men they'd known in their youth all the way to Havenwood Mountain Park. As Dee's car climbed higher and higher into the blue green hills, the sky began to darken, turning a smoky pewter.

"This is what I hate most about winter," Dee said. "How early night comes. It's not even five and I can see the moon already."

"And it's so cold," Ella Mae said. "I don't remember it being this cold. Look at the lake. It's covered with a shimmer of ice."

Below them, Lake Havenwood sparkled like a mirror. The town seemed frozen too. The shops and houses huddled together around its shore like children gathered around a campfire.

Dee pulled the car into the lot near the entrance to the park's hiking trails. "Where's your friend?" she asked Ella Mae.

"Eira's bully of a husband probably refused to let her meet me."

Sissy put her arms around Chewy, who gave her a lick on

the cheek. "Poor woman. From what you told us, it sounded like she was keen on seeking sanctuary in our grove."

"We'd best get goin'," Reba said. "We've got lots to tell Adelaide."

At the mention of her mother's name, Ella Mae was suddenly impatient to unburden herself, to share her worries and cares in the tranquility of the glade where her mother stood, graceful and alone.

She hurried up the winding path, turning her face away from the sharp, probing wind. Because she had a head start on Reba and her aunts, Ella Mae was by herself when she rounded the last bend in the trail. To the right, a sea of treetops stretched on and on. Straight ahead was the rock wall that signaled the path's end for anyone who wasn't magical. But something else was there at the base of the boulder.

Ella Mae hesitated just long enough to realize that the crumpled mass was a body. A woman's body.

"Reba!" she shouted. Rushing forward, she dropped to her knees.

The woman was lying in the fetal position with her long legs pulled up to her chest. She wore only a gray sweater, an ivory skirt and tights, and a pair of silver ballet flats. Her face was milk white, as were her lips and fingers. Her eyes were closed.

"Do you know this girl?" Reba asked softly.

There was a sheen of frost covering the young woman from her crown to the tip of her shoes and as the last rays of the setting sun shone on her face, the miniscule pieces of ice sparkled like tiny stars. She looked like a fairy-tale princess, cursed to sleep until a prince would come along and free her. But no man could wake this princess with a kiss. The girl who'd once danced the dance of the snowflakes had become one herself. White and cold and fleeting in its beauty.

Ella Mae reached out, her fingertips hovering above the

dead woman's hand. Bowing her head, she whispered, "This is Eira. This is the woman who asked for our help, who needed sanctuary." She turned to Reba, tears pooling in her eyes. "She was so close. So close."

Chapter 4

"You'd best not touch her," Reba said softly, putting a hand on Ella Mae's shoulder. "Come away now."

Ella Mae allowed Reba to pull her a few steps back, but her eyes never left Eira's lovely, ice-covered face. "Why didn't she go into the grove?"

Reba frowned. "I don't know, hon. It doesn't make sense to me either."

She turned to warn Verena, Dee, and Sissy about the dead woman, but it was too late. Sissy gave a cry of alarm and then quickly clamped both hands over her mouth. Her eyes were round as moons.

Dee moved next to Ella Mae and slid a strong arm around her waist. "Is that your friend?"

Ella Mae nodded, too upset to speak.

"She doesn't even have a coat!" Verena shouted angrily. "And she's two feet from safety!" She turned to Reba. "Are there any signs of violence?"

Reba shook her head. "None that I can see. But I'm not

going to touch her. She's not from around here and we don't know anything about her, so we'd better leave this to the police."

Sissy began to weep. "Look at her," she whispered. "She's like the Little Match Girl from that awful Hans Christian Andersen tale. Except that girl died with rosy cheeks and her mouth curved into a smile—lost in happy memories. This girl is just lost."

"Unless her husband found her," Ella Mae said darkly. "And wasn't happy about her being here." She pulled away from Dee's supportive arm and gestured at the silent trees and towering rock wall. "Someone drove her to the park. Saw her walk up that trail, even though she wasn't dressed for cold weather. And then, when all she had to do was put her palms against the boulder and take one more step into safety, she didn't. She froze to death instead."

"We don't know how she died, Ella Mae," Reba said. "But I know this. You need to be protected from whatever happened. Let us deal with the cops. You go on inside and stay with your mama."

Verena pulled a cell phone from the pocket of her hound-stooth coat and removed her fuchsia gloves in order to dial. "Reba's right. You can't get mixed up in this, Ella Mae. You have responsibilities to your people and to the folks coming to Havenwood from Tennessee. Nothing good will come of your involvement! I know that you felt a connection to this poor girl, but you can still honor her wishes by helping her friends and neighbors."

"I can't leave her," Ella Mae protested. "She—"

"We'll take care of her," Dee said gently and moved to stand over Eira's body. "She won't be alone for a moment. I promise."

Ella Mae wiped a tear from her cheek. "All right, but I don't like this. She came here to meet me and I'm abandoning her."

"You're no good to anyone stuck at the police station for the rest of the night," Reba said. "I'll be back to pick you up as soon as I can."

"Don't leave until you've seen how Robert Morgan reacts to the news of his wife's death," Ella Mae said, her voice low and menacing. "If he did this, so help me, I will make him pay for it."

Sissy, who was the most sensitive of the four LeFaye sisters, squatted next to Eira and began to hum, as if she were lulling a child to sleep. Ella Mae recognized the beautiful and haunting melody as "In the Bleak Midwinter."

Verena listened for several seconds before turning away to call the police. For a moment, Ella Mae wondered what reason her aunt would give for being on the mountain so close to dark, but she knew that whatever Verena said, the police were bound to believe her. After all, she was the mayor's wife.

Verena had never been able to speak sotto voce and her conversation with the emergency operator echoed into the woods and floated out over the valley below, disturbing the peacefulness of Sissy's song. Ella Mae cringed when she heard her aunt say the words, "dead body."

The daylight was fading fast and the shadows were multiplying all around them. Ella Mae didn't think it was possible, but she felt colder than before. The chill sank so deep into her bones that she began to feel numb.

"Go," Reba commanded, pointing at the boulder. "Your mama will help you through this. She'll help with all of it, but she can't do a thing if you insist on standin' out here, shiverin' like a leaf."

Ella Mae looked at Eira one last time. "I'm sorry," she whispered.

Sissy began to sing very softly. "Snow had fallen, snow on snow. Snow on snow."

The song tugged at Ella Mae's heart. She leaned over the beautiful frozen woman, wishing she could touch her hand just once in farewell. Her breath plumed over Eira's pale hair—a curlicue of regret and sorrow. And then, Ella Mae stood and pressed both palms against the boulder.

As usual, she felt instantly dizzy and nauseated. Her skin felt stretched taut and her blood surged like a rushing river. The intense physical discomfort was over almost as soon as it had begun, and before she knew it, Ella Mae was on the other side of the rock wall.

She sucked in a deep breath and steadied herself. Entering the grove always made her feel as if she'd been turned inside out. But the discomfort was always worth it. No place on earth was as lovely and tranquil as the grove. The air was always warm, a playful breeze rustled the tree branches, and glorious flowers bloomed all year long.

Seasons were different here too. Outside, it was blustery and gray. Here, the sky was a soft blue tinged with streaks of silver and lilac. The tree leaves turned brilliant colors in the autumn, their crimsons, oranges, and golds as bright as bonfires, but in the winter, all the color leaked out of them. The entire grove turned a pure and gleaming white, from the tree trunks to the leaves to every blade of grass. It was a glittering white, holding all the magic of the first snowfall or the sparkles inside a snow globe. And because Adelaide LeFaye was the Lady of the Ash, there were roses everywhere.

Ella Mae stepped under an arch covered with a tangle of wild roses. The blooms smelled of sugared marzipan and opened wide as she passed by. Any other time, Ella Mae would have stopped to drink in the amazing variety of scents her mother's flowers produced. In December, she'd walked from bush to bush, inhaling hints of candy canes, fir trees, cinnamon, roasted chestnuts, and wood smoke. Now she was too upset to pay attention to the ethereal beauty of her surroundings. She hurried through the apple orchard, barely noticing that the apples had turned from gold to silver and raced up a low hill to where her mother stood, tall and magnificent, on its crest.

I'm here, Mom! Ella Mae shouted wordlessly. She never needed to speak when she and her mother were together. Their thoughts and feelings were exchanged in silence—a knot of complex emotions flowing between them like air currents.

Ella Mae fell to the ground and wrapped her arms around the ash tree's trunk. The rough bark scratched her skin, and for the hundredth time, she wished her mother were herself. Someone made of flesh and blood. Someone who could return an embrace. Who could smooth Ella Mae's hair with long, graceful fingers.

Why are you crying? The voice whispered inside Ella Mae. Absently, she raised a hand and touched her wet cheek. Closing her eyes, she formed a picture of Eira in her mind so her mother could see what she'd seen.

She then called forth images and memories of the Gaynors' party, sharing the news about the burned Tennessee grove and Eira's plea to help her friends and neighbors.

"I'm going to let them stay at Partridge Hill," she said. Speaking the words out loud gave them more strength.

Invite them and you invite danger in as well, her mother replied.

"Maybe so." Ella Mae pressed her face against the bark. She smelled roses and crushed herbs and moonlight—her mother's unique perfume. "But I've been in danger since I came back to Havenwood. And while I might be putting myself at risk, I can't sit by and let these people suffer. Even if the arsonist ends up under our roof, I'm going through with this."

I wouldn't expect any less of you.

Ella Mae switched subjects and began to talk about the winter carnival. She described the pies she planned to make, and how she intended to increase the pie shop's business, but her mind kept returning to Eira.

Time worked differently inside the grove. On previous

occasions, Ella Mae had spent hours with her mother only to find that on the other side of the rock wall, she'd been gone for a less than fifteen minutes. Now, she wondered what was going on out there. Had the police arrived? Was the coroner examining Eira? Were they taking photographs of the body in situ, the camera flashes lighting up the dark woods, forcing the shadows to retreat for the moment?

Ella Mae felt something land on the back of her neck. Reaching up to touch the spot, her fingers closed around a silky smooth rose petal. More petals fell about her head and shoulders, brushing against her brow and cheeks and hands. Each one felt like a warm kiss. Her mother was trying to comfort her.

It's not enough. The thought escaped unbidden. *I need you back and I know how to free you. There's a magical flower at the bottom of Lake Havenwood. I just have to figure out exactly where it is and how to get it.*

The branches of the ash tree whipped around as if caught in a high wind. Ella Mae knew that this was her mother's way of saying no. The petals swirled feverishly, twisting on frantic eddies of air until they looked like massive snowflakes.

Call the butterflies, her mother commanded. Her branches stopped moving and the roses blooming around the glade folded into tight buds. The tree had taken over, forcing the woman inside into a twilight sleep.

Ella Mae knew better than to plead with her not to go. In the beginning, she'd been so frightened by the abruptness with which her mother's presence vanished that she used to rage at the tree, beating its trunk and crying, terrified that her mother was gone for good. And though she always returned, Ella Mae noticed that her mother's sentences were growing shorter and shorter with each passing visit. By the next harvest, she would be able to speak to her daughter only once a season.

Picking up one of the white petals, Ella Mae curled her

fingers into a fist. Her mother's advice made no sense. Ella Mae had learned months ago that she could see through the eyes of any moth or butterfly, but there were no such creatures in Havenwood during the winter.

"What could they show me anyway? Who came here with Eira? Who torched the Tennessee grove? What monster guards the Flower of Life? That would certainly be useful." She looked down at the crumpled petal, which rested just above her clover-shaped burn scar. Pushing down on the smooth, puckered skin, she cast a final glance at the ash tree and then returned to the orchard. She'd walked past two neat rows of ancient trees when she ran into Reba.

"It's over," Reba said. "Your aunts are with the cops. Verena's already planted a seed that Eira's husband wasn't exactly the kind and gentle sort, so they'll be askin' him plenty of questions tonight."

Ella Mae shook her head sadly. "What if that's not enough? What if they only see Robert Morgan as an influential businessman in town to look at property? What if he spins a bunch of lies about Eira or claims that she was unstable? Will the cops still insist on a full investigation? With the winter carnival approaching, I could see them wanting to hush this up to maintain the illusion that Havenwood is a safe place . . . a place that is on the verge of welcoming hundreds of tourists."

Reba snorted. "Are you forgettin' who the mayor is? If Verena doesn't plan on lettin' this girl's death go unnoticed than neither will your uncle Buddy." She put a hand on Ella Mae's arm. "You should have seen Verena out there tonight, Ella Mae. She made up this wild story about how we all come up here every year for a sunset ritual. She told them we each write down our New Year's resolution on a leaf. And then we send the leaf off on the wind." She smiled. "The cops looked at us like we'd lost our marbles, but they bought what she was sellin'."

Ella Mae smiled. "Actually, her idea sounds lovely. Maybe

we'll put it into action right now. She yanked a leaf from the apple tree. "Do you have something I could write with?"

Surprised, Reba dug around in her pocket and then handed Ella Mae a silver glitter pen. Ella Mae wrote on the smooth leaf and then gestured at the silver apples. "What happens to them when they're removed from the orchard?"

"They transform into Galas or Golden Delicious or Granny Smiths dependin' on the season. Most times they end up pretty withered. Everybody tries to take one at least once, but even the folks who've managed to get an apple out in good shape say they taste real bitter. Why?"

"I need an extra dose of magic. I don't have much time to make the pie shop boom and it needs to become the town's biggest hot spot real fast. If I could make a few dozen enchanted hand pies, I could have people all over the county lining up to eat with us." She cupped her palms around the closest apple. "Normally, I'd feel like a slime using magic to net new customers and fill our cash register, but every dime will go toward helping the Tennesseans."

Reba pulled a short knife from her boot and was about to slice the apple from the branch. "Might as well give it a try," she said when Ella Mae stayed her hand.

"I'll enchant my own apples. Let's leave these where they belong."

Nodding, Reba put her knife away. "I don't know how you're gonna figure out who needs help now that your friend is gone."

"I guess I'll have to talk to Robert Morgan."

"Not necessarily," Reba said. "Her friends will be at her funeral. You've got to track down that girl from the coffee shop in Eira's town. The one who knows everything about everybody."

"Yes," Ella Mae agreed. "I need to find Jenny." She wrote the word "courage" on the leaf and put it in her pocket to release once they left the grove. "I started off the weekend by crashing a party. Despite the fact I was completely uncomfortable with that, I'm going have to take my rudeness a step further. Now I need to crash a funeral."

After leaving Havenwood Mountain Park and tossing her leaf into a breath of cold wind, Ella Mae had Reba drop her off at Canine to Five. She was a little early for her date with Hugh; she needed to see him. Even though she couldn't reveal that she was of a race of magical beings, she could tell him that the beautiful young woman she'd met at the Gaynors' party had been found dead. She wanted Hugh to gather her in his arms, to rub her back while she put her face on his shoulder and took in his scent of wet grass and summer rain.

Waving good-bye to Reba, she opened the front door and walked past the unmanned reception desk and down the corridor toward the small pool where the dogs were allowed to take their daily swim. She entered the spacious room and let out a gasp. Candles burned everywhere. Hundreds of candles of every shape and color. They were grouped on tables and lined the entire perimeter of the pool. Dozens more, shaped like lily blossoms, floated in the water. Soft light reflected off the walls and the surface of the water, making the room almost as magical as the grove.

Hugh had arranged a picnic near the shallow end. Ella Mae approached the table, smiling as she noted a glass wine decanter, china dishes, a moss-green vase filled with pink carnations, and a plate of chocolate-dipped strawberries.

As she reached out to warm her hands over the candles on the table, Hugh came out of the kitchen carrying a bottle of red wine. "You're early!" he said and pointed at her purse. "I hope you remembered your suit. We're having a starlight swim." Seeing Ella Mae glance up at the ceiling in confusion, he smiled. "Watch this."

Setting the wine on the table, he jogged over to the wall. He pressed a button on the stereo and Billie Holiday's "It

Had to Be You" floated through the speakers. He then switched off all the overhead lights, allowing the candle flames to glimmer and wink in the dimness.

Ella Mae dropped her purse on the floor and knelt by pool's top step. The water was warm and inviting.

"How does it feel?" Hugh asked, coming to stand beside her. "I thought we could eat and then—"

She silenced him by pressing her fingers over his mouth. Kicking off her shoes, she yanked off her socks, unzipped her jeans, and wriggled out of them.

"Oh," Hugh said, watching her.

Ella pulled her sweater over her head and tossed it away. Wearing only her bra and panties, she stepped into the pool. With the water lapping at her ankles, she turned and held out her hands. Hugh took them and bent to kiss her.

"I guess you don't have much of an appetite," he teased.

"Not for food." Ella Mae began to unbutton Hugh's blue shirt. As she slid each button free, she told him about Eira. She touched his chest with trembling fingers.

Grabbing her wrist Hugh raised her fingers to his lips and kissed each one. "You're upset. Maybe this"—he gestured at the room at large—"isn't a good idea."

She looked up at him. "I've always wanted you, Hugh. But right now, I *need* you. And I do have an appetite. Take off the rest of your clothes, come into the water, and I'll show you exactly what I mean by that."

Hugh didn't hesitate. He shucked out of his shirt, threw his pants on top of Ella Mae's, and dove into the pool. Arching his body, he sailed right over the top three steps and entered the water without a splash. He was like an arrow piercing a piece of blue silk. Breaking the surface, he smiled impishly and pulled her so that she lost her balance and fell into his arms. Cradling her tightly, he walked deeper into the water. And then he gave her another mischievous smile and buckled his knees, submerging them both. When they rose to the surface again, they were both completely wet.

To Ella Mae, Hugh had always looked like a merman, but never so much as at this moment. His dark, wavy hair was slicked back and fat droplets clung to his handsome face, his sculpted chest, and his muscular arms. He belonged to the water. Even his eyes, which were the brilliant blue of a Grecian sea, rippled with waves of light.

I don't know what you are, Ella Mae thought. *But you are no ordinary man.*

That was the last lucid thought she had. After Hugh bent to kiss her neck just below her earlobe, her senses could focus only on the feel of his lips and his hands. She barely noticed when he carried her out of the water, naked and dripping, to a makeshift mattress made of two pool floats. All she knew was that she wanted Hugh Dylan. And now, the moment she'd been dreaming about since she was a teenager was finally happening.

Smiling in joyful expectation, Ella Mae lay back and closed her eyes against the candle flames, which winked and flickered in the darkness like a host of fireflies.

Much later, wrapped in soft towels and happiness, Ella Mae and Hugh ate a cold supper.

"The Parmesan chicken was a nice choice. It tastes good hot or cold." Ella Mae grinned and gestured at the cucumber salad and the bowl of noodles tossed with garlic, olive oil, and tomatoes. "If I hadn't known better, I'd have said you prepared an entire meal that didn't need to be heated."

Hugh grinned. "I had other things on my mind when I came up with the menu." He passed her a basket filled with slices of French bread. "You were hungry as a bear."

Ella Mae took a heel of the crusty bread and glanced at her empty plate. "I guess so."

The two of them laughed and talked of everything and nothing. They filled each other's glasses and savored the sweet strawberries. And by the time they'd eaten all the food and drunk all the wine, the candles were sputtering and the night felt old.

Suddenly, the mood shifted. Ella Mae didn't know why, but she could feel it. She pulled her towel tighter around her shoulders and looked at Hugh. He was staring at her with a tender expression. But there was sadness in his eyes too. "What's next for us?" he whispered. "I want to share my life with you, Ella Mae. So what do we do about this weird thing between us? We don't even talk about it, but it's not exactly normal that we both have to be soaking wet to avoid setting each other on fire."

Ella Mae had been anticipating this conversation for months now. She was unsurprised that Hugh had picked this moment to talk about their unusual problem. After all, they'd both just allowed themselves to be completely vulnerable, letting go of any inhibitions and doubts. They should have been giggly and starry-eyed, but theirs was a different kind of intimacy. They'd already overcome obstacles to be together. They'd have to overcome many more if they wanted to stay together.

Ella Mae got out of her chair and sat down on Hugh's lap. His arms automatically closed around her. "I don't know why we're like this," she said. "There must be something in us that combines to create the burning sensation. But how do we discover what that something is? Or why our bodies react this way? We can't go to a doctor or a therapist. Can you imagine how they'd look at us?"

"Like we were total nut jobs." Hugh laughed. "We can share a padded room until we both grow old and gray." He tightened his grip and rested his chin on her shoulder. "That would still be better than the alternative: life without you. We can figure it out, Ella Mae. I don't know how, but I feel like we can do anything together."

She put her hand over his. "We're going to be taking lots of baths, showers, and dips in the pool. Maybe we should move to a tropical island. We can swim all year long."

They fell quiet until the Billie Holiday CD started over for the sixth time. "I have to turn that off," Hugh said and Ella Mae stood up. She watched him walk away, feeling wretched that she couldn't be honest with the man she loved.

Can I continue to do this? she wondered silently. *To keep secrets from him day after day, let alone year after year?*

Feeling cold, Ella Mae got dressed. When she was done, she turned to find Hugh looking at her with questioning eyes. "Can I help you clean up?" she asked.

He shook his head. "No. This place is closed tomorrow, so I can do it then." He put his shirt on and began to button it. "I guess you don't feel like sleeping on those pool floats, do you?"

She knew he was teasing, but she had a better idea. "Come home with me," she said.

"How about tomorrow night?" He took her by the shoulders and kissed her lightly on the forehead.

She hugged him tightly. So much had happened over the last twenty-four hours that she could use a little solitude to process all of it, and yet, she didn't want the night to end. Not like this. "I wish we could be like everyone else, but I know that we belong together. That's all that matters."

"Trust me, I don't want to be like everyone else," he said. "From the outside, you and I might look like a complicated mess. But to me, what we have is nothing short of magic."

Ella Mae smiled over his choice of words. "Come home with me. I'm not ready to let you go."

"How can I argue with that?" Hugh gestured in a wide arc, indicating all the candles. "But you'll have to help me put these out. It wouldn't look good for one of Havenwood's volunteer firefighters to burn down his own business."

"No, it wouldn't," Ella Mae agreed, feeling warm and happy again. She leaned over to blow out the nearest candle flame, and unbidden, her mind formed a picture of a charred and blackened grove. She moved to the next candle and snuffed its fragile light, wishing she could extinguish the arsonist with similar ease.

And then she came upon a white candle covered in silver snowflakes and she thought of how Sissy had compared Eira's frozen corpse to that of the Little Match Girl. Like the child in the fairy tale, Eira had been cold and alone when she'd breathed her last, lacy breath. As Ella Mae blew out the flame, she could only hope that Eira had slipped away as if she'd slowly drifted off to sleep, dreaming of music and dancers, the stage lights and the applause of a delighted audience warming her like a thousand suns.

Chapter 5

Ella Mae had grown accustomed to sleeping with Chewy curled up at her feet and an empty space beside her, so it felt strange and wonderful to wake and find Hugh there instead. Less wonderful was the fact that Dante, Hugh's Harlequin Great Dane, was stretched out across Ella Mae's legs.

"Dante. Get down," she whispered and tried to extricate her feet from beneath his bulk. He was not a light dog. In fact, Ella Mae was certain he weighed more than she did. She wriggled her legs again. "Dante. Off."

The Great Dane raised his massive head, yawned, and went right back to sleep.

"Chewy!" Ella Mae hissed. "Wake up! Chewy! Breakfast!"

Chewy stirred to life. He stood up and stretched.

"Breakfast," Ella Mae repeated.

Wagging his tail, Chewy dashed out of the room, arousing Dante's curiosity. The big dog lurched to his feet and followed the little terrier. Ella Mae winced as sensation returned to her legs.

Pulling on her robe, she wriggled her feet into slippers and went downstairs to feed the dogs and brew coffee. She let Chewy and Dante outside and was just shaking the dew from the Sunday edition of the newspaper when the phone rang.

"Hope I didn't wake you!" Aunt Verena bellowed.

"No, I'm up. Are you calling to tell me something about Eira's case?"

Verena put her hand over the speaker and shouted for Buddy to turn the oven off. "Sorry, hon. I had a hankering for cinnamon rolls this morning and they're ready. The timer could beep from now until next Tuesday and Buddy would act like he didn't hear a thing." She sighed. "I don't have any more information on the poor girl, but I made a few phone calls last night to learn more about her husband. Some of Opal's party guests are my friends too."

"And what did they say?"

"That Robert Morgan is a businessman with a reputation for ruthlessness. No wonder Opal is welcoming him to Havenwood with open arms! He and Eira were married for two years, and from what I could glean from the gossip shared among the folks from Oak Knoll, Morgan had been in perfect health prior to becoming engaged to Eira. He only asked her to marry him after his so-called accident. According to one of my friends, the Tennesseans clammed up when asked why Morgan needed a wheelchair."

Ella Mae wasn't sure why Robert Morgan's physical state was relevant. "Do you think he was faking his disability? That he drove Eira to the park, possibly drugged her, and left her there to freeze to death?"

"I wish I knew!" Verena sounded frustrated. "But I heard Morgan talking to a police officer at the station last night and I was getting tingles all over. He's a liar, Ella Mae. Every other word out of his mouth was a lie. You know I can tell when someone's being dishonest, and if this man were

Pinocchio, a dozen birds would be perched along the length of his nose!"

"I'm going to call Eira's friend Jenny in a little while. I don't know if her coffee shop is open on Sundays, but I have to contact her. I bet she's heard all the dirt on Robert Morgan."

Verena wished her luck and then hung up, no doubt eager to get her hands on a tray full of warm cinnamon rolls. Ella Mae poured herself some coffee and began to fry bacon strips. While the bacon was sizzling, she opened her laptop and looked up coffee shops in Oak Knoll. There was only one. It was called Lulu's Lattes and was open seven days a week.

"A man could get used to waking up to this," Hugh said when he came into the kitchen. "You, looking beautiful, and bacon."

Ella Mae glanced down at her bathrobe and laughed. "You don't have very high standards, do you?"

"The highest." Hugh crossed the room and kissed her. The kiss was light, but Ella Mae felt a spark of heat against her lips. She pulled away, ostensibly to save the bacon from burning. Cracking eggs into a bowl, she asked Hugh to pour two glasses of orange juice and set the table.

"I thought I felt the bed lurch to one side last night." Hugh opened the refrigerator and peered inside. "Did Dante crush you?"

"I couldn't feel my legs, but he kept me warm."

Hugh frowned. "Hey, now. That's my job."

"No, your job is to find the orange juice," she teased.

They shared a leisurely breakfast, while watching the dogs through the window. Chewy and Dante were playing a game of tag on the lawn. They barked noisily and raced back and forth over the frost-covered grass, their exhalations drifting into the air like puffs of smoke.

"I'm going to have tenants in Partridge Hill," Ella Mae told Hugh. "I hope they all like dogs."

Hugh gestured at the main house with a piece of bacon. "You're letting strangers move in? Why?"

Ella Mae shrugged. "Mom won't be back until spring. Maybe even later. She doesn't want the house to sit empty in the meantime." She made herself smile. "It'll be nice to see lights on at Partridge Hill during the long winter nights. And the renters can help with the housework. I have enough trouble keeping my own place clean."

Hugh examined his empty plate. "Speaking of messes, I'd better get down to Canine to Five and take care of the one we made. If my staff sees what I left behind, you and I will be the topic of conversation at every water cooler in Havenwood on Monday." He collected the dirty dishes and carried them to the sink. After washing everything by hand, he refilled Ella Mae's coffee mug. "What are you doing today?"

Ella Mae pointed at the newspaper. "After I read this, I'm going to create the menu for The Charmed Pie Shoppe booth at the winter carnival. Is the fire department sponsoring an activity again this year?"

"We're responsible for the bonfire and the Polar Plunge. Someone usually comes close to having a heart attack after they dive into the lake, but it's one of those events that raises tons of money so we keep doing it. I overheard your uncle saying that he has over a hundred pledges already." Hugh put on his coat. "Is Havenwood's mayor a good swimmer?"

Ella Mae got up and walked him to the door. "Not really. If Uncle Buddy's taking the plunge, you'd better be dressed in a wetsuit and have a defibrillator on hand."

Hugh didn't seem concerned. "I don't really get cold in the water. Must be my alien DNA." He kissed her on the cheek. "After I clean up Canine to Five, I'm going to try to solve our mystery, Ella Mae. Starting today, I plan to check out every Internet site that so much as hints at our situation."

"If you do a search for sparks between lovers, you're going to end up with a bunch of romance novel titles or links to porn sites."

Hugh flashed one of his characteristic impish grins. "Sounds like the perfect Sunday."

After Hugh left, Ella Mae called Lulu's Lattes and asked for Jenny.

"That's me," a woman said in a light and merry voice.

Her cheerfulness gave Ella Mae pause. Unless she was an incredible actress, Jenny didn't know about Eira's death. *No one called her.* With dismay, Ella Mae realized that she would have to be the one to tell Jenny the terrible news.

She gave Jenny her name and explained that she owned a pie shop in Havenwood. "I met Eira at a party Friday night. She asked for my help."

"Oh, thank goodness. Can you do anything for us?" Jenny's tone was laced with both hope and fear.

Ella Mae heard the hiss of milk being steamed and the pleasant din of customers talking in the background. "Yes, but maybe we should have this conversation later."

"No way," Jenny said. "Give me your number and I'll call you back from my car. I always listen to audio books on my break. I'm a book and junk food addict."

She's going to fit right in, Ella Mae thought after Jenny hung up. She moved to the window seat and gazed out at her mother's dormant garden, wishing she didn't have to be the one to shatter Jenny's world. But she doubted Robert Morgan would call Eira's friends to tell them what had happened. He might not even invite them to her funeral. If there was a funeral.

Less than a minute later, Jenny was back on the phone. "It was so nice of you to call, Ella Mae. I can't tell you how worried I've been about our future. The closest grove is in the North Carolina mountains, and while it's beautiful there, there isn't much work to be had. A few people have gone to Colorado or as far north as Montana, but I hate the cold. There are at least twenty of us looking to start a new life in a place not too different from Oak Knoll, and as soon as Eira told me she was headed to Havenwood, I started researching the town. It seems like the perfect place for all of us."

Ella Mae assured her that she was welcome to come for a visit and to stay at Partridge Hill. "Jenny, we have our share of troubles here. Even though I wanted to touch base about relocating you and your friends, I also have something really difficult to tell you."

"It's Eira, isn't it?" Jenny's voice was suddenly taut with anxiety. "She checks in with me every day. When I didn't hear from her on Saturday, I had this terrible feeling. . . . Her bastard of a husband keeps her on such a short leash. What's he done to her now?"

"I'm so sorry, but Eira's dead." Ella Mae spoke as gently as possible. There was no point in delaying the pain any longer. "I don't know how she died, but I will find out. I promise you."

Jenny went silent. She didn't scream or burst into tears, she just seemed to disappear. Ella Mae couldn't even hear her breathing, so she just kept talking. "I was the one to find her. We were supposed to meet at our grove. When I arrived, it was already too late. She looked like she'd been there all night." Ella Mae spoke quickly, knowing that every word was like a dagger. "She said she needed sanctuary. Who was Eira scared of, Jenny? Her husband?"

There was no answer.

"She looked as if she'd gone to sleep within inches of the grove's entrance," Ella Mae went on. "For some reason, she didn't go inside. She was lying on the ground with no coat. No hat. Nothing. Someone had to have dropped her off. Who would have driven her to our park? Robert? Barric?" She waited for a moment and then spoke more firmly. "Jenny, I know this is devastating, but Eira's death is all wrong. If someone hurt her, I want them to pay. Don't you?"

Jenny let loose an enraged howl. Ella Mae flinched as a

high note of grief and fury burst through the phone speaker. She waited while Jenny released another guttural cry and then murmured, "It'll be okay. Shhhh. Shhhh. Talk to me, Jenny. Talk to me."

"Why should I?" Jenny demanded. "I don't know you. I don't know anyone from your town. How can I trust you? My best friend is dead, my grove's been burned, and I have no place to go. In a few minutes, I'm supposed to go inside and serve coffee as if nothing happened. It's too much. I can't take another blow. I can't take any more. . . ."

"I know exactly how you feel," Ella Mae said after a moment. "Listen. Please. My mother is the Lady of the Ash. My role is to serve my people, and I promised Eira I would do my best by her people too. Come to Havenwood. Help me find justice for Eira and create a new future for you and the others who've lost their grove."

Jenny was silent for several seconds. "I don't have any other choice but to trust you. I'll be there in three hours." She expelled a deep breath. And then another. Jenny was pulling herself together, steeling herself against her grief. At that moment, Ella Mae knew that Jenny Upton was made of stern stuff. She was glad of it. She needed Jenny to look after the people who'd be relocating to Havenwood.

Ella Mae had so many questions for Jenny, but she knew that they would have to wait. She gave Jenny directions to Partridge Hill and, after saying that she was sorry about Eira once more, said good-bye.

Chewy jumped onto the window seat cushion and put his head in Ella Mae's lap. She stroked his neck and velvety ears and stared out the window, where a male cardinal was flitting from branch to branch on the dogwood tree. The flash of his red feathers was a stark contrast to the rest of the gardens' beiges and browns. Ella Mae looked for the cardinal's mate, but the female was nowhere to be seen.

"She has more camouflage than the male," Ella Mae murmured to Chewy. Inadvertently, she thought of how

Eira's ethereal beauty stood out in a crowd. There was one person who would have hated to share the spotlight with such a lovely, young woman. Someone who would have viewed Robert Morgan as excellent husband material. That person was Loralyn Gaynor.

"Could she be involved?" Ella Mae asked Chewy. "Or do I just want her to be a suspect?" Chewy sighed and licked her palm. Ella Mae ran her fingers through her dog's fur and wondered how long it would take the medical examiner to get Eira's lab results back. Without knowing how Eira had died, Ella Mae couldn't begin to figure out who'd had a hand in her death. Not unless she could discover who had driven her to the park in the first place.

Carefully easing Chewy off her lap, Ella Mae showered and dressed for church. The familiar hymns and rituals of the late morning service always calmed her. And while her mind often wandered during the sermon, it didn't today. The minister seemed to be looking right at her as he spoke of beginning the new year with honesty. "Be truthful to others and to yourself." He gazed down at the congregants from the pulpit. "Speak the truth in your heart before you speak with your voice."

Thinking of how often she lied to Hugh, Ella Mae shifted uncomfortably in her seat. She preferred to focus on more pleasant memories, like having him next to her in bed or the way he devoured six pieces of bacon. Smiling, she looked down, feigning great interest in the announcements listed on the back of the worship program.

The sermon went on longer than usual and Ella Mae's thoughts turned to the winter carnival. She'd attended the carnival as a girl, and had always enjoyed herself immensely. But she hadn't liked chili when she was young and she knew that the spicy entrée often upset the stomachs of the elderly townsfolk. Ella Mae needed to create an attractive alternative to chili, a menu that would appeal to people of all ages.

It would be nice to do without forks, she mused silently

as the minister began the Scripture reading. Taking a pencil from her handbag, she began to write notes next to the list of those in need of special prayers. *Cheeseburger pie for the kids. Mini shepherd's pie for the adults. Desserts: Mini maple pecan pies. Warm apple caramel hand pies. Piecrust cookies in the shape of mittens?*

Her vision of the charming display of cookie cutters she'd seen the last time she'd visited the restaurant supply company in Atlanta was interrupted by a burst of organ music. The congregation rose to sing the final hymn and Ella Mae hurriedly riffled the pages of her hymnal in hopes of catching up before the first verse was over. When she found the page, she didn't join in, but simply listened as the voices of her neighbors rose to the vaulted ceiling. The sun streamed in through the stained glass and painted rainbows across the pews. For a moment, the room was as warm and colorful as a spring day.

Several people stopped Ella Mae on the way out, hoping to learn what she had on the menu for the upcoming week.

"I'll let you in on a secret," she said with an enigmatic smile. "The pies will make you feel so relaxed and content that you'll swear you've spent a week on a Caribbean cruise instead of an hour in my shop. Bring your friends. Grab a coworker. You don't want to miss out."

Ella Mae was thrilled to hear people talk about eating at The Charmed Pie Shoppe. They made lunch and tea dates or promised to meet for breakfast and then rushed to their cars, eager to escape the winter wind.

As for Ella Mae, she went home, fixed herself some lunch, and spent the afternoon creating the specials for the following week. "A winter vegetable tart," she said while examining an old issue of *Bon Appétit* magazine. "And another with potatoes, ham, caramelized onions, and Taleggio cheese. And to round off the savory selections, a nice chicken tortilla pie." She focused on desserts next and then double-checked her shopping list. She was trying to remember if she had enough buttermilk on hand when she heard the sound of a car coming down the driveway.

Chewy was on his feet and barking before Ella Mae could cap her pen. She looked out the picture window to see a yellow Camaro pulling alongside her pink Jeep. A woman got out, briefly glanced around, and strode purposefully toward the cottage. Ella Mae met her at the door.

"You must be Jenny," she said, smiling and extending her hand.

The other woman was in her late twenties but had the wary, watchful eyes of a much older woman. She took Ella Mae's hand and shook it heartily, and then squatted in front of Chewy. "Who's this handsome fellow?"

"That's Charleston Chew. Chewy for short. He's all bark, no bite. But look out, he'll try to lick you to death." As if to prove her point, Chewy covered Jenny's outstretched fingers with a series of wet, slobbery kisses.

"I love your place." She pointed at Partridge Hill. "Are you seriously offering *that* house to a bunch of strangers?"

"I prefer to think of all of you as friends I've yet to make," Ella Mae said. "Come on in. Would you like some coffee?"

Jenny laughed. "No, thanks. Can't stand the stuff. I'm a sweet tea drinker."

Ella Mae opened her refrigerator. "I always have a pitcher ready." She poured two glasses and asked Jenny to take a seat.

Clearly too restless to sit, Jenny took her glass and paced around the small kitchen and living room. "I quit my job today," she said. "The owner is closing shop in two weeks, so I figured I might as well spend some time in Havenwood. To be honest, you seem too good to be true, but I guess I just don't trust anyone anymore. But I'll try. I really appreciate what you're doing for us."

Ella Mae took Jenny's empty glass and put it in the sink. "Before we make any plans, I need to take you to the grove. I have to make sure you're not a Shadow Child."

Jenny threw back her head and laughed. The sound was low and throaty. "Me? An assassin?" She raised her arms. "My cardio boxing sessions must really be paying off."

"I'm afraid I'm serious," Ella Mae said. "We need to trust each other if this is going to work."

"Fine by me." Jenny moved to the door and then hesitated. "That's where you found Eira, isn't it?"

Ella Mae nodded.

"I know it sounds stupid, but can we stop somewhere first? I'd like to get her some flowers. When she and I said goodbye last week, I had no idea it would be the last time we'd talk." Jenny's voice wavered.

Acting on instinct, Ella Mae took Jenny's hand and held it. "She seemed happy at the party Friday night. She danced. She was amazing. Radiant."

"Tell me everything," Jenny said, blinking back tears. "Please."

"I will. Right down to the smallest detail. Let's head to the grove and then we can come back here and spend the evening figuring out how to honor Eira's last wish."

Jenny zipped her leather jacket and stepped outside. "Okay, I'm ready. For all of it."

She's tough, Ella Mae thought. *Good. Havenwood could always use another strong woman.*

"You remind me of someone," she told Jenny as they drove away from Partridge Hill. "Her name is Reba. She and I work together."

Jenny, who'd been studying the scenery, glanced at Ella Mae. "Speaking of work, could you use any help at the pie shop? I know how to brew a mean cup of coffee. And when I touch people, they get a little zing of energy. It's my put-a-skip-in-your-step superpower."

Ella Mae grinned. "Get Reba's blessing and you're hired."

"Can she be bribed?" Jenny asked.

"We'll pick up a jumbo pack of Twizzlers while we're at

the store. Give her those, and you'll be on her good side right from the start."

Later, after Jenny had laid a wreath made of lilies and dried lavender on the spot where Eira had lain, Ella Mae led her into the grove. Ella Mae hung back as Jenny paid respects to the Lady of the Ash and tried to mask her sorrow when her mother didn't speak to her. Jenny was a keen observer, and once they were back in the car, she turned to Ella Mae and said, "I guess we've both lost people."

Ella Mae nodded but chose not to elaborate. She didn't know Jenny, and until she did, it was better not to tell her about how she intended to set her mother free. However, the two women talked about other things, and by the time they returned to Partridge Hill and Ella Mae finished giving Jenny a tour of the house, she knew that Jenny had an older brother named Aiden, had recently broken up with a long-term boyfriend, and had always lived in Oak Knoll. She loved junk food and maintained her athletic figure by lifting weights and spending an hour a day attacking the punching bag suspended from the ceiling in her garage.

Reba arrived in time to overhear Jenny describing her exercise routine. "I like a girl with a mean right hook," she said, giving Jenny the once-over.

"And I like a woman who can't live without a certain kind of candy." Jenny smiled and offered Reba the Twizzlers.

Reba put down the grocery bags she'd been carrying and shook Jenny's hand. "You're not in the clear yet, but this is a good beginnin'. Why don't you come into the kitchen and help me make supper? Ella Mae's aunt Verena will be here in thirty minutes and if we don't have food waitin' on the table, things could get ugly."

"I'm not much of a cook, but I can take orders," Jenny said. "Give me a job."

Ella Mae had her set the table and chop vegetables for the salad. The three women sipped Syrah and chitchatted as they worked, moving around one another in the kitchen like dancers following a choreographed routine. By the time Reba's turkey Tetrazzini was done baking and Ella Mae's aunts arrived, it felt as if Jenny had been with them for years.

After introducing Jenny to her aunts, Ella Mae said, "Not only is she new to Havenwood, but she's the newest employee at The Charmed Pie Shoppe."

"How *wonderful*!" Sissy exclaimed and enfolded Jenny in her arms. "We're so sorry about Eira. I really wanted to meet her. And I would have loved to have seen her dance."

Jenny thanked Sissy and received another hug from Dee. Verena was impatient to talk business, so as the women sat down to eat, she asked Jenny to tell them all about the magical folk from Oak Knoll who wished to move to Havenwood.

"Do you think the arsonist could be among this group?" Verena twirled noodles around on her fork, but Ella Mae knew her aunt was on alert. She would immediately know if Jenny told a lie. "Can you be certain that we're not inviting a murderer to live among us?"

"There's already a killer in Havenwood," Jenny said darkly. "Someone killed Eira. She didn't walk up that path with the intention of freezing to death. For the first time in many months, she was hopeful. About living here and . . ."

Ella Mae gave Jenny a nod of encouragement. "Go on."

Jenny was clearly reluctant to continue, but she knew she had no choice. "I guess you can't take all your secrets to the grave," she murmured. "Eira was pregnant." Jenny paused and took a long swallow of wine. "With Barric's baby. She didn't expect Robert to be around when the kid was born. She said that it was only a matter of time before he was punished again and then she'd be free."

The rest of the women exchanged befuddled glances.

"Punished?" Dee asked. "For what crime?"

"Robert Morgan was in perfect health before he and Eira

got married," Jenny said. "He was paralyzed from the waist down after bragging about his abilities. To those *not* of our kind."

There was a collective gasp of shock from around the table.

"Why would he do something so stupid?" Reba wanted to know.

"For money. For power," Jenny said. "There was a ton of competition to land some A-list client and Robert needed an edge. Eira told me that it was a multimillion-dollar deal, and since no one had been punished in years, Robert didn't think anything too horrible would happen to him. That man has such an incredible ego." She frowned in disgust. "Even after he lost his magic and was wheelchair-bound, he boasted that the pain and the physical sacrifice was worth the seven-figure payoff."

"What a *fool*," Sissy whispered, aghast. "He's lucky to be alive."

"Why did Eira marry him, Jenny?" Ella Mae asked. "He sounds like a monster."

Jenny pushed her plate away. "He is. And if he's moving to Havenwood, it's because he must believe that he's found people sympathetic to his cause—people interested in enacting radical changes. Robert wants to *purify* our kind. At Oak Knoll, he was trying to convince the Elders to excommunicate all those with gifts he considered unworthy. He wanted to cut these folks off from the renewal ceremonies until their magic withered and died, leaving only the rich and well bred retaining their powers. As ludicrous as his vision sounds, he had plenty of support."

Ella Mae felt a prickle of unease. "Robert Morgan seems to be quite cozy with the Gaynors. This sounds like an agenda they've sought for decades."

"Well, isn't this just fabulous?" Reba muttered. "Another snake to add to Havenwood's viper pit."

Verena banged her fist against the table. "We are LeFayes!

Adelaide is the Lady of the Ash! That makes us the first family of Havenwood. Not the Gaynors. And certainly not Robert Morgan. He's nothing but an interloper!"

Putting a hand on her aunt's arm to calm her, Ella Mae looked at Jenny. "Morgan was punished before your grove was burned, wasn't he?"

When Jenny nodded, Sissy sucked in a sharp breath. "That means he can't be the arsonist. He couldn't have gotten inside the grove to start the fire."

"No," Jenny said. "I admit that whoever destroyed our grove might be one of the people hoping to move here. The arsonist could also have already relocated to another town. Personally, I'm more concerned with finding Eira's killer. And I know that her husband had something to do with it. He must have found out about Barric or the baby."

"We have several serious issues to tackle," Ella Mae said to Jenny. "And I can't address any of them without you. When can you move into Partridge Hill?"

Jenny hesitated. "It depends. I can't leave Miss Lulu behind and I'm not sure if she's welcome here."

"Miss Lulu?"

"She's a Schipperke," Jenny said.

Ella Mae was puzzled. "Excuse me?"

"That's a type of dog breed," Dee said to her niece. "Miss Lulu is small and black with foxlike features. I'd guess that she's also smart, joyful, very active, and occasionally too willful."

"That's Miss Lulu to a tee." Jenny laughed softly. "I love her to death, but she could use an obedience class. Shoot, she could use a live-in obedience tutor."

"Is your coffee shop named after her?" Ella Mae asked.

The humor in Jenny's eyes vanished. "Yeah. I came up with the name Lulu's Lattes when the coffee shop changed hands last year. The man who bought it carried Lulu in his arms the day he came in to meet the current staff. I'm not sure who I fell in love with first. Curt or Miss Lulu."

Ella Mae saw the hurt in Jenny eyes when she spoke the man's name. "Is Curt the ex you mentioned earlier?"

Jenny nodded. "That's him. Things had been going downhill between us for a while, but we lived and worked together, so our breakup was complicated. Until you called, that is." She gave Ella Mae a sad smile. "Suddenly, things became very clear. I told Curt he could have all of my stuff if I could have Miss Lulu. I can live without my furniture, but I can't live without that dog. We bitches need to stick together."

"Now that's a toast!" Reba exclaimed and raised her glass.

"I'll hang a sign on Partridge Hill's front lawn," Ella Mae said, lifting her own glass. "Bitches welcome."

The women laughed and then continued to make plans. By the time the food and wine were gone, the room was filled with warmth and fellowship. Ella Mae felt invigorated. She had a renewed sense of purpose. People to fight for. As she glanced around the table, she marveled at the beauty she saw in each woman's face.

That's what hope looks like, she thought. *Hope. The most powerful kind of magic.*

Chapter 6

Ella Mae spent Monday morning grocery shopping and making piecrusts. She had little time to prove to tourists and locals alike that The Charmed Pie Shoppe was Havenwood's best eatery. With only a week to go until the winter carnival, she needed tales of her wondrous pies to go viral.

In the shop's sun-filled kitchen, Ella Mae sat on a stool in front of her worktable. She scooped up a handful of flour and let it fall between her fingers, watching the wood surface of the table turn powdery white.

"I need a shortcut," she mused aloud. "If I can infuse a week's worth of piecrusts with feelings of happiness, then every dish I serve will be charged with magic." She opened a bag of salt and rubbed a few grains between her thumb and forefinger. "Does magic have a shelf life?"

She looked over the ingredients on her shelves, waiting for a spark of inspiration. Last week, she'd done her best to fill the pies with warmth and cheer, but she couldn't do the same thing again or her customers would grow used to the enchantment. She needed to surprise them with new tastes and sensations each time they dined at The Charmed Pie Shoppe.

The radio was tuned to the country station, but Ella Mae couldn't get into any of the songs. She tried generic pop, oldies, and light jazz, but nothing worked. Finally, she hit scan, hoping that some random song would burst out of the speakers and ignite an idea. Instead, the rotating digits stopped on a talk radio station, catching the disc jockey in the middle of wishing a caller a happy eightieth birthday.

"My great-granddaughter and I were both born today," the woman was saying. "She's having a princess party this afternoon and I'm invited. Everyone will be wearing tiaras and corsages, including me. I've never had a tiara before!" The woman giggled.

The sound of the old woman's mirth was exactly what Ella Mae needed to hear. She searched through mental snapshots of childhood, trying to recall when she'd felt as giddy as the old woman. Closing her eyes, she found the perfect memory.

She remembered one Halloween night in particular. Dressed as Dorothy from *The Wizard of Oz*, Ella Mae had wriggled all through supper, impatient to start trick-or-treating with her friends. The second she finished her meal, she was at the front door, calling for Reba to hurry.

"I cannot believe you talked me into wearin' this getup," Reba shouted from the next room. And then she appeared in the hall wearing her Cowardly Lion costume and Ella Mae had giggled. Those giggles soon turned into peals of laughter, because Reba was the epitome of silly. She wore a mane of brown yarn, had apple red cheeks, and had used eyeliner to create her black nose and whiskers. But it was her tail that got Ella Mae laughing with every twitch or wiggle. Made of yellow felt sewn around a length of wire, the tail was too long and seemed to have a mind of its own. Reba would turn to the right and the tail would go left. All the children trick-or-treating with them that night had more fun chasing Reba's tail than collecting fistfuls of candy.

Ella Mae held on to that memory as she made ball after ball of dough. Dough that would later be rolled out on a lightly floured surface and turned into piecrusts. The majority of the dough balls were cocooned tightly in plastic wrap and put in the freezer, but Ella Mae left out a dozen or so. One at a time she rolled these out, set them into pie plates, and fluted the edges.

After stopping to eat lunch and read what the newspaper had to say about the upcoming carnival, she got back to work. She still had graham cracker and shortbread cookie crusts to make, and because the Halloween memory had lost its freshness she focused on a different one.

"The Easter Egg Hunt," she said, crumbling graham crackers over her mixer bowl. "The year I won the chocolate duck."

She smiled as she recalled pulling a burlap sack up to her waist and hopping across the wide lawn behind the church. A pocket, shaped like an Easter basket, had been sewn on the front of her sack and Ella Mae, and dozens of other children were supposed to collect eggs and stick them in their basket pockets. The more the kids bounced, the harder it was to keep the eggs tucked inside the pockets. Not only that, but some of the eggs were filled with jellybeans. Those bounced and rattled with every hop, making the children laugh, which, in turn, made it harder to jump.

The biggest challenge was reaching the eggs scattered at the bottom of the lawn's only slope. Weighed down by eggs and unbalanced by the burlap sacks, most of the contestants fell somewhere on that hill. Ella Mae was always among them. However, the children would just roll the rest of the way down, giggling like mad and getting grass stains on their shirts and the top halves of their Easter dresses. The year Ella Mae had fallen the hardest and somersaulted all the way to the bottom was the year that she'd stood, dizzy and laughing, and hopped to the nearest tree to find the coveted prize: a chocolate duck wrapped in gold foil.

By three o'clock, even this delightful memory was used up and Ella Mae was exhausted. She was unused to putting magic into everything she touched. Up until now, she made only some of the pies enchanted. This was the first time she'd injected feelings into each crust, and the effort had taken its toll.

She looked at the flour-covered floor and knew that she didn't even have the strength to sweep. "I need coffee," she mumbled wearily and left her untidy kitchen. Locking the back door, she trudged to the Cubbyhole, shocked by how weak she felt. She had to stop more than once to catch her breath, and when she was only a block away from the bookstore, she collapsed onto a bench and sat there for several minutes.

"Are you all right, ma'am?" a man asked. "You sat down kind of hard."

"I'm just worn out," she said. "Too much work and not enough play." She tried to smile, but the muscles in her face wouldn't comply.

The man nodded. "We all have days like that." His voice was kind. "But the tough times don't last. Just keep that in mind."

"Thank you." Ella Mae gave him a grateful smile. "I'm meeting a friend at the Cubbyhole. Seeing her will give me a boost."

Satisfied that she wasn't ill, the man told her to get some rest and walked away. Ella Mae watched him leave, vowing to store away the warmth she felt over the stranger's concern. *When a friend or family member is solicitous, it feels good*, Ella Mae thought. *But when a person you don't know from Adam cares about your welfare, there's something special about that. It strengthens your faith in your fellow man, makes you believe that goodness is everywhere, just waiting to show itself.*

Buoyed by this notion, Ella Mae made her way to the end of the block and entered the Cubbyhole. She stumbled past the display of snow-themed children's books and dropped into one of the soft reading chairs.

"Look what the cat dragged in," said a familiar voice.

"Hello, Loralyn." Ella Mae didn't bother glancing up. She was too tired to raise her head and she had no interest in exchanging verbal barbs with her nemesis.

And then Suzy's face was in front of hers. "You look awful. Like you've pulled too many all-nighters. Want some coffee?"

"Please," Ella Mae whispered.

"Loralyn, I think you need to talk to Ella Mae. She was at the party too and might have a different perspective."

Loralyn snorted. "She won't help me. Even if she could, I wouldn't want her help."

"You two need to get over yourselves," Suzy chided. "Now sit down until I get back. Each of you has something the other person wants. If Ella Mae can help protect your family's reputation from the rumors that are bound to start circulating and you can play your part in getting her mama back, then you'll both win."

Suzy moved off and Ella Mae caught a glimpse of toned calves and a leopard-print skirt as Loralyn took the seat opposite her. She didn't say a word, and when Suzy returned with Ella Mae's coffee, she clicked her tongue in disappointment.

"Seeing as you probably can't think clearly at the moment, just focus on getting this down your throat," she said.

Ella Mae immediately complied. She drank the coffee in greedy gulps, ignoring the heat in her mouth and throat.

"You used too much magic today. A common novice mistake," Loralyn said haughtily. "But I keep forgetting that you're new to all this."

"It's true," Ella Mae confessed. "But it'll be worth it."

"Start talking," Suzy said to Loralyn. "I'm going to grab Ella Mae a huge glass of water. She probably doesn't even realize she's dehydrated."

Loralyn waited until Suzy was out of earshot before saying, "I've just spent two miserable hours at the police station. Suzy's a good listener, but she can't imagine how grueling the experience was. How humiliating. You can, of course, since you've been interrogated . . ." She frowned in mock concentration. "How many times is it now?"

Ella Mae ignored the question. "What happened? Does this have anything to do with Eira's death?"

"Wouldn't you like to know?" Loralyn examined her French manicure.

"I would and you will tell me. I am the Lady's daughter and a dead woman was found just outside our grove." Ella Mae glanced behind her to make sure that none of the other patrons were listening, but she saw only a mother showing her toddler a picture book about snowmen. The toddler was talking loudly enough to obscure anything Ella Mae had to say. She turned back to Loralyn. "Why were you questioned?"

"Because we were the hosts, of course. The last time Eira was seen alive was at our house. Such a nuisance. Why couldn't you have taken her to your place for a piece of pie and a nice chat?"

"I wish I had," Ella Mae said. "She might still be with us. I liked her, you know."

Loralyn gave an eloquent shrug. "She was pretty enough in a waif-like, tiny dancer kind of way. Not much personality though. Like I told the cops, I can't imagine why anyone would bother killing her. She has no money of her own. It's all Robert's. And it's not like he'd bump her off to get her life insurance payout. That sum is pocket change for men like Robert Morgan."

"It's not always about money, Loralyn. And why are you so certain she was murdered?" Ella Mae strongly believed that Eira had met with foul play, but she wanted to know everything that the police told the Gaynors.

"According to the lab results, Eira ingested several sleeping pills along with some alcohol. One pill would have been enough to send her off to dreamland, but the amount found in her bloodstream was enough to render a bull unconscious, so our men in blue have concluded that she was barely breathing when she was brought to the park. Assuming she was brought there involuntarily, that is. She could have committed suicide for all we know."

Ella Mae frowned. "I don't think so. Her best friend said she was excited about moving here. Hopeful. People with hope don't lie down and submit to hypothermia."

"Then who would do this to her?" Loralyn puzzled.

Ella Mae pictured a man carrying Eira in his arms, her limp limbs dangling as he walked. She imagined how the moonlight had shone on Eira's pale hair and clothes, making her look like a ghost long before she became one. "She was taken to the park and left there. Left to freeze to death. That kind of cruelty isn't about money. It speaks of rage. Or revenge. Her killer must have been filled with a cold hatred."

"Well, I don't know who the murderer is and neither does my mother, so don't bother asking. It's totally inconvenient for us to be involved in this investigation at all. Worse than that is the negative media attention that's certain to follow. That's not good for our reputation. And anything that compromises our family name is bad for business."

Suzy returned with a second cup of coffee, a large glass of water, and a protein bar. Ella Mae drank the water and started in on the protein bar. She was feeling a little stronger, but not much.

Loralyn was studying her. "So now you know what's going on. Do you really think there's anything you can do to help?"

"Yes," Ella Mae said. "I've just hired Eira's best friend. She knows most, if not all, of the partygoers from Oak Knoll. Eira didn't have a connection with anyone from Havenwood, so I think it's safe to assume that someone from her town was out to do her harm."

"How far can some BFF's gossip get us?" Loralyn scoffed. "We need an eyewitness."

Ella Mae took a sip of coffee. "Oh, I don't know about that. For example, Jenny might know who suffers from insomnia and might have a prescription for sleeping pills."

Loralyn lifted her brows. "All right. Maybe you and this Jenny person could prove to be useful. And I assume you want something in return, aside from protecting our community and defending truth, justice, and, oh, just fill in the blank with the idealistic principle of your choosing."

Ella Mae glanced at Suzy. "Did you ask Loralyn about the missing pages from *Lake Lore of the Americas*?"

Suzy nodded. "I showed her the book. She thinks she might know where they are."

Hope bloomed in Ella Mae's heart, burning in the center of her chest like a sun. She had to fight against her desire to grab Loralyn by her fur-trimmed collar and shake her until she promised to deliver the pages. However, she mastered her desperation and returned Loralyn's cool look with measured calm.

"I don't think you or your mother are involved in Eira's death," she said and turned to Suzy. "Opal wouldn't have done anything to upset Robert Morgan. She and he are finalizing some major real estate deal in which she's sure to make an enormous profit. She'll want to keep Morgan happy until the ink is dry." Ella Mae focused on Loralyn again. "I will do everything I can to find Eira's killer. If I succeed in removing all suspicion from the Gaynors, then you must let me borrow those pages."

"Agreed," Loralyn said, looking a little too smug for Ella Mae's comfort. Were the pages useless? Were they damaged? Completely unreadable?

She's just trying to mess with you. Don't fall for it. Ella Mae held out her hand. "Then we have a pact."

Loralyn hesitated. A pact between members of their kind

was taken seriously. An oath breaker could be punished by being denied the right to use their gifts for a set amount of time, and Ella Mae knew how much Loralyn enjoyed manipulating men with her enchanted voice. But she finally took Ella Mae's hand and said, "We have a pact." She then rose and smoothed her leopard-print skirt. "I'll leave you to it. If you need assistance from our end, you should ask my mother. I have important things to see to, like planning the winter carnival fashion show."

When Loralyn was gone, Suzy gave Ella Mae a triumphant look. "See? That wasn't so bad. You two can get along when you try."

"I would have gone after Eira's killer without the promise of the missing pages," Ella Mae said and then jerked a little as her cell phone rang. Pulling it out of her jeans pocket, she saw that it was Jenny calling. "I am so glad to hear from you. Are you in Havenwood?"

"Just passed the town limits sign," Jenny said.

"I need a huge favor. Let me tell you how to get to the Cubbyhole bookstore. I'll be waiting for you here."

Suzy raised her brows in a silent question but couldn't wait for Ella Mae's answer as the mother carrying the toddler was waiting to purchase several items. By the time Suzy had bagged two books on snowmen, one book on Jack Frost, and a cookbook for fussy eaters, Ella Mae had her eyes closed and was minutes away from sleep. She heard Jenny's Camaro pull up to the curb before she saw a burst of yellow through the display window. And then Jenny was squatting down next to her, peering at her with concern.

"This is going to take more than a little zap," she said and put both hands on Ella Mae's shoulders. "Here comes the skip in your step."

A wave of heat flooded Ella Mae's body. She felt as if her blood had turned to molten gold. It wasn't an unpleasant sensation and was utterly unlike the burn of Hugh's kiss. This was like an injection of sunshine—a jolt of pure energy.

"Wow," Ella Mae said, holding on to Jenny's arms for a moment. "That was amazing."

Jenny stepped back, smiling. "You overdid it, didn't you? I've seen that look before. Your muscles went all doughy and your eyes glazed over."

"I feel much better now."

"That's because I gave you the equivalent of ten shots of espresso," Jenny said and then glanced at her watch. "I hope you don't mind, but I haven't come alone today. I was leading a mini caravan of folks from Oak Knoll, including my brother. They're headed to your place as we speak."

Ella Mae handed her a set of keys hanging from a brass partridge key ring. "By all means, let them in."

Jenny left along with another of Suzy's customers. "Did she say she had a brother?" Suzy asked, watching the yellow Camaro turn south onto Soldier Street.

"She did. His name's Aiden."

"In that case, I'm closing early." She flipped the open sign over and turned off the lights. "If Aiden looks anything like his sister, then I want to be the first one to welcome him to Havenwood."

The next day, after staying up too late helping Jenny, Aiden, and a middle-aged couple named Shirley and Joe settle into their rooms in Partridge Hill, Ella Mae unlocked the back door of The Charmed Pie Shoppe and looked around at her untidy kitchen.

"This won't do," she said, tied on an apron, and got to work.

Reba showed up early, as did Jenny and Aiden. Jenny took one look at the shop's coffee machines and shook her head. "You need to upgrade these. I can't make espressos. I can't even steam milk."

"Just you wait. The money will start rollin' in." Reba handed Jenny an apron. "And Ella Mae means to use it to

help your people. So our customers will have to make do
with regular cups of joe until you're all standin' on your
own two feet."

Jenny blushed. "I didn't mean—"

"You can always speak your mind around Ella Mae and
me. The three of us are gonna be spendin' lots of time
together. We've got to be free to be ourselves." Reba turned
to Aiden, who towered over her. In fact, Jenny's brother was
one of the biggest men Ella Mae had ever seen. He was well
over six feet tall and was as brawny as a bull. His arms were
tree-trunk thick, and despite the cold temperatures, he wore
nothing but an orange Sunkist soda T-shirt. "As for you, my
strappin' young buck, Ella Mae wants to put you in charge
of deliveries this week. I know it's not the kind of work
you're used to, but reckon you'll get some big tips walkin'
around in that tight shirt. I bet the ladies at the hair salon
will call here every hour."

Aiden smiled. "I hope they don't mind waiting. I have
no idea where anything is in this town. Good thing my
phone has GPS." He patted his pocket. "The way I see it,
this job will give folks a chance to get to know me. That
should help me find, uh, different work."

"A more manly job?" Jenny flicked her brother with the
tail end of a dishtowel. Aiden snatched the towel from her,
crumpled it between his massive hands, and threw it at her
as if it were a snowball.

Reba drew out a licorice stick and thwacked him on the
forearm.

"Ow!" The big man examined the red mark on his skin
and gave Reba a wounded look. "What was that for?"

She grinned saucily. "I know all sorts of ways to get a
man's attention. Want me to show you some more?"

Ella Mae knew it was time to restore order. "Listen up!
We need to get ready for a packed house. Reba, you show
Jenny the ropes and I'll see how Aiden fares as a sous chef."

"Oh, no." Aiden paled and gestured at the kitchen doors.

"I know all about furnaces and fuse boxes, heat pumps and AC units, but, Ms. LeFaye, I can't cook. Unless you want me to start a fire, I don't think you want me back there."

His remark about starting fires gave Ella Mae pause. She and Reba exchanged wary glances before Ella Mae took Aiden by the elbow. "We'll start with knife training. Learning how to chop, slice, cube, and mince can come in handy."

"Especially with a murderer on the loose," Jenny said, her eyes flashing with anger. Fortunately, her dark mood didn't linger. By the time the tables were set with fresh flowers in the bud vases and the coffeepots had finished brewing, Reba came into the kitchen to tell Ella Mae that the pie shop's new employee was humming and polishing flatware with the edge of her clean apron.

"And there's a line outside. Folks are chompin' at the bit to get in."

Dusting cinnamon sugar from her fingers, Ella Mae grinned. "Good. And the Upton siblings?"

"Aiden's on the porch with his fists tucked under his biceps. He looks like a bouncer at some seedy bar, but his smile is electric. He's tellin' folks about our new delivery service, and Jenny's pimpin' the specials. That girl's a natural." Reba gave her apron a tug. "I'm ready. You?"

Ella Mae nodded. "Yep. Every piece of pie, slice of tart, and wedge of quiche has been baked with a little something extra. We should expect lines for lunch too. I think the word will spread quickly."

"What's the special ingredient?"

"Glee." Ella Mae tossed a pinch of sugar into the air. The tiny grains caught the morning light, winked like diamonds for half a heartbeat, and dropped back to the worktable. "Pure, childlike, unapologetic glee."

"Sounds good enough to eat." Reba pointed at the clock mounted over the sink. "Fire up the ovens, darlin'. I'm going invite our first wave of customers inside."

That was the longest conversation Ella Mae had with

Reba until after the tea service. Between the lunch and tea services, Ella Mae was finally able to catch up with Jenny and Aiden as they grabbed something to eat. Both siblings seemed happy with their work and were surprised by the friendliness of Havenwood's citizens.

"They're good tippers too," Aiden said after swallowing a large bite of chicken tortilla pie.

"I'll say." Jenny gave her apron pocket a satisfied pat.

"We have one more service to go," Ella Mae said while she loaded the dishwasher for the fifth time. "You guys are doing great. Reba? Everything okay?"

"Couldn't be better." Reba tore into a package of Twizzlers. "I've heard lots of giggling and Mrs. Declan skipped down the path on her way to the car. Don't know if that was because Jenny touched her hand or because she had a double helpin' of dessert, but it's probably been twenty years and a hundred pounds since that woman has been that light on her feet. It was a treat to watch her, I tell you. It's had me grinnin' for the past hour."

At that moment, Ella Mae happened to peer out the window over the sink. "Jenny, you and I may have given these ladies an overdose of youthful energy. Come and look."

Reba, Jenny, and Aiden joined Ella Mae at the sink. Their eyes went wide when they saw three elderly women playing hopscotch in the parking lot.

"Check out Ms. Harvey." Ella Mae smiled in delight. "She jumped the whole thing on one leg. Isn't she almost ninety?"

"I think they stole the chalk from our menu board," Reba said with a mixture of wonder and admiration. "Sly devils."

The employees of The Charmed Pie Shoppe witnessed similar scenes for the rest of the day. There was a great deal of giggling, silliness, and skipping. In the middle of teatime, Mr. Patel, the stern-faced bank manager, broke into the bubbles he'd bought for his young nephew and began blowing them across the room. The rest of the customers darted about, popping them with their forks while the bank tellers stuck spoons to their faces. According to Jenny, even the Methodist minister had a dozen spoons hanging from his cheeks, chin, and forehead by the end of the tea service.

"You have talented customers," she teased Ella Mae.

An hour later, Reba pushed through the swing doors wearing an expression of relief. "Sweet Lord, if I have to listen to Mrs. O'Shea tell another knock-knock joke I am gonna lose my mind! I'll give you a little taste. Knock, knock."

"Who's there?" Ella Mae asked.

"Pecan."

"Pecan who?"

"Pecan somebody your own size."

Ella Mae laughed while Reba rolled her eyes in annoyance.

Finally, the last customer left and Reba locked the front door and sagged against it. Ella Mae brewed a pot of tea and invited her three employees to sit down. She filled their teacups and served them slices of apricot crumble tart.

"Here's to the first of many successful days together," she said and toasted Jenny, Aiden, and Reba. "And I haven't forgotten about Eira," Ella Mae said to Jenny when their plates were empty. "Have you been able to find out whether she or Robert were taking sleeping pills? I know I only asked you about that last night and you were in the middle of moving into Partridge Hill, but what are your thoughts?"

"There's no way Eira would have voluntarily swallowed any kind prescription drug," Jenny said firmly. "She was so paranoid about her pregnancy that she wouldn't eat peanut butter, fish, or anything that might contain a trace of caffeine."

"But there was alcohol in her system when she died." Ella Mae argued gently. "Maybe she was desperate. Maybe she was looking for an escape. A permanent one. She did seem unhappy, though you'd know better than the rest of us if she was even capable of such an act."

"No!" Jenny shot to her feet so quickly that her chair fell over. "No. I refuse to believe that."

Someone knocked on the front door. Without bothering to turn her head, Reba shouted, "We're closed! Come back tomorrow, ya hear?"

The knocking continued.

"I'm already up. I'll see who it is," Jenny said.

After peering out through the glass, Jenny's body stiffened. She flung open the door but didn't give the man on the stoop a chance to enter. Ella Mae couldn't see him clearly, but something about the lines and angles of his face seemed familiar. She was just about to invite him in when Jenny's right fist shot forward. It connected with the man's nose with a sickening crunch.

"It's about time you showed up!" Jenny hissed, rubbing her knuckles. "Well, don't just stand there bleeding on the welcome mat. You have some major explaining to do."

Chapter 7

At the sight of blood, Reba grabbed a napkin and moved behind Jenny. Jenny didn't hear her approach and stepped backward, right onto Reba's foot.

"Sweet mercy, girl! Are you hell-bent on inflictin' as many injuries as possible?" Scowling at Jenny, she beckoned for the bleeding man to enter. "It's all right. She won't haul off and cold cock you again."

"Says who?" Anger rolled off Jenny's body like waves of summer heat. "I should throttle him until he tells us where he's been. Or where he was when Eira was freezing to death!"

Ella Mae got up and touched Jenny's arm. "Have a seat. You need to calm down so we can all listen to what he has to say."

When Jenny hesitated, Ella Mae gave her a little push. "Go on." She then coaxed the stranger forward. "You're Barric Young," she said. "I saw you dancing with Eira at the Gaynors' party. Please. Come in and join us."

Glancing warily at Jenny, Barric took the chair next to

Reba. She tapped gently on the napkin covering his nose. "May I? I'd like to see if your beak is broken."

Barric nodded and turned to face her.

"If it's not broken, I can try again," Jenny muttered.

"Doesn't look crooked," Reba said when she was done. She put a hand on Barric's shoulder. "But I'm afraid it'll turn a pretty shade of purple. Kind of like blueberry pie filling." She offered him a clean napkin. "Keep applyin' pressure, hon."

Ella Mae gestured at the teapot. "Could I pour you a cup?" When he shook his head, she explained who she was. "I've been trying to find out what happened to Eira. I . . . My aunts were the ones who found her on the mountain. I'm so sorry, Barric. I could tell she was really special to you." She waited for a moment and then asked, "When did you last see Eira?"

"A little after ten o'clock," Barric said. Due to his pinched nostrils, his voice sounded high-pitched and juvenile. There was nothing humorous about the agony etched on his face, however. When Ella Mae had seen him at the Gaynors' party, he'd been an attractive young man twirling a beautiful woman across the dance floor. He'd shone nearly as brightly as Eira, but now his golden hair was a dirty blond shade and his skin was wan. His proud bearing was also absent. He sagged in his chair, shoulders hunched, staring blankly at the teapot. "I don't mean to be rude, but I'd rather not talk to you about her," he said to Ella Mae. "I don't know you."

Ella Mae's heart hurt for the young man across the table. Every inch of him was weighed down by grief.

"You can trust her," Aiden said to Barric. "She and her friends and family have given a bunch of Oak Knoll folks a place to stay. And she's helping us find work. She's their Lady's daughter."

Barric lowered the napkin and twisted it between his fingers. "It's so hard to say this, but the last thing Eira and I did together was . . . well, we had a fight. God, I wish I could change that. I wish I could take back everything I said, but I can't. I was out of my mind at that moment. She had me so upset. I didn't think—"

"Yeah, you've had issues with forgetting how to think before," Jenny snapped.

"And I paid the price, didn't I?" Barric shot back, anger surfacing in his eyes. "But I don't go around burning things when I'm pissed off. Like our grove, for example." He pointed at Aiden. "I've seen you messing around with fire. You can make a fire burn even from a distance, can't you? Were you involved in some scheme with Morgan? Did he pay you to torch our grove? Did he have something on you? Because he sure as hell had something on Eira."

Aiden's neck and cheeks flushed a deep red, and he slammed his fists against the table. "Watch it, boy. You're not the first to accuse me of that crime. Do you want to find out what I did to the other people who dared say that to my face?"

Barric made to rise when Ella Mae thrust her arms outward, looking like a traffic cop during rush hour. "This is my shop," she barked. "You will both be civil or I'll throw you out." Her steely expression made it clear that she was completely serious.

Both men were quick to apologize and Ella Mae lowered her arms. She turned to Barric and gestured for him to continue. "I know this is difficult, but we can't help you if we don't know the whole story. No one will interrupt you again, I promise. Please. Go on."

After a long pause, Barric resumed his narrative. "I didn't know Eira was pregnant. She led me into some guy's office to tell me the news. I was furious. I said some really terrible things to her." His forehead glistened with perspiration and he pulled at the collar of his shirt. "I didn't want a baby. Not ever. You can all understand why. When a magical couple has a child together, horrible things usually happen. Because of that stupid curse placed on our kind all those years ago by Myrddin, one of the parents pays a price for daring to defy the odds. I can't tell how many times I've heard of a parent being injured or killed. It always looks like a freak accident to the outside world, but we know the truth, don't we?"

Everyone at the table nodded. Ella Mae's own father had been crushed in a cave-in shortly after her birth. The risk was too great for most magical couples, and she understood why Barric didn't want to take a chance.

"I couldn't imagine losing Eira. Not in exchange for a child. She wanted children more than anything in this world, but I didn't. I never did and she knew that." Shifting uncomfortably in his seat, Barric wiped his brow with a napkin. His hands were shaking. "I guess she was going to have a baby no matter what. But to get pregnant when she was still married to Morgan? That was pure insanity. I knew he'd punish her for making him look like a fool. Everyone knows he can't father a child."

Ella Mae touched Barric lightly on the hand. "I promised not to interrupt, but I have to ask why Eira married Robert Morgan in the first place. Why would a lovely and talented dancer marry such a creep? You mentioned that he had some hold over her."

"She wouldn't tell me what it was," Barric said. "I guess she married him—"

"Because Barric couldn't keep it in his pants," Jenny said, crossing her arms over her chest.

"Jenny." Ella Mae held up a warning finger and her new employee fell silent, but Barric lowered his eyes in shame.

"Eira and I grew up together," he said. "We were in the same kindergarten class. We spent our free time running through the woods or sailing paper boats in the stream behind her house." The timbre of Barric's voice changed. Ella Mae could hear the smile creeping into it. Watching him, she knew that he had returned to his boyhood. A boyhood filled with images of his best friend—a thin, graceful little girl named Eira.

Reba leaned over and whispered in Ella Mae's ear. "Sounds like a good country upbringin'. No wonder he misses that girl. She was his past. Should've been his future too. He doesn't know who he is without her. She was a part of him."

"We even broke a bone at the same time," Barric continued wistfully, unaware that Reba had spoken. "I fell out of the tree house I was building for her and fractured my left arm. Later that day, after she wrote all over my new cast, Eira tried to jump from one of the big rocks in the forest to another. She would have made it if it hadn't been for that patch of moss." He winced at the memory. "She missed and broke her foot. I had to carry her home. Trust me, I didn't mind a bit. We were freshmen in high school and were so in love. We'd been in love forever by then. We were everything to each other." He seemed to hit a wall at this point in their history. Looking up, he met Jenny's eyes. Ella Mae was surprised to see her give him an encouraging nod.

Maybe she's realizing that he's been punished enough, Ella Mae thought. *Whatever he did, he couldn't deserve this anguish.*

"We didn't go to the same college," he went on. "I wanted to be a farmer—my name actually means 'grain farmer.' Eira had always had her heart set on being a dancer. But we picked schools within a decent driving distance so we could still see each other." He rubbed his temples, as if he could erase the memories he was forcing to the forefront of his mind. "One night, during our senior year, we had our first blowout. It was about whether we'd get married and start a family after graduation. I was fine with the marriage part."

"But not the kid part," Reba said helpfully.

Barric nodded. "Eira was so mad that she kicked me out of her dorm room and wouldn't take my calls for weeks. It was the longest we'd ever gone without talking and I didn't handle it well. I went to a bunch of parties. Drank too much. Started thinking I should date other girls. I was curious about . . . sex." His cheeks turned pink. "Eira and I weren't going to sleep together until after we got married. Not many people abstain these days, but we decided it would be more special that way."

Aiden's brows rose. "Seriously? Man that must have been tough." He coughed in a sudden fit of embarrassment. "I'm not trying to be crude, ladies, but when I was in college, I spent half of my time chasing girls. That's what guys my age did. And it also might account for why I'm an electrician and not a nuclear physicist."

"What you do is important," Jenny said firmly. "You can create a Christmas display that can be seen from outer space. And you're a people person. Who would carry the old ladies' groceries if you were holed up in some lab making weapons of mass destruction? Be proud of what you are. I am."

Aiden grinned. "Thanks, sis."

Everyone looked at Barric again. The camaraderie between the siblings must have reminded him of his childhood with Eira, but he swallowed the lump in his throat and plodded on. "I was at a frat party and had had way too much to drink when this girl who'd been flirting with me all semester starting hitting on me. To make a long story short, I slept with her. The next day, I was so guilt-ridden that I drove to Eira's school and told her everything. I begged her to forgive me, but she couldn't. She refused to speak to me. No matter what I did, I couldn't earn her forgiveness." His breath caught on the last word and he fixed his gaze on the tablecloth.

Ella Mae poured Barric a cup of tea. "Drink this." She then turned to Jenny to complete the narrative. "So Eira became a dancer and later met and married Robert Morgan after he saw her perform. Did she marry him to punish Barric?"

Jenny shrugged. "Maybe. Then again, when they got engaged, Morgan was rich and influential and wanted a big family. She never told me that she loved him, so I figured she just wanted the security he could offer."

"Eira went through some hard times when she was a girl," Barric added quietly. "Her mom left when she was in the first grade and her dad wasn't always right in the head. He drank and took pills for depression. The booze and meds didn't mix well, so Eira spent half of her life at my house. She knew she'd have a hot meal and a comfortable place to sleep. Nothing was ever certain at her place. One day, her dad might cook a feast and the next, he'd throw every ounce of food into the woods because he thought it was poisoned."

Reba made tsk-tsk noises. "Poor girl. Where'd her mama go?"

"She fell for a man at work," Barric said. "One day, when Eira was at school and her dad was on some job, Eira's mom packed her things, wrote a quick note saying that she was sorry, and vanished. She was never heard from again." Barric shot Ella Mae a nervous glance, but when she didn't react, he continued. "After her mother left, Eira's world started to unravel. Her dad went downhill fast, and Eira spent her time dreaming of growing up and creating a family that wouldn't be anything like her own."

Ella Mae felt a knife-twist of grief in her stomach. Her world hadn't been the same without her mother, so she understood how alone and scared Eira must have been.

You'll get her back, she told herself. *You won't have to live without her. You're not Eira.*

Reba reached over and squeezed Ella Mae's hand.

"I'm sorry you two fought," Jenny said to Barric. "But are you sure that's the last time you spoke to Eira? You didn't see her leave the Gaynors' house?"

He shook his head.

"Was she drinking anything when you were with her?" Ella Mae asked.

Barric seemed startled by the question. "I don't remember. She dropped a pretty big bomb on me. I don't think I would have noticed much at that point."

Again, his forehead was covered with a sheen of perspiration and Ella Mae couldn't help but wonder if he was being completely forthright. She wished Aunt Verena were here. Not only could she tell if Barric was lying, she could also ask Aiden if he knew more about the fire in Oak Knoll than he let on. But Verena wasn't around and Ella Mae knew it was up to her to discover those answers and more.

Ella Mae tried to process everything she'd heard. "Our next step is clear. I need to find someone who saw Eira after Barric left. I also want to know who else she talked with and what frame of mind she was in by the end of the party."

"How can we help?" Aiden gestured at himself and his sister.

"Talk to the people from Oak Knoll at the carnival this weekend. I'll make a few special pies that will loosen their lips, encourage them to say if they witnessed anything unusual at the party." Ella Mae glanced at her watch. "It's almost suppertime. Barric, do you have a place to stay?"

"I have a room at the resort," he mumbled.

Jenny whistled. "Fancy. How are you swinging that on a farmer's salary?"

"Hey, now. Leave the guy alone." Aiden said. "He's been through enough. Besides, you already gave him a nose-bleed."

"Sorry about that," Jenny told Barric. "I was taking everything out on you. All of my grief. You didn't deserve that."

"Yes, I did. A punch in the face isn't nearly enough," Barric said. "I should have been protecting her. I knew Morgan would lose it when he found out she was pregnant, but I thought she'd be smart enough to hide it from him. I guess she told him that night and he had one of his goons deal with her."

Ella Mae didn't think Eira would risk her own safety or that of her unborn child by confessing that she was carrying another man's baby. "A more likely scenario is that someone overheard your conversation at the Gaynors'. Exactly where were the two of you when she told you about the pregnancy?"

"A man's office. It had a huge desk and one of those globes that opens up to reveal bottles of liquor. But the door was closed. No one could have heard us," Barric insisted.

Barric was clearly unaware of the number of hidden panels within Rolling View. Like Partridge Hill, the grand house was built to help protect its magical owners, and though Ella Mae didn't know the exact locations, she was certain that the Gaynor mansion was replete with passageways, niches, peepholes, and trompe l'oeil.

"Why don't you leave that pricey hotel and come stay with us?" Jenny asked Barric and then checked herself. "If that's okay with Ella Mae."

"No." Barric was quick to refute the offer. "I can't . . . I need . . ." He wiped his forehead with the napkin again. "Thanks, but I can't."

Something isn't right about him, Ella Mae thought. She had no clue what he hadn't told them, but he was hiding something. As with the concealed compartments in Rolling View, one would have to know which button to press to reveal Barric's secrets, but that would prove difficult with him staying at Lake Havenwood Hotel. Suddenly, she had an idea. "Did you come to Havenwood in search of work?"

"Yes." Barric released a defeated sigh. "I must have knocked on every farmhouse door in the county, but no one's hiring right now. I was told to come back in the spring. I really wanted to buy my own place, but I can't sell my Oak Knoll farm. I'm upside down on the mortgage." He studied his knuckles.

Ella Mae tried to relieve his embarrassment. "But you have experience with animals, right?"

"Cows and horses mostly. I grew grain and produced high-quality animal feed on my farm. All organic. The best feed on earth."

Ella Mae smiled. "My friend Chandler Knox is a large-

animal vet and he's been looking for an assistant. I'll tell
him to expect your call. It's not farming, but it's something
to tide you over in the meantime." She passed him a business
card with Chandler's number on the back.

"Thank you." Barric put the card in his pocket and stood
up. "I don't have a cell phone, but if you learn anything about
Eira, call me at the hotel. Night or day. I won't be sleeping.
Not anymore."

A heavy silence descended over the pie shop.

"Is your nose okay?" Jenny asked quietly. "I could get
you some ice."

Barric looked at her, and for just a moment, Ella Mae
saw that lightning flash of anger in his eyes. "My nose will
heal. Other parts of me never will."

And with that, he was gone.

That night, Hugh brought Ella Mae supper. He was waiting
for her in the driveway, an extra-large pizza and a DVD from
Redbox resting on the hood of his truck. Ella Mae was
thrilled to see him, especially since she'd struck out at the
Gaynors' house. She'd been hoping to question Opal about
Barric and Eira, but no one had answered the door and there
were no lights on inside the stately mansion. Ella Mae
decided that she'd have to stop by Loralyn's nail salon the
next day after work. Until then, she was determined not to
think about Eira, burning groves, or her mother.

After Chewy jumped down from the Jeep to greet Dante,
Ella Mae gave Hugh a hug and then ushered everyone into
her cottage. While Hugh entertained the dogs, she fixed a
salad of field greens, plated the pizza, and opened a bottle
of red wine. Snuggled up close, she and Hugh ate on the
sofa, bookended by their dogs.

"Drool all you like," Ella Mae admonished Chewy. "I
refuse to share a single bite of pepperoni and sausage."

"Same goes for you, big man." Hugh gave Dante's head

a quick scratch. "Hold out until the movie starts. I have a surprise for you both."

Ella Mae handed Hugh a cold bottle of beer and sighed in contentment. "This is just what I needed. A peaceful evening in with my favorite men."

A dog began to bark from somewhere in the garden, causing Dante and Chewy to jump up and dash to the front door. When no one opened it for them, they raced to the window seat and peered into the darkness. Seeing nothing, they darted back to the door, barking fervently.

Hugh got up, looked the dogs in the eye, and said, "No." The word was heavy with authority and they ceased their barking immediately. "Do you have a canine visitor?" he asked Ella Mae.

"Partridge Hill has new tenants. One of them is a Schipperke named Miss Lulu." She told Hugh about Jenny and Aiden.

"Should we introduce our boys to the new lady in town? We won't be able to concentrate on this movie until they've met her. They'll just run from the window to the door and back all night."

Ella Mae grabbed Chewy's leash. "We'd better keep them reined in. We don't know how Miss Lulu will respond to our canine Romeos."

The couple led their eager dogs across the frost-brittle grass and into the garden. They found Jenny seated on a stone bench whose legs were made of kneeling cherubs. In the spring, the bench would be nearly obscured by a riot of yellow and silver white roses, but now it looked cold and uninviting.

Miss Lulu took one look at the Jack Russell and the Great Dane prancing at the ends of their leashes and grinned coyly. While the dogs sniffed one another and rubbed noses, Ella Mae introduced Jenny to Hugh.

Jenny removed a thick woolen mitten and shook his hand. "Miss Lulu is used to all kinds of people and pets. Dogs

were welcome in our coffee shop and we even had a customer who brought her cat every day. The cat, Mrs. Pickles,
would sit in the lady's bike basket and drink warm milk
from a saucer while she read the paper and sipped her
cappuccino.

"Sounds like a cool place," Hugh said.

"It is. Luckily, I found another cool place." After winking
at Ella Mae, Jenny got to her feet and rubbed her arms. "I'd
better go in. Miss Lulu and I just got home from a walk and
I thought I'd sit here for a minute and enjoy the stars, but
I'm freezing." She looked at Ella Mae. "Can I leave Miss
Lulu out for a little longer?"

Ella Mae gestured at Chewy and Dante. "Sure. The boys
will keep an eye on her. They know not to wander off the
property."

Jenny wished them a good night and went inside. Ella
Mae glanced up at the windows on the second floor. It made
her happy to have lights shining upstairs again. She particularly liked how they cast a warm glow across the slumbering
garden.

"Let's get back to our movie." She took Hugh by the
hand. "I've got microwave popcorn and a blanket big enough
for the both of us."

Hugh smiled. "We should make this a Tuesday-night
tradition. Just think of how many movies we could see over
the next forty-odd years."

"And how many miles I'll have to run to burn off that
pizza," Ella Mae joked.

"I can think of more interesting cardio exercises," Hugh
said.

Ella Mae swatted him in the stomach. "What are we
watching, by the way?"

"This awesome action flick about a guy who fights ter-
rorists and rescues a boat full of kidnapped sorority girls."

Rolling her eyes, Ella Mae said, "Seeing as you deliberately picked this trash, I can promise you that it'll be all the action you'll see tonight."

Hugh's laughter burst from his mouth, bending into a translucent curlicue before dissolving into blackness. Watching his breath vanish into the air, Ella Mae found herself holding him just a little tighter.

Wednesday passed by in a flash. Customers shivered in the cold as they waited expectantly on the porch or stamped their frozen feet on the sidewalk, hoping for a seat in The Charmed Pie Shoppe to become available soon.

All day long, Aiden darted in and out of the kitchen, his arms loaded with takeout boxes and his pockets stuffed with cash. "I feel kind of awkward driving around town in a pink Jeep," he complained after returning from a delivery. "I'd use the Camaro, but that car is a ticket magnet. Cops go out of their way to leave Jenny expensive love notes under the wiper blade. Of course, that might also have something to do with her habit of parking ten feet away from the curb."

Ella Mae laughed. "I noticed that when she parallel parked outside the Cubbyhole. She practically needed a drawbridge to reach the sidewalk."

Aiden opened a pink bakery box and Ella Mae eased a chocolate bourbon pecan pie into it and watched as he deftly tied the box with string. "The Cubbyhole? That's the shop Suzy owns, right?" His mouth curved into a secretive grin. "She's really cute. And smart."

"I'll tell her that you said so."

"I need to stop by her place and thank her. I told her that I had no idea where to put my stuff in your house—how to arrange it, you know—and she came over and took care of everything. That woman could read me, well, like a book." His cheeks and neck reddened.

Ella Mae wondered if she should encourage Aiden's

interest in Suzy. She liked her new employee well enough, but until she could be sure he had nothing to do with the fire at Oak Knoll, she didn't want her best friend to get involved with him. The person who needed to get close to Aiden Upton was Verena. Verena would have to ask only a single question and then Aiden would be in the clear. Either that or he'd prove to be a murderous arsonist.

I'll have her call in a takeout order tomorrow, Ella Mae thought.

To Aiden, she said, "You'd better hit the road. Mrs. Frazier said she needed that chocolate bourbon pecan pie badly, so we have to get it to her ASAP."

Aiden raised his brows. "What's the rush?"

"She's the mother of five-year-old triplets. Boy triplets."

"Holy crap. I'd better get going."

Ella Mae couldn't help but smile as she watched the burly man in his peach apron rush out to a pink Jeep carrying a pink bakery box. "He looks good in pastels," she said to the cheerful kitchen and prepared to serve the last customers of the day.

After closing, Ella Mae made her way to Loralyn's nail salon. Perfectly Polished was busy and nearly every chair was occupied. The majority of Loralyn's clients were women, but there were also several men receiving treatments. Ella Mae tried to picture Aiden in the pedicure chair having his toes painted a delicate rose pink and had to stifle a giggle.

"May I help you?" the receptionist asked with overt dislike. Ella Mae wasn't exactly her favorite person. She wasn't a client and only stopped by when she had a bone to pick with Loralyn.

"I'm here to see your boss." Ella Mae smiled politely.

The girl glanced down at her appointment book. "I don't see your name written here, Ms. LeFaye."

"That's because this is a private matter. I am here at Ms.

Gaynor's request and she'll be very unhappy if our meeting is delayed."

The idea of earning her employer's displeasure struck a chord with the receptionist. She told Ella Mae to wait and strode to the back of the salon where Loralyn's office and the massage, facial, waxing, and tanning rooms were located.

Loralyn appeared a moment later. She sidled up to Ella Mae and gave her the once-over. "I don't think there are enough hours left in the day to help you. You need a facial, a mani-pedi, a paraffin treatment, and lots of waxing." Pointing at Ella Mae's chin, she said. "Beards are not sexy on a woman."

Refusing to take the bait, Ella Mae said, "Can we talk in your office? It's about the party."

"I asked you to deal with my mother over that subject. I'm in the middle of finalizing the carnival fashion show lineup."

"I only need a few minutes."

Loralyn surveyed the menu board listing the salon's services. "We'll chat during an express facial. Just some hydration and a few extractions. My new esthetician works miracles with blemishes. She's also hearing impaired, so I can have her turn her hearing aids off during your treatment. Follow me."

Ella Mae had no choice but to agree. The receptionist shot her a triumphant look and said, "Enjoy being perfectly polished."

Inside a room decorated like a beach cabana, Loralyn told Ella Mae to lie down on the spa table. She then beckoned to someone in the hall and a moment later, a petite Asian woman entered the room. The woman gave Ella Mae a shy smile. Loralyn tapped her own ear and said, "This will be a silent service, Yuri." The woman bowed, made the necessary adjustment to her hearing aid, and began lighting the candles positioned in each corner of the room. She then moved behind Ella Mae's head, placed a finger on either side of her temple, and applied gentle pressure. "We begin."

Ella Mae exhaled. She felt more relaxed already. Loralyn dimmed the lights and perched on a stool at the foot of the spa table. "Well?"

"I had a chance to talk with Barric Young yesterday. I don't know if you met him at the party, but he was—"

"The hotheaded farmer. I didn't bother speaking with him. He doesn't interest me."

"Because he's poor?"

"And unrefined. I'm sure he crashed our party. I don't remember seeing his name on the guest list."

Yuri tied a towel turban around Ella Mae's hair and wiped her skin clean with a warm washcloth that smelled of eucalyptus. Using a cosmetic brush, she began to paint Ella Mae's face with a thick cream scented with mint. The cream quickly hardened into a mask and Yuri began to rub Ella Mae's knotted shoulders, making it hard for her to focus on the purpose of her visit.

"I think he just wanted to be near Eira. They were lovers." The mask made Ella Mae's cheeks and chin feel stiff. It was difficult to speak clearly. "What makes you call him a hothead?"

Loralyn laughed derisively. "The same thing that lets me say that you're totally wrong about he and Eira being lovers. I overheard them talking and I can assure you that they've never done the deed. Actually, I should amend that previous statement. Eira was talking. Barric was *yelling*."

Ella Mae propped herself up by the elbows. "About what?"

"I found the entire argument extremely dull." Loralyn feigned a yawn. "After all, the subject matter was such a cliché. Girl tells boy she's pregnant. Boy rages because baby isn't his. Girl cries. Boy storms off, wounded to the core. Total soap opera material."

"The baby wasn't Barric's?" Ella Mae gaped, forcing a crusty piece of mask to fall from her upper lip.

Loralyn shrugged. "According to what I heard, Mr.

Twinkle Toes never got past second base. And he obviously thought his lady love was pure as a snowflake. That boy was furious." She paused thoughtfully. "Everyone knows to expect vengeance from a woman scorned. But what about a man scorned? What does he do?"

"A man consumed by fury can react without considering the consequences of his actions," Ella Mae said, gesturing for Yuri to hand her a washcloth. She scrubbed the mask off her face and then met Loralyn's curious stare. "He can be driven by impulse, by a desperate need to lash out. He can feed his anger until it commands him. Until he obeys it. And that leaves me wondering this: Was Barric angry enough to murder the love of his life?"

Chapter 8

Loralyn didn't answer the rhetorical question. Having realized that Ella Mae had nothing to offer in exchange for the information she'd provided, she signaled for Yuri to turn on her hearing aid and left the room in a cloud of indignation.

"Relax. It's okay." Yuri convinced Ella Mae to lie back down.

While the aesthetician treated her skin with deft fingers, Ella Mae tried to make sense of what Loralyn had said.

Who had fathered Eira's baby if not Barric? Ella Mae had no doubt that he and Eira had been in love, but Barric had freely admitted that he never wanted a child. Had he avoided being intimate with the woman he loved because he was afraid of getting her pregnant?

Ella Mae's shoulders tensed as she realized that Barric was much more than Eira's grief-stricken lover. He was the second man Eira had jilted. The first had been her husband. And, like Robert Morgan, Barric had become a suspect in Ella Mae's eyes. After all, Barric had admitted that Eira had made him very angry the night of the party—that she'd dropped a bomb on him. Hearing the news that the woman he loved was pregnant with another man's child must have torn a hole in his heart. Had Eira's duplicity led to her death?

Ella Mae knew all too well what betrayal did to a person. Less than a year ago, she'd discovered her husband *in flagrante* with two redheads who lived in the same apartment building. Though it had become less and less painful as the months passed, the memory was forever seared into her memory. For a time, she couldn't think of her husband without feeling a white-hot rage—the kind of rage that's birthed when love turns into hate.

There was a thin line between the two, Ella Mae knew. Some people were able to cross it and return again. To forgive and forget. Not Ella Mae. Her anger had eventually dulled, but any trace of affection she'd once felt for her husband dissipated along with it, leaving her feeling nothing at all.

Barric hadn't had the chance to reach that stage of numbness. His overt anguish told Ella Mae that he was being wracked by grief and regret. And possibly, by overwhelming guilt as well.

Had he killed Eira? Ella Mae could picture Barric carrying his unconscious lover in his arms, holding her close to him as he climbed the mountain path. Was he truly capable of leaving her to freeze to death? To die alone in the dark?

"This is full of vitamin C and will tingle a bit." Yuri applied a cream that smelled of oranges to Ella Mae's skin and then massaged it into her cheeks, forehead, and neck. When she was done, she advised Ella Mae to drink plenty of water and to return for another facial in six weeks.

"Thank you. That was wonderful," Ella Mae said. "I'm sorry that I kept moving around."

"You must learn to be still. In here." Yuri smiled and touched her heart. "You are very beautiful. Full of light. I hope you'll come back and see me."

The compliment buoyed Ella Mae. She practically floated to the receptionist's desk where she paid an exorbitant price for her service and left Yuri a generous tip.

After collecting Chewy from Canine to Five, Ella Mae headed for Aunt Dee's house. Her aunt's calm and quiet demeanor was just what Ella Mae needed. Dee had a deep sense of tranquility about her. A stillness of the heart, as Yuri had indicated.

Pulling up in front of a converted barn her aunt used as a studio, Ella Mae let Chewy out to play with Dee's pack of rescue dogs and rapped on the massive sliding door.

"Come in!" Dee called.

Ella Mae stepped inside, expecting to see her aunt sculpting a metal replica of someone's beloved pet. She'd seen countless numbers of cats, dogs, birds, hamsters, goldfish, and all sorts of reptiles come to life in Dee's studio, but she'd never slid open one of the heavy barn doors to find her aunt crafting a piece of furniture.

"Are you diversifying?" Ella Mae teased. "I thought you already had more work than you could handle."

Dee pushed her welder's mask off her face. "I do, but I promised to help the animal rescue center with their bed. If they win, they'll use the prize money to build a cat play area. There are more homeless cats than ever these days and there isn't enough room for them to exercise."

She stared at the white and blue flame of her welding torch and Ella Mae could see her aunt's resolve to aid the shelter. Dee loved all animals, but animals in need of rescue held a special place in her heart.

Ella Mae edged closer. "So this is for Saturday's bed race?"

Dee nodded. "I've made it as light as possible. The shelter volunteer who'll be sitting in this bed weighs less than some of my dogs, so this baby should fly. And the four runners have been practicing all year. They really want to win one of the cash awards."

Ella Mae peered at the headboard, admiring the design her aunt had engraved into the metal. A dog and cat were nestled together on top of a plaid blanket. In a dream bubble above their heads was an image of a charming little house. The animals were clearly fantasizing about being given the chance to live in such a home. "That picture alone will elicit lots of donations," she said.

Dee gestured at the footboard. "Check out the rest of the story."

Walking to the end of the bed, Ella Mae couldn't help but smile when she saw the engravings of two sleeping children. To the left was a boy who dreamt of throwing a ball to a small dog with a spotted coat. On the right was a girl who dreamt of dangling a piece of yarn before a fluffy kitten.

"How did you do it?" Ella Mae asked. "The eyes of the dog and cat—they're glowing. I thought you could only do that with a sculpture—that you needed to have a feel for what the real animal was like in order to bring its spirit to life inside the metal."

"These two are real animals. The dog is a beagle mix named Scout and the cat is a domestic longhair named Snowball. They're at the shelter, waiting to be adopted. I've gotten to know them quite well over the past few weeks."

"I hope I'll be able to get away from the pie shop booth for a few minutes to watch the race," Ella Mae said. "From what I've heard, the costumes have been getting crazier every year."

Dee shook her head in wonder. "I can't believe what a draw this race has become."

The bed races were a relatively new component of the winter carnival. Havenwood's major competition had always been the annual Fourth of July Row for Dough boat race. That event took place during the height of the tourist season and routinely filled the town coffers. Because of its incredible success, Uncle Buddy had proposed that a race be added to the winter carnival program as well.

The first bed race was relatively small, but thanks to a bunch of riotous YouTube videos, word quickly spread and the number of teams entering had tripled by the second year. Now, teams came from all over the South to compete. The registration fees had also increased, as had the cash awards. If Havenwood's animal shelter could secure one of the three top prizes, beating out teams of triathletes or structural engineers, it would be a real coup for the volunteers who worked there.

"I suspect you'll see plenty of unfamiliar faces in the pie shop starting tomorrow. I heard that lots of teams, including the circuit's most infamous team, The Naughty Nurses, checked into the resort last night."

Ella Mae rolled her eyes. "Naughty Nurses? Seriously?"

Dee grinned. "These ladies wear very short, very tight uniforms with white garters, and many a competing team has been distracted by their, ah, assets. The Naughty Nurses have caused dozens of crashes. They have a loyal following too. People travel from all over to watch them race. And they're fast. *Really* fast."

"Can the shelter gals take them?" Ella Mae asked.

"I hope so. I've been researching lightweight metals and different types of wheels for nearly nine months now." Dee put a hand on the metal frame. "If the Barkers Beauties can avoid a collision, I think they have a strong chance of winning." She put her welder's mask on her workbench and began to polish the footboard. "Is there something on your mind, hon? I have a feeling you didn't come here to talk about the bed races."

Ella Mae filled her in on the investigation. "I need Verena's help. But how can I get Barric and Aiden and the rest of the Oak Knoll folks to open up to her?"

Dee tapped on the bed. "Get her to chat with them at the carnival or while they're watching the race. If they're distracted, they're unlikely to realize that they're being grilled by a woman who can tell whether they're lying or not."

"You're brilliant, Aunt Dee." Ella Mae gave her a hug. "I always find answers when I come over here."

"It's the animals," Dee said. "They settle us—give us the kind of peaceful calm we need to be able to think straight." She slid the door open and was immediately rushed by three dogs and an orange tomcat. Dee's pets gazed at her with adoration. She leaned over to ruffle their fur and coo at them. "Theirs is an unselfish kind of love. They ask so little, yet give so much. People aren't like that, Ella Mae. Look at Eira and Barric. Both of them were unfaithful. They made promises they couldn't keep. They hurt each other deeply. That isn't an unselfish love."

"No, it isn't," Ella Mae agreed. "But what about the man who gave Eira what she most wanted? The chance to have a child of her own? Could she have been in love with him?"

Dee considered this. "I'm not certain she was capable of loving any man. She was married to Robert Morgan, made promises to Barric, her childhood sweetheart, and still, she had another lover. A man who doesn't want to be known."

"Why do you say that?"

"Because he's stayed in the shadows instead of coming forward to seek justice for her," Dee said. "If he loved her, he'd act."

"Maybe he's safe as long as he hides. I'm sure both Robert and Barric would try to punish him for sleeping with Eira," Ella Mae said. She watched a black cat slink into the woods, instantly disappearing in the dark. "On the other hand, this third man could be the killer. In that case, he'll stick to the shadows to protect himself."

"Why did all these men fall for her?" Dee mused. "She had a fragile beauty, I could see that. But what made her truly special was long gone by the time we found her that night on the mountain. What was it?"

"Her dancing," Ella Mae said without hesitation. "That was her gift. It must have had the same effect on men as Loralyn's voice. Eira could seduce through dance. I assumed that she was sweet and innocent, but she may have been more manipulative than I could ever imagine. Even Loralyn doesn't toy with three men at once. She usually limits herself to two."

Dee seemed lost in thought. Scooping up an orange tom-cat, she began to stroke the fur under his chin. He purred and rubbed his pink nose against her cheek. "Where did this third man see her dance? Perhaps Eira's friend can tell you."

Ella Mae groaned. "The things I've learned today are going to tear Jenny apart! She thought she was Eira's closest friend, but look at all the secrets Eira kept from her." Ella Mae squatted down to pet a yellow lab who'd grown tired of trying to get Dee's attention. "I hate to cause her any more pain. She's strong, but she's been through so much already."

"Having Eira's murderer behind bars will help everyone heal," Dee said softly. "It's the unanswered questions that keep our wounds from closing."

Whenever Dee spoke so morosely, Ella Mae wanted to ask what had happened to give her aunt such insight about pain and loss. Reba had once told her that Dee had had her heart broken, but no one would elaborate any further.

Hasn't everyone had at least one broken heart? Ella Mae thought as she glanced at the animals Dee had taken in. It suddenly occurred to her that her aunt surrounded herself with these homeless cats and dogs because loving them was less risky than engaging in a relationship with another human being. Ella Mae didn't know who'd caused Dee to don such thick armor, but it must have happened many years ago, because her aunt had been alone as long as Ella Mae could remember.

As if sensing her thoughts, Dee said, "My questions were never answered and I never got over my first heartbreak. I'll tell you all about it, but not today. I have a bed to finish and you have far more important tasks to accomplish." She let the squirming tom jump from her arms. Ella Mae watched the cat run off to seek cover under the nearest bush, said good-bye to Dee, and then ushered Chewy into the Jeep.

"Let's go home," Ella Mae said to her terrier. "A hot bath and a big glass of wine are calling my name."

She carefully edged away from the animals and drove down her aunt's long and winding driveway. Overhead, the moon was an insignificant sliver and the stars were concealed behind a curtain of dark clouds. The trees lining the road were black hulking shadows and the forest felt close. Too close.

Ella Mae tried to picture her mother's garden in summer, to call forth an image of sunshine and colorful butterflies hovering over silky petals, but the night seemed to grow darker still. She sped up, in a sudden hurry to reach her cozy house.

Once inside, she turned on all the lights and fed Chewy. She then lit a fire, poured herself half a glass of wine, and called Lake Havenwood Hotel. When she asked to be put through to Barric Young's room, the desk clerk hesitated.

"I'm sorry, ma'am," he said. "Mr. Young has checked out."

"What?" Ella Mae couldn't conceal her astonishment. "Oh, but I really need to reach him. Do you have a contact number?"

The clerk cleared his throat officiously. "I am not permitted to share that information."

"Of course." Ella Mae knew it was useless to argue, but she had to locate Barric. "Did he leave a message? A forwarding address?"

"I'm afraid not." The clerk's polite tone was tinged with impatience. "Is there anything else I can do for you this evening?"

"No, thank you." Ella Mae hung up and sank down on the sofa. She wrapped the chenille throw Aunt Sissy had given her for Christmas around her shoulders and threw a slim piece of wood from the hearth basket into the fire. The flames diminished for a moment and then leapt over the fresh wood, crackling and snapping as they enveloped it.

Chewy finished his meal and came to sit beside her. The terrier closed his eyes while Ella Mae continued to stare into the fire. A scrap of paper floated just out of the reach of the hungry flames and Ella Mae followed its perilous flight, thinking of Eira and how she'd danced with danger.

"You played with people's hearts," she whispered when a tongue of fiery yellow eventually consumed the paper. "That's far more reckless than playing with fire. And yet, you were left to freeze to death. Fire and ice. Love and hate." She pulled the throw tighter across her shoulders. "And now, a murder suspect's gone missing." Running her fingers through Chewy's fur, she sighed and picked up the phone again. It was time to tell the police why they needed to find Barric Young without delay. Maybe they could track him down, question him, and declare the case closed before the winter carnival.

Touching the four-leaf-clover-shaped burn on her palm, Ella Mae took a deep breath and dialed the station.

The next day passed in a flurry of baking. The Charmed Pie Shoppe was packed to capacity from the moment it opened until closing time. Ella Mae didn't untie her apron and leave at four in the afternoon as she usually did. Instead, she worked until late in the evening preparing food for the carnival.

By the time Friday afternoon rolled around, Reba came into the kitchen to announce that the streets of Havenwood were crowded with unfamiliar faces. "Every hotel within fifty miles is booked solid. Our regulars are all out of sorts because they have to wait even longer to eat at 'their pie shop' because a bunch of 'snowbirds' decided to visit. I asked Jenny to give the locals an extra shot of zip-a-dee-doo-dah."

"How's Jenny doing?" Ella Mae asked. She knew the Upton siblings had left for the day, and regretted having been too busy to talk with them much.

"She's lost some of her sparkle," Reba said. "No surprise, seein' what she's learned about her best friend. I'm glad she's got Aiden. He dotes on her."

Ella Mae smiled. "Did you see his face when Suzy stopped by and invited them to her place for supper? I've never seen a man his size blush such a deep shade of red. His cheeks were the same hue as cherry pie filling."

Reba raised a warning finger. "He's not as transparent as we'd like to believe. Verena called and asked him to deliver a caramel apple pie today. She did her best to grill him about the Oak Knoll grove while pretendin' to dig around in her purse for her wallet. No luck. She said that he avoided answerin' every question she asked about the fire."

"Do you think Aiden's hiding something?"

"Yes, but I don't know what. He and Jenny have a secret. I can tell by the way they shoot quick, nervous looks at each other."

Ella Mae slapped a ball of dough onto the worktable, sending a cloud of flour into the air. "Maybe Suzy can get something out of him. What about Robert Morgan? What's he been up to besides cremating his wife without ceremony?"

"I hear he's gettin' nice and cozy with Opal Gaynor." Reba wriggled her brows suggestively. "He's at Rolling View all the time. But according to the rumor mill, the master of the house is comin' home tomorrow, and I don't think Jarvis Gaynor is the type of man to sit by and watch his wife flirt with another man."

"Maybe Opal's spending time with Robert to show the community her sympathetic side. After all, the *Daily* has been full of articles on Eira's death," Ella Mae said. "Did you see this morning's edition? The front page showed a photo of the Gaynors' house from the night of the party with

a headline proclaiming that Rolling View was the last place
Eira was seen alive."

A wicked twinkle appeared in Reba's eyes. "Opal and
Loralyn are always tryin' to hog the spotlight. Well, now
it's shinin' down on them, nice and bright. They're like little
bugs under a magnifyin' glass. Shoot, I can practically smell
the smoke."

"Did someone mention smoke?" Hugh poked his head
in through the back doorway. "Should I call my buddies at
the fire department?"

Reba gave Ella Mae a disgruntled glance. There were
things Hugh shouldn't overhear and Ella Mae knew that
Reba didn't like him entering the pie shop without knocking
first. However, she was quick to hide her displeasure. Turning to Hugh, she said, "I could find a way to get those boys
ready for action without usin' a telephone." She punched
Hugh playfully on the arm. "Don't keep Ella Mae up too
late, you hear? She's been workin' double shifts every day
this week and needs rest."

Hugh saluted her. "My intentions are completely innocent, ma'am. I thought I'd help her clean up so she can get
out of here faster." He raised a grocery bag. "And I'm going
to fix supper. I'm not much of a cook, but I can get a pot of
water to boil."

"Just by lookin' at it, I bet." Reba smiled, squeezed Hugh's
cheek, and left.

Hugh came around behind Ella Mae and kissed her on
the nape of her neck. "Let me take you home, sweetheart."

Ella Mae leaned back against his chest, feeling the warm
and comforting solidness of his body. He wrapped his arms
around her and held her tight. Neither of them spoke. It was
enough just to stand close to each other.

"I'm so tired. You might have to carry me to my car,"
she whispered.

"I need to tidy up first. You sit and order me around."
Hugh pushed Ella Mae onto a stool, wrapped the dough in

plastic wrap, and placed it in the refrigerator. He then wiped the counters and the work surface and swept the floor. When he was done, he pulled Ella Mae to her feet and, without another word of warning, lifted her over his shoulder.

"I was only kidding!" Ella Mae cried. "I'm not *that* tired." Her hair broke free from its clip and fell in whiskey-colored waves. She nearly dropped her purse and lost a shoe as well.

"Stop wiggling and hit the lights." Hugh thumped her on the bottom.

"Do you manhandle all of your victims like this?" She laughed and flicked the light switch.

Outside, the winter air took Ella Mae's breath away. Her coat was still in the pie shop. "Oh, it's cold! Come on, Hugh. You can let go of me now."

"Never," Hugh said and squeezed her tighter. "I'm going to carry you home when you've had enough. I'm going to rescue you from work and from loneliness and from anything else that troubles you. That's my job and my promise. I'm going to rescue you. Over and over again, if necessary. So quit your squirming and get used to it."

Ella Mae smiled but said nothing. She'd been right, as a young girl, to have fallen in love with a boy named Hugh Dylan. He was one in a million. And he was hers.

The morning of the winter carnival dawned gray and cold. Rumors of snow circulated throughout the town, increasing the anticipatory air already permeating every inch of Havenwood. Even in January, snow was rare in the Georgia mountains. The promise of the tiniest flurry sent children scouring the house for buttons and carrots on the off chance they'd be able to make a snowman.

"We're supposed to get anywhere from a dustin' to two inches. All this science and still there isn't a weatherman on this earth who can actually predict the weather," Reba said. She sat in the pie shop's kitchen, eating a meat pie for breakfast. "These are really good. I hope you made enough." She gestured at a takeout container meant to hold salad dressing. "What's in here?"

"Paprika aioli. It's for the meat pies. I thought it would be nice to serve a sauce with a little kick. I made basil buttermilk mayo for folks who prefer something mild."

Reba dipped a corner of her crescent-shaped hand pie into the aioli and took a bite. Her eyes widened. "Whoa. That sent a jolt of heat right down to my toes." She studied Ella Mae. "You've worked some serious magic with the carnival food. Did you sleep at all last night?"

"About five hours. But I feel strangely energized. It's not just the possibility of snow either. I feel like something's going to happen today." Ella Mae touched the burn scar on her palm. "Maybe I'll find Eira's killer. Or, at the very least, discover the identity of her lover."

"Your aunt Verena is hell-bent on pinnin' down Aiden today. She'll get an answer out of that boy about the Oak Knoll grove fire if it's the last thing she does." Reba smirked. "I hope he doesn't get mad and start burnin' stuff. That could be a disaster."

Ella Mae paused in the middle of packing a tray of mini cheeseburger pies. "I hope you're armed. Aunt Verena can't defend herself against fire."

"Oh, I'm armed. And dangerous." Reba winked. "And I'm wearin' my new red cowboy boots. These beauties were custom made."

"So there's an entire arsenal stashed between your knees and your toes?"

Reba nodded. "Exactly. And yet, they're as cozy as a pair of slippers." She leaned over to examine Ella Mae's fur-lined boots. "I know you're not packin' heat in those Eskimo shoes. Where's your piece? In your apron?"

Ella Mae knew Reba was referring to the Colt Forty-five she'd taken from the gun cabinet in Partridge Hill a few months ago. "In my purse, where I hope it'll stay. If we corner a killer or an arsonist today, I'd like to let the police handle the arrest."

Reba snorted. "Oh, right, 'cause they were so grateful when you called to tell them about Barric and Eira's mystery man. Her baby daddy, as they say on those stupid talk shows. The cops don't even know where Barric is, let alone the identity of her other boyfriend. And I thought *I* liked to juggle men. That girl could've had her own circus act."

The arrival of Jenny and Aiden put an abrupt end to that conversation.

"Coffee," Jenny croaked. She looked as if she hadn't slept in days.

"It's too bad you can't zap yourself," Reba said, hastening to pour Jenny a cup.

Aiden put a hand on his sister's shoulder. "She'll be all right. She's tough and we've got a big day ahead of us." He pointed at the trays filled with bite-sized pies and tarts. "Which ones are we supposed to pass out to the Oak Knoll folks?"

"Let me handle that. You just tell me who they are," Ella Mae said. Because she couldn't put complete trust in the Upton siblings, she wanted to serve the enchanted food herself. And for the first time, the magical fare wasn't pie.

The last thing she'd made before Hugh had shown up Wednesday evening was a special batch of piecrust cookies. Shaped like snowflakes, the crisp, buttery cookies were covered with cinnamon sugar. When Ella Mae sprinkled the sugar mixture over the dough, she'd thought back on the dry, autumn evening when her high school class had gathered around the Homecoming bonfire.

The bonfire, which was a long-standing tradition, was always supervised by the fire department. However, no one could have predicted that an inebriated senior would grab a burning branch and race into the woods, the branch held high overhead. Havenwood hadn't had rain for weeks and the pine needles crackled beneath his feet. The firemen gave chase while the student's classmates cheered. It wasn't long before the boy stumbled over a root and fell flat on his belly. The burning stick went flying and came to rest at the base of a pine sapling. The small tree caught fire with a loud *whoosh*. Ella Mae remembered exactly how she and the other spectators had stood in horrified awe as flames raced up the trunk and spread across the branches. The pine needles looked like Fourth of July sparklers as they blazed yellow and orange against the night sky. And then another tree caught. And another.

Luckily, the fire engine was parked nearby and the volunteers soon had everything under control. Years later, Ella Mae had stood in her pie shop kitchen recalling how everyone had been completely hypnotized by the hungry flames.

"Show us your love for fire," she'd whispered to the cookie dough. "Tell us of its power. Of how it could turn a grove into ash. Be compelled to boast about it. You are proud of what you've done. The fire you created was magnificent. Beautiful. Describe it to someone."

Now, with an hour remaining until the winter carnival would begin, Ella Mae put her hand on the lid of the tray containing the snowflake cookies and prayed that the enchantment would work.

"Time to load the Jeep," she said brightly, feeling that tingle of anticipation again.

Aiden and Jenny grabbed two trays apiece while Reba propped open the back door. However, Aiden didn't step outside. He stopped in the threshold and inhaled, his mouth curving into a twisted smile. "Fire," he murmured.

Ella Mae glanced down. The tray of cookies was still in front of her. Aiden hadn't eaten any, so he wasn't responding to their magic. What then, was he talking about? "What fire?" she asked sharply.

Aiden turned to her. "I see smoke. It's about two blocks away. What's over in that direction?"

Joining him at the door, Ella Mae saw a column of smoke

twisting upward into the gray sky. She paled. "That's where we're headed. Everything's there. The grandstand, the out-door games, vendor tents, the start of the bed race. It's the heart of the carnival."

For just a moment Aiden's eyes were filled with sparks of light. Tiny flames flickering from deep within the black pupils. He pointed at the smoke and said, "Then the heart of the carnival is burning."

Chapter 9

Grabbing the last aluminum tray from the counter, Ella Mae hopped into the Jeep and drove toward the smoke, Jenny and Aiden following close behind in Jenny's Camaro.

Members of the Havenwood Volunteer Fire Department were already on the scene and the engine blocked Ella Mae's view of what was burning, so she parked her car behind the pharmacy and she and Reba ran around the building to get a closer look.

"There!" Ella Mae shouted. She pointed at the beds clustered together behind a starting line made of caution tape. The bed in the very center of the pack was obscured by bright flames. They snapped and crackled in the cold air, chewing hungrily through the mattress and an upholstered headboard. A crescent moon mounted on the center of the headboard was turning from yellow to black while smoke formed a dark halo around the moon's topmost point.

The bed appeared to be the source of the fire, but it wasn't the only thing burning. Half a dozen beds were smoldering and Ella Mae saw sparks jump from one to another. There

was a zealous energy to their movement, like children leap-
ing from stone to stone to cross a stream.

"No!" she yelled, seeing multiple wisps of smoke appear
on the thin mattress covering the animal shelter bed.

Reba followed her gaze, her mouth tightening into a thin,
angry line. "What kind of jackass would try to ruin this race?"

"Someone who wants to win it," Ella Mae said, frantically searching for Hugh. It was impossible to differentiate
between the firemen, however. They were all shouting and
hurrying and dragging heavy hoses at the same time.

There was nothing the spectators could do but stand by
and watch. Two firemen gripping the end of a hose signaled
to the engine. Suddenly, a stream of water burst from the
nozzle. The elements clashed, fire and water battling as the
flames coughed up a fresh wave of smoke. The acrid air
smelled of charred cloth, melted metal, and chemicals.

"The fire on the bed in the center isn't going out," Aiden
said from behind her in a strange, faraway voice. "Something keeps feeding it."

Jenny grabbed her brother's massive arm. "Can you help
the firemen?"

Aiden's eyes were fixed on the dancing flames. "There's
gas and oil. It smells like an engine fire."

"An engine on a bed? That's against the rules," Reba said.
"You're not supposed to use any kind of mechanical propul-
sion. Just four people runnin' their hearts out and one person
on the bed, yellin' incentives. Four people, four wheels." She
spread her arms as if to encompass the chaos surrounding
them. "But folks cheat, don't they? Especially when there's
money involved."

Once again, Ella Mae tried to locate Hugh. And then she
saw him, edging the hose closer to the bed with the moon
on its headboard. Just as he approached, there was a deafen-
ing boom. Pieces of metal exploded, ricocheting into the air
and skittering across the surface of other beds.

"Hugh!" Ella Mae cried, terrified that he'd been struck,

but Hugh hadn't moved an inch. He was holding the heavy hose with one hand while touching the water pouring forth from its nozzle with the other. Because of the dense smoke, Ella Mae couldn't completely trust her eyes, but she thought she saw a glimmer pass from his fingers to the water. Hypnotized, she tried to track the glint in the water. It surged forward, blanketing the cloud of white-hot flames enveloping the area where the metal had erupted so violently.

Ella Mae didn't know much about firefighting, but she was pretty sure that one wasn't supposed to douse a chemical fire using water.

"What's that damned fool doin'?" Reba whispered, staring at Hugh in horror. "He'll get himself killed."

As if responding to her prediction, the fire surged toward Hugh, momentarily obscuring his body in a wall of flame. Ella Mae screamed, but just as quickly as the fire lashed out, it retreated again. Hugh was still standing there, braced against the weight of the hose. Once again, Ella Mae caught a glimpse of something sparkling in the water. And then, as if it had never been there, the fire abruptly winked out.

"Did you see that?" Ella Mae asked Reba.

"I saw a boy with a death wish, if that's what you mean," Reba said and put an arm around Ella Mae's waist. "Your man might not have the sense the good Lord gave a gnat, but he's got a lion's share of courage." She swept her sharp gaze around the damaged beds. "I hope Dee's isn't a total loss, but I can't tell from here. Come on, let's get a little closer."

Now that the fire was extinguished, leaving only a veil of smoke drifting upward to mingle with the bank of low, gray storm clouds, Aiden's dreamy expression was gone too. He surveyed the scene, looking as distressed as the rest of the bystanders.

He wasn't involved. He was with me when this fire started, Ella Mae told herself. Besides, what motive would

Aiden have for damaging the beds or carnival tents? He and his people needed the carnival to succeed.

Luckily, most of the tents were empty. It was too early and too cold for anyone to be manning them, and the majority of the merchants, Ella Mae included, had rented booth space inside the community center. The tents lining the road were set aside for carnival games and live entertainment.

Reba slowed as she passed the Havenwood School of the Arts tent, and Ella Mae was surprised to see an unfamiliar woman was inside, pressing a wad of glossy brochures to her chest. Ella Mae assumed that the woman was an Oak Knoll transplant because both Suzy and Aunt Sissy had taken in boarders this week, and her theory was proved correct when the woman waved at Jenny and Aiden.

"It is so nice to see some familiar faces!" she called out. "Here I am, my first week in a strange town and *this* happens." She gestured in the direction of the smoke. "Do you think the carnival will be canceled?"

"Not a chance," Jenny said with confidence. "The people of Havenwood aren't going to let a little fire ruin the day. Just ask my boss. Cadence, this is Ella Mae LeFaye."

Seeing the fear in Cadence's eyes, Ella Mae greeted her warmly. "The carnival will go on," she assured her. "There might be a delay while this mess is cleaned up, but all of the morning's events take place inside the community center, so I imagine the firemen will ask everyone to make their way there." She checked her watch. "The fashion show will be starting any minute now, and we need to run. Our booth has to be ready by the time the show is over. Stop by when you get a break and we'll serve you some coffee and cookies."

Cadence shifted the brochures in her grasp. "It's very nice of you to offer, but I'm afraid I only drink herbal tea. Coffee isn't good for my voice and I'm hoping to get a job as the chorus teacher at your aunt's school. To do that, I need to be able to sing at the top of my form."

You'll need to do more than that, Ella Mae thought. She doubted this buxom, matronly woman was the Oak Knoll arsonist, but she also knew that Sissy wouldn't take any chances when it came to the safety of her pupils. "I look forward to hearing you sing. And while we don't have tea on hand, try to swing by The Charmed Pie Shoppe booth anyway. I promise that today's special treat will have you singing your sweetest songs. They're free of charge to anyone from Oak Knoll."

"How delightful. I've been so impressed by the people of Havenwood thus far," Cadence said, relaxing a bit. "It seems like the town was well named. Perhaps it will become a haven for us all."

"I truly hope so," Ella Mae said. "Jenny, you and Aiden wait here with Cadence. I'll be back in a minute." She gave Cadence a quick smile and then caught up to Reba, who was waiting for her near the smoking beds.

It wasn't mere nosiness that propelled the two women forward, but a concern that the Oak Knoll arsonist was now targeting their town. If that was the case, they needed to know what had motivated him or her to act. And Ella Mae also wanted to make sure Hugh was unhurt.

Many of the spectators had left the area, discouraged by the smoke and the frosty air. A stream of people headed toward the community center and part of her longed to follow them, to escape the stinging in her eyes and in the back of her throat, but she had a duty as the Lady's daughter and so she stayed.

"Loralyn will have a full house for the fashion show," she said to Reba.

Reba smirked. "One of the nail techs came into the pie shop during her break yesterday and told me all about the opening act. Loralyn's gonna strut down the catwalk in a teeny, tiny glittery silver bikini and toss out coupons for her tannin' beds. After that, she'll put on a captain's hat and show folks what to wear on their next cruise. Like all of us are settin' sail for the Bahamas next week."

"I wish we were," Ella Mae said wistfully. "I like the idea of sitting in the sun, sipping fruity cocktails, and reading until I fall asleep. Instead, here we are in Havenwood, sharing our streets with a murderer and an arsonist. Today started with a fire and it'll probably end in snow." She took Reba's arm. "Maybe, in between those two events, we can be heroes. Catch some crooks, sell a bunch of pies, and restore peace and order to our town."

"You've got some lofty goals, sugar."

Ella Mae approached the starting line and slowed her pace when she saw the ruined beds up close. "Barkers Beauties had lofty goals too. Do you think they can still race?"

Reba ducked under the caution tape and drew alongside the animal shelter's blackened bed. "The mattress is trashed, but the frame's okay. It's not as pretty as it used to be, but those gals don't need pretty to win. They need speed and smarts."

"And a mattress. It's part of the rules. Despite the fire, I doubt the judges will grant any dispensations. Not when the grand prize is ten thousand dollars." Ella Mae tapped her chin. "You have an empty bed in your guest room, right?"

"It's ready and waitin' for someone from Oak Knoll. Not just any someone either. I'd like a hot guy like Aiden to darken my door. I don't want a diva songbird like Sissy's got or an old granny like Suzy has. I'm holdin' out for a hunky, silent type. A man who can light a fire in a woman's body just by—"

"Let's focus on *this* fire," Ella Mae interjected. "From here, it definitely looks like the fire originated from the bed with the moon. I wonder if someone was targeting this team, because someone obviously went out of their way to make sure their bed was in no condition to race."

She was scrutinizing the charred remains when Hugh

strode up to her. His mask was off, but he still wore his helmet and his pants and jacket were covered with soot. He fixed her with an expression of stern disapproval, but all Ella Mae could do was smile.

"You're all right." The words came out as a sigh of relief.

Hugh's clenched jaw relaxed a little. "I am, but you shouldn't be here. This area is hazardous."

Reba pointed at a piece of twisted metal at her feet. "Was this from the moon bed?"

Hugh nodded. "Someone concealed an engine inside the mattress coils. Obviously, they had no idea that it was leaking fuel. It dripped onto the asphalt and pooled at the foot of the bed. Something—a cigarette butt most likely—ignited the fuel. The flames spread over the bedding and then the engine exploded. We're lucky the station is so close or this could have been much worse."

"So you don't think the fire was set deliberately?" Ella Mae asked.

Hugh stared at her, perplexed. "What makes you ask that?"

She shrugged. "There's a big pile of money at stake."

"Our fire investigator said there's no sign of arson," Hugh assured her. "The guy has had limited exposure to arson cases, but we all believe it was an accident. An unfortunate one created by a bunch of lowlife cheaters, but an accident all the same."

Another fireman called Hugh's name and he waved in response. "I know you have work to do," Ella Mae said. "I just needed to see that you were okay. When I saw the engine blow up, it looked like the fire had swallowed you. It was really scary." Her eyes ran over him once more. "But you're not burned at all."

Hugh winked at her. "What can I say? My superhero powers must have been activated." Leaning over, he gave her a quick kiss. "I'll drop by your booth later. I know we'll all have worked up a monster appetite by the time we're done here."

"Send a few of those hungry firemen my way!" Reba shouted as he walked off.

Ella Mae took a final look at the bed Dee had so carefully crafted. The gleaming metal was mostly black, but the animals' eyes were still lit by tiny sparks of light.

"Can you take Aiden home and have him tie your spare mattress to the roof of your car?" Ella Mae asked Reba on their way back to the Havenwood School for the Arts tent. "The Barkers Beauties are going to compete in today's race. All of us—the animal shelter staff, my aunts, you, me—we need something to cheer for. These gals might be the underdogs, but they're Havenwood's underdogs. Wouldn't it be amazing if they crossed the finish line first?"

Reba shook herself, as if she'd nodded off for a second. "Sorry, hon. I didn't hear a thing you said other than, 'take Aiden home' and 'tie' and 'bed.' Was there somethin' else?"

"You're incorrigible!" Ella Mae laughed. "See you at the booth. And hurry. I expect Jenny and I will have our hands full."

"I'm hopin' to have mine full too." She wiggled her pointer finger at Aiden. "Come with me, big boy. I want to put those huge muscles of yours to good use."

Inside the community center, Loralyn's employees were strutting down a catwalk dressed in winter white pants and jewel-tone blouses. At first, Ella Mae was disoriented by the strobe lights and loud music, but Suzy appeared from behind her Cubbyhole booth and offered to carry a tray of pies. "Don't worry, the finale's up next so you'll have a few minutes to set up while everyone swarms to the Perfectly Polished booth," Suzy said. "Loralyn's giving half-price express manicures to the first fifty people. The fashion show has been a huge hit. I wish you'd been here to see the whole thing."

"I was sidetracked by the fire." Ella Mae raised her voice over the music.

Suzy's cheerfulness faltered. "It's awful, isn't it? I heard the team of cheaters has taken for the hills. They can't hide forever though. Havenwood's finest will get their names and addresses from the carnival committee and the idiots will face charges. I just hope they're not locals."

"Me too," Ella Mae said. After setting the trays on a table at the back of her booth, she attached a peach Charmed Pie Shoppe banner to the marquee and began to arrange paper plates and napkins. Jenny arrived shortly afterward and added another stack of trays to the table. She paused just long enough to set out a sandwich board listing the menu and prices and then hurried outside to fetch another load of pies.

Suzy waited for her to leave before withdrawing a book from her voluminous purse. "I wanted to show you this before things get too busy."

"Who's looking after your booth?" Ella Mae peered at the faded gilt letters on the book's supple leather cover. *The Encyclopaedia of Magick.*

"I left Granny in charge."

Ella Mae grinned. "Doesn't the woman have a first name?"

Suzy shrugged. "She does, but she prefers Granny. It suits her too. You should see her with the kids. They absolutely adore her. My Tuesday- and Thursday-morning story times are going to be the talk of the preschool circle."

"I'm glad. Now, what's special about this book?"

Suzy gingerly opened the old book to an illustration of a bare-chested man rising from a pillar of flames. "I've been researching fire magic."

"Fire magic or Aiden?"

"Both," Suzy admitted. "I like him, Ella Mae, but he

could be dangerous. Especially if he's one of these." She pointed at the subheading.

"Fire elementals?" Ella Mae frowned. "Is this for real?"

Suzy seemed entranced by the illustration. The man had the powerful shoulders and thick legs of a body builder and a penetrating stare. "Elementals are very rare. Like one-in-a-million rare." She tapped on the black-and-white drawing. "Male elementals are headstrong, passionate, destructive, creative, unpredictable, quick to anger, and possess a nearly irresistible sexual magnetism."

"Do you think Aiden is one of these . . . beings?" Ella Mae asked. She thought of Reba's theory about Aiden and Jenny sharing a secret. Is this what they were trying to hide?

"I hope not," Suzy said in a small, dejected voice. "Elementals don't operate by our rules. They don't need to enter a grove twice a year to have their energy restored like we do. Their power is innate. It doesn't fade, but they also can't control it like we can. They're wilder—influenced more by emotion than by reason."

Ella Mae skimmed the first few paragraphs and then turned the page. The next illustration showed the male fire elemental locked in a passionate embrace with a beautiful woman. Her eyes were closed and forehead was creased in ecstasy or agony, Ella Mae couldn't tell. "Can elementals enter a grove?"

"I don't know," Suzy said. "But if Aiden got inside the Oak Knoll grove, he could have started a powerful fire."

"But why would he?"

Suzy eased the book from Ella Mae's hands. "Maybe someone used magic to hurt him or a person close to him and so he wanted to put an end to magic in Oak Knoll. I have no clue. This is pure conjecture at this point. Anyway, I've memorized everything in this book, and I thought you might want to read it next."

Ella Mae glanced up to see Jenny heading toward them, her arms full of aluminum trays. "I will, thanks. But, Suzy, what are you going to do? Aiden is clearly smitten with you. He blushes every time someone says your name."

"If he's an elemental, then this reaction doesn't mean a thing. Male elementals act like that with every woman they want to seduce. They're supposedly less volatile when they're wooing a new sexual partner, which might be why we all find Aiden so charming and sweet." She sighed. "Elementals aren't interested in relationships. They want brief, fiery flings and that's not what I'm searching for, Ella Mae. I want a man to look at me the way Hugh looks at you. Like he sees the entire universe in your eyes. The past, present, and future." She glanced at her booth. "Oh, I have quite a line. Talk to you later!"

Suzy rushed off and Ella Mae hurried to help Jenny. "How many loads are left?" she asked.

"At least three," Jenny said, setting the trays on the table. She was about to say something else when a roar of applause echoed throughout the building.

Ella Mae turned to look at the catwalk. Loralyn stood at its end, dressed in a stunning gown of cobalt blue. Her golden hair spilled over her shoulders and a necklace of diamonds and sapphires glittered around her neck. After thanking everyone for coming, she invited the crowd to join her at the Perfectly Polished booth, and gave a regal wave. The applause continued until the house lights came on.

Jarvis Gaynor was waiting to help his daughter step down from the stage. He beamed at Loralyn, who took his hand and gave him a quick peck on the cheek before trotting off to her booth. Ella Mae hadn't seen Jarvis for months. In fact, since she'd moved back to Havenwood she'd only run into him twice. The man was always away on a business trip. At the Gaynors' party, Ella Mae had overheard a local couple talking about how Jarvis spent more time attending breeder and horseracing conventions or meeting with prominent Thoroughbred owners and guild members than he did at Rolling View.

And now that the head of the Gaynor family had finally returned, he didn't look very happy to be home. Ella Mae followed his dark gaze to where Opal was sitting beside Robert Morgan. She was laughing and slapping Robert's hand as if he'd just told her the funniest joke in the world, oblivious to her husband's disapproving stare. A woman next to Opal interrupted to show her an image on her cell phone. While Opal and her friend examined the screen, Robert raised his head and looked directly at Jarvis. There was no mistaking the challenge in his stare. The two men remained that way for a long moment, communicating their mutual hatred as loudly as if they'd shouted at each other across the room.

Ella Mae wondered if Opal had the slightest clue that two of the most powerful men in Havenwood were exchanging venomous glares because of her. But then the fashion show spectators began to leave their seats and Jarvis disappeared.

"Are you okay?" Jenny asked. "You seem lost in thought."

"There have been way too many distractions this morning," Ella Mae said. "Come on, let's focus on selling all of these pies."

By noon, the line in front of their booth stretched all the way to the restrooms. Jenny and Aiden took orders, Ella Mae plated pies, and Reba handled the money. They didn't serve many Oak Knoll transplants, but whenever one of them showed up, Jenny sent Ella Mae a signal by dropping a napkin on the floor. Ella Mae would then give the newcomer a free meal, an enchanted cookie, and offer them a seat at a table reserved just for them.

No sooner had they taken their first bite of Ella Mae's delectable pie than they suddenly found themselves sharing the table with Verena. Ella Mae's aunt was decked out in a black woolen dress with a white faux-fur collar and a pair of hot pink boots. Having already eaten with five people from Oak Knoll, she should have been too full to swallow another mouthful of pie. However, Verena had a voracious appetite, and when Ella Mae seated a man at the reserved table, Verena worked her way through her fifth meat pie with gusto.

This cycle continued until two o'clock in the afternoon. Most of the savory pies were gone and Ella Mae was close to exhausting her supply of magical snowflake cookies. Unfortunately, Verena had had no luck with her tablemates.

"Not one of them mentioned the fire in their grove!" she complained during a lull. "With this morning's drama, I had the perfect segue, but all they wanted to talk about was how the destruction affected their income. I know they've been through a tough time, but not one of them is mourning the loss of their Lady or expressing concern for those without homes or gainful employment. And now these snobs are *our* neighbors." She harrumphed. "Buddy and I will have to set them straight. They need to learn how to be charitable. A little lesson in compassion would do them good!"

"I can't think of a better teacher than you," Ella Mae said and then lowered her voice. "What about Aiden?"

"I haven't gotten my hands on him yet," Verena admitted. "He's been avoiding me."

Ella Mae glanced at Aiden. He was staring across the room at the Cubbyhole booth, a small smile playing at the corners of his mouth. "I caught a tiny glimpse of his gift today," she whispered, gesturing to the table where they'd lined up the aluminum trays. "These buffet servers come with a pair of fuel cans. They only work for a few hours. We lit them too early and the hot pies were in danger of growing cold before the lunch service had even begun. When I mentioned the problem to Aiden, he simply stood over them and *zap*, the flames were bright and strong and the cans have been burning all day long. See?"

Verena put a hand near the closest tray. "So he can create fire and keep it burning as long as he wills it to? A remarkable gift. And very powerful!" She picked up a snowflake cookie and absently nibbled a crisp edge. "I'm going to have to involve Suzy. She's clearly the object of his adoration, so he's more likely to answer if she asks him about the fire. Wait until today's closing ceremony. We'll get the truth from him then!" She cocked her head and then gave a little jump. "Oh, that's my phone."

Reba had heard Verena's Aretha Franklin ringtone and grabbed the phone from Verena's purse. "It's Dee," she said, examining the screen.

"Answer it!" Verena commanded.

Putting the phone to her ear, Reba listened for several seconds and then took Ella Mae by the hand. "We have to go! The bed race just started and the Barkers Beauties are givin' the Naughty Nurses a run for their money. If we hurry, we can make it in time to see the thrillin' conclusion."

"I'm coming too!" Jenny said and told her brother to watch the booth. Aiden was too busy mooning over Suzy to move, so the four women dashed out of the community center, none of them pausing to grab their coats.

Outside, the press of the crowd and the sound of raucous cheering greeted them. The leading teams were about two blocks away, and though Ella Mae could make out a group of beds, she couldn't identify the individual teams.

"The one in the front has a Jolly Roger flag," Reba said. Her vision was far superior to Ella Mae's.

Verena was squinting up the street. "Can you see Dee's bed?"

Reba's face was a study of concentration. "Yes! The Barkers Beauties are in third place, right in front of a bunch of *Sesame Street* characters and a team of clowns. The Naughty Nurses are in second. Man, those gals must be really well endowed for me to be able to spot their assets bouncin' from here." Suddenly, her eyes widened and she cried, "Whoa! Whoa!"

Ella Mae saw the pirate bed swerve. "What's happening?"

"I think one of the nurses lost her uniform. I'm seein' a helluva lot more skin than I did a second ago." She cackled. "Guess the pirates noticed her wardrobe malfunction too."

The beds were approaching fast and the crowd gave the runners a wide berth. The Naughty Nurses were veering all over the road, and with only one block to go, they abruptly cut in front of the pirates. The move forced the team of men, each costumed like Captain Jack Sparrow, to crash into a sidewalk bench. The Barkers Beauties, who wore headbands with dog or cat ears paired with striped or spotted bodysuits, pulled ahead.

Ella Mae would have loved to say that she saw the animal shelter team overtake the nurses in the last fifty feet, but something fluttered onto the lashes of her right eye, causing her to blink and look away. She was just reaching up to touch her lashes when another small, wet object stuck fast to her cheek.

Lifting her face skyward, she shouted, "It's snowing!"

By the time she glanced back at the street to catch the race's thrilling finale, the top three beds had already crossed the finish line. Her smile widened as she watched the Barkers Beauties exchanging embraces and high fives. Aunt Dee rushed over to the exhausted women and was immediately enveloped in a group hug.

Ella Mae was looking at her aunt, whose cheeks were flushed with cold and happiness, when she spotted a familiar face in the row of spectators on the opposite side of the street. She sucked in her breath—a sharp and startled hiss.

And suddenly, the face was gone.

"What's wrong?" Reba asked, raising her voice to be heard over the crowd. "You look like you've seen the devil."

"I think I have." Ella Mae pointed across the street while star-shaped flakes fell onto her trembling finger. "Barric Young didn't leave town. He's here. And he's angry. Very, very angry."

Chapter 10

Reba didn't hesitate. She took off, racing across the street in a blur of arms and legs, and Ella Mae felt a twinge of fear. She knew Reba was armed to the teeth—there was a shoulder holster concealed beneath her shirt, a throwing star tucked into the waistband of her jeans, and another weapon stashed in her new red cowboy boots, but the miniature arsenal didn't alleviate Ella Mae's concern.

"What if Barric's an elemental?" she asked the falling snow. Someone bumped into her and offered a hasty apology, but Ella Mae didn't even notice. "If she corners him, he might react without thinking. That quick temper could blaze into life. He might start a fire. Reba could get . . ." The thought was too terrible to voice.

Pivoting, Ella Mae searched the crowd for a policeman, but the bed race contestants obscured her view. She edged past a Cookie Monster talking to a Naughty Nurse, two clowns with rubber noses and rainbow wigs laughing it up with a pirate, and two cats from the Barkers Beauties team receiving congratulations from two women dressed as fairy tale characters. Ella Mae thought she saw a cop standing behind Snow White and Little Red Riding Hood, so she maneuvered around them, only to have her path blocked by someone in a wolf costume. She stared at the wolf's yellow eyes and bared teeth until he raised his paw in a hello wave. She smiled an awkward little smile and edged around him.

Rushing up to the policeman, Ella Mae blurted, "Officer, I just saw a suspect in the Eira Morgan murder case. That way!" She pointed in the direction Reba had gone. "It's Barric Young. You guys have been searching for him for days. Can you radio for backup?"

The cop looked at her, his face an unreadable mask. He made no move to use the radio attached to his uniform shirt. "What's your name, ma'am?"

Ella Mae told him and then went on to add that it had been her family members who'd found Eira's body and that she was responsible for informing the police about Barric's suspicious behavior in the first place.

"Is that so? Who took your statement?" the officer asked, his voice betraying his disbelief.

"Officer Hardy. Jon Hardy." Ella Mae was doing her best to rein in her impatience, but this man's indifference was fueling her anxiety. "Please. Call *someone* before Barric gets away. He could be very dangerous. The man's a *murder* suspect!"

Her emphasis on the word murder seemed to break through the cop's studied cool. He canted his head and spoke into his radio, receiving a string of static-riddled code in reply. "Hardy's in the community center with the mayor," he said to Ella Mae. "Can you describe what Young was wearing?"

Ella Mae pictured Barric again. She'd seen only his face and those furious, laser-point eyes. "Not really. I caught a glimpse of a dark coat. No scarf or hat. He was standing behind other people, so I didn't have a clear view."

The officer passed on her inadequate description to his

colleagues, and Ella Mae felt the roiling in her stomach sub-side. The cops were on it. Reba wasn't alone. She had backup.

"Hardy would like to speak to you," the officer said. "He's at the community center right now, but later, he'll be by the lake."

Ella Mae raised her brows. "He's doing the Polar Plunge?" She knew Jon Hardy well enough to be surprised by the idea. Even though their acquaintance had begun when Hardy arrested her on suspicion of murder within weeks of her return to Havenwood, Ella Mae had come to like Hardy. He was a decent man and a good cop who loved his wife, his job, and his two headstrong Boxers. Ella Mae had seen him in The Charmed Pie Shoppe on a regular basis too, and judg-ing from the way he could put away a big meal and then linger over coffee and cherry pie, Ella Mae hadn't pegged him as someone who'd deliberately jump into a lake in the middle of one of Havenwood's coldest winters on record.

"No, Hardy isn't going in." The cop grinned. "Half of the force has signed up to freeze their rumps off, but not Hardy. He'll be there to maintain order and assist the para-medics if necessary. I'm sure he'll have his hands full. Someone always stays in the water too long or cuts a foot on a stone. If it didn't bring in so much money for the Wounded Officer Fund, I'd say cancel the whole crazy thing. But dozens of families have made it through rough times because of the donations." He sighed. "I was even dumb enough to volunteer this year. I've never done it before and I'm not looking forward to it."

Ella Mae had been listening with only half an ear. She was already making plans to check in at the pie shop booth before tracking down Hardy. However, her Southern upbringing forced her to smile and wish the young man luck with his inaugural plunge. She then hustled back to the com-munity center.

Inside, a troupe of girls had taken the stage. Dressed in black leotards hung with sequined fringe, they performed a tap dance routine that included complicated moves involving top hats and canes. The space reverberated with the clacks and clicks of their shoes striking the floor and a tinny recording of "All That Jazz," which Ella Mae found preferable to the disjointed techno music of Loralyn's fashion show.

At The Charmed Pie Shoppe booth, Jenny and Aiden were busy serving coffee and dessert. From what Ella Mae could see, all was running smoothly.

"What an amazing finish to the bed race!" Jenny exclaimed when Ella Mae joined her behind the makeshift counter. "Your aunt must be so happy."

"I think she is, but I didn't get a chance to talk to her," Ella Mae said. "I was going to go over, when I spotted Barric Young on the other side of the street. I had to find a cop before Barric could get away again."

Jenny and Aiden exchanged a look of surprise.

"What is that guy thinking?" Aiden asked. "He must know that he's a wanted man. Why would he risk his neck to come back to Havenwood? And why today? He could have been halfway to Canada by now."

"Is that where you'd go if you had to flee from the law?" Ella Mae asked, wondering if the question would fluster Aiden, but he was completely unperturbed.

"Nah. Too cold. I don't even want to leave the building. I am not a fan of the cold and I hate snow."

Jenny was staring at Ella Mae. "I don't know what Barric wants, but I don't like this. Should we help the cops look for him? We know his face on sight and we're almost out of food anyway. There are half a dozen pies left and about the same number of cookies. And the cash box is so full that we can barely close it."

Ella Mae took in the stacks of empty aluminum trays. She would have loved to celebrate their success, but she was too preoccupied by the idea that Barric could be hatching some malicious plot. "Aiden, I think we can extinguish the fuel cans now. If you'd prefer to stay indoors, you can sell the rest of our food, pack our things, and then maybe give Suzy a hand."

Though Aiden's eyes lit up at the mention of Suzy's name, he shook his head. "No way am I going to let the two of you chase after Barric without me. He could get violent."

"You'd like that, wouldn't you?" Jenny said. "You've wanted to knock Barric Young's lights out for weeks now."

"Ever since Jenny told me that he cheated on Eira, I haven't liked the guy. They had one fight and he jumped into bed with another girl. That's not cool." Aiden shrugged and began to blow out the tiny flames in the fuel cans.

Ella Mae was on the verge of asking him if he'd ever hurt someone he loved when Opal Gaynor appeared.

Assuming she was a customer in need of service, Jenny gave her a bright smile. "Can I help you?"

"No, thank you, I'd like to express my displeasure to the owner personally."

Jenny stiffened, but Ella Mae put a hand on her shoulder and told her everything was okay. Opal walked several feet away from the booth and beckoned for Ella Mae to join her. While she complied, Ella Mae glanced around for any sign of Officer Hardy. Unfortunately, several spotlights were trained on the tap dancers, making it hard to see beyond the circles of light onstage.

Cleary irritated by Ella Mae's lack of attention, Opal waved a manicured hand in front of her. "Hello? Remember me? I'm the woman who's spent most of the carnival dodging questions and refuting insinuations. You pledged to help our family, to prevent our reputation from being tarnished, and you've done nothing to help. May I remind you that I held up *my* end of the bargain?" She gestured at The Charmed Pie Shoppe booth. "It was because of me that the committee asked you to be a vendor at this very lucrative event."

"And I appreciate that. Truly. I'm doing everything I can to investigate on my own and to assist the police with the case as well." Ella Mae lowered her voice. "In fact, one of the suspects is at large, somewhere in town, this very minute. The police are searching for him and I was just about to join them."

"Well, that does sound promising." Opal was slightly mollified. "As you can imagine, Mr. Morgan is also interested in having his wife's killer brought to justice. Seeing as how his company will boost our local economy, we should do all we can to prove that we're on his side."

Ella Mae frowned. "You might feel compelled to fawn over him, but as far as I'm concerned, Robert Morgan isn't in the clear when it comes to his wife's murder. You saw them together. They were hardly a loving couple."

Opal threw her head back and laughed. "How nice it must be to live in fantasyland, Ella Mae. Allow me to explain, as someone who inhabits the real world, that very few successful marriages endure due to some vague storybook notion known as true love."

"What about you and Jarvis? It wasn't love that brought you together?" Ella Mae looked around again, and while she noted that Robert Morgan was parked close to the stage, his gaze fixed on a little blond girl dancing a solo, she didn't see Jarvis anywhere.

"Marriages between important families are based on more substantial things, my dear. Bloodlines, breeding, and a proclivity toward rare and powerful talents. But I don't want to delay you discussing things you wouldn't understand, so run along. I believe you have a villain to find."

Ella Mae didn't care for Opal's tone. "Yes, I do. But I want you to know that I made a promise to myself, to the people of Havenwood, and to Eira. I vowed that I wouldn't let her death go unpunished. Unlike you, I don't care how much money a person has or if they can trace their lineage to a famous monarch. I only care about the fact that an innocent young woman was given an overdose of sleeping pills and then left alone on a mountain to die. I'll hunt for

Barric, but your Robert Morgan had a strong motive to kill his wife. Perhaps you'd better take a moment to consider whose reputation is more important—Morgan's, or yours?"

And with that, Ella Mae pivoted on her boot heel and marched away. She was annoyed, but more at herself than at Opal. The conversation had served to remind Ella Mae of how little progress she'd made with any of her goals. Eira, Hugh, her mother. Nothing was resolved. Things were not much clearer than they'd been the night she found Eira's frost-covered body.

Fists clenched, Ella Mae strode outside, hoping she'd run right smack into Barric. Recalling how Jenny had punched him at the pie shop, she fantasized about having the opportunity to do the same. But throttling him would serve no real purpose. Barric had to be forced to talk. He needed to sit in a holding cell until he told the whole truth about his relationship with Eira.

"I'll tell Officer Hardy about the look in Barric's eyes. I have to make him see that finding Barric is more important than escorting the mayor or babysitting the Polar Plunge participants." Ella Mae's words came out of her mouth in terse, rhythmic puffs. She looked like a steam engine as she made her way to the lake.

Signs calling attention to the Polar Plunge marked the narrow tree-lined road leading to the water. Over the years, it had become a tradition for family and friends to wish the swimmers good luck by posting signs along the path. Other signs, which beseeched spectators to donate to the Wounded Officer Fund, featured color photographs of policemen and women from across the state and taglines like, "Give to Those Who Protect and Serve."

Ella Mae paused a moment in front of a sign reading, "They Stand Between Us and Fear." If only there'd been someone to stand between Eira and fear that fateful night on the mountain. Or to shield Oak Knoll's Lady of the Ash. Two women taken unawares. Two women with no champions. Ella Mae silently renewed her vow that no one else would come to harm.

Sliding her hand into her purse, she touched the cold barrel of her Colt. "I'll be ready," she told the falling snow.

The Polar Plunge was the carnival's final event. Because its kickoff was less than an hour away, Ella Mae expected to find a few people hanging around the lake's edge. However, when she left the copse of pine trees behind and stepped out into the open, she found herself totally alone.

"I guess it's just too cold," she said and then considered the irony of that statement. The participants would soon be disrobing and deliberately racing into the frigid water. Until then, they probably wanted to stay warm and dry.

There were two vehicles parked close to the lake: an ambulance and a trailer with the fire department's shallow-water rescue boat hitched to a commercial-grade pickup truck. Ella Mae whistled at the number of camping tents dotting the shoreline. The swimmers kept towels and a change of clothes inside. Immediately after their plunge, they'd rush into the tents, strip down, and put on thick wool sweaters and heavy sweatpants. There'd be roaring camp-fires too. After changing out of their swimsuits, the partici-pants would celebrate by making s'mores or roasting hot dogs over the fires.

"Dozens of campfires," Ella Mae murmured anxiously. "If Barric's an elemental, he could set this whole beach ablaze. All the tents. The trees. The paper signs along the road. Everything."

It was easy to envision such a fire. Each campfire would grow brighter and hotter, higher and wider, as people stared in horrified fascination. Next, sparks would leap onto tents and towels and clothes, chewing hungrily. The smells of burning plastic and wool would pollute the air, followed by the first terrified screams. Then the pine needles would catch, just as they'd done during the bonfire when Ella Mae was in high school. Flames would rush up the trees and fiery branches would fall onto the narrow path leading to the main road. There'd be nowhere to go. They'd be trapped. Panicked people would seek refuge in the cold lake water. Water that would quickly wrap them in a fatal embrace. If they didn't stay on the shore and burn, they'd wade into the lake and risk freezing to death.

"Burn or freeze. Fire and ice." The theme kept repeating in Ella Mae's mind.

Walking closer to the water, she could imagine its mirrored surface reflecting the pine trees as they turned into smoking torches. She saw how the yellow and orange flames would stretch into the sky, searing the snowflakes as they fell.

Ella Mae thrust her fingers into the water, hoping the chill would dispel the images she'd conjured. That's when she noticed something odd resting beneath the surface. It took a few seconds for Ella Mae to comprehend what she was seeing, but she knew that the object, which was about twenty feet from the shore, did not belong in the lake.

It was a boot. A heavy-duty work boot made of tan leather. A man's boot.

Withdrawing her hand, Ella Mae stood up and peered at the spot. She had to wait for the ripples she'd created to dispel, but when the water was still again, she could see the boot quite clearly.

Then she noticed a second boot. The toes of both were pointing skyward, the laces gently bobbing in the invisible current.

"What on earth?" She moved as close to the water's edge as she could and stared, unblinking, certain that her eyes were playing tricks on her. But it appeared as though something was attached to the boots. A pair of legs.

Ella Mae glanced over her shoulder, hoping to spot someone, anyone, on the path. Seeing that she was still alone, she pulled off her own boots and socks. She then rolled her pants up to the knees and waded into the water.

"Damn, it's *cold*!" she cried as the water's sharp chill shot through her feet and up her body.

She moved gingerly, making slow progress. As she made her way deeper in, the tan work boots seemed to recede, as if invisible hands were dragging them away from shore to an even colder, darker place.

Ella Mae wanted to hurry but couldn't. There were slick, uneven stones under her feet, and at one point, she nearly lost her balance and tumbled sideways. Luckily, she was able to windmill her arms and remain upright. She wished she could move faster. The cold sank into her veins and pumped into her heart. She could almost imagine her blood turning a glacial shade of blue.

Her toes grew numb as she shuffled closer to the boots. By now, the water was well past her knees. It soaked her pants, but she barely noticed. Her attention was fixed on the face gazing up at her. She'd found a male Ophelia, floating in a watery grave.

Ella Mae couldn't see his features clearly, because her movements had made too many ripples in the water. Ignoring her shivering hands, she bent down and caught hold of one of the boots. The water's biting cold seeped into her chest and rushed up her arms, but she squatted even lower to grasp the second boot. Tugging, she managed to move the drowned man a few inches, but the rough stones on the lake bottom refused to release their hold on his heavy coat.

"Let go!" Ella Mae commanded, shivering more violently now. She shifted her weight to her heels and pulled again. "Let go!"

The body came free without warning, causing Ella Mae to tumble backward. The water closed over her head, drenching her completely. The shock of it was like nothing she'd ever felt. Her heart thudded wildly in her chest. *Thump thump thump.* An agitated bird trying to escape its cage. Ella Mae tried to get up, but it felt like an iron chain was pulling her down.

I will not drown in three feet of water!

Twisting and pulling, she managed to shrug off her heavy coat and finally push to her feet. The air stung her lungs and snowflakes stuck fast to her wet skin, but she grabbed the man's boots again.

This time his body came willingly, floating to her with the buoyant ease of an empty fishing hook.

What kind of fish is on my line? A magical one? Will I get three wishes? Ella Mae wondered, feeling strangely distant from her own body.

Ella Mae knew the cold was getting to her. She'd read the hypothermia warnings printed on the Polar Plunge sponsorship form and guessed that she was experiencing most of the symptoms, but all she could think about was reaching the shore so she could rest. Lie down and have a long, long rest. She was so tired, and as she looked back to see how much farther she had to go, the swirling snow confused her. The tents were blurry and too far away.

She focused on pulling again and the man's face bobbed to the surface, jellyfish white and terrifying. Ella Mae recognized his features. She knew whose boots she held. Whose corpse she was dragging out of the water.

"Barric Young," she whispered, desperately trying to hold on to the lucid thought. "Barric Young, Barric Young, Barric Young . . ."

Suddenly, her muscles turned to liquid. She was just about to drop onto the pebbled shore when she felt herself being lifted. Someone swift and strong carried her into a tent. Ella Mae's eyes were closed, but she sensed the heat of a fire. And then warm fingers were removing her dripping clothes. She forced her lids to open for a second and saw that the person undressing her was Aiden. She tried to talk, to protest that his touch was painful, that he shouldn't be undoing her bra, and that Barric was in the lake, but her tongue was thick and useless.

Groggily, Ella Mae glanced down at her naked flesh. It

was covered with gooseflesh and tiny rivulets ran from her hair and over the swell of her breasts. Aiden wrapped an oversized towel around her, unzipped a down sleeping bag, and helped her wriggle inside.

"Barric," she croaked after he'd zipped her into the cocoon of flannel.

"He's not going anywhere," Aiden said matter-of-factly. "You, on the other hand, stayed in the water way too long. I'm going to carry you outside to the fire now." He scooped her up again as if she weighed no more than a child. "I'll make it hot enough to dry your hair quickly. You're losing too much heat through your head."

Ella Mae murmured a "thank you" into his chest, which had the comforting scent of wood smoke and pine.

Aiden shushed her and kicked aside the tent flap with his foot. He stepped outside, cradling Ella Mae in his arms, and came face-to-face with Hugh Dylan.

Chapter 11

To Hugh's credit, he didn't immediately jump to the wrong conclusion. Anger flared in his eyes and his jaw muscles tightened as he realized that the woman he loved was being held in another man's arms. But then his gaze swept over her wet hair and limp body and his frown softened.

"Did she fall into the lake?" he demanded.

"More like waded in. She took her boots and socks off first." Aiden jerked his head, indicating Hugh should move out of the way. "Listen man, I need to get her to the fire."

Ella Mae reached out for Hugh. Her arm felt like jelly, but he caught her hand and gave it a gentle squeeze before falling into step alongside Aiden.

"There's a body in the lake," Ella Mae whispered. "That's why I went in."

She didn't see Hugh's reaction but heard his sharp intake of breath. "I'll take care of it. You focus on getting warm. And drink this." Hugh pulled a water bottle out of his coat and wedged it into the snow-dusted ground near the camp-fire. Ella Mae noted that the bottle had no label. She'd had

Hugh's mystery water once before. Back in June, when her mouth and throat were coated with a film of soot and her strength had been completely sapped, he'd offered her a similar bottle. The water inside had tasted like nothing she'd ever known. It was cool and crisp and reminded her of spring rain. After finishing the bottle, the smoke-tinged air she'd inhaled became a distant memory and her flagging energy had been restored. At that moment, Ella Mae had believed that Hugh must be one of her kind, but she'd been mistaken.

"Close your eyes," Aiden said as he set her on the ground and knelt down beside her. "I need to be quick about this. We can't have your non-magical guy catching a glimpse of what I can do."

Ella Mae nodded and Aiden slipped an arm around her shoulders and eased her toward the crackling flames. The heat on the back of her head was so intense that she was certain her hair must be on fire, but she didn't smell anything burning.

Less than ten seconds went by before Aiden helped Ella Mae sit upright. She ran her hand over her hair. Every strand was dry and warm. She widened her eyes in wonder. "That's amazing. Can you touch fire without being hurt?"

"I sure can. Made for an awesome party trick in college. I'd hold my finger over a candle longer than the other guys just to get free beer." Grinning, he opened the water bottle and handed it to her. "Shoot, I could have jumped into the fireplace and sung all the verses of our fraternity song, but that might have raised a few eyebrows."

Ella Mae took a long drink of Hugh's water. Feeling was returning to her muscles, and the sensation was unpleasant. She winced. "I feel like I'm being poked by a thousand tiny needles."

"Good." Aiden smiled and pushed a knit hat over her head. "That'll keep the heat in. Let's hope Hugh doesn't notice how fast your hair dried. If he's like most guys, he won't. Plus, he's got a dead man to deal with."

Withdrawing a bare arm from the sleeping bag, Ella Mae grabbed Aiden's hand. "You saved my life. How can I ever thank you?"

Aiden looked taken aback. "You already have. By giving Jenny and me jobs and a place to live, you saved us. You treated us like family right from the get-go. Because of your kindness, we'd do anything for you and yours. I'm just glad I happened to come down here when I did."

"Why were you here?" Ella Mae searched his face. "I thought you hated cold and snow."

Aiden didn't have the chance to explain, for at that moment, a woman screamed.

Ella Mae turned to see a group of people standing at the end of the path, their mouths forming wide O's of shock. The woman gave another theatrical shriek and pointed at Barric's corpse.

Hugh had dragged the body out of the water and was standing protectively in front of it. He spread his arms and made a "get back" gesture to the civilians. After informing them that he was a fireman, he warned them not to come any closer.

"We'd better get you dressed," Aiden said. "I can't dry your clothes now. Too many witnesses. So we'll have to scrounge around in the tent for something suitable." He glanced at the tittering spectators and then pointed at the sleeping bag. "You can't really walk in that. Should I just pick you up again?"

Smiling, Ella Mae said, "Sure. I love being carried like a sack of flour."

"You feel lighter than that. All thanks to my love of bicep curls." Aiden made a fist and pretended to kiss the bulging muscle on his upper arm. He then scooped Ella Mae off the ground and brought her back to the tent. "I'll leave you to rummage. In the meantime, I'm going to help Hugh with crowd control."

Ella Mae had qualms about borrowing another woman's turtleneck, wool sweater, and sweatpants, but she had no choice. She dressed in haste, too focused on what was happening outside to care that her sweater was covered by designs of dancing polar bears or that the sweatpants had the word "Angel" written in glittery pink letters across the rear.

Stepping out of the tent, she found that the crowd had swelled to twice its size. Ella Mae hustled to where Hugh and Aiden stood. The men were staring warily at the fascinated onlookers and talking to each other in low tones. Neither of them saw her move close to Barric. She gazed down at him, at the water pooling beneath his sodden corpse, and felt a rush of pity.

Unzipping the sleeping bag she'd taken from the tent, she gently spread it out over him. She was just about to drop the cloth over his face when she paused. There was something in Barric's hair. At first, Ella Mae assumed that it was mud from the lake bottom, but when she leaned in for a closer look, she saw that his blond hair was matted with blood. The shape of his skull was wrong too. It was caved in at the back, just above his neck. His head appeared deflated, as if someone had let air out of a balloon. Her hand flew to her mouth, stifling a cry.

"Who did this to you?" she whispered hoarsely and glanced at the people milling about by the path's entrance. She scanned their winter pale faces until her eyes fell upon Aiden's broad back. What was he doing by the lake? He hated the cold. And yet, he'd also admitted that he disliked Barric. Had he struck Barric with a rock and then waded in, thigh-deep, and dumped his body in the lake? Was he avenging Eira's death?

Ella Mae's gaze traveled to his boots. They were totally dry, which meant that he hadn't worn them in the water.

Then again, he used the fire to dry my hair in seconds. He could probably do the same to his footwear, she thought. And the blunt object Barric had been struck with could be anywhere. Most likely, it rested on the bottom of the lake. Ella Mae pictured tiny fish swimming in zigzags around a crimson-stained rock, agitated by the scent of blood in the water.

The sound of sirens penetrated the crowd's excited murmuring, and Ella Mae turned back to Barric. "I hope you and Eira find each other," she said softly. "I hope you can dance together again." Resisting the urge to close the dead man's eyes, she let the sleeping bag fall over his face. She then walked up to Hugh and leaned against him.

He immediately enfolded her in his arms and held her so tightly that she couldn't breathe. "Thank God for Aiden," he said when he finally let her go. "You were in serious trouble when he found you, Ella Mae. What were you thinking? Why'd you stay in the water for that long?"

"Because I knew him." She pointed at the shrouded body. "Not well, but I recognized him. I had to get him out of the lake. I didn't think it would take long, but his coat got caught on something and I lost my footing." She shook her head. "Believe me, I'm completely embarrassed that I had to be rescued."

"I'm sorry to say this, but the man you knew was dumped in the lake. There's a trail of blood leading from an area near the tents to the water. I only caught a glimpse of the wound, but judging from the angle and the depth, someone hit him hard. There's no way he could have gotten that injury by accident," Hugh said gravely. "This place will be crawling with cops in under a minute."

"I saw his head, Hugh. He was murdered," Ella Mae said. "Someone was either incredibly arrogant or totally foolish to commit homicide with hundreds of police nearby. And the cops won't be happy. The Polar Plunge will be canceled now."

As if on cue, the sirens grew deafeningly loud. The crowd reluctantly parted to allow passage for Officer Jon Hardy and a small group of uniformed men and women.

"All right folks, show's over!" Officer Hardy called. "Go back inside where it's warm." When no one moved, he threw out his arms in exasperation. "If you insist on gawking and snapping pictures while you catch your death, then I need you to take twenty steps backward. *Now.*" He turned to a young female officer. "Officer Ross, count for them, will you? Jacobson, rope off this whole area. No one else gets in."

Striding up to Hugh and Ella Mae, Hardy dipped his chin in greeting and then studied Ella Mae closely. "Ms. LeFaye. Do you need medical attention?"

"No, thank you. I'm fine." Ella Mae watched as a cop carrying a black duffle bag and a policewoman holding a camera approached Barric's body. "And I know you need to talk to me."

"Ms. LeFaye exhibited symptoms of hypothermia and should be examined right away," Hugh said in his official fireman's voice. "Hypothermia can cause lingering effects."

Hardy glanced at the body and then at Ella Mae again. "I'll get a full statement later, but if you could provide us with a brief description of what happened before you leave, I'd be grateful."

Putting a hand on Hugh's arm to stop him from protesting, Ella Mae gave Hardy a succinct summary of how she'd spotted the corpse in the lake. Hardy's eyes opened a fraction wider at the mention of Barric's name, and when she described Barric's damaged skull, the lawman stiffened. It was a subtle movement, but Ella Mae knew that he was angry. Hardy now had two murder cases to deal with, one of his prime suspects was lying dead in the mud, and he had an audience of hundreds observing his every move.

"Thank you," he told Ella Mae in a tone of polite dismissal. "I'll be in touch." He turned to Hugh. "Would you see that Ms. LeFaye is given the care she needs?"

"Of course." Hugh slung an arm around Ella Mae's shoulders. "Come on, there's a blanket with your name on it in the ambulance."

Hardy, who'd started walking toward Barric's body, suddenly swiveled. "Ms. LeFaye?" he said. "One more thing. Where did you get this sleeping bag?"

Ella Mae pointed at the appropriate tent. "From that blue tent. Along with these clothes. Could you tell the owners that I'll return everything I borrowed as soon as possible?"

Hardy waved off her request. He wasn't interested in the clothes. "Did anyone else go into the tent with you?"

"Yes. Aiden Upton. He's right over—" She stopped, her raised arm falling to her side. "He was helping to keep the public away from Barric's body, but he might have gone back to the community center once you and your team showed up."

Hardy nodded absently in acknowledgment. The pull of Barric's corpse was just too strong. Ella Mae could practically feel the police officer's urgency to lay eyes on the dead man. He wanted to begin unraveling the mystery of Barric's death to reach the starting point of the maze in order to get to its other side. "Aiden Upton. Got it," he called over his shoulder and then turned his full attention to the body lying on a bed of mud and stone.

Hugh led Ella Mae to the ambulance and asked her to sit on the gurney. He wrapped a wool blanket around her and then knelt on the floor and put his hands on her knees. "I know you don't like being fussed over, but I need to make sure you're all right before I leave to get my truck. As soon as I come back, I'll drive you home. First, show me your fingers. I want to make sure you don't have frostbite."

"Can I use them to call Reba first? She can bring me a coat and a pair of gloves." Ella Mae smiled tenderly at Hugh. She could hardly blame him for being upset. He'd been scared because he loved her. And even though the fear had dissipated, he needed to be assured that she was really okay. Ella Mae suspected that Hugh might also be unhappy because he hadn't been there to rescue her. Instead, a burly younger man had taken her from the frigid water, stripped off her clothes, and warmed her.

Hugh returned her smile and handed her his phone. He was starting to relax, to let go of the fear that he might have lost her. "Here. I'll examine your toes while you talk."

Reba picked up after the first ring. Her voice was shrill. "Where are you?"

"In an ambulance parked near Lake Havenwood. I'm not hurt," she added quickly. Hugh's reaction was tame compared to what Reba's would be when she found out what happened. "But Barric's dead."

"Serves him right. He got away from me by knockin' over the Girl Scouts' table. I just couldn't step on their cookie boxes, so I lost the bastard." Reba was clearly seething. "You stay put, you hear? You can tell me how he breathed his last in about five minutes."

Ella Mae tried to shut out the image of Barric's glassy stare. "He didn't die peacefully. It's pretty bad, Reba." She closed her eyes and tried to focus on the feel of Hugh's fingers on her skin as he removed her borrowed sock. "Could you bring me a coat, please? Mine's all wet."

Reba growled. "Why do I get the feelin' that this has nothin' to do with the snow?"

"I fell in the lake," Ella Mae admitted sheepishly. "But I'm fine. Hugh's examining me right now."

"I bet he is." Ella Mae could almost picture the wry grin on Reba's face. "But if he plans to warm you up the way I'd want to be warmed up, make sure the gurney brakes are on or your *examination* will be over right quick."

"Reba—" Ella Mae's tone made it clear that she wasn't in the mood for coarse humor.

"I know, honey." Reba was instantly contrite. "I'm makin' jokes when there's nothin' to laugh about. Truth be told, I'm furious with myself for failin' to catch Barric alive, because now we need to consider an awful possibility. Let me ask you a question before I continue. Did Barric kill himself?"

Ella Mae felt her throat constrict, but she couldn't say much in front of Hugh. She'd never told him that she was investigating Eira's murder. "Not a chance."

"Then you're probably thinkin' what I'm thinkin'," Reba

said darkly. "If someone bumped off Barric, then we might
have more than one murderer runnin' loose in Havenwood."

An hour later, Ella Mae was standing under a stream of
scalding water. The glass doors in her shower were fogged
over to the point that she could no longer see Chewy. He
liked to curl up on her bath mat and wait for her to open the
shower door and reach for her towel. The moment she did,
he'd zip into the shower and start licking the tiles. Sometimes, he'd walk right by his water bowl and stand expectantly, all four paws on the fluffy white mat, until Ella Mae
turned on the shower and let it run long enough to form a
small puddle around the drain. He was on the mat now, but
Ella Mae was enjoying the feel of the hot water running over
her too much to rush on his account.

Hugh had driven her home and planned to accompany
her to the police station, but he was called back to the lake
to help some of the other firemen search for the murder
weapon.

"Tonight?" Ella Mae asked after he'd told her that he had
to leave. "It's dark. Besides, dozens of cops have been hunt-
ing for it all afternoon. Why do you have to go now?"

"I'm on the water rescue team and they've asked us to
search the lake near where Barric's body was dumped. It
really doesn't matter when we dive because it's dark at the
bottom anyway." Hugh had kissed her hand. "The cops are
really riled up, Ella Mae. This benefit was really important
to them and they won't rest until the murderer's caught."

Ella Mae had been relieved to think that in addition to
having the entire Havenwood police force out looking for
clues, the visiting cops were helping as well. "There must
be a hundred men and women involved," she'd said.

Hugh had nodded. "They've combed every inch of
woods, path, and shoreline and have taken inventories of

every tent. However, none of the visiting lawmen packed dry suits in their bags. The whole point of the plunge was to jump in wearing as little as possible, remember? Besides, it seems pretty likely the murder weapon was tossed in the water. It's a convenient place to get rid of an incriminating piece of evidence."

"It's also a big lake. All kinds of things could be down there," Ella Mae had pointed out in a distracted whisper. Her thoughts had turned to the magical object growing in the deepest part of Lake Havenwood.

"And a cold one. We'll go down in pairs and take fifteen- to twenty-minute shifts," Hugh had said. "We have two underwater light cannons, but even those will only help so much. The water's pretty murky away from shore and, according to the ME, we're probably looking for a rock. A rock in a lake filled with rocks." He'd shrugged. "Still, we have to try."

Ella Mae hugged him hard. She hadn't liked the idea of him swimming down to the bottom at night, his rubber fins cutting through the moving shadows, swirls of silt clouding the water. She imagined the branches of aquatic weeds grabbing at his arms and legs. Ella Mae would never have conjured such images before reading Rupert Gaynor's book, but she'd thought of his descriptions of malicious water spirits and deadly serpents and held Hugh even tighter. "Be careful, okay?"

"I'll be fine," he'd promised. "After all, I'll be in my element."

He kissed her cheek and threaded a strand of hair behind her ear. "We might be out on the lake for hours. You should rest and have someone check on you. Could you ask Reba to spend the night?"

"Why not Aiden?" Ella Mae had teased. "He's right across the garden. I could just call over there." She pointed at Partridge Hill.

Hugh had scowled. "I think he's seen enough of you for

one day." He gave her another kiss, more forceful and possessive than the last. "If he hadn't saved your life, I'd have to kill him."

Gently pulling away, Ella Mae had opened the car door and stepped out into the cold. The snow had stopped falling and a row of icicles glinted like translucent daggers from the roofline of her cottage. "I think we've had enough killing for one day," she'd murmured to herself and hurried inside.

Now, bundled in flannel pajamas and a robe, Ella Mae decided to make tea. Just as the kettle starting whistling, Reba arrived. She wiped her feet on the mat, shrugged out of her coat, and wiggled her index finger at Ella Mae.

"I don't want any of that herbal decaf crap." She plunked down an unopened bottle of Jack Daniel's and a bag of coffee grounds. "Jenny gave me the recipe for Tennessee Coffee and that's what I'm havin'. After I'm done tellin' you what I saw, you'll want one too, so I'm gonna go ahead and make two cups."

"I don't like the sound of that." Ella Mae frowned and put the kettle aside. She handed Reba a pair of glass mugs and opened the bottle of whiskey. Chewy greeted Reba with several licks and then jumped on the sofa and yawned. He stretched out and laid his head on his paw, his eyelids drooping.

"Oh, to be a dog." Reba smiled indulgently at Chewy. She then dumped three tablespoons of coffee grounds into Ella Mae's French press and used the water from the kettle to wet the grounds.

Ella Mae poured milk into a saucepan and dug around in her drawers for her immersion blender. "Start talking, Reba."

Reba added more water to the grounds. "Before I came over, I went to check on the progress at the lake. Lots of folks are there. Looks like a damn tailgate party. The campfires are roarin', people are sharin' fried chicken and hot dogs and passin' flasks and bottles of Bud around. Of course, they've had to move their tents away from the action. A huge area is off-limits, even though the cops haven't found a single piece of evidence."

"What about Hugh and the rest of the divers?" Ella Mae plugged in the blender.

"They were in the water, lookin' like sharks in those black rubber suits." Reba poured espresso into the glass mugs. "It was kind of spooky. You could see their lights sink as they dove down and they created this weird, greenish glow. Reminded me of ghost lights." She shrugged. "The divers kept complainin' that there was almost no visibility near the bottom. Seems like the whole endeavor is pretty pointless."

Ella Mae frothed the milk. "It was certainly a long shot," she said over the whirr of the blender. "If Barric was struck by a rock, what were the chances of someone finding it? A million to one."

Reba stirred a shot of whiskey and a teaspoon of sugar into each cup of coffee. She then stepped aside so Ella Mae could add the milk. When the drinks were ready, Ella Mae touched Reba's glass with her own.

"*Cha ghéill sinn gu bràch*," she said softly. She'd read the Gaelic war cry in an old scroll in her mother's library and liked the sound of the old language. It was both strange and familiar.

"*Cha ghéill sinn gu bràch*," Reba repeated. "What's it mean?"

" 'We'll never fall back.' " Ella Mae took a sip of the Tennessee Coffee. It filled her mouth and throat with welcome heat. "This is delicious; now tell me why I need it. What did you see at the lake?"

Reba wiped a smear of frothed milk from her upper lip. "While I was there, two of the divers called it quits, but Hugh wouldn't give up the search. With his partner sittin' in the boat, freezin' his tail off, your man wouldn't get out of the water. He didn't seem to get tired or cold. He'd stay down for fifteen minutes at a time. Then twenty. The last time, he was under for twenty-five minutes. I timed him. And then he finally called it a night and headed back to shore."

"Go on."

"I waved and tried to get his attention to see if he needed food or somethin' hot to drink. I know what he means to you, honey, and he'd been given a miserable job." She took of gulp of coffee. "He didn't hear me callin' so I edged along the caution tape until I was close to his truck. He got out of the boat, took off his fins, and came to his truck to get a towel. That's when I saw the hose—the one that goes from his breathing thingy to his tank. It wasn't attached all the way, Ella Mae. That thing was leakin' the whole time he was underwater."

Ella Mae had been scuba diving several times and knew exactly what Reba meant. "The hose connecting his regulator to his tank wasn't connected?" She paused to think. "Maybe it came loose when he climbed back into the boat."

"No. He spotted the problem when he took the tank off and glanced around, guilty as a kid caught sneakin' cookies before supper, to see if his buddies were watchin'. No one was, so he let out a bunch of air so that it would look like he'd used what was in his tank. I could hear it hissin'. He was under that last time for twenty-five minutes! The world record for breath holdin' is nineteen minutes and change. I looked it up. So what the hell was he breathin' down there?"

The two women stared at each other.

"What is he?" Ella Mae said uncertainly. "He's not our kind. If he's not human, then what is he?"

Reba shook her head. "Damned if I know. I never thought you two should be together. At first, I didn't want you to fall for him because he was under Loralyn's thrall, but the truth is, I've been wonderin' about Hugh Dylan for years. Like how he could beat anyone in a swim race even when he was real little. Or how his skin never got wrinkly, no matter how long he stayed in the water. He'd splash and float and dive like an otter, like he belonged in the lake or the swimmin' hole. Like—"

"He was in his element," Ella Mae said, using the exact words Hugh had spoken earlier. Shaken, she asked Reba to give her a minute and went upstairs to find the book Suzy had leant her.

For a moment, she stood next to her bed, staring at the book on the nightstand as if it were toxic. And then she turned to the chapter on water elementals and began to read.

Chapter 12

Later, Ella Mae came downstairs to find Reba waiting for her on the sofa. One glance at Ella Mae's face and she gestured at the glass of whiskey and soda on the coffee table.

"It's that bad?" Reba asked.

Ella Mae showed her an illustration of a male water elemental. He was beautiful. Not handsome, but beautiful. With his waves of dark hair, large eyes, proud nose, strong jaw, and full lips, he looked like a Greco-Roman sculpture. The man also had a swimmer's body—a pair of wide shoulders tapering to a narrow waist.

"Lord Almighty. He could be Hugh's twin." Reba took a swallow from the tumbler she'd poured for Ella Mae. "When was that book printed?"

"At the turn of the nineteenth century." Ella Mae motioned for Reba to pass her the glass. "Water elementals are typically female," she said after taking a sip. "A male is rare and is incredibly attractive to humans and to all types of water spirits."

Reba groaned. "Like Loralyn Gaynor."

"Exactly." Ella Mae pointed to a paragraph below the illustration. "These elementals must live near the water and can become weak or seriously ill if they don't immerse themselves in a natural water source on a regular basis." She glanced up. "You know, Hugh left Havenwood for a period of time to travel the world. He told me once that he wanted to learn more about where his people came from, but maybe he was really trying to discover what he was. I wonder if those destinations were all close to an ocean, river, or lake."

Frowning pensively, Reba said, "Remember how often he was at the swimmin' hole when you were kids? It was like he owned the place.

Ella Mae thought back to those days. "Maybe he did. Water elementals choose a body of water to guard. If not the swimming hole, then maybe he's claimed Lake Havenwood. If that's the case, do you know what that means?"

Reba started to shake her head and then stopped, her eyes going wide. "He could be the guardian? The creature you need to fight to get that flower for your mama?"

"If the love of my life is truly a water elemental, then he might be able to transform, to adopt the physical attributes of certain aquatic animals." Ella Mae closed the book. "Of course, I have no idea of this author's findings are accurate. It doesn't seem possible that he could know so much about our kind."

"You'll have to ask Suzy about that. Let's get back to the subject of Hugh. Is there a test or somethin' you can give to see if a person is an elemental? Because two men who are real close to you seem to fit the bill. You've got a man livin' in your mama's house who might juggle fireballs in his spare time, and you're sleepin' with a man who could be part fish."

Ella Mae shook her head. "The odds of having two elementals in one place are extremely small. And I don't care if Aiden's an elemental, one of us, or a genie released from a lamp. The fact is that we still have no idea why he was down by the lake when I found Barric's body. I think he was following Barric. He may even have killed him. Aiden's strong as a bull. He could have struck Barric, dumped him in the lake, tossed the bloodied rock into the deep water, and then thoroughly dried himself using his gift. The whole thing would have taken less than five minutes."

Reba's brows rose. "What's his motive? I know he didn't like Barric, but there are plenty of folks I can't stand and I don't go around knockin' them senseless."

"Aiden and Jenny are keeping a secret, remember? Something they're scared to have brought to light," Ella Mae said. "Maybe Aiden was sweet on Eira. Maybe *he's* the third man. The father of her unborn child."

"He does seem to like the ladies," Reba muttered and the two women exchanged worried glances.

At that moment, the phone rang. Reba leapt to answer it. She listened to the caller for a few seconds and then pursed her lips in defiance. "No, sir. She's done in. I've sent her to bed. You can talk to her first thing in the mornin'." She paused and then glowered. "No, that's an ungodly hour for anyone to be out and about. She'll be there at eight and not a minute earlier."

"Who was that?" Ella Mae asked after Reba put the phone down.

"Officer Hardy. He wanted to question you tonight, but I put a stop to that. Your man was right; someone needs to make sure you get lots of rest."

Ella Mae tilted her tumbler, watching the amber liquor slosh back and forth inside the glass. "My man. Whatever else he may be, he's mine." She thought of all the times she'd seen him swim, of how often she'd compared him to a merman, and of how he'd seemed so at home in the water. She'd always felt a little in awe of him. But afraid? Never. "Maybe Hugh's being an elemental could turn out to be a good thing. It might explain our bizarre reaction to each other." She picked up Suzy's book again. "Suzy said that a fire elemental is unable commit to one person. What if that's true for water elementals too?"

Reba took the book away and pointed at the stairs. "No more of this now. March on up to bed. You've got a police interview in the mornin', and then you and I need to dig into Barric's past. It's nice to have the cops involved, but Eira and Barric were both our kind and they were probably killed by our kind as well. When magic and murder are paired, the clues can be too hard for regular folks to spot. Decent, determined people like Officer Hardy don't stand a chance against an enchanted killer."

"Do we?" Ella Mae asked. "Murders. Ruined groves. Elementals. Flowers growing on the bottom of our lake. The world gets crazier every day." She hugged Reba tightly. "You're the one constant in my life. What would I do without you?"

"Drink less booze, I'd imagine." Reba kissed her on both cheeks and then sent her up to bed.

As Ella Mae climbed the stairs, she heard Reba shooing Chewy off the sofa. "It's time for you to turn in too, Charleston Chew. I'm gonna sit and read for a spell. This old dog needs to learn some new tricks. The kind that'll keep that precious girl of ours safe. Her man might guard some puddle of water, but I guard her. Just like you do, boy. You and I need to keep the monsters at bay. You got that?"

Chewy gave a little bark in reply and then Ella Mae heard his quick, light tread as he trotted upstairs and into the bedroom.

Ella Mae patted the covers and Chewy scrambled onto the bed. She ruffled his fur and kissed his black nose and then watched as he performed three lazy circles before finally settling down near her feet. Ella Mae smoothed a wrinkle in the quilt her mother had placed at the foot of the bed in the beginning of September. It had been made by

Ella Mae's grandmother and was divided into equal panels, each depicting a garden during one of the four seasons.

Ella Mae kept the quilt folded so that the spring and summer scenes were on top because the colors matched her comforter. Now she turned it over and spread out the other side, tracing the path of yellow and orange leaves drifting onto a cluster of chrysanthemums and asters. Her fingers moved to the winter panel, which featured delicate snowflakes swirling around holly leaves, firethorn berries, and camellia blossoms. Examining the needlework more carefully, Ella Mae noticed that some of the snowflakes resembled tiny white butterflies. Others looked like four-leaf clovers. Upon closer inspection, she saw those shapes in each of the four panels.

"Call the butterflies," her mother had said. The advice still made no more sense to Ella Mae than it had in the grove. "I'll think about it tomorrow," Ella Mae whispered sleepily. She pulled the quilt over her and turned off the light.

She dreamt of a fire in the pie shop's kitchen. Smoke poured from the oven, so thick that Ella Mae couldn't get close enough to see what was burning. She heard sirens, and then the scene abruptly dissolved and she was wading into Lake Havenwood dressed in her Charmed Pie Shoppe apron and winter boots. The water was black and oily and she was afraid.

Without warning, a massive tentacle snaked through the water and wrapped around her right ankle. Another slimy appendage coiled around her arm. The thing tried to pull her under, but she twisted and squirmed and fought to stay on her feet. She could hear Hugh calling her name and she screamed for him to help her. And then, she saw that he was the creature grabbing her. He wasn't at all the Hugh she knew. The nightmare Hugh had scales instead of skin. His eyes were no longer bright blue but the flashing silver of startled minnows. And when she looked down at the hand clamped around her wrist, she saw that it was webbed. She screamed again, and managed to wrench free of his grasp.

●

She splashed out of the water, her heart pumping wildly in terror, and raced into the woods. She ran all the way up the mountain trail, finally coming to a stop at the boulder wall. She put her hands out but couldn't get into the grove. Sliding to the ground, she pulled her knees to her chest and remembered that this was the very place where Eira had died.

An owl called forlornly in the distance and Ella Mae cried out in her sleep.

She didn't dream any more that night.

The next morning, Ella Mae told Officer Hardy what she could about Barric Young. There wasn't much to say that he hadn't already heard when she'd called to tell him that she believed Barric should be considered a suspect in Eira's murder. Ella Mae felt a fresh twinge of guilt over leaving out the part in which Jenny slugged Barric at the pie shop, but nothing good would come of the police investigating the Upton siblings. Hardy had little chance of discovering their shared secret. That task was Ella Mae's to complete.

"So that's it?" Hardy was staring at her intently, making it clear that he didn't believe she was telling him the whole story. "He glared at you from across the street and then turned and ran?"

Ella Mae nodded. "Yes, but he was looking at someone else first. There were people everywhere, so I don't know who was the original target of his anger."

Hardy grunted. "But he shifted his gaze, the two of you locked eyes, and he suddenly bolted?"

"Like a spooked deer. Though I didn't think he was running off for good. His expression was determined. Defiant. I got the feeling that he wasn't going to leave until he did what he came here to do." She shrugged. "Whatever that was."

Hardy looked doubtful. "You deduced all that in one glance?"

"His eyes were full of a cold rage," Ella Mae insisted.

"Believe me, I'm not here to waste your time or tell you colorful stories. I'd rather be doing other things on a Sunday morning." She gestured around the conference room. "This place doesn't exactly bring back fond memories."

Hardy ignored the reference to the time she'd been considered a person of interest in a murder investigation. "Okay. After informing Officer Weiss that Mr. Young was a suspect who needed to be apprehended, you headed to the community center to look for me. When you didn't find me, you went to the lake next. Can you explain how you happened to come across Mr. Young's body? It's an unusual coincidence that you were the one to discover him not long after seeing him in town."

"As I said, I was looking for you, but no one was at the lake yet." Ella Mae couldn't keep a defensive note from creeping into her voice.

"Unfortunately, I was delayed by the mayor. He cornered me about—" He waved his hand. "That's not important. I should have been there, but I wasn't. Please continue."

"I walked near the water, caught up in thinking about all the crazy people who'd be swimming in it soon. That's when I saw one of Barric's boots. I got as close as I could without getting wet. Close enough to notice the second boot." Ella Mae described how the boots were both pointing skyward, and yet still seemed anchored to the muddy bottom. "I realized I was looking at a body, so I went in. Later, I fell trying to pull Barric out."

Hardy examined his notes. "Luckily, Aiden Upton came along and carried you to safety."

"That's right." Ella Mae hoped she wouldn't have to go into detail about Aiden's having to remove her clothes. However, Hardy seemed more interested in learning what he could of Aiden's background and his movements during the rest of the day. Once he'd exhausted that subject, he wanted to know more about Barric's head wound and any other observations Ella Mae could make about the body's appear-

ance. "He didn't look human anymore." She finished by
saying, "He was white and wet and whatever had made him
Barric Young was gone."

"Yes," Hardy agreed. "But not forgotten."

They looked at each other for a long moment and Ella Mae
knew that Hardy would do everything in his power to solve
Barric's case. In that way, she and he were alike, only Hardy
didn't know that Ella Mae was investigating the murders on
her own. She dropped her gaze and he cleared his throat and
got to his feet.

"Thank you for your time," he said. The interview was
over.

Ella Mae stepped into the hall, where Loralyn was pacing
back and forth like a caged leopard. When Ella Mae saw
her face, she paused in surprise. Loralyn's skin was splotched
and her eyes were puffy from crying. Ella Mae had never
seen Loralyn cry before. She found it very unsettling.

"Are you all right?" she asked Loralyn quietly.

"The stupid cops have been questioning my mother for
over an hour!" she spat. "And I can't imagine what's taking
our idiot attorney so long to get here. I called him right after
these cretins showed up at our door and 'requested her presence at the station.' " She was practically snarling as she
repeated the police officer's words.

Ella Mae took Loralyn by the elbow and led her down
the corridor. She stopped in front of a pair of plastic chairs
facing a water cooler. "Does this have anything to do with
Barric's death?"

"You should have left him in the water." Loralyn's anger
rolled off her in waves. "Because of your little body-fishing
expedition, the cops are reviewing our statements from the
night of the party. The entire catering staff is being questioned, and they have a search warrant for Rolling View. A
bunch of lowlifes are rifling through my things as we speak!
All thanks to *you*."

"I don't blame you for being upset," Ella Mae said sooth-ingly. "But I can't help you without knowing what triggered a renewed interest in your family. What piece of information came to light? Did the cops find something on Barric's person?"

Loralyn frowned in confusion. "On Barric? No. They're trying to link the sleeping pills they found in Eira's system to my mother. She has a prescription for the same pills. She's taken them on and off for years, usually when she's about to sell one of our Thoroughbreds to the highest bidder. My mother had her prescription refilled the day before the party, which is completely logical, seeing as she'd just finalized a million-dollar land deal. She'd never have gotten any sleep without those pills. Between the land deal and the party, she was too wound up."

Opal Gaynor had always been the picture of composure, so it was difficult for Ella Mae to imagine her tossing and turning or watching late-night television until she was finally able to sleep.

"Were pills missing from your mother's bottle?"

"The whole thing's gone," Loralyn said miserably and then her fury returned and pinpricks of cold light appeared in her eyes. "What does that prove? Anyone could have taken the pills. My mother didn't think she had to lock her own medicine cabinet."

Ella Mae thought about how flirtatious Opal had been with Robert Morgan at the winter carnival. Were the two of them accomplices? Ella Mae considered the possibility. Though Opal couldn't have drugged Eira and then left her own party to drive the unconscious girl to the park, she might have spiked Eira's drink and had someone else take her to the grove. Could Barric have been in collusion with the Gaynors? Or had he and Robert Morgan formed some sort of alliance? It sounded crazy, the idea of the jilted hus-band and lover uniting in order to punish the woman they'd once loved, but maybe Barric already knew that Eira was carrying another man's child. Perhaps his surprise was feigned.

"Well?" Loralyn interrupted Ella Mae's fruitless conjectures.

"Officer Hardy and his team must be looking for your mother's pills. Those pills were in your house the night of the party and someone stole them and used them to drug Eira. Either that, or they wanted to make it seem like your mother was guilty of doping Eira," Ella Mae said. "What about the catering staff?"

Loralyn shook her head. "We've used them dozens of times. They're trustworthy. After all, my family is very influential. One bad word and no one would ever hire them again. They wouldn't dare do anything to incite our displeasure."

Ella Mae knew this was probably true. "Okay, let's focus on Eira's drink. You said that it looked like apple juice, but the lab results state that she'd ingested alcohol. Did someone force her to swallow brandy? Or bourbon?"

"How? By pinching her nose in the middle of the party?" Loralyn smirked. "Maybe she actually wanted something stronger than apple juice."

"No way." Ella Mae dismissed the idea immediately. "She was pregnant."

A shadow flitted over Loralyn's face. She turned away in a sudden hurry to fill a paper cup with water from the cooler.

"What were you thinking just then?" Ella Mae demanded. "What do you know that I don't?"

Loralyn took a dainty sip of water. "I asked the bartender—he's catered at least twenty parties for us—if he had apple juice on hand that night. He didn't. Cranberry, tomato, orange juice, and pineapple, but no apple."

Ella Mae sat down on one of the plastic chairs. She closed her eyes and revisited every scene from the party in which she'd seen Eira. It was then that she realized who'd been sipping amber-hued liquid throughout the evening.

"It wasn't apple juice," she said. "The pills must have been mixed in with whiskey. Robert Morgan was drinking whiskey at the party. I remember that his glass was different from those the catering company provided. His was made of fine crystal. Where did he find that tumbler?"

Loralyn tried to produce one of her trademark shrugs, but the flicker of alarm in her eyes belied her show of indifference. She was scared, and Ella Mae knew that the only thing that could frighten Loralyn Gaynor was a threat to her family.

"I know what you're going through, Loralyn. I lost my mother during the harvest festival and I'd do anything to get her back. If your mom's in trouble, then let's find a way to save her." Ella Mae paused, but Loralyn remained silent. "The land deal with Morgan is a fait accompli, right?"

"Your French accent is as bad as it was in high school, but yes, the papers have been filed and the funds transferred."

Ella Mae lowered her voice. "Then why is Opal still so solicitous toward Morgan? Your father's home from his business trip. I saw him at the winter carnival. He was watching your mom with Morgan and he didn't seem at all happy about how cozy the two of them were together."

Loralyn crushed the paper cup in her fist, forcing drops of water to leak from between her fingers. "You don't know anything about my parents or their relationship. They're fine, you hear me? Everything's *fine*. I'm sure Morgan's in love with my mother. Lots of men fall in love with her. It's the same with me. Men just can't help themselves."

"That's because you enchant them with your voice, leaving them with no free will. I'm not impressed by your ability to manipulate men," Ella Mae said, momentarily forgetting her feelings of empathy as she recalled how Loralyn had enchanted Hugh again and again. "If that's how your mother acquirers her admirers too, then the pair of you deserve to be in the mess you're in. Enchanting Robert Morgan might be profitable down the road, but it might also explain why your father isn't here to support your mother."

Loralyn flushed and glanced at her cell phone. "It looks like our bumbling attorney has finally arrived. I'll go meet him in the lobby and remind him what will happen to him should he fail to put an end to this nonsense. And since my mother had nothing to do with either Eira's or Barric's demise, she doesn't need your help. None of us do. Consider whatever arrangement my mother had with you null and void. Go back to minding your own business and stay out of ours."

Uncertain as to what to make of Loralyn's mercurial behavior, Ella Mae watched her march down the hall, her heels clicking angrily on the polished tiles.

"She's protecting her mother," Ella Mae murmured. "But from what? What has Opal done? And has it driven Jarvis Gaynor away?" She took out her phone and dialed Suzy's number. "Are you busy?" she asked.

"Nope. I'm drinking my third cup of coffee while pretending to read the paper." Suzy sounded dejected. "I can't focus on anything. I keep thinking about Aiden. It doesn't help that he stopped by last night with an armload of flowers and a story about saving your life. And then he told me about Barric. What's going on?"

Ella Mae grabbed her handbag and started for the front door. "I'll tell you everything when I get there. In the meantime, can you work some magic on the computer and see what you can find on Barric Young? I've never really thought about him beyond the fact that he was Eira's lover, but now I'm wondering if he had some connection to the Gaynors."

Suzy let loose an exasperated sigh. "Does everything have to be their fault?"

"No, but the killer might be trying to make it look like it is," Ella Mae said. "I know you do research better on a full stomach, so can I bring you anything?"

"Sure. How about Aiden? Stripped of his elemental powers and his clothes, thank you very much." Suzy laughed.

"You'll have to settle for a sausage, egg, and cheese biscuit. See you in a bit."

Ella Mae didn't often find herself in the drive-thru lane of Havenwood's only fast-food restaurant, but every now and then she felt a powerful craving for an egg and cheese biscuit. Reba got her hooked on the breakfast sandwich over twenty years ago, and she sensed Suzy would enjoy what Reba called "a bit of heaven wrapped in yellow wax paper."

She was right. Suzy stuck her nose in the bag, inhaled deeply, and then gave Ella Mae a grateful smile. "Okay, I forgive you for being naked in front of the man I'm obsessing over. Come into the kitchen, I want to show you something interesting."

Ella Mae said hello to Jasmine while Suzy gave her poodle a rawhide chew. "That'll keep her busy. Granny's been spoiling her terribly. She reads to her too. I swear Jasmine understands every word." Suzy pulled her breakfast sandwich out of the bag. "I really like Granny, but I'm glad she's at the shop. Sometimes a girl just wants to be alone with her coffee, her books, and her dog, you know?"

Suzy's kitchen table was completely cluttered with books. Her laptop was propped on a coffee table book about James Bond films, her coffee cup rested on *Joy of Cooking*, and her salt and pepper shakers were perched on a stack of vintage Frances Hodgson Burnett novels. Ella Mae examined the blue book on the top. Its title was *Queen Silver-Bell*.

"Is she a fairy?" Ella Mae asked, pointing at the cover. A woman with long, golden hair and a pair of diaphanous wings danced barefoot through a patch of wildflowers. She wore a Grecian robe, a crown of leaves, and a secretive smile.

"The queen of the fairies, no less," Suzy said, unwrap-

ping her biscuit. "In this book, she tells stories to get people
to believe in fairies like they once did. Speaking of fascinating stories, check out what I uncovered about Barric." She
took an enormous bite of her breakfast sandwich and then
gestured at her computer screen. A piece of bacon fell onto
Queen Silver-Bell's nose.

Ella Mae sat down in front of the laptop and began to read.
A few seconds later, she turned to Suzy in astonishment.
"Barric's farm is owned by Morgan Industries? As in Robert
Morgan?"

Suzy nodded. Ella Mae opened a new window and did a
Google search on Young's Farm of Oak Knoll, Tennessee.
The home page showed a bucolic stretch of fields planted
with oats and alfalfa. There was also a photo of a trio of
Thoroughbreds galloping near a stable that looked remark-
ably like the one at Gaynor Farms. Ella Mae read about
Barric's special horse feed and then clicked the testimonials
link. There, on the bottom, was a quote from a man named
Rand Dockery. Ella Mae drew in a sharp breath.

"What is it?" Suzy asked.

"Barric, Robert Morgan, and now Dockery," Ella Mae
said. "It's straight out of Shakespeare."

Suzy looked confused. "I don't get it. Who's this Dockery
guy?" She studied the man's photograph. "He's good-
looking in a rugged, cowboy way."

"He's also the head trainer at Gaynor Farms. According
to this testimonial, he's been buying feed from Barric Young
for years." Ella Mae sat back in the chair, her eyes fixed on
the screen. "Barric, Robert Morgan, and the Gaynors.
They're connected. But what do these connections have to
do with Eira's death? Or Barric's?"

"I hate to say it, but you need to have a frank talk with
the Gaynors."

Ella Mae nodded. "I know. And I'm not going alone. I'm
taking Reba and my aunts with me."

"What if things turn violent?" Suzy chewed her lip.

"Then Reba will be delighted. She's waited for decades to kick a little Gaynor ass." Ella Mae smiled ruefully. "And I don't think I'll be too inclined to stop her."

Chapter 13

Ella Mae said good-bye to Suzy and Jasmine and headed out to her car. She told Chewy to hop into the Jeep, but he stubbornly refused. Instead, he sniffed the ground near the front tire and started to growl.

"What is it, boy?" Ella Mae idly wondered whose scent he found so offensive.

Chewy's lips curled back, revealing his sharp little teeth. He swung his head from side to side and then released a torrent of furious barks.

He was so agitated that Ella Mae became concerned. "What's wrong?"

Chewy jumped up and placed his front paws on the Jeep.

"No! Down, boy," Ella Mae scolded. "You'll scratch the—" She suddenly noticed the slip of paper tucked under her windshield wiper. Pulling it free, she unfolded the piece of cream-colored cardstock and read the typed words:

        The dead are dead.
        Let them be.

> If you don't
> another lady will burn.

Ella Mae shoved the note into her coat pocket and scooped Chewy into her arms, holding him tightly. Normally, he'd lick her on the cheeks once or twice and then squirm until she let him go, but he seemed to sense that she needed comfort. He nuzzled her neck with his nose and grew still in her grasp.

"It's a threat," Ella Mae whispered to her terrier. "They'll set fire to our grove. Destroy our magic forever. Murder my mother. Mom!" She choked on the last word and pressed her face into Chewy's fur, inhaling his familiar aroma of dirt and damp grass. She then put him in the car, shut the door, and spread her hands over the metal side panel. Ella Mae wanted to punch something. She wanted to scream in rage. She wanted to find who'd written the note and wrap her hands around their throat. But none of those things would help her protect her mother, so she got in the Jeep and called Reba.

"Are you still at the police station?" Reba asked, incredulous. "I told you to let me drive you. If I'd been there, Hardy wouldn't have dared to keep you that long."

"I'm just leaving Suzy's," Ella Mae said, fighting to keep her voice steady. "She found out that Robert Morgan's company owns Barric's farm. We also discovered that the Gaynors have been buying feed from Young's Farm for years. I'll explain in more detail later. Right now, I need a huge favor. An illegal favor."

Reba chuckled. "It's about damn time. Will I be bustin' knee caps, stealin' evidence, breakin' into the Gaynors' house, or all of the above?"

"I'd like a copy of the ME's report on Eira," Ella Mae said. "I want to know everything there is to know about her, starting with that file. Jenny's given me Eira's recent history and I believe Barric was telling us the truth about Eira's childhood, but I want to see if the ME listed what kind of drugs and alcohol he found in Eira's system or anything else that might have been noted that could help me figure out what happened to her the night she died."

"Does this mean you want me to get friendly with the ME's assistant?" Reba didn't sound pleased.

"I thought you were already friendly. Didn't you used to date him?"

"Toby and I went on one date over a year ago. The man smells like tuna fish." Reba sighed wistfully. "It's a shame too. You know I have a weakness for bald men and Toby's head is as round and smooth as a billiard ball. But when he moved in for a kiss at the end of our date, I wanted to hose him down with Lysol."

"Reba, things have taken an urgent turn. You need to meet with him today."

"On a Sunday? Unless he's in workin' on Barric, he'll be at home."

Ella Mae considered this wrinkle. "I'll make a pie for him. Something with turkey and an extra dose of drowsy. If he eats the pie at the office, you can easily copy both Eira's and Barric's files. And if you meet Toby at his house, you'll have to steal his keys, copy the reports, and return his keys before he wakes up. That's much riskier. Are you up to it?"

"I like livin' dangerously. That's when I feel the most alive," Reba said. "Now tell me what's got you so tense."

"More like terrified, Reba. The arsonist is definitely in Havenwood and I need to find them or someone else will die. Not might die. *Will* die." Ella Mae allowed her fury to bubble forth. "The bastard left me a warning, Reba. A note saying that if I don't back off, they're going to torch our grove. I *must* stop them. I have to protect our people and my mother!"

Reba's growl was nearly identical to Chewy's. "Where was this note?" When Ella Mae told her, Reba said, "Someone is trackin' your movements. I'm gonna see where the

Upton siblings are. They'd better be able to account for every second of their day or I'll have to introduce them to my throwing stars."

"It could have been Robert Morgan," Ella Mae pointed out. "He has a driver. Or one of the Gaynors. Their house was being searched this morning, but that doesn't mean they're all standing around watching the cops."

"Rolling View is bein' searched? What for?" Reba asked.

"Sleeping pills, I'd guess," Ella Mae said. "Opal's mother conveniently misplaced hers the night before the party. I don't know what other evidence the police are hoping to find. Everything will be listed in the warrant, but the Gaynors aren't likely to share that information with me. I ran into Loralyn after my interview with Hardy." Ella Mae pictured Loralyn pacing the hall in the police station. "She was crying, Reba. She's scared and I think it's probably because someone close to her played a role in the murders."

Reba was silent for several seconds. "All right, let's get movin'. You bake Toby's pie. I'll feed it to him and get the ME's reports. Meanwhile, have a sit-down with Verena and the Uptons. Make sure Aiden answers Verena's questions. Use force if necessary."

"Yes, it's past time we learned the Uptons' secret," Ella Mae agreed. "I'm adding one more thing to my agenda. You won't like this, Reba, but I'm not waiting until spring to go after the Flower of Life. I'm going for it now. Well, as soon as I can borrow a dry suit from the fire department."

"I know you want to save your mama, but you can't just jump into the lake and swim to the bottom. You've only been scuba divin' with Sloane in calm, clear Caribbean waters. Lake Havenwood is dark and deep, and some terrible creature is down there. You need to know how to fight it."

Ella Mae released a guttural cry of anger and frustration. "I will kill anything that stands between me and that flower. No one is going to burn my mother! Do you hear me?"

"I know you're fierce as a lioness, but your Colt won't be

much help below the surface. You need to know your ene-my's weakness before you go into battle." Reba spoke softly. "Find somethin' to offer the Gaynors in trade for those mis-sin' book pages. If that means gettin' the cops off their backs for a spell, so be it. If they're involved in the murders, we can deal with them after your mama's safe."

Ella Mae saw the sense in that. "I'll have Verena talk with the Elders. We need guards at the grove until the arson-ist is caught." She turned the Jeep's engine on and set the heater to high. Yesterday's snow was already gone, but the chilly winds that had carried the storm to Havenwood had yet to retreat. "Once I bake the pies for Toby and Hugh, I'll call you to come get yours." She shook her head. "I never thought I'd be giving my own boyfriend enchanted food, but I need his keys to the fire station."

"Just make sure he never finds out," Reba warned. "He'll never trust you again.

"I'm keeping so many secrets from him already. What's one more?" Ella Mae was struck by a fresh wave of guilt and remorse, but she shoved the feelings aside. She could analyze her relationship with Hugh later. Now, it was time to act. To fight, if need be. And Ella Mae's weapons were about to be baked into two pies.

At The Charmed Pie Shoppe, Ella Mae made a makeshift bed for Chewy in the dining room. She waited for him to settle down on a flattened cardboard box lined with dish-towels and then tied on her apron and got to work.

Her first step was to turn the thermostat to high, making the kitchen as hot as she could. Next, she cut fresh onions, tomatoes, mushrooms, parsley, and the meat from a cooked turkey breast into bite-sized pieces. After caramelizing the onion in butter, she added white wine to the frying pan. Her original recipe for puff pastry turkey pie called for chicken broth, but she decided the wine would help increase the feelings of somnolence she intended to put in the filling.

Tuning the radio to the classical station, she buttoned up her heavy wool coat and stood next to the oven. She dropped the mushrooms into the onion and wine mixture and stirred the vegetables. All the while, she thought back to a time at the end of her junior semester in college when she had to write a research paper for her geology class. She'd signed up for the class because she thought it would be an easy way to fulfill her science requirement, but the class turned out to be both difficult and dull. Ella Mae had put off working on her final project until the eleventh hour, but finally, she'd had to sit down and finish the long and tedious paper.

She had a clear memory of being in the overly warm library with books and notebooks spread across a polished wood table as she tried to eke out enough words to complete the assignment. The hours passed with agonizing slowness, and she'd worked late into the night, until her writing began to blur and her eyelids felt so heavy that she had to fight to keep them open.

I want to sleep, she remembered thinking. She also recalled how the weight of her fatigue coaxed her head down closer and closer to the table. And then she'd made a pillow of her arms and closed her sore eyes. Her muscles went flaccid and blissful darkness had filled her vision.

Ella Mae held on to this memory as she removed the onions and mushrooms from the stovetop and added them to the bowl of turkey, tomatoes, and parsley. "Sleep," she whispered while sprinkling salt and pepper over the mixture. "You are *so* tired."

After lining two pie pans with her puff pastry dough, she poured in the turkey filling and then grabbed a fistful of Parmesan cheese. "Go on. Close your eyes and sleep." She let the grated cheese drift onto the surface of each pie. "Sleep long and deep."

Sliding the pies into the oven, she set the timer and then immediately took off her coat and hung it up. She was sweating and her hands and forehead were clammy, so she stepped outside and invited the cold air to chase away her drowsiness. As the kitchen filled with the aroma of the baking pies, Ella Mae stood on the steps until she could feel her arms break out in gooseflesh.

When her temperature felt normal again, she went back inside and popped in a CD by HardDrive, her favorite bluegrass group, and set about making piecrusts for the upcoming week. By the time the turkey pies were done, she'd sung every song and had a small mountain of dough balls cocooned in plastic wrap ready for the refrigerator.

She'd just brewed a pot of coffee when Reba and Verena entered the kitchen.

"Reba told me everything!" Verena bellowed. She thrust out her hand. "Let me see that note."

Ella Mae took the offending paper from the pocket of her coat and laid it on her aunt's palm. Verena unfolded it angrily and read, Reba at her elbow.

"This person dares to threaten my sister?" Verena's voice rose angrily. "Fool! The Oak Knoll community was taken by surprise, but that won't happen to us. The first sentries are already in place." Her brow furrowed. "Look at this paper. This is fine stationery. And the syntax? This was not written by some hillbilly."

"He or she has a laser printer too," Reba said, sniffing the note and examining it closely. "This isn't typewriter ink."

Ella Mae nodded. "The wording doesn't remind me of Aiden or Jenny, but we can't be sure." She wrapped the turkey pies in foil and handed one to Reba. "You take care of Toby. Aunt Verena and I going to Partridge Hill to have a chat with the Uptons."

"I reckon that other pie's for Hugh." Reba looked concerned. "You're not thinkin' of takin' a late-night swim, are you?"

"For now, I just want to copy his keys. I'll try to get the missing pages from Loralyn first, but even if I fail, I have to go after that flower. I can't sit at home, hoping that whoever wrote this letter is convinced that I'm not a threat." Ella Mae put a hand on Reba's arm. "If we're dealing with a fire elemental, then it won't matter how many people we have standing guard over our grove. He'll get in. Suzy told me that only someone with powerful water magic can stop him. Like a water elemental."

Verena said, "That Suzy is quite an asset to our community."

"I was hoping Jenny and Aiden would be assets too. It's time to find out if I was right." Ella Mae showed her aunt the gun in her handbag. "Are you armed?"

"I sure am!" Verena's mouth curved into a wicked grin. "Reba gave me a Taser. If Aiden so much as lights a match, he'll rue the day he came to Havenwood."

At Partridge Hill, they saw Jenny's yellow Camaro parked in front of the house and Aiden out on the lawn, throwing a tennis ball for Miss Lulu. He waved as Ella Mae pulled up next to Jenny's car and smiled as Chewy jumped out of the Jeep to greet him.

Chewy and Miss Lulu engaged in a friendly tussle until they were distracted by a squirrel chattering from the edge of the lawn. The two dogs responded to the other animal's taunt immediately. They darted for the woods, quivering noses raised high.

"Nice to see you again, Ms. LeFaye," Aiden said to Verena. "I'd shake hands, but mine are covered by Miss Lulu slobber." A flash of anxiety in his eyes belied his friendly smile and relaxed posture.

"It's too cold to talk out here anyway." Verena pointed at the house. "Let's all go into the house and have a cup of something hot. Do you think we could get your sister to do the honors?"

Aiden's smile slipped. "Yeah, sure." He stood to the side, allowing Ella Mae to lead the way inside.

Jenny was already in the kitchen pouring hot water into a ceramic teapot shaped like a hen. When she turned to find Ella Mae and Verena standing in the threshold, she seemed genuinely delighted. "What perfect timing. Would you like a cup of Ceylon black? This pot makes the world's best tea."

"Please," Ella Mae said, coming closer. "My aunt Dee has a bunch of animal-shaped teapots. A bluebird, a tabby cat, and an elephant. When I was a kid, the elephant was my favorite because its trunk was the spout. Dee would pour out lemonade and tease me by saying that the elephant had a bad cold."

Jenny laughed. "Aiden bought me this hilarious toilet-shaped pot as a joke. I broke it by accident, I swear!" Crossing her fingers, she looked at her brother. "Remember that hideous thing?"

Aiden's expression was grim. "I don't think they're here to talk about your teapot collection, Jenny."

Taken aback by his solemn expression, Jenny glanced between Ella Mae and Verena. "No, I guess they're not."

"Let's go to the sunroom," Ella Mae suggested. "It's the warmest spot in the house."

Once they were all settled, Jenny took her time pouring tea and setting out Adelaide's sugar bowl and a small pitcher of milk. Aiden shook his head when she offered him a cup. "It's time for me to tell them, Jenny."

Nodding miserably, Jenny dropped a sugar cube into her teacup. She kept her eyes fixed on the sugar, pushing it this way and that with her spoon, as if mesmerized by the dissolving granules.

"You have a secret," Ella Mae began. "And we have two murders on our hands. Both victims are from Oak Knoll." She focused her gaze on Aiden. "Why were you at the lake yesterday? Did you kill Barric?"

Aiden shook his head. "I was looking for you. I waited

until Jenny went in the other direction in search of Barric, and then I headed to the lake. I wanted to tell you my story where no one else could hear us. But when I got there, you were on the verge of passing out and Barric was beyond my help."

Ella Mae cast a sideways glance at her aunt, but Verena didn't even arch an eyebrow. Aiden was telling the truth. "Well," she prompted gently, "I'm here now."

Aiden rested his hand on his sister's shoulder and drew in a deep, fortifying breath. "Not long before our grove burned, I was working on wiring a house in a new development. The general contractor was behind schedule and I told him I'd stay late to get the job done. So, I was alone when Eira showed up. She'd brought me supper—fried chicken, cornbread, butter beans—which I figured had been Jenny's idea. Jenny spoils me."

Jenny reached up to touch his hand with hers. "You're all I've got, despite the fact that you're a total idiot."

Her eyes were full of affection and Aiden shot her a quick grin before continuing. "Eira didn't come just to feed me. She had an agenda. While I ate, she told me about the terrible things Robert did. He'd lock her in her room if she didn't act exactly how he wanted and he tried to control everything about her life. He picked out her clothes and food and even chose the books she read and the music she listened to. Made it sound like she lived in a prison."

"If that place was anything like the house Mr. Morgan purchased here in Havenwood, it must have been a fancy prison," Verena said.

"Oh, yeah. Big mansion. Servants. The best clothes, jewelry, and all that," Aiden said. "But Eira told me she didn't care about those things. Her dream had always been to teach dance to kids and to perform for an audience. That was never going to happen though because she was only allowed to dance for her husband."

Ella Mae took a sip of tea. It was hot and strong. "Dancing

was her gift. She could enthrall people, men especially, whenever she danced."

"I didn't know that until the night of the Oak Knoll fire," Aiden said. "It's not like we all go around discussing our abilities, and Eíra never mentioned hers in front of me. And as you might have guessed, I've never been to the ballet. I'm more of a country fair kind of guy." He shrugged. "Anyway, after she was done telling me her sob story, she turned up my radio and started to dance. She danced all through that empty house. I felt something inside go all tingly watching her. Like my brain had gone fuzzy."

"She enchanted you!" Verena cried and drained her tea in one gulp.

"Absolutely," Aiden agreed. "She had to use magic because I wasn't attracted to her. Not even close. I'm not into delicate flower types. I like a pretty, feisty, sharp-witted woman. Like Suzy Bacchus." He smiled when he spoke Suzy's name.

"Keep the train on the tracks, bro." Jenny punched her brother's thick arm.

Aiden rubbed the spot and continued. "So after Eira put me in this trancelike state, she asked me to get rid of her husband. She wasn't subtle about it either. She kissed me and whispered in my ear that if I killed Robert, we could be together."

Ella Mae was stunned. "My Lord, I completely misjudged Eira. She was far more than a talented dancer. She was also a skilled manipulator and actress. Did you ever see that side of her, Jenny?"

Jenny's eyes filled with tears. "I knew she was miserable with Robert, and I knew her history with Barric. I honestly believed she still loved him. I didn't find out that she tried to use Aiden to kill Morgan until the night of the fire in our grove." She squeezed the handle of her teacup so hard that Ella Mae was afraid it would snap right off.

"What happened?" Verena asked Aiden. "Did you go after Robert Morgan?"

"I meant to," Aiden admitted guiltily. "I wasn't in my

right mind, okay? I came up with a scheme to electrocute him. I'm okay with fire, but electricity is my specialty."

At this, he received another punch from his sister. "Seriously, Aiden. This is not the time to brag."

"I almost went through with it," he said. "Eira gave me the house security code and said that Robert would be alone in his study all night. Luckily, I didn't drive straight to their place. I went to the grove to give my already amazing powers an extra boost." He danced out of the way as Jenny tried to swat him again. "Being there cleared the fog in my head. Not totally, but enough for me to realize something was wrong. I sat down to think. The grass in our grove was pillow soft and I only meant to lie down for a few minutes, but it was so peaceful and I'd had a long and tiring day. To make a long story short, I fell asleep."

Ella Mae wasn't surprised. She'd stretched out in the clearing of their grove more than once, breathing in the sweet air and letting the serenity of the place wash over her. It made for the perfect napping place. "When did you wake up?"

"In the middle of the fire." Aiden passed his hands over his face. "The whole grove was burning. I heard . . . somehow . . . I heard our Lady screaming." He paused to collect himself. "I didn't start the fire. I'm no arsonist. Besides, I need fuel to get a fire going. A match, gasoline, flint and steel, lightning. I can keep flames burning but I can't produce fire from nothing. My gift is really about encouraging the flow of energy, which is why I became an electrician. Heat, lights, air conditioning—that's all energy. Jenny's gift is similar. She increases the energy flow in people."

Verena had been watching Aiden without blinking. "So you refused to answer my questions about the grove because you'd gone there to premeditate murder?"

"Yes, ma'am. I didn't think you'd want me working for Ella Mae once you knew." Aiden threw out his hands. "It sounds like a total load of crap to me and I was *there*, so I didn't expect either of you to believe me."

"I believe you, son," Verena said. "I don't suppose you have any idea who the real arsonist is?"

Aiden narrowed his eyes. "If I did, he'd be dead by now."

"Or she," Jenny added.

"This *person* destroyed our sacred place, murdered our Lady, and drove us from our homes. The arsonist took everything we knew and destroyed it." Aiden knelt next to Ella Mae. "Jenny and I told you that we wanted to help you find this scumbag. We meant what we said."

Ella Mae covered his hand with hers. "Both the violence in Oak Knoll and the murders in Havenwood seem to be connected to Eira. If we can identify the third man, the father of her child, then I believe we'll have our answers."

Jenny rose to her feet. "Let us assist you somehow. Please. You've done so much for us."

"All right," Ella Mae said. "Try to gain access to Eira's things. Maybe she kept a letter inside one of her books or owned a jewelry box with a hidden drawer. We need a clue that'll reveal the identity of the third man." Ella Mae jotted down the address of Robert Morgan's house. "Maybe you can ask him for a keepsake. After all, Eira was your best friend."

"No, she wasn't." Jenny shook her head angrily. "Friends are honest with each other. True friends trust each other with their hopes and dreams. With their secrets."

Ella Mae could see the pain in Jenny's eyes. "I'm sorry to ask, but did you know that Morgan owned Barric's farm?"

For a moment, Jenny didn't move. "That must be it!" she cried. "All this time I couldn't understand why she married that brute, but she must have done it to protect Barric's livelihood. His farm was in trouble. Big trouble. He was about to go bankrupt and then Morgan came along and fell for Eira. She married him to save Barric. Even after he'd cheated on her. Even after she said she'd never trust him again. *That* was the Eira I knew. She saved the boy she'd loved since childhood and deliberately placed herself in a loveless marriage. All she wanted from Morgan was a child and then that chance was taken from her when he was punished. Oh, Eira!" Her voice caught. She bent her head, covering her mouth with her hand, and sobbed noiselessly until Aiden moved to her side and put his arm around her shoulders. "After what she sacrificed for Barric—how could she turn away from him for this other guy?" she muttered into her brother's shirt.

"Because Barric didn't want a child," Ella Mae said softly. "She had to find someone who'd grant her heart's desire. And apparently, that desire also included the murder of her husband."

Verena clucked sympathetically. "Eira might not have been open with you, but you were a good friend to her. You were as close as she dared come to having a real relationship. Don't you ever forget that!"

Jenny sniffled and wiped her face with a napkin. "Thank you. Whatever else may have happened, at least we found our way to Havenwood. To you, Ella Mae, and the pie shop." She managed a smile. "So what's next, boss?"

"I'm heading to Rolling View," Ella Mae said. "I need to see if the Gaynors' stable manager, a Mr. Rand Dockery, looks like father material."

Chapter 14

Ella Mae didn't head straight to Rolling View from her house. Instead, she drove to their stables hoping to get a good look at Rand Dockery. Rand had worked for Gaynor Farms for many years and was a familiar figure around town, and though Ella Mae had seen him from time to time, she'd never spoken with him. She had no intention of questioning him about Eira or Barric on his own turf, and she already had a story prepared to cover her reason for visiting the farm. All she wanted was to get a sense of the man. She wasn't so naïve as to believe that she'd be able to tell whether he was a murderer or not just by exchanging a few inane phrases, but she believed she could gain some insight as to what sort of man he was just by interacting with him.

However, Rand wasn't inside the largest of the heated stables, which was where the staff offices were located. A few horses peered at her over the doors of their stalls and two of them nickered when Ella Mae walked in, but no one else was around. Rand Dockery's office was dark. His door was locked. Though it was Sunday, Ella Mae knew the

Gaynors wouldn't leave their valuable animals unguarded, and that someone was bound to come along any moment, so she decided to have a quick look at the photographs on the wall outside Rand's office and then leave.

Most of the photos featured a jockey mounted on a stunning Thoroughbred whose neck was decorated by a flower horseshoe. Rand Dockery was in many of the pictures—always with a possessive hand on the horse's bridle. Ella Mae assumed that Rand attended many of the races to maintain a personal level of contact with owners and trainers, and also to watch the horses he'd raised compete. Judging from the photomontage, Rand and Gaynor Farms had produced many winners.

Moving closer to an image of Rand standing behind a long-legged colt, Ella Mae could see why women would find him attractive. In his late thirties, with the weathered skin of a man who works outdoors, he was ruggedly handsome. As Suzy had said, he looked like a cowboy, but what was most appealing about him was that he wore an expression of contentment. He seemed like a man who was doing exactly what he was meant to do. There was both warmth and pride in his dark eyes as he posed with the colt.

"You obviously like beautiful things," Ella Mae said to Rand's satisfied face. Deciding that she was unlikely to discover additional clues about him in the stables, she got back in the Jeep and drove through a pair of imposing iron gates and up Rolling View's driveway.

There were no police cars outside the Gaynors' mansion, but the house carried an air of affront. It seemed to have closed in upon itself following the invasive search. The curtains were drawn and there was an unusual stillness to the place. Even the birds had gone quiet, as if sensing that it would be impolite to call to one another from the bare branches of the magnolia trees after witnessing the intrusion of Hardy and his team.

Pulling the lapels of her coat tight against the afternoon

chill, Ella Mae rang the doorbell and then waited. When no one responded to the lengthy chimes, she rang it again, expecting to see the shadow of the housekeeper's eye darken the peephole. Instead, Loralyn swung the door open and sneered. "What do you want?"

Behind Loralyn, a uniformed maid mopped the checkered tile floor while another polished a mahogany side table. They were so intent on their work that they didn't even glance up to see who stood on the welcome mat. Ella Mae could hear the sound of multiple vacuums being run on the second floor, and somewhere to the left, she heard someone promise to see to the tarnished silver immediately. It was evident that the Gaynors were in a hurry to remove all signs that the police had been in their home.

"I know that the man who got Eira pregnant is from Rolling View," Ella Mae began without preamble. She had no proof of this allegation, but she said it anyway. It was imperative that she come away with the missing book pages and put an end to the violence in Havenwood. "I don't know what went wrong between them, but he traveled to Oak Knoll for business. He and Eira started having an affair, and his visits to Oak Knoll became even more frequent."

Loralyn went pale, but she did her best to recover her aplomb. "What proof do you have?"

"Honestly? Not much. But I'm sure the police could examine his travel records, hotel bookings, and other transactions and arrive at the same conclusion." The maid with the mop was drawing closer, so Ella Mae lowered her voice. "How could you protect him, knowing what he's done?"

"I wasn't certain until I heard him arguing with my mother last night. And you might not think very highly of me, but I'm fiercely loyal to the people I care about. Loyal to the death." Her blue eyes were cold and threatening. She had yet to invite Ella Mae inside, but kept one hand on the open door as if she might slam it on Ella Mae's face at any moment.

"Well, I'm not going to turn around and run to the police. I'll give you a little time to talk him into giving himself up," Ella Mae said. "On one condition."

Loralyn stared at her in irate disbelief. "And what's that?"

"Hand over the missing pages from Rupert Gaynor's book."

"In exchange for a few hours' reprieve?" Loralyn released a dry, humorless laugh. "No deal." Her mouth thinned into an angry line. "Swear to leave him alone. Say that you'll let my family handle this internally and I'll give you the pages. I know why you need them, Ella Mae. You want to free your mother from our most ancient of spells, despite the fact that this particular spell was put into place to ensure the survival of our kind. And yet you can't understand why I didn't confess everything to Officer Hardy while he was rifling through our things?"

Ella Mae thought there was a world of difference between saving a parent and an employee, but she didn't say as much. "I won't turn my back on two murders, Loralyn. The man you're protecting threatened to burn our grove. What do you think the Elders would say if I showed them this letter?" She handed Loralyn the note she'd received and waited for her to read it. "I don't believe they'd give him the option of turning himself in. No. I'm pretty sure he'd be punished immediately. Knowing what he did to the Oak Knoll grove, they wouldn't hesitate. They'd state their case to my mother and I'm quite certain the Elders would pool all of their powers to ensure that his penalty was far more severe than Robert Morgan's. Partial paralysis would be mild compared to what—"

"Stop it!" Loralyn shouted. "Please. Stop. I'll give you the pages. But you must promise not to speak to the authorities for three days. We need time to . . . to confront him. He's extremely dangerous. Very volatile."

"You have twenty-four hours from this moment," Ella Mae said firmly. "And if I smell so much as a whiff of smoke anywhere near me, my family, or the grove, I'll contact the Elders immediately." She'd never seen Loralyn so deflated. Her whole body sagged and she leaned heavily against the doorframe. "I'm sorry that it has to be this way," Ella Mae added. She was moved by Loralyn's misery, but couldn't let her sympathetic feelings interfere with what had to be done. "Eira and Barric didn't deserve to have their futures cut short. I speak with the Lady's voice when I say that they will both have justice. Get me the pages, please."

"Wait here," Loralyn whispered and walked over the wet floor toward the library. She returned a minute later with a sealed envelope and an expression of icy hatred. "This is what you wanted. Now go away."

Ella Mae started to say thank you when Loralyn shut the door on her.

It took every ounce of restraint not to read the pages right there on the stoop, but Ella Mae managed to drive all the way home before removing them from the envelope. She'd read two sentences describing the creature's habitat when the sound of a car engine coming up behind her had her glancing nervously in her rearview mirror.

Darkness was falling around the trees and the shadows were multiplying. The headlights from the oncoming car momentarily blinded Ella Mae and she tucked the book pages into her purse and stepped out of her Jeep, ready to draw her Colt. When she recognized Hugh's truck, she exhaled in relief and then immediately tensed again. She'd been so focused on stopping a killer that she'd pushed Hugh from her mind. He'd called her three times today and she hadn't even listened to all of his voice mail messages.

"This is perfect!" she called brightly as he got out of his truck. "It's as if you knew I'd made you a special supper. I was going to call you," she lied. "Now I don't have to."

Dante jumped to the ground, barked twice in greeting, and shot past her in search of Chewy. Hugh had eyes for only Ella Mae. "You wanted me to come over tonight?" He was clearly surprised. "And here I was, wondering if I should even swing by. I'm glad I listened to my gut." His face broke into a relieved smile and Ella Mae felt another sharp prick of guilt. Hugh was a good man. He deserved more than she had to offer, especially when it came to honesty. She thought of how hurt Jenny had been to discover Eira's duplicitous nature. How would Hugh feel if he knew how many lies the woman he loved had told him?

Ella Mae didn't want Hugh to notice her troubled expression, so she ducked back inside the Jeep to grab her purse. Meanwhile, Chewy had spotted Dante through the cottage window and was barking wildly. "The boys can race around the yard while I preheat the oven," she said, unlocking the front door. Chewy darted outside in a blur of brown and white fur, and Ella Mae caught a glimpse of a wagging tail and a flash of pink tongue before he disappeared into the garden.

She and Hugh stood in the doorway for a moment, watching Dante give chase.

"I think they're playing hide-and-seek," Hugh said when both dogs were out of sight. Dante's low bark rumbled across the lawn and Hugh laughed. "He doesn't realize that he's too big to hide under a rosebush."

Ella Mae stepped inside and was about to unbutton her coat when Hugh took her hand. "I've been really worried about you. You found a dead man, had hypothermia, and spent the morning talking to cops. And yet, without saying more than two words to me since Aiden pulled you out of the lake, you're suddenly cooking me supper? I feel like you're keeping me at arm's length, Ella Mae. I don't want to be here." He indicated the space between them and then took a step forward, closing the gap. His bright blue eyes bored into hers. "I want to be here."

Ella Mae leaned her head against his chest, feeling a powerful rush of love for her wonderful man. It wasn't a hot, lustful feeling this time, but the warm, comfortable sensation of coming home at the end of a very long day. She lifted her face and kissed him on the lips, but it wasn't long before the kiss turned painful.

Hugh broke away first. He gazed at her tenderly and tucked a lock of hair behind her ear. "So what are you feeding me tonight? I need to know how many miles I'll have to run tomorrow."

"Puff pastry turkey pie, salad, and wine. If you have any room left after that, I could make you a chocolate mousse."

Groaning, Hugh reached for the door handle. "I might as well start right running now."

Ella Mae gave him a playful shove. "You're not going anywhere but into the kitchen. Your job is to decant the wine. It's not the greatest vintage, but maybe, if we let it breathe for an extra-long time, it'll taste halfway decent."

Hugh saluted her and followed her into the kitchen. Ella Mae washed her hands, turned the radio on low, and took out salad ingredients from the refrigerator. She'd just begun to slice the cucumber when Hugh said, "Talk to me, Ella Mae. You don't have to put on a brave face. What happened yesterday—it's a big deal."

"I know," she said and caught her reflection in the knife blade. She was pale and drawn, as if the lake's cold water had drained the pink from her skin. Suddenly, she saw Barric's face and got caught up remembering a dozen tiny details, like the blond stubble on his chin, and that his upper lip was chapped. There was a small mole below his left eye and a lock of hair curled over his forehead, bobbing gently in the current like the tail of a seahorse. She shared these memories with Hugh. "It was hard enough to look at those blank eyes or watch the way he was floating just below the surface, but seeing his head. The blood and—" She stopped to take a swallow of wine. "I wonder who could have hated him that much. Someone snuck up behind Barric and felled him like a tree. What kind of person can pick up a rock and turn it over and over? Test the weight of it? Test the grip?

And then, satisfied that he's chosen the right weapon, set forth to use it. What kind of man can do that?"

Hugh wrapped his arms around Ella Mae's shoulders. "Don't worry, Hardy will find him." He shook his head, his hair brushing against her neck. "I should have been with you last night. I was working when I should have been with you."

"No," she insisted, pivoting to face him. "What you did was important. Neither you nor the police would have slept a wink without doing everything that could be done to find the murder weapon. Besides, I wasn't alone. Reba was with me. You know she's like a second mother to me." She smiled. "Not that it wouldn't have been nice to have you sleeping next to me, but I was so tired that I barely remember going to bed."

"What about this morning? I thought you might want company at the police station."

She turned and resumed slicing the cucumber. "You work so hard, Hugh. I wasn't going to ruin your day off by having you sit on one of those uncomfortable chairs in the station's lobby." She scooped the cucumbers into a bowl and started cutting a tomato into wedges. "I wasn't nervous at all about talking with Hardy. He and I have come to know each other by now. And you're right. He won't rest until he nails this guy."

Hugh opened the front door and called the dogs. Once he'd petted and praised them both, Hugh began to talk about the underwater search. Ella Mae really wanted to ask if his regulator hose had malfunctioned, but she couldn't do so without revealing that Reba had spied on him. She also knew that this wasn't the time to determine whether her boyfriend was a water elemental or not. She had a fire elemental to deal with first.

The oven beeped and Ella Mae took out the hot pie and set it on a heart-shaped trivet. The scent of melted butter and roasted turkey wafted through the room. Hugh leaned over the pie, inhaled, and grinned. "That smells like Thanksgiving."

"I hope you're hungry. I nibbled on stuff while I was making dough at the pie shop, so I'm sticking to salad."

"Sure, fatten me up like my name was Hansel." Hugh tapped on the nearest wall. "Nope. Not gingerbread." He kissed her cheek. "And you're far too beautiful to be a witch."

I wouldn't count on that, Ella Mae thought ruefully and served Hugh his supper.

As they ate, Hugh told her about a particularly rowdy Dalmatian who'd been enrolled at Canine to Five on Friday. "I think he just needs attention." He went on to describe the dog's personality in detail, and though Ella Mae tried to listen, her thoughts kept flitting between the missing pages in her purse and the wall of photographs featuring Rand Dockery.

Ella Mae wondered if she'd done the right thing by bargaining with Loralyn. She didn't trust any of the Gaynors, but she'd had to get those pages. It wasn't as if she could march into the police station and tell Officer Hardy to arrest Rand. She had no concrete evidence that he'd been involved in either Eira's or Barric's deaths. She'd made a wild assumption, which, based on Loralyn's reaction, turned out to be correct, but the police couldn't arrest a man based on hearsay. And there was something else to consider. Anyone, being of a magical nature or not, who tried to put handcuffs on a fire elemental could be seriously injured. Or killed.

As Hugh cut himself another wedge of pie, Ella Mae considered the likelihood of Rand Dockery surrendering to the authorities. It was all too easy to envision him packing a bag in preparation to start a new life elsewhere. Ella Mae's stomach knotted with anxiety at the thought. And if he wasn't busy buying plane tickets, was he still watching her? Had he seen her talking with Loralyn? While she enjoyed Hugh's company, was Rand planning to punish her by burning the grove and murdering her mother?

Hugh put down his fork and yawned. "Sorry," he said, his voice sounding thick and groggy. "It's so nice and warm in here. And I'm really full." He leaned back in his chair, his shoulders drooping. His entire body relaxed and he gave Ella Mae a drowsy, boyish smile that she found completely endearing.

If you knew what I've done, you wouldn't look at me that way, she thought and put an arm around his back. "Come on. Let's move this party to the sofa."

She'd barely gotten Hugh settled before his head lolled back on the throw pillow and he closed his eyes. "So tired," he murmured as Ella Mae pulled off his boots. She helped him stretch out and then covered him with a blanket. Chewy hopped onto the sofa and curled into a tight ball by Hugh's feet while Dante flopped down on the hearthrug. It wasn't long before Hugh's snores mingled with the steady breathing of the two contented dogs.

Hoping that Hugh had eaten enough pie to keep him in dreamland for several hours, Ella Mae ran upstairs and packed a tote bag with two beach towels, her heaviest wool sweater, and a pair of thick cotton sweatpants. She then scooped Hugh's key ring off the coffee table, bundled up in her coat and hat, and left.

As soon as the lights of Partridge Hill vanished in her rearview mirror, she called Suzy. "I got the missing pages. Were you able to pinpoint the deepest part of Lake Havenwood?"

"Yes. I found a free database on the world's lakes. You'll need to dive about one hundred and fifty feet down. And from a very useful geological database, I discovered that the exact spot is really close to the island in the middle of the lake. It's like the world just falls away from the island's southern shore."

Ella Mae felt her heart lift. "Reba and I can row our boat there. Our dock points right at the island."

"Back up a second," Suzy said. "What do the pages say about the creature?"

"I don't know yet. I'll stop over and we can read them together. But as soon as we're done I'll need to run. I fed

Hugh an enchanted pie and he's sleeping like a coma patient, but I don't know if I'll have all night to do what I need to do."

"Which is what?" Suzy said. "Don't tell me you're going after the Flower of Life *tonight*!" She groaned. "Actually don't answer that. Just hurry up and get here, okay?"

Ella Mae did as Suzy requested, and ten minutes later, the two friends were bent over the pages from Rupert Gaynor's book.

"Oh, here's the part about the creature!" Suzy exclaimed, but Ella Mae was a sentence ahead of her and her throat had turned so dry that she was unable to speak.

Legend speaks of a guardian bearing a resemblance to a Nile crocodile, Gaynor had written. *However, this predator has flippers in lieu of legs, allowing it to move with astonishing speed.*

Ella Mae recalled a television documentary she'd seen showcasing the world's fiercest reptiles. The show had featured a clip of a Nile crocodile attacking a wildebeest. The wildebeest had been wading in the shallows when the massive croc struck without warning, dragging the doomed animal into the water. She remembered the froth of churning water and the shrill, wrenching noises of panic and pain the wildebeest had made as it struggled in the croc's viselike jaws.

I'm going to face something even deadlier, she thought fearfully. According to Gaynor, Lake Havenwood's monster was more agile, and twice as long as a Nile crocodile.

"This thing sounds like a *Liopleurodon*," Suzy said, her voice quavering. "An aquatic dinosaur from the Jurassic period. I remember a particularly frightening illustration in a book called *Top Prehistoric Predators*." Reaching for her laptop, she hit a few keys and then pointed at the screen. "That's a *Liopleurodon*. Kind of looks like a croc with a dolphin's body and a turtle's flippers."

"I like those last two animals, but if the creature in Lake

Havenwood has teeth like this dinosaur's . . ." Ella Mae trailed off.

"How can you possibly fight this thing?" Suzy asked. "I'm not doubting your courage. Not for a second. But you're not trained for combat. Even Reba would be powerless against such a creature. You'll be entering its domain in a dry suit, sucking on oxygen, and leaving a bubble trail a mile long. You'll be blind and slow and completely at its mercy." She gripped Ella Mae's arm. "You aren't prepared for this kind of battle. You need to find someone who is."

"It has to be me and you know it," Ella Mae said. "Everything we've read about the Flower of Life makes it clear that the person in need of the flower must go after it themselves. It's my quest, Suzy. No one can stand in for me. At least I'm going down there armed with the most important thing."

Suzy nodded, smoothing the loose book pages. "Purity of heart. No one seeking the flower can succeed without it. You aren't interested in personal gain. You'll use the flower to break the spell cast on your mother while establishing a permanent source of magic for our grove. You're willing to risk your life for the greater good." Suzy tightened her hold on Ella Mae's arm. "Okay, yes, you pass the greatest test before dipping a toe in the water. But *that* thing will still be waiting for you!" She gestured wildly at the screen. "You could die." Her eyes filled with tears. "There must be some other way."

Ella Mae took her friend's hands in hers. "You know there isn't."

Suzy stepped back, grabbed a tissue from the counter, wiped her nose and eyes, and then resolutely squared her shoulders. "All right. I can see that I can't talk you out of this madness. So how do you plan to arm yourself?"

"I'm going to ask for Aiden's help." Ella Mae stared at the blood-chilling image of the *Liopleurodon*. "If I ever hope to return to the surface with the flower, I need to kill this thing with one strike. In this case, I'm thinking of a lightning strike."

"Underwater?" Suzy asked doubtfully.

"Yes. My best chance is to hit the monster with an incredibly powerful jolt of electricity," Ella Mae said.

Suzy's eyes widened. "Like a shark prod?"

"Exactly. I have no idea why, but Reba owns a cattle prod. If Aiden can supercharge the thing, then it won't matter if it gets wet. I'm hoping that a high dose of magical electricity will be enough to fry this fish."

Suzy was aghast. "You're going to put your life in *Aiden's* hands? The man is—"

"Not an elemental. Nor did he start the Oak Knoll fire." Ella Mae watched as comprehension, followed by relief and happiness flooded Suzy's face. "He's innocent of any wrongdoing and he definitely has feelings for you."

The corners of Suzy's mouth turned up, but she refused to allow the smile to form. "Well, he'd better do everything in his power to help you or he'll have to answer to me."

"I haven't even asked him yet. I was hoping you'd do that." She held out Hugh's keys and shook them until they jingled. "As for me, I'll be borrowing scuba gear from the Havenwood Fire Department."

Chapter 15

Reba was correct in saying that most of Ella Mae's dive experience had been acquired in relatively shallow Caribbean water. However, her last scuba trip had taken her to a depth of one hundred and thirty feet. The shipwreck dive had required a specialized training course that both Ella Mae and her then-husband, Sloane, had passed with flying colors. Because it was their first deep dive, the couple hadn't been allowed to spend much time on the wreck, but the dive had gone smoothly and Ella Mae wasn't afraid to dive down another twenty feet tonight. She had something else to fear.

Ella Mae knew she'd have to follow the same meticulous procedures that she'd learned in her deep-water course, including the addition of multiple decompression stops during her ascent. The thought of stopping to eliminate nitrogen from her system while being hunted by a giant crocodile was more than a little unsettling, but getting the bends or losing consciousness would be fatal, so Ella Mae calculated her stops and then checked the equipment she'd taken from the fire station for the third time.

After loading everything into her Jeep, she headed back to Partridge Hill. "Now for the weapon," she said grimly, wishing Chewy sat in his usual spot on the seat, smearing the window with his nose and leaving white fur all over the dash.

Chewy wasn't waiting for her at her mother's house, but everyone else was. She'd expected to find Aiden, Jenny, Reba, and Suzy there, but her aunts had caught wind of her plans and were also gathered, pinched-faced and silent, in the kitchen.

"This is madness!" Verena cried the moment Ella Mae entered the room.

"Probably," Ella Mae agreed and then turned to Aiden. "Did Suzy explain what I needed?"

He nodded and pointed at the cattle prod on the stovetop. It was glowing with a bright yellow light. "It's charged. Press the button and enough juice will come out of there to sink a battleship. It'll stay lit the whole time you're under water too. I figure it would be better than your going down holding a dive light. I'd rather you kept two hands on your weapon."

Ella Mae could tell that Aiden had poured as much power as he could into the prod. He looked completely drained. "Thank you, Aiden."

Jenny took a step forward. "I want to give you an advantage too. After you're changed into your dry suit, let me give you a megadose of energy. It'll help you swim faster and be more alert. Your reflexes will be quicker and you'll be less likely to get dizzy or confused at the bottom on your way back to the surface."

"A magical cure against the bends." Ella Mae smiled. She felt a surreal sense of calm. Ever since her mother had volunteered to be the Lady of the Ash, Ella Mae had known that her destiny had forever been changed. And now that the moment of trial had arrived, she was ready to prove that she could be as brave as her mother.

As if sensing Ella Mae's thought, Sissy put her hands

over her heart and said, "You've never reminded me *so* much of Adelaide as you do right now."

Dee reached into the front pocket of her overalls and drew forth a necklace. "I made this for you a while ago. I'm not giving to it you now because you need luck. You don't." Her voice was a soft whisper. "This is my way of being with you down there. Another light in the darkness." She took Ella Mae's hand and let the necklace coil onto her palm. The pendant, a silver four-leaf clover, came to rest on top of Ella Mae's clover-shaped burn scar.

"Thank you." Ella Mae hugged each of her aunts. "Don't worry, okay?" She gazed from one familiar face to another. "Just knowing you're all here together gives me the strength I need. Now it's time for me to go. I can feel it."

Reba zipped up her parka, donned a fur-lined hat, and grabbed the cattle prod. "I'll get the boat ready and load your tank and flippers. You get your gear on and meet me at the dock."

When Reba left, Miss Lulu started barking from somewhere upstairs. "I thought I'd better lock her in my room," Jenny said. "If she got outside, she'd run right over to your place to see if Chewy wanted to play. I figured the sound of three barking dogs might wake Hugh."

Ella Mae had put Hugh out of her mind, and the image of him sleeping on her sofa with Chewy nestled on his lap nearly undid her. Part of her wanted to curl up beside him and forget about the Flower of Life, and the lake, and the creature waiting for her where the land fell away into deep, cold darkness. No one would blame her for turning away from such a perilous quest, but Ella Mae's love for her mother and her desire to protect her people won over the temptation. She gave Jenny a nod of gratitude and went into the bathroom to change into her dry suit.

Once dressed, she went out through the back door without saying good-bye. Jenny followed close behind and the two women walked across the lawn in hurried strides. It was another frigid night and they were both shivering by the time they reached the dock.

Drawing to a stop alongside the boat where Reba waited, Jenny put her hands on Ella Mae's neck and closed her eyes. "I'm going to give you all I've got," she said. "Ready?"

Ella Mae didn't even have the chance to nod before her body began to shudder. Jenny's gift shot through her muscles like a flaming arrow, electrifying her blood, and heightening her senses. "I feel like a superhero. Thank you." She hugged Jenny and then bent down to unwrap the dinghy's stern line from the cleat.

She handed the rope to Reba and boarded. Reba waited for her to get settled in the bow before raising and lowering her battery-powered lantern three times. She then picked up the oars and started to row, her eyes fixed on the island in the middle of the lake.

As the small craft moved away from shore, someone began to turn on all the lights in Partridge Hill. Ella Mae watched as, one by one, each window filled with rectangles of soft yellow. The house blazed bright as a moon, a beacon of love and safety shining across the black water.

Neither Reba nor Ella Mae spoke. Ella Mae kept herself occupied by checking her gauges and reviewing the digital dive computer she'd taken from the fire station. The dive computer would help Ella Mae keep an eye on her depth, direction, pressure, dive time, and gas mixes. During her ascent, she'd use the timer to regulate her compression stops.

"Your mama wouldn't like me sittin' in this boat while you go in alone. Divers are supposed to have partners," Reba said.

"My mother would know that you're not slacking off as my protector," Ella Mae said. "And, yes, divers need partners, but this quest has its own rules, remember? I have to go alone. Every legend about the flower says that same thing."

Reba didn't reply, and for a few minutes, both women listened to the sound of the oars cutting through the water.

"I realize that it's probably going to be harder for you to wait in this boat than it is for me to get in the water and face a monster, but knowing you're here is what'll keep me going when things get bad." Ella Mae glanced behind her. The shadowy shape of the island was coming up fast. "And it's going to get bad. We both know that. If it were easy, someone would have picked the flower by now. You're my life buoy, Reba. If I can get the flower, shock the beast, and point my face toward the light of your lantern, then you can take me back to Partridge Hill."

Reba's eyes filled with tears. "I'll be up here shinin' like the brightest damn sun you've even seen. You just swim to my light, baby. Get that flower and swim on home to me."

Ella Mae's throat tightened. She soaked in Reba's tender gaze before finally shrugging off her coat and strapping her tank onto her back. She then took another few seconds to steady her racing heart by fixing her eyes on the lights of Partridge Hill. The water lapped at the side of the boat, rocking it gently. Ella Mae had been playing in the lake since she could walk. She'd swum and raced boats with other children from one dock to another for years. It was not her enemy. Even though there was no sun now—just a sliver of moon glaring down at her from a starless sky—the lake was as much a part of her as the rest of Havenwood. The only thing she had to fear was the creature guarding the flower. And it was time to enter its world.

Ella Mae watched her breath plume into the air once more before drawing her hood and mask on. With gloved hands, she placed her regulator in her mouth and positioned herself on the gunwale with her back to the water. Turning her diver's headlight on, she took a firm hold of the charged prod. She then winked at Reba and went over the side and into the lake.

The shock of entering the water robbed Ella Mae of her senses. For several seconds, she forgot all she knew of scuba diving. She frantically turned her head to the right and left, the beam of her headlight searing the darkness, and tried to think, but everything looked and felt so alien.

You're sinking, she told herself and glanced at the dive computer readout.

That small movement allowed her to regain control. She angled her body downward and started to kick her feet. Her heart rate slowed a little, though its beats were far from normal. Every cell in her body was firing with adrenaline, fear, and Jenny's magical energy. Ella Mae knew that staying as calm as possible for the entire dive would be a challenge.

That, and facing a monster, she thought and continued to sink.

As she descended, she performed an exercise she'd learned years ago to equalize the pressure in her ears. While she worked to open her Eustachian tubes, she considered how her immersion into this world had all the subtly of an alarm gong. Her trail of bubbles, her noisy breathing, the ripples from her fins, the glow of her headlight, the hum of the electrified prod—all sent a signal to the lake's occupants that an unfamiliar creature had entered their territory.

And yet she hadn't seen a single fish. It was as if the underwater domain were holding its collective breath.

Ella Mae didn't trust the stillness.

Glancing at her dive computer, she realized that she was only twenty feet from the bottom. She pivoted her right arm so the light from her prod covered a greater area, but all she saw was darkness. Somehow, she felt there was no need to brace for an attack from the guardian until she actually tried to take the Flower of Life. However, she never considered the possibility that she wouldn't be able to locate the flower in the first place. In Suzy's Gilgamesh storybook, the magical plant had radiated so much light that the hero had had no difficulty swimming directly to it. Ella Mae feared that she wasn't going to be that lucky.

I've come to claim the Flower of Life, she shouted in her

mind. This was how she communicated with her mother, and Ella Mae hoped it worked on all things in the magical realm. *I seek the flower for my people. To preserve and protect their magic. I offer all I have—all that I am—if you would reveal yourself to me!*

She looked at her depth reading. Five feet from the bottom. There was nothing here. Nothing but the lumpy shadows of rocks.

Fighting despair, Ella Mae's left hand went to the outline of the clover pendant tucked beneath the dry suit. And suddenly, she knew what to do.

Planting her finned feet on a patch of gooey silt, Ella Mae thrust out both arms. *I am the Clover Queen! I have come for the Flower of Life. I am worthy to claim you!*

A flash of blinding white light erupted in the darkness. It was so powerful that Ella Mae was forced to close her eyes against it. When she dared open them again, she saw a dome several feet away. As Ella Mae swam toward it, she could felt a hum of energy moving through the water. It was a song with no words and no melody, but a song nonetheless. And somehow, it was familiar. Deep in her bones, she knew that she had passed the test. An ancient magic had examined her heart and was inviting her to take what she'd come for.

The dome looked as if it were made of glass. It was covered with an oily film of rainbows and yet was still completely transparent. Beneath the dome, looking small, fragile, and heartbreakingly beautiful was the Flower of Life.

The white flower was a single stalk growing from a tangle of roots in a pristine circle of sand. If a star fell to earth and merged with a rare orchid, the result would be this flower. It seemed hardy and healthy and nearly crackled with life. But it was also delicate and ephemeral, like a snowflake on one's palm.

Without hesitating, Ella Mae thrust her arm through the dome. It separated as if it were made of gelatin. The humming in the water increased and Ella Mae sensed the flower was calling to her. Recognizing her. Granting her permission.

She cupped her left hand under its root ball and paused. What would happen once she took the flower from this place? Would it begin to die and shrivel the moment it was separated from its web of enchanted roots? And would the guardian immediately emerge from the dark with its mouth open wide, its daggerlike teeth ready to strike?

Ella Mae took a shallow breath and tugged. The flower floated into her hand, its light undiminished. She glanced at it for a brief moment of joyous wonder before tucking it into the thigh pocket of her dry suit.

The moment the flower was hidden, the dome vanished and the humming in the water became a shrill, high-pitched keening. It was a frightening noise that set Ella Mae's teeth on edge. She tensed for attack.

The guardian's been summoned, she thought, a wave of terror rushing through her.

Gripping the electric prod, she began the most challenging part of her quest. Keeping one eye on the water surrounding her and the other on her dive computer, she slowly ascended ten feet. Then fifteen. Then twenty. Physically, she felt surprisingly normal. Her faculties were sharp and she experienced no discomfort. Jenny's gift was working to its full effect, but Ella Mae knew that she needed to take her first decompression stop.

She followed protocol and treaded water while casting about for signs of the guardian. Continuing her ascent, she paused for her second stop. It was then that she could feel a shift in the water temperature. A wave of ice passed right through her, and the throbbing that had surrounded the magic dome abruptly ceased.

It's coming! The guardian's coming!

Ella Mae expected the beast to attack from below, but it came straight at her. A black shadow longer than the dingy appeared just out of range of her headlight beam. It was moving fast, circling her. Assessing her. Ella Mae raised the prod, her heart hammering in her chest. She knew she'd have only one shot. One chance to save herself and her mother. She must stay calm. If she didn't, if she somehow managed to miss, all would be lost.

Suddenly, the monster veered to the left just beyond Ella Mae's halo of light.

God help me, Ella Mae prayed as she took in the rows of enormous jagged teeth crowded into its impossibly long snout. The beast was watching her through an icy blue eye. The black pupil narrowed into a malicious slit, and the look it gave her was oddly familiar, almost human in its contempt.

My heart is pure enough to take the Flower of Life, but I still have to face this monster! Magic can be so cruel. The absurd thought passed through Ella Mae's mind while she slowly swiveled, her eyes tracking the creature as it swam into the gloom.

She wasn't foolish enough to believe it was gone for good, but she had to take advantage of its disappearance, so she began to swim to her next decompression stop. As she rose, she searched for the creature in front of her, then down, and then she turned to glance behind her. Because she never lifted her gaze, she failed to see the dark shadow looming overhead. Without a sound, the monster's powerful tail shot through the water, seared the light cast by her prod, and swatted the weapon right out of her hand.

The force of the blow sent a wave of pain up Ella Mae's arm. She watched in horror as the prod sank. Within seconds, it was out of reach and Ella Mae knew she had no chance of catching it.

Heaven help me, she repeated, drawing out a small knife with her left hand. She kicked her legs, instinctively seeking escape now that she'd lost her weapon.

As she arrived at her last decompression stop, the beast swam in a wide, lazy circle around her. For half a heartbeat, Ella Mae considered skipping the stop and swimming desperately for the surface, but there was a chance she'd pass out. She still had her knife, and though she doubted she could use it to inflict any real damage, she didn't plan on surrendering without a fight.

As if reading her mind, the creature pivoted its head to stare at her once more. Again, Ella Mae got the sense that it was judging her—that it found her contemptible—and once again, its calculating gaze seemed inexplicably familiar.

Another icy current of water swept over Ella Mae. The monster opened its great and terrifying mouth and swung around, swimming directly for her. It was moving fast. So fast that its tails and flippers became a blur.

Ignoring the pain in her right arm, Ella Mae took the knife in both hands and held it out in front of her. Just as the beast moved to strike, she jerked to the side and plunged the knife down through the scaly hide of its shoulder.

It jerked away, blood billowing in its wake, and Ella Mae knew that she'd given it only a flesh wound.

There was only one thing left to do now. She had to swim. Faster than she ever had before. She had to swim for her life.

She lifted her arms into a V and pumped her feet hard, trying to guess where the next attack would come from. If possible, she'd shove her gas tank into the monster's maw and hope it would get lodged there, giving her enough time to reach the surface and the safety of the boat.

I dare you to follow me all the way up, she thought wildly. *Reba will riddle you with bullet holes and then turn you into a pair of boots.*

Ella Mae's mind was a tangle of images. Hugh, as she'd left him sleeping on the sofa with Chewy; Suzy, Jenny, Aiden, and her aunts standing in Partridge Hill's kitchen; Reba, sitting in the boat, a pair of guns on her lap; the rose petals that had fallen the last time Ella Mae had leaned against the ash tree that was her mother. It wasn't Ella Mae's life flashing before her eyes but a catalogue of those she loved. Thoughts of them gave her courage and strength, pulling her up and up out of the water. Away from danger.

But suddenly, the monster was back. It raced at her like a missile and her heart stopped beating. Despite being numb with terror, she yanked off her tank. Still swimming, she held it against her chest like a mother embracing a child. She knew she'd reached the moment of truth. She would die now or buy herself a few more precious seconds.

Screaming in fear and rage, Ella Mae thrust the tank forward and the creature butted it aside with its sharp nose. Clinging to the tank, Ella Mae raised her legs to kick at the monster's hostile eye, at the rows of serrated teeth.

And then in an instant, the beast was abruptly sucked backward and entrapped inside a giant bubble made of pale light. It thrashed frantically, biting at the bubble walls, striking them again and again with its powerful tail, but failed to escape.

Ella Mae didn't wait around to see what would happen next. Letting go of the tank, she started to swim. She kicked once before she was enclosed within her own bubble of light.

There was no water inside the bubble. It was filled with pure oxygen. After drawing in a deep breath, Ella Mae glanced behind her in search of the bubble's source.

What she saw made her gasp.

Suspended in the water, his arms held out to the side and a grim look on his beautiful face, was Hugh.

Ella Mae blinked behind her scuba mask. Once. Twice. But it was Hugh, his eyes glowing a bright and angry blue. Ella Mae had never seen such fierceness in his eyes before. His naked skin also had a bluish cast, but the shade was cold, reminiscent of deep ocean trenches and subterranean caves. His hair floated in loose, lazy waves and a school of tiny silver fish darted through the strands.

Hugh didn't move. He simply floated, staring at her.

Ella Mae pulled off her mask and reached out to touch the bubble wall. Before she had the chance, Hugh lifted his hand, palm facing skyward, and Ella Mae's bubble began to rise. She looked back and saw that the bubble cage containing her attacker was descending.

"Thank you," she mouthed to Hugh, though she knew that he was not the Hugh she knew. Not at this moment. He was something else entirely. Something magnificent and frightening. Beautiful and unpredictable. A water elemental.

Ella Mae had nearly reached the surface. She could make out the outline of the boat above her head. Hugh had risen with her, those electric eyes never blinking, his body relaxed as the water did his silent bidding. His lips were stretched into a thin, tight line of disapproval.

The bubble halted several feet below the surface and Hugh raised an arm.

He pointed at her pocket, the one holding the Flower of Life. His eyes bored into her and he made a "give me" gesture with his hand.

"No." Ella Mae covered her pocket with her palm. "I have to save my mother."

Hugh didn't react. He simply repeated the gesture.

"No," she said again, louder this time.

A shadow rippled across Hugh's face and the silver fish scattered in alarm. Seeing them dart away, Ella Mae knew she should be frightened. This version of Hugh did not seem to recognize her. He simply wanted the flower and she would not give it to him.

She pushed at the bubble, but it wasn't like the viscous dome that had covered the flower. This film didn't give. It was solid as steel. She pounded on it while Hugh studied her with a displeased expression.

I can't have come this far only to fail now, she thought, wishing Reba could see what was happening. But they were directly under the boat and its hull blocked the bubble from view.

I need to signal her. But how? And then it came to her.

Her mother's advice. The last words her mother had spoken, the ones that had sounded like lunacy at the time, lit up in Ella Mae's brain like a neon sign. Her mother had told her to call the butterflies. In the dead of winter, she'd told her to call the symbols of summer. The custodians of flowers.

Ella Mae opened her pocket and withdrew the Flower of Life. It shone like a star in her gloved hands. On the other side of the bubble wall, Hugh nodded in satisfaction. He thought she planned to do as he'd commanded. Ignoring him, Ella Mae stared at the flower petals and imagined orange monarchs, purple swallowtails, red lacewings, blue morphos, painted ladies—a rainbow of butterflies.

Wake up! Ella Mae shouted in her mind. *I summon you! Wake and come to me!*

The flower's radiance intensified. Rays of white light shot outward, tearing holes in the bubble wall. Water began to stream in through the openings, but Ella Mae didn't move. She kept her eyes locked on the petals and repeated her command.

Within seconds, the water reached her waist and was so cold that she felt as if her blood was freezing in her veins. The bubble was turning into ice. Ella Mae looked away from the flower and saw that Hugh was glaring at her, his fingers curling inward as he used his powers to make the water colder. He would trap her in ice to get the flower from her. He was willing to kill her for it.

You can't have it, Ella Mae thought and smiled triumphantly. She could feel the butterflies approaching. In her mind's eye, she could see them swooping low over the lake, aiming for the small boat off the southern shore of the island.

Ella Mae channeled every ounce of will she could muster into the flower, bidding it to shatter the bubble of ice. Suddenly, Ella Mae heard a muted tinkling, as if someone had dropped a crystal glass on a hard floor a million miles away, and saw that she was free. Holding the flower overhead, she swam to the side of the boat and surfaced.

The second her hand burst from the water, the butterflies swarmed. They grabbed hold of her shining burden and lifted it high into the air.

Ella Mae gasped for breath, feeling dizzy, sick, and numbingly cold.

Take it to the grove, she whispered and could feel Reba's fingers close around the material of her dry suit. She heard Reba's voice, hoarse with urgency, and tried to make out the words. And then she was lying down inside the boat and a blanket of butterflies had settled over her. Their touch felt like June sunshine. Her muscles drank in their heat and she felt herself drifting, surrendering to a magic as old as time, a magic that whispered to her, painting pictures of ancient forests with colossal trees, snow-covered mountains tall enough to pierce the sky, and verdant grasslands stretching as wide as a sea. And then she heard a woman singing. The language was unfamiliar, but the melody was so lovely that Ella Mae ached to hear it for the rest of her days.

And then another woman, Reba perhaps, was pleading to her. Telling her to stay. Begging her to come home.

Home. The word exploded in Ella Mae's heart like a fireworks display. Then, a string of names danced into her mind, followed by a collage of beloved faces. The faces burned in her heart like a hearth fire.

She wanted to be with them. She wanted to go home.

And so she opened her eyes.

Chapter 16

Ella Mae's body felt like rubber. She was no longer cold or wet, but she was almost too exhausted to speak.

"Drink this," Reba said, holding a cup to her lips.

"I can hold it," Ella Mae protested. She tried to lift her arm, but it felt like a boulder was weighing it down.

Reba clicked her tongue. "Come on now. One sip."

Ella Mae took a swallow of hot tea spiked with whiskey and then let her head fall back against the sofa cushion again. Verena tucked a wool blanket around her feet while Sissy plumped the pillows. Dee stood quietly in front of the fireplace, her hands stuffed into the pockets of her overalls.

"You gave us quite a scare," she said and gestured at the fire. "Are you warm enough?"

Sissy started pacing behind the sofa. "Is there anything we can get you?"

Reba shushed both sisters. "Let me get this down her throat first." She held up the cup of tea again.

This time, Ella Mae was able to hold the ceramic mug herself, though it felt anvil heavy. She drank the tea quickly, feeling its heat in her throat and belly, and said, "No time for questions. I need to get to the grove. The butterflies are waiting for me."

Verena shook her head. "You're in no condition to—"

"I have to go. Right now." Ella Mae turned to Aiden, who was standing at a discreet distance in between Suzy and Jenny. "I know you've done so much for me already. But can I beg another favor?"

Suzy understood immediately. She put a hand on Aiden's arm. "You need to carry her up the path. She's too weak to walk."

Aiden dipped his chin. "I'd be honored."

"I must get the flower in the ground," Ella Mae said. "I don't know how long it'll last, and the butterflies are agitated. I can feel them calling to me."

Verena rose to her feet. "Then we'll all go. We know you had to retrieve the flower by yourself, but you'll finish this thing with an entourage!"

Ella Mae touched Reba's sleeve. "Bring your Taser. Someone might try to stop us on our way to the grove."

Reba grew tense. "Forget the Taser. I'll pump them so full of bullets that they'll set off the metal detectors in the Atlanta airport."

"No," Ella Mae said, her voice leaden with sorrow and weariness. "That someone is Hugh. He's . . ." She paused and Reba squeezed her hand gently. "He's an elemental." She glanced at the concerned faces surrounding her. "He was down there, under the water with me, and he was really angry that I took the flower. You should have seen him. The way he looked at me." A tear slipped down her cheek. "He didn't know me. Nor I, him."

Sissy ceased pacing and gaped at Ella Mae. "Oh, my dear."

"Maybe he was compelled to protect the flower," Dee whispered. "I know it's not much comfort right now, but I don't think he would have threatened you without a reason."

Jenny raised her fists and boxed the air. "If he tries to hurt you, I will demonstrate all of my mixed martial arts skills on him."

Ella Mae gave her a weak smile. "I'd rather you helped me into my coat."

Later, a pair of cars drove through a dark and deserted downtown, heading north for the parkland. Ella Mae was nestled between Dee and Sissy in the back seat of Reba's Buick, and all three of them were being pitched about like buoys in a stormy ocean as Reba drove even more erratically than usual.

"Are you trying to kill us before we get there?" Verena demanded from the front seat. "You're going twenty miles over the speed limit!"

"Verena's right," Sissy said, gripping the door handle for dear life. "How can you even *see* where you're going? The roads aren't lit and they're as curvy as a snake's back."

Dee reached over Ella Mae to pat her sister's hand. "Reba has the night vision of an owl. We'll be fine."

They pulled into the parking lot and Reba helped Ella Mae out of the car. Ella Mae tried to walk to the trail's entrance on her own, but stumbled after only a few steps. She only had to look at Aiden and he was at her side. Without a word, he picked her up and started to climb the narrow trail.

Reba took the lead, flashlight in one hand, Taser in the other, while Jenny covered the rear. She had a rifle slung over her right shoulder and promised not to fire on Hugh unless absolutely necessary.

They walked without speaking, and in the silence, Ella Mae found herself thinking of Eira. She'd probably been carried just as Ella Mae was being carried. On another cold, moonless night, a man had held her close. A man had made his way along the trail until its end. There, at the foot of the boulder wall, the killer had set his burden down. And then he'd turned and disappeared into the darkness, leaving Eira to her lonely death.

I have not forgotten you, Ella Mae promised, as if communing with the young woman's ghost. Her thoughts were a jumble. This close to the grove, she had trouble focusing on anything but the agitated buzz of the butterflies.

Finally, Aiden rounded the last bend. And when he did, he gasped.

Butterflies covered every inch of the boulder wall. A rainbow of fluttering wings formed a veil between this and the magical world, and Ella Mae knew that she'd be the only one permitted to pass through. Despite Verena's wish to be involved, this was still Ella Mae's quest and it wasn't over yet.

"Thank you, Aiden," she said as he gently let her feet drop to the frozen ground.

Jenny's face was lit with wonder. "Where did they all come from?"

"And how can they survive in this cold?" Suzy asked.

"They live in the grove," Ella Mae said. "They only came out because I needed them. They'll return with me and sleep until spring."

Sissy leaned close to Verena and whispered, "Can this flower truly bring Adelaide back to us? Do I *dare* hope?"

Verena put an arm around her younger sister. "If our niece says it can, then I believe it with every fiber of my being." She regarded Ella Mae with a new deference. "Go on, my girl! Take that flower and rescue my sister."

Ella Mae cast a lingering glance at Reba and her aunts and then faced forward again. She raised her hands and the butterflies began to part. As she placed her palms on the wall she heard Jenny say, "Ella Mae told me how you sang to Eira—the day you found her. Would you sing it again while we wait?"

"Of course, dear," Sissy said.

Ella Mae heard a few hauntingly beautiful notes of "In the Bleak Midwinter" before stepping into another world.

The butterflies crossed to the other side with her. They set the Flower of Life on a soft patch of grass and hovered protectively above it. To Ella Mae's incredible relief, the flower looked just as radiant as it had on the bottom of the lake. It sat on the emerald grass, pulsing like a heart waiting to be transplanted. A heart filled with magic.

Silently thanking the butterflies, Ella Mae picked up the flower and held it gingerly in her cupped palm. She walked through the orchard, past the meadow and the rows of rose-bushes to the clearing. Her eyes traveled up the shallow rise to the top, where the ash tree presided over the enchanted garden.

As Ella Mae drew alongside the tree, she realized that she didn't know where to plant the flower. With her free hand, she touched the ash tree's bark.

"You're the master gardener. Tell me what to do," Ella Mae murmured to her mother. When there was no reply, she began to dig a hole at the base of the tree using the diving knife she'd slipped into her coat pocket. She scraped away the dirt for several minutes and then placed the flower in the hole. Pushing the soft soil over its roots, she gave the turned earth several firm pats and then sat back on her heels and held her breath.

Nothing happened.

Ella Mae watched and waited. The flower looked the same. So did the ash tree. Everything was the same.

She was doing something wrong.

Ella Mae wondered if the flower needed water but immediately dismissed the notion. It had grown over a hundred feet below the surface of a lake without receiving an ounce of fresh water or sunlight. It must have absorbed its nutrients from the maze of roots growing on the lake floor.

"You were tapped into a source of life," she said, her gaze falling on the knife blade. "If I think of you as a beating heart ready to be transplanted, then you need a host. A new source of life."

Suddenly, she knew what to do.

"Forgive me," she said, hoping her mother heard her plea. She then pinched one of the ash tree's thin roots between her fingers. It curved above the ground like a tiny bridge and disappeared into the grass again directly below the trunk. Ella Mae hesitated. She looked at the veins on the back of her hand and thought about how they carried blood and oxygen to the rest of her body. The flower needed to be grafted to the tree's veins. After listening to her own heart for a moment, she sliced into the tree root with her knife.

A scream of pain bloomed inside her mind, but Ella Mae steeled herself against it and sawed deeper into the root. Another cry of agony echoed inside her head, shrill and terrible, and Ella Mae's mouth twisted in anguish.

"Hold on," she whispered to her mother. Gently pulling the flower out of the dirt, she cut the tip of a root at an angle and pressed it into the wet cavity she'd created in the ash tree root.

The flower instantly fused with the tree. For a brief second, all was still. And then the entire grove starting shaking. Ella Mae reached out to grab hold of the tree trunk, but a violent tremor knocked her backward. She lay sprawled on the grass as the canopy of branches over her head twitched and trembled. Leaves rained down on her and a frenzied wind hurled twigs and petals and bits of bark into the air.

Ella Mae tried to keep her eyes on the flower, but they were watering against the sting of the wind. Squinting, she saw the flower's glow spread outward, like a star going supernova. Its pure white light was so blinding that Ella Mae had to hide her face in her hands.

"Mom!" she cried. Had she made a grievous error in grafting the flower to the tree? Had she destroyed everything? *"Mom!"*

Abruptly, the wind stopped and the ground ceased

roiling. Ella Mae's body trilled with energy. Every ounce of fatigue vanished from her cells. She felt powerful enough to lift the ash tree and balance it on her shoulders as if it were a broomstick. She felt like Atlas. Like she could carry the whole world on her back.

Rising to her feet, she opened her eyes and saw wavelets of silver sweeping across the meadow. Like ripples moving over a stagnant pond, the flower's magic was permeating every blade of grass, every plant stalk, every stone and tree. It flowed through Ella Mae's bloodstream and she felt light enough to fly.

The entire grove was quickly consumed by white starlight and glittering silver. And then, just as abruptly as it had flared, the light winked out. The moment it disappeared, the ash tree started to twist and buck. With an inhuman groan, a large rent appeared in its trunk and Adelaide LeFaye was ejected from within. She pitched forward, limp and lifeless, and fell into Ella Mae's open arms.

Her mother was coated with a sticky, saplike film from her crown to her feet. Her eyes were closed and she didn't seem to be breathing, but her flesh was warm to the touch.

Ella Mae wiped the sap away from her mother's mouth. "Breathe," she whispered. "Come on, Mom. Breathe. You're not a tree anymore. You're Adelaide LeFaye. Adelaide LeFaye. Adelaide. You're my mom, and you need to breathe."

Her mother's lips parted and she drew in a wet, ragged breath.

"Yes, yes! That's it. Keep going." Ella Mae smoothed her mother's hair while tears blurred her vision.

Her mother blinked and breathed, blinked and breathed, as if waking from a very long slumber. Ella Mae sat cradling her mother's head and felt her heart swell in her chest. A lump formed in her throat and she started to cry. She let go of all the fear she'd held at bay since she'd put on the dry suit hours before. Hot tears streamed down her cheeks and dripped into her mother's silver hair.

Ella Mae sobbed in relief first. And then, after her mother whispered her name aloud, from joy. Her mother could speak again. In the days to come, the two of them could sit and talk as other mothers and daughters did. And Ella Mae had so much to tell her mother. So many questions to ask. And now there would time for that.

Ella Mae helped her mother sit up. They stared at each other, each of them drinking in the familiar contours of the other's face, cherishing each angle and plain, every line and freckle.

"You saved me," her mother said, her voice as faint as a distant breeze. She held Ella Mae's cheek in her palm and smiled.

"I didn't want to be without you." Ella Mae swiped away the tears pooling in her eyes and took her mother's hand. "No one will ever again have to make the sacrifice you made. That part of our history is over."

Her mother nodded and a lock of hair fell over her shoulder. She took it between her fingers and frowned.

"You've gone silver all over," Ella Mae said. "Guess we'll have to make you an appointment at the hair salon."

Shaking her head, her mother said, "No. This will remind me of what you and I have survived. Of what's most important."

Ella Mae stroked her mother's silver tresses and thought of all she'd been through since her mother had sacrificed herself for the good of her kind. "I don't need reminders. I'd like nothing more than to forget what we've endured. I'd give anything to lead a normal life for a little while. A life without magic or monsters. Without murderers or superhuman boyfriends."

Her mother said nothing, and though Ella Mae knew she would never lead a normal life, she wanted to at least enjoy this moment to its fullest. Her mother was weak as a sparrow hatchling, but she was alive. She was a woman of flesh and blood. She could laugh and sing and move through the rooms at Partridge Hill. She could tend her gardens and take up her matchmaking rituals once more.

Overwhelmed with happiness, Ella Mae gave her mother a fierce hug. She then pulled away and draped her coat over her mother's naked body. "There are some people waiting outside who are very eager to see you. Rest here and I'll get them."

Her mother grabbed her by the hand to stay her. "Before you do, I want to tell you how proud I am to be your mother." She smiled. "You were always with me, you know. Even when I couldn't reach out to you. You were in here." She touched her heart with her free hand and her words carried all the love and tenderness of a caress. "My darling daughter. My light in the darkness."

The lump in Ella Mae's throat kept her from answering. She returned her mother's smile and then ran to invite the others to share in her amazing news. Crossing to the other side of the boulder wall, she shouted, "She's here! She's back!"

And then she followed the others to where her mother leaned against her former prison. Ella Mae cherished every cry of jubilation, every euphoric hug and kiss, every moment of tearful reunion between the four sisters. Reba pushed past Verena, Dee, and Sissy and threw her arms around her lifelong friend. Finally, Suzy, Jenny, and Aiden moved forward to pay their respects to the former Lady of the Ash.

"I feel like we should be drinking champagne!" Verena bellowed and danced a merry jig on the grass. Dee and Sissy laced their arms through hers and they spun around, heads thrown back, their laughter drifting into the silver sky.

Ella Mae joined the beautiful women, feeling as if her entire body were filled with tiny bubbles of light. If her aunts weren't holding her, she was sure she'd float away. And she didn't want to go anywhere. There was no place she'd rather be.

Separating from the ring of dancers, she dropped on the ground at the foot of the ash tree. She took her mother's hand in her own and stared at her, drinking her in. The smile of tenderness and pride in her mother's hazel eyes enveloped Ella Mae and she knew that she'd discovered the true meaning of magic.

Eventually, the deliriously happy but bone-weary group returned to Partridge Hill.

"It's *so* hard to say good night to you, Adelaide," Sissy said as they all stood in the kitchen. "But you look worn out."

"Won't it be lovely to sleep in your own bed?" Verena said. "We'll be back in the morning, but you should rest as long as you can. This experience must have taken its toll on you."

"I do feel strange," Ella Mae's mother admitted. "To be walking and talking, to move my arms and feel air on my skin." She stopped. "It's going to take time to become myself again. I heard and saw and sensed things when I was part of the tree . . ."

Reba made a shooing gesture. "That's it, folks. The lady needs some shut-eye." She looked at Ella Mae. "I'm stayin' here. I'll watch over the place while you both sleep."

Ella Mae nodded gratefully and accompanied her mother to her room.

"I'm glad you opened up our home to Jenny and Aiden," her mother said and sat down on the edge of her bed. "The house feels more alive with them here. Tell them that I'd like them to stay."

"I'm glad. I've grown very fond of them." Ella Mae opened a dresser drawer and took out a flannel nightgown. "Why don't you take a long, hot shower? I'll check on Chewy and then come back and brush out your hair."

Her mother smiled. "That sounds like heaven."

Ella Mae closed the door and went downstairs. The kitchen was deserted, and when she glanced at the clock over the stove, she was surprised to find that it was after midnight.

Chewy would be sound asleep, but Ella Mae felt the need to have him near. She was just putting on one of her mother's coats when Reba appeared at the back door, shotgun in hand.

"He could be waitin' for you," she said softly.

Ella Mae had been so wrapped up in her mother's return that she'd managed to put Hugh out of her mind. "I hope not," she said. "But if he is, let me try talking to him. And that gun stays here. The Taser's enough."

Reba adopted a guileless expression. "How'd you know that I had that on me too?"

"I wouldn't be surprised if you pulled a stick of dynamite out of your bra." Ella Mae grinned and opened the door. "After you."

Ella Mae's house was exactly as she'd left it. The only difference was that her sofa was missing its occupant. The fire had gone out and yet the dark space felt restful. The entire atmosphere was one of peaceful slumber and didn't hold a hint of malice. Relaxing a little, Ella Mae motioned for Reba to follow her upstairs.

Turning on the hall light, Ella Mae whispered her dog's name. She didn't want to startle Chewy or Dante, so she repeated her whisper and then tiptoed into her bedroom.

She took two steps and then froze. Hugh was sound asleep, a wave of dark hair falling across his forehead, his arm thrown out to the side as if searching for Ella Mae.

"That sure as hell ain't Goldilocks," Reba muttered under her breath.

"Stay here," Ella Mae told her and crept around to her side of the bed.

She stood there for a long moment. Dante and Chewy were both curled up near the footboard, but upon seeing her, Dante raised his massive head and stretched out, taking over the space she'd normally claim. Chewy grunted once in his sleep but didn't wake.

Relieved to find him safe and snug, Ella Mae went into the bathroom. She expected to see a crumpled towel on the

floor or some other sign that Hugh had been in the lake's
freezing water earlier that night, but nothing was amiss.
Wondering if his pillowcase would be damp, she eased herself onto the bed and reached over Dante. Her fingertips met
with warm, dry sheets.

"Hey, you," Hugh murmured, startling her. She withdrew
her hand as though it had been burned.

Hugh's voice was thick with sleep, and yet the sound of
it put Ella Mae on full alert. She sat on the very edge of the
bed, ready to move at a moment's notice. "Sorry, I didn't
mean to wake you."

Keeping his eyes closed, he slung an arm over his dog's
shoulders. "I don't remember coming upstairs. Did Dante
drag me?"

Ella Mae was at a loss for words. Was Hugh telling the
truth? Didn't he realize that he'd tried to encase her in a
bubble of ice? Or was it possible that the elemental part of
him was a separate entity? Either that, or he'd learned to
mask it so effectively that he could fool anyone. Even the
woman he supposedly loved.

"A full belly and a roaring fire did you in," she whispered.

"Ah, another thrilling date with Hugh Dylan." Opening
his eyes, he propped himself up on one elbow and pushed
Dante out of the way. "Did my horse of a dog force you out
of bed?"

"No," she said quickly and smiled to conceal her nervous-
ness. "Actually, my mom's back. I know it's late, but I'm so
excited to see her that I'm going over to the main house to
catch up with her." She covered Hugh's hand with hers. It
was warm and familiar and she desperately wanted to
believe that he wasn't the same man who'd glowered at her
with those frightening, electric eyes. "Do you mind?"

He released a drowsy sigh. "Of course not. The boys and
I can spread across the whole bed now." He reached out to
squeeze her hand. "I'm glad your mom's home. I know you

missed her. And I'll try to remember to put some clothes on when I go out to get the morning paper."

Ella Mae couldn't help but laugh. "That sounds like a good idea."

After planting a soft kiss on her palm, Hugh burrowed deeper under the covers. "Give your mom my best," he said and closed his eyes.

Chewy was sleeping so peacefully that Ella Mae didn't want to disturb him, so she smoothed the fur on the top of his head, grabbed a pair of pajamas and her toothbrush, and left the bedroom. Putting her finger to her lips to forestall any noise from Reba, she tiptoed down the stairs.

"Did you hear everything?" she asked once they were outside.

Reba nodded. "I don't know what to make of it, but I don't trust him. Neither should you."

"I'll deal with him tomorrow. Tonight, I just want to enjoy my mom."

"Lord knows you deserve a little happiness. It's all gonna be better now. You'll see."

The two women returned to Partridge Hill arm in arm, but Reba didn't accompany Ella Mae inside. Holding up Hugh's keys, she said she'd return the scuba gear and put his keys where Ella Mae had found them.

"Don't know what we can do about the missin' gas tank. I'll have to order one online and sneak it into the fire station later on." Reba looked quite pleased by the idea. "Let's just hope the water rescue team doesn't suit up for a while."

Ella Mae pictured the tank resting on the lake floor and shivered. She gave Reba a quick hug and hurried into the house. Upstairs, she knocked softly on her mother's bedroom door. There was no answer, so she entered as quietly as she could.

Her mother was curled up on top of the covers, her hands folded under her chin, her shoulders gently rising and falling. She'd left the curtains open and starlight shone down on her face and hair. Though she was in incredible physical condition, and had amazingly unlined skin for a woman in her sixties, her mother seemed old and fragile. There was something in the troubled furrow between her brows and in the pinch at the corners of her mouth that made Ella Mae's heart wrench.

Magic always exacts a price, she thought. She then picked up her mother's hairbrush and slowly drew it through the long silver locks. Her mother sighed and the tension in her face eased a little.

"You've done enough," Ella Mae whispered. "It's time for you to rest. I'll take care of everything from now on."

She sat there for a long time, brushing her mother's hair with careful, tender strokes until it looked like spilled moonlight. Eventually, Ella Mae laid a quilt over her mother and curled up beside her. She was afraid her sleep would be punctuated by frightening memories of the lake monster, but her dreams were filled with beauty. Lying beside her mother, she dreamt of butterflies and a garden filled with flowers and summer sunshine. It was as if Ella Mae's subconscious finally surrendered to the belief that the worst of her nightmares had finally come to an end.

Chapter 17

She woke the next morning to find the bed empty.

During the night, her mother had covered her with a blanket, and now Ella Mae kicked it off and luxuriated in a full-body stretch. She felt amazingly alert and energized. The magic that had coursed through her after she'd grafted the Flower of Life to the ash tree was still humming in her cells. She knew she'd need it too, since the day promised to be a challenging one.

After washing her face and brushing the tangles from her hair, Ella Mae descended the stairs. The sound of clanking dishes and the aroma of coffee and bacon drew her into the kitchen.

"I made a pie," Reba said upon seeing her. "Your mama looked like she needed a big dose of protein, so I fixed her a breakfast pie with eggs, cheese, and sausage. Then I added this bacon lattice on top. What do you think?"

Ella Mae looked at the crisscrossed strips of oven-baked bacon and smiled. "Very creative. Can I steal that idea for the pie shop?"

"Let's see how it tastes first." Reba waved in the direction of the sunroom. "Your mama and your coffee are in there. Chewy too. I went over to fetch him after I got up. Hugh was already gone. He made the bed, neat as a pin, but left no signs of havin' been in the lake last night. Nothin' I could find anyway."

"I'll stop by Canine to Five later and try to get a read on him." Ella Mae sighed. "But I can't make Hugh a priority today. I gave the Gaynors a deadline. If Rand Dockery doesn't turn himself in, Verena will have to call a meeting of the Elders. Then they'll have to figure out what to do with him."

Reba cut into the breakfast pie. "How will they punish him if he doesn't show up at the police station? The grove is self-sufficient now. There's no Lady. That means there's no one to penalize folks who break the rules."

Ella Mae had never stopped to consider the negative consequences of injecting the grove with an unwavering source of power. She'd been so caught up with saving her mother that she hadn't imagined she could be making a mistake.

"I'm not findin' fault with you, hon." Reba slid a large wedge of pie onto a plate next to a handful of ruby red strawberries. "The Elders can run things like a democracy now. It's about time we modernized. Stirred things up a bit." She plated another slice of pie. "Sure, we survived doin' things the old way, but don't you think it'd be great if we did more than survive?"

"Definitely. I'd like to see our kind flourish. And a little unity would help. Here I thought I was making progress with the Gaynors, but now I know we'll never trust each other. They've been harboring a killer, Reba."

Reba handed her the two plates. "You'd better fuel up, because someone has to go to Rolling View and make sure that their murdering scumbag is behind bars by the end of the day. And, my girl, that someone is you." She smiled.

"I'm comin' too, of course. I don't want to miss out on a chance to manhandle a Gaynor."

Laughing, Ella Mae carried breakfast into the sunroom.

Seeing her mother at the table with the newspaper spread out before her made Ella Mae's smile stretch even wider. "A tiny part of me was afraid you wouldn't be here when I woke."

"And miss being treated like a queen?" Her mother gestured at the silver coffeepot and the plates in Ella Mae's hands and grinned. Her levity vanished almost immediately, however. She filled Ella Mae's cup, wearing a grave expression. "Reba told me everything. About Eira and Barric. And Hugh." She pushed a manila folder across the table. "Reba wanted you to see this. She said it came from her sleepy friend, Toby. I have no clue what she means. This report is equally confusing. I guess I'm having a hard time processing all that's happened."

"You and me both," Ella Mae said, reaching for the pitcher of cream. She doctored her coffee and opened the folder. After several minutes, she slammed the cup down, causing coffee to slosh onto the table. "Eira wasn't . . ." She shook her head in disbelief. "This is crazy." She read more of the ME's notes. "Maybe Eira *was* crazy. I don't know whether to pity her or be disgusted by her. I don't know what to feel."

Her mother touched her hand. "You sought justice for her. No matter what, she deserved that."

Ella Mae searched her mother's face. "I came to the grove right after she was killed. Do you remember that? Or any of my visits?"

"My memories are jumbled," her mother said. "I processed information differently when I was one with the tree." She pushed her fork into the breakfast pie and then set it down again. "I felt more than heard. I sensed your distress, but I can't recall details. In order for me to help you now, you'd better tell me everything from the beginning."

Ella Mae did. She talked, drank coffee, and polished off Reba's delicious pie. When she was done, she noticed that her mother had eaten only her strawberries. "Are you feeling all right?" she asked her.

"I think I'm between two worlds," her mother said. "I hope to feel more human as the days pass, but I barely slept and I have no appetite. Coffee tastes awful, the idea of eating meat is repulsive, clothes feel strange, and I long to be outside." She smiled faintly. "I'm tempted to give Chewy my pie to avoid insulting Reba."

Ella Mae shook her head. "His stomach couldn't handle all that bacon and sausage." She glanced out the window. "I have some time before I have to pay my visit to the Gaynors, so if you're up for it, we could take a walk. Chewy could use some exercise. He's slept most of the winter away."

Her mother readily agreed and Ella Mae ran home to shower and dress. She met her mother in the garden.

"Noel did a wonderful job winterizing," she said. "Are he and Kelly around?"

"They've spent the past six weeks in Florida. Noel's mom hasn't been well."

Her mother reached out to touch the brown stem of a rosebush. "The season has been hard for so many people. And yet, I look at this dormant stalk and know that it is merely waiting to change into a glorious bloom."

"I've felt like this bush since I came back to Havenwood," Ella Mae said.

"You're finally emerging from your cocoon. The grove's magic is inside you. I can sense it. It's like music playing far off in the distance."

Ella Mae moved away from the bush and gave Chewy his lead. "That's not necessarily cause for celebration. Magic is messy. Not to mention complicated and confusing."

Her mother shrugged. "Depends on what you do with it."

Ella Mae grew thoughtful. "If I could, I'd use it to bring our kind together. All the descendants of Guinevere and

Morgan le Fay. I'd use it to break the curse that Merlin laid on our line and see that our kind was able to marry and have children without fear. I'd use it to fight the last of the Shadow Children and learn how to befriend elementals."

"I believe you're capable of accomplishing those things," her mother said. "But you need to restore peace to Havenwood first."

Ella Mae nodded. "After our walk, I'll go straight to Rolling View. I want to make sure the Gaynors do the right thing."

"They might not be able to control Rand. Not if he's the fire elemental." She put a hand on Ella Mae's arm. "And if they can't, how will you?"

Ella Mae looked into her mother's lovely, world-weary face and thought about what she'd read in the ME's file. "I'm not going to reason with him. I'm going to break his heart."

Ella Mae didn't think her mother should come to Rolling View, but Adelaide insisted. "I'm not as weak as I appear," she said. "And my presence might convince them to behave. The Elders expect Rand Dockery to show up at the police station by sunset. If he doesn't, the Gaynors will be permanently banned from our grove."

Though the punishment sounded dire to Ella Mae, the Gaynors weren't easily intimidated. "Are you sure you can handle Dockery?" Ella Mae asked Reba for the second time.

"I told you, I've got a blow dart that'll send him right to dreamland. He'll wake in a jail cell with a hole in his neck and a nasty headache. The slightest whiff of smoke and I'll fill him with so many darts that he'll look like a porcupine."

Satisfied, Ella Mae parked her Jeep in the Gaynors' driveway and rang the doorbell.

A woman in a maid's uniform invited them into the entrance hall and then bustled off to inform Opal that she had company.

When Opal strode into the room, her eyes went wide. "Adelaide," she whispered, clearly awestruck. "You're free."

"Yes." Ella Mae's mother pointed at Opal's left shoulder. "And you're injured. What happened?"

For a moment, Opal was too stunned to speak. Her hand seemed to move of its own accord, hovering protectively over her shoulder. "Nothing."

"Your wound's reopened," Ella Mae's mother said softly. "I can smell the blood."

Ella Mae had never seen Opal Gaynor frightened, but she was definitely scared now. She backed away several steps and then seemed to recall that she was in her own house. "Please, go into the library. I'll be with you shortly."

Reba went in first. After peering behind curtains and under the desk, she said, "Don't let your guard down. There's at least one secret panel in here. Anyone could be listenin' or watchin'."

Ella Mae joined her mother on one of the room's leather sofas. "You smelled Opal's injury?"

"Yes. I think the wound is fairly deep. I wonder what caused it."

"A knife." The words were just wisps of air. "I stabbed her. Opal was the creature in the lake. She tried to kill me after I took the flower."

Reba snarled. "Why that—"

"She couldn't help it," Ella Mae said quickly. "I'm sure she was assigned that role. Maybe born to it. I doubt even Opal Gaynor enjoys having to turn into a monster."

"Perhaps you're the monster," Opal said from the doorway. "My family has been protecting the flower for generations. To think it would eventually be taken by a LeFaye? It's reprehensible. If Hugh Dylan hadn't interfered, you would never have succeeded." Her eyes were shining with cold hatred and Ella Mae knew why the lake creature's glare had seemed so familiar. She'd seen it for years.

Ella Mae got to her feet. "But I did succeed. My mother

has returned, and the Elders know that you're sheltering a murderer. Will you give him up?"

Opal's mouth twisted into a smile. "He's all yours. I've been done with him for years."

"No!" came a shocked and angry cry from the other end of the room. They all turned to find Loralyn stepping from a large opening in the wall. "How can you say that? He's my father!"

Ella Mae stood very still, staring at Loralyn. She suddenly understood how mistaken she'd been. She thought about the crystal glass Robert Morgan had balanced on the tray of his wheelchair the night of the Gaynors' party. Both the tumbler and the whiskey had come from Jarvis Gaynor's office. Jarvis, who took frequent business trips that kept him away from his family for weeks at a time. Not that Opal seemed to mind. She'd told Ella Mae that her marriage to Jarvis wasn't a love match. She'd picked him for his bloodline and because he possessed a powerful magical gift. If Jarvis was the fire elemental, then it was in his nature to pursue beautiful women. Had Eira become a victim of his passion or had he fallen under her spell?

Reba shot a confused glance at Ella Mae and whispered, "Rand Dockery isn't her daddy, is he?"

"No. Her father is Jarvis Gaynor. And he's a killer," Ella Mae said, loud enough for everyone to hear. "He had an affair with Eira Morgan." She turned to Opal. "I suspect he had a string of affairs."

Opal shrugged. "He did, but this was his last. That girl made a fool of him. She used her gift to entrance him. He was utterly captivated. And when he heard she was pregnant, he was beside himself with joy. There's nothing like a baby to help a man recover from a midlife crisis."

"No!" Loralyn gasped. "He wouldn't!"

"I'm sorry you had to find out this way." Opal walked toward her daughter, hand outstretched, but Loralyn shrank from her touch.

Thoughts were swirling in Ella Mae's mind like a dust storm, but all the motes abruptly settled and she saw the complete picture with absolute clarity. "Jarvis didn't plan on drugging Eira. Robert was his target. He wanted to get Eira's husband out of the picture. But somehow, Eira ended up drinking the spiked whiskey."

"Did you know?" Loralyn asked her mother. "What Dad was going to do?"

Opal shook her head. "Of course not. Do you think I'd seek that kind of negative publicity? I wasn't even aware that your father had returned from his latest jaunt. I realize now that he remained invisible in order to avoid suspicion."

"When Eira was killed, your only concern was for your family's reputation?" Ella Mae was stunned. "The fact that your husband drugged an innocent young woman and left her to die didn't matter to you at all?"

Opal took a seat behind the writing desk. "No, it didn't. In fact, I saw an opportunity to forge an alliance with Robert. He and I are very much alike. With Eira dead, Robert was freed from her enchantment, and he discovered a kindred spirit in me. Eira could never satisfy his ambition, but I can. Jarvis did Robert and me a favor by getting rid of her." She looked at Loralyn again. "We're better off with Robert, my dear. Your father has always been a loose cannon. I allowed him his paramours, but he took this affair too far. He was willing to ruin everything I've worked so hard to build. He didn't care about shattering your world either. Do you really want to protect him when he never stopped—not for a fleeting second—to consider how his actions would hurt you?"

Loralyn leaned against the bookshelves. She wore a glazed look. "Don't you see?" She spoke slowly. "You have it all wrong, Mom. Once Dad realized Eira had been drugged by mistake, he took her up the mountain. He knew she was meeting Ella Mae there, so he was probably trying to frame the LeFayes. He must have done that because he was trying to make things right. To protect our family from being accused of murder."

"And Barric?" Ella Mae could feel her anger rising. "How did killing him make things right?"

Loralyn fell silent.

"Why didn't you share all of this with the cops?" Reba directed her question at Opal. "Barric might still be alive if you'd spoken up."

Opal scowled. "I didn't know what Jarvis did to Eira. This house has several secret passages and I never saw Jarvis the night of the party. He didn't show himself to me until the winter carnival. I only had to look at him later that night to realize what he'd done." She began tidying a stack of papers. "Our name will be tainted because of his poor decisions. Our business will suffer. But not forever. Once Jarvis is out of my life, Robert and I will marry. We'll make a new empire together."

"How can you say these things?" Loralyn shouted. "*You* might be willing to hand my father to the cops, but I'm not."

"It's over, Loralyn." Opal gestured at the recess in the wall. A dark gap yawned in the middle of the polished oak paneling. "Tell him to join us. I know he's near. I've felt him watching us."

Loralyn didn't move. "I won't let you do this. He can go away. He can leave and never come back. You can't turn him in. He's my father."

"We have no choice," Opal said. "He's guilty, Loralyn. The police will come for him soon enough. Officer Hardy is reviewing Jarvis's travel records. At the end of his search, he's certain to draw the logical conclusion. What do you suppose would happen to him and his men should they make your father angry?"

"I don't care if he burns the whole town!" Loralyn cried. "I can live somewhere else. And since you don't need to guard the lake anymore, you can move too."

Opal's smile was dangerous. "I would never have been put to the test if you'd have kept Rupert's book from Suzy Bacchus. And handing over the missing pages to a LeFaye? I never expected you to be so naïve."

"I was buying time for Dad," Loralyn snapped. "You might be willing to sacrifice him so you can marry that rich cripple, but I'm not. I'm getting Dad out of Havenwood right now."

"Then he'll make a fool of you." Opal's voice was low and cold. "Jarvis only cares about himself. He doesn't care about you. You were his greatest disappointment, Loralyn. He wanted a son more than anything in the world, but he didn't get one. As for me, I only wanted a girl. I wanted *you*. Once you came along, I refused to have any more children. Why take the risk? But your father has never stopped dreaming of a son, and when he fell under the spell of that dainty dancer, he believed his dreams might come true."

Ella Mae threw out her arms in exasperation. "Then why leave her to die? And why outside the grove?"

"Because she lied to me," Jarvis said, stepping through the opening in the wall. He brushed a cobweb from his sweater and calmly studied each of the women in turn. "Eira wasn't pregnant. Hers was a case of hysterical pregnancy."

Opal rolled her eyes. "Honestly, Jarvis! You never learn. The girls you're attracted to are always such train wrecks."

"At least they're not cold, unfeeling, moneygrubbing socialites," he shot back. "Eira was passionate. She danced like a fire was lit in her soul. She wanted a child. I wanted a child. A new beginning for both of us. I burned the Oak Knoll grove so she would lose her powers. If I had a child with a non-magical mother, then we stood a better chance at happiness. Elementals may or may not be susceptible to Myrddin's curse, I don't know. I didn't want to take that chance with Eira. You and I were able to have a child, Opal, but I paid a price, all right. My life was a living hell from the moment you gave birth. You changed. Suddenly all you cared about was that baby." He glared at Opal. "And *you* had to invite the bluebloods from their grove to come here. At first, I was furious. Then, I decided to use the party to get rid of Eira's husband. I promised to free her and she made promises to me in return."

Ella Mae's mother spoke for the first time. "Eira knew you meant kill her husband?"

Jarvis nodded, his mouth curving into an amused grin. "I'm relieved to see you back with us, Adelaide. I won't have to hurt you now." He cocked his head to the side. "Your silver hair is quite fetching, by the way."

"You mean to say that you're still plannin' on torchin' the grove?" Reba asked. She looked completely relaxed, but Ella Mae knew Reba was prepared to strike at the first sign of danger.

A flicker of malice surfaced in Jarvis's eyes. "I'm done with Havenwood. With this marriage, this town, and this life." He turned to Opal. "Why should you get your happily ever after? Why should any of you?"

"Dad," Loralyn began and then faltered. She was fighting back tears, her face a mask of sorrow. Despite all of their differences, Ella Mae hated to witness Loralyn's anguish, but she was powerless to stop it. Ella Mae had come to Rolling View to break Rand's heart. She'd planned on showing him the ME's report and then watching as he was brought to his knees by the news that the woman he loved had never been pregnant. With his defenses lowered, Reba would have hit him with a tranquilizer dart and then called the cops. However, she couldn't apply the same tactics to Jarvis. It was clear that he already knew about Eira's hysterical pregnancy. He had probably killed her as soon as he found out.

"How did you know that Eira wasn't with child?" she asked, hoping to have more questions answered and to give Loralyn time to collect herself.

"I overheard her conversation with her farmer boy the

night of the party. They were in my office and I have a very comfortable false closet in that room. Eira was holding the glass of whiskey I'd prepped for Robert. I knew it was the same one because I keep a crystal tumbler and matching decanter on a silver tray on my desk. No one uses that crystal but me," Jarvis said with a trace of arrogance. "When Eira told Barric about her pregnancy, he reminded her that she'd deluded herself once before. He brought up a time during college in which he'd cheated on her and she'd broken up with him, only to show up a few months later claiming that she was expecting another man's child. She'd missed a few cycles, gained some weight, and even had a positive result on a home pregnancy test, but it was a false positive. Apparently, it took counseling for her to accept that she wasn't having a child."

Opal examined her fingernails and yawned. "Two hysterical pregnancies? She was a complete nutcase. Not exactly the best mother material, Jarvis."

"Barric told us that her father struggled with mental illness," Ella Mae said quickly before Jarvis could be distracted by Opal's remark. "If Eira struggled with those issues too, then she deserved a chance to get help, not to be drugged and dumped on a mountain trail."

Jarvis folded his arms over his chest. "Really? She deceived her husband, her old boyfriend, and me. That's why I carried her to the entrance of the grove. To make a mockery of the next chapter of lies and deceit she was about to embark upon. You were next, Ms. LeFaye. You and everyone in Havenwood. She would have manipulated all of you given the chance. But I took that chance away and let her sleep inches from the place she most wanted to be. It's what she deserved."

"She deceived herself too," Ella Mae pointed out. "Eira wanted a child so badly that she would have moved heaven and earth to have one. She'd been misused by everyone she cared about, and I think she believed that the only way she could experience true and unconditional love was to have a child of her own."

"I concur," Jarvis said. "I came to the same conclusion as I listened to her talk with Barric. She didn't love me. She wanted me to get rid of her husband and to father a kid, but she would never love me. She never got over her mother's abandonment, her daddy's mental health issues, or Barric's betrayal. She cared about Barric the most. If not, she wouldn't have asked Morgan to finance his farm. But he wouldn't give her a child. As for Morgan, she tolerated him for a little while, but once she knew he couldn't have a kid, she began to work her magic on me."

Opal snorted. "And after a few twirls and pirouettes you succumbed."

Ella Mae shushed her without taking her eyes off Jarvis. "So you forced her to drink the whiskey you'd prepared for Robert." Jarvis dipped his head in assent. "And Barric didn't leave town because he suspected you. Why?"

"He saw me at the resort. I checked in the day of the party and he found out who I was." Jarvis rubbed his chin. "I suppose he started following me. The day before the winter carnival, I had some words with Robert Morgan at the resort's bar. I'd tracked him to that spot in order to warn him to stay away from my wife. I wasn't going to let Opal humiliate me in my own backyard." He shot his wife a venomous glance. "Morgan thanked me for getting rid of his wife—a fact my own dear viper of a wife must have shared with him—thus making him free to marry again. Things would have escalated at that point had I not spotted Barric out of the corner of my eye."

Reba whistled. "That poor boy. Attractin' the attention of a fire elemental isn't very smart."

Jarvis puffed out his chest. "No, it wasn't. I've been known to have a difficult time controlling my temper."

"Enough!" Opal shouted and stood up. "You killed two people, Jarvis. You care nothing for your wife, your daughter, or your family's reputation. I married you because you were a distant cousin and our union was supposed to lead to great things. I was wrong, but I won't suffer your faults any longer. Either allow the LeFayes to bring you to the police station or I'll call and invite the cops to collect you."

Jarvis laughed. It was a deep rumble that started in his chest and roared out of his throat. "My bags are packed, Opal dear. I only joined this little party to tell Ms. LeFaye that she should have heeded the note I left on her car. Because she refused to listen, I will reduce the grove to ash on my way out of town." He glanced from Reba to Opal. "Get in my way, and you'll burn too."

"Go ahead," Opal said nonchalantly. "Make a fireball. I dare you."

Loralyn rushed forward and grabbed her father's arm. "Dad, don't! *Please!*"

Jarvis shook her off. The motion was smooth and detached. He didn't even acknowledge her presence. Ella Mae could see that his indifference caused Loralyn more pain than if he'd struck her full in the face. She reeled away from him, too stunned and hurt to do anything more.

"I never thought we'd come to this point, but you've pushed me too far," Jarvis snarled at Opal and raised his right hand. His cheeks and neck went red with fury. Ella Mae, believing him to be on the brink of creating fire, shot an anxious glance at Reba. Reba responded with a cool nod.

Opal opened a desk drawer and was suddenly brandishing a handgun. She pointed it at Jarvis. "You're finished. You just don't realize it yet."

Jarvis let loose a feral cry and thrust his arm forward. Nothing happened. Surprised, he repeated the motion. When his hand stayed the same, his mouth fell open in shock. Opal smiled in triumph as Jarvis stared at his clenched fist. "For once, Ella Mae has done me a great service. Because of her late night swim, the source of your power has been severed.

She took the Flower of Life. Its connection to the outside world of Havenwood is gone and so are your abilities." Her gaze flicked to Ella Mae. "I'd read several ancient texts hinting that elementals gathered near these rare flowers, but I wasn't completely sure of their accuracy. And as we all know, magic is rather fickle. Which is why I'm holding a loaded gun. The only thing that ever attracted me to Jarvis Gaynor is gone and now I'd like him to be gone." Aiming the gun at her husband's chest, she held out her cell phone. "Loralyn, I'd like you to call the authorities. If we cooperate, we won't be seen as accessories." When Loralyn hesitated, Opal softened her tone. "Your father was about to burn you alive. Is he still worthy of your loyalty? Of your love? No, my sweet. He isn't."

Weeping, Loralyn moved to take the phone.

Without warning, Jarvis grabbed her around the neck and pulled her in front of him. "You might be as cold as the deepest circle of hell, Opal, but you won't shoot your daughter. She's your greatest accomplishment. A chip off the old icicle." Jarvis began dragging Loralyn toward the opening in the wall.

"Dad!" Loralyn's voice was a strangled squeak of fear and despair.

Opal lowered the gun. "Don't you hurt her! I swear, if you—"

Just then Jarvis's hand flew to his neck. He paused, faltered, and released his hold on Loralyn. His eyes went round in astonishment and then he pitched sideways, hitting the floor with a resounding thud.

Reba spun the blowgun in her hand, looking as if she were leading a marching band onto the field. "Go on and call the cops now, Opal. He won't give you any more trouble."

Ella Mae hurried to Loralyn and slid an arm around her waist. "It's going to be all right," she said. As Opal dialed Officer Hardy's number, Ella Mae led Loralyn, who was trembling violently, to the sofa. Her mother took one of Loralyn's hands and stroked it gently. Ella Mae picked up the other. The LeFaye women comforted Loralyn as she wept, her mascara dripping onto her white silk blouse, leaving a permanent record of the moment when her world fell apart.

Justice is similar to magic, Ella Mae thought. *They both exact a price. And sometimes, the price is unfair.*

The man who'd killed Eira and Barric would pay for his crime, she knew, but his family would pay too. Opal would feel ashamed, though not for long, but Loralyn was bound to suffer her father's rejection for the rest of her days. Now, as Ella Mae held the hand of the woman she'd once viewed as her greatest enemy, she vowed to help her heal.

Ella Mae turned to Reba and the two women smiled at each other. It was the kind of smile shared between family members. A slight curve of the lips and a glimmer in the eyes that said, "I know you. I love you. I'll always be with you."

And when Ella Mae returned her gaze to her mother's face, she saw the same smile lifting the corners of her mouth. Ella Mae could feel the invisible threads joining her to her mother and to Reba. She imagined that if one were to strum them, the sound they'd produce would be like the ringing of tiny silver bells. And if the threads became visible, they'd shine like starlight.

Ella Mae shut her eyes. She rubbed Loralyn's back and murmured softly to her. Her hand moving in gentle circles, Ella Mae's thoughts turned to another woman with a halo of golden hair. A woman who Ella Mae hoped had leapt out of her frozen body to dance right off the mountainside and into the moonless sky. She thought of Barric and of the burned grove in Oak Knoll.

Inexplicably, a strange peace fell over her. She held Loralyn, and in a voice barely above a whisper, she sang a verse from "I See the Moon," an old lullaby Reba used to sing to her when she couldn't sleep.

Over the mountain, over the sea,
Back where my heart is longing to be,
Please let the light that shines on me
Shine on the one I love.

Chapter 18

In the days following Jarvis Gaynor's arrest, Ella Mae tried to put the ordeal behind her. She wanted nothing more than to return to a life of baking pies, playing with Chewy, and sharing meals and laughter with her family and friends. She'd also been trying to catch a few moments alone with Hugh.

He'd been avoiding her, she knew, citing issues at work, and would stop by the pie shop only for quick visits. Coming in through the back door, he'd sit on a stool and chat amiably while Ella Mae, Reba, Jenny, and Aiden did their best to keep pace with the ever-increasing number of orders.

Ella Mae could barely concentrate on the baking, plating, and garnishing, let alone having to discern whether or not her boyfriend remembered seeing her in the lake Sunday night. All she knew was that a chasm was opening up between them. Hugh still made her laugh, like when he made a smiley face garnish out of two cucumber slices and a tomato wedge and dared Reba to serve it to one of Havenwood's grouchier residents, but his levity felt forced. He still kissed her too, but his touches were brief and without tenderness. When his lips brushed hers, she sensed a lack of presence, as if his thoughts were elsewhere.

But Ella Mae wasn't the kind of woman to sit around and wait for change. Since her return to Havenwood, she'd learned what mattered most in life, and her love for Hugh mattered. She wasn't going to let what they had go cold without a fight, so on Friday, when closing time drew near, she rolled out a ball of dough and fetched a heart-shaped cookie cutter from a large plastic tub she kept in the storeroom.

She'd just retrieved a container of red raspberries from the walk-in when Jenny entered the kitchen carrying two dirty plates. "Officer Hardy is here. He wants to know if he can come back and talk to you. He's not in uniform or anything. In fact, he just polished off a slice of pear and almond tart followed by three mini maple pecan pies."

"Hey, if a paying customer wants to check out the kitchen, that's fine by me."

Jenny finished loading the dishwasher and then hesitated. "The dining room's empty. Do you want me to stay and keep you company? I don't mind."

"No, you go on ahead." Ella Mae smiled at her. "And tell Reba and Aiden they're done for the day as well."

"Aiden will be out the door in seconds," Jenny said. "He has a date with Suzy tonight. It's just supper at her place, but Aiden's been checking his watch for the past two hours. He'll spend more time primping than Suzy will, I swear."

Ella Mae laughed. "Just warn him that if he ever hurts her, I'll bake him an arsenic pie."

Jenny saluted on her way into the dining room.

A moment later, Jon Hardy pushed the swing door open. "Is it safe to enter?"

"As long as this isn't an impromptu health inspection."

Hardy gazed around the room, clearly liking what he saw. "It's warm, bright, and clean in here. Exactly how a kitchen should be." He pointed at the stool pulled up to the worktable. "May I?"

"Of course. Do you mind if I make some noise before we talk?" She pointed at the food processor. "I'm making a white chocolate and raspberry filling."

Hardy waved to indicate she should continue with her work and Ella Mae blended the filling and began to spoon it onto the heart-shaped pieces of dough. She didn't add any enchantment to Hugh's treat. She vowed to never use magic on him again. "Are you interested in becoming a pastry chef on the side?"

"No, ma'am. I'll leave that to experts like yourself." There was a glint of amusement in his eyes. "Though you seem to get caught up in my job more than the average citizen."

Ella Mae paused in the act of covering the white chocolate raspberry filling with another piece of heart-shaped dough, wondering if Hardy expected her to appear contrite. "I guess I have been entangled in a mess or two since I came back to town."

"I'm actually here to thank you," Hardy said. "Opal Gaynor stated that without your intervention, her husband might have fled before we had the chance to apprehend him. We knew that he'd been romantically involved with Eira Morgan, but we had to wait on the Oak Knoll Sheriff's Department to obtain the proof we needed before making an arrest. Mr. Gaynor paid for most things—hotel rooms, restaurant bills, gifts—in cash, but when the deputies distributed photos of Gaynor and Eira Morgan to neighboring towns, many people remembered seeing them together. Apparently, they acted like a couple madly in love."

"That wasn't love," Ella Mae murmured.

Hardy spread his hands in a show of capitulation. "I agree. Theirs was more of a dangerous passion. Crimes of passion are about possession and betrayal, and this one had a lion's share of both." He watched Ella Mae seal the edges of the tiny pie using the tines of a fork. "I also came to tell you that Eira Morgan wasn't pregnant. The details of this case will be public knowledge before long, but I wanted to tell you this one myself. She wasn't well, Ms. LeFaye. She suffered from delusions and paranoia. She was seeing a professional when she was in college but stopped shortly after graduation. Apparently, that was the first time she was convinced that she was carrying a child, but she wasn't pregnant then nor prior to her death."

"If only she'd gotten help," Ella Mae said sadly. "All of this could have been avoided."

"Her life might have been spared," Hardy said hesitantly. "But Jarvis Gaynor was a ticking bomb. I've encountered men like him before. Always too quick to anger. Always burning with a quiet fury. People like Jarvis stoke their fires until they explode. Sadly, Eira Morgan was in his path when it happened."

Ella Mae fell silent, wondering if Jarvis's propensity toward anger was exacerbated by Opal's coldness, if her disdain had fanned his rage. Jarvis had said that what he wanted most was to start a new life far away from his wife.

"I'm surprised he confessed," she mused aloud. "I expected him to go down swinging."

Hardy nodded. "I did too. But as our interview wore on, he told me that he'd lost everything that defined him, and it no longer mattered if he had his freedom or not. He indicated that you were responsible for his ruin, though that doesn't hold much water with me. People always want to blame someone else when they realize they have nowhere left to run."

"Did he admit Robert Morgan was his original target? What if he'd succeeded? What would he do with Morgan's body?" Ella Mae opened the oven door and slid the heart-shaped pies inside. When she turned around, Hardy was pushing granules of sugar around the worktable with the pad of his index finger and frowning.

"He was going to dump Mr. Morgan into the lake." Hardy shook his head in disgust. "Roll his wheelchair right off the end of a dock."

"That's awful." An image flashed in Ella Mae's mind of the terrifying creature she'd seen in the lake. The knowledge that she'd known the beast in its human form all her life made Ella Mae shudder.

She rubbed her arms and smiled at Hardy. "Can I offer you a decaf? I need something hot to drink."

"No, thank you. I've overindulged already, especially on your magical pies."

At his use of the word "magical," Ella Mae's smile nearly faltered, but she kept it in place and poured the remains of the coffee into her mug. She couldn't help but feel that Hardy was studying her, analyzing her facial expressions and body language, but for what purpose she couldn't say. Stirring cream into her coffee, she picked up the mug and gazed at him expectantly over the rim.

Hardy cleared his throat. "One final question before I go. Mr. Gaynor was involved in an arson case in Oak Knoll, Tennessee. Two of your employees are from that same town, correct?"

"Yes."

"Did you know about the fire before you asked Jenny and Aiden Upton to live in your house and work in your pie shop?"

Ella Mae didn't know where he was going with this line of questioning, but she decided to tread carefully. "I heard about the fire for the first time at the Gaynors' party. I had no idea it was set deliberately until much later," she lied. "Jenny and Eira were friends, and Eira mentioned that Jenny and her brother were ready to relocate. Since I was in serious need of help, I called Jenny and asked her to drive down for an interview. Knowing she'd be a great fit, I offered her the job right away."

Hardy looked confused. "The fire didn't destroy a single home or business, so why did so many people leave Oak Knoll? Especially to come here?"

Ella Mae shrugged. "I can only speak for Jenny. She was

involved with her boss and they had a bad breakup. Trust me, when a romance at work goes sour, it's best to start over again in a new place. And Eira was moving to Havenwood, so it made sense for Jenny to be near her best friend and for Aiden to follow his sister. As for the others who left? I have no clue. Did you ask Robert Morgan? Perhaps he could shed some light on the Oak Knoll exodus." She idly sipped her coffee.

"I did ask, in fact. Mr. Morgan told me that his company had outgrown its current office space and that he'd gotten an incredible buy on a large tract of land just outside Havenwood's town limits. Most of his executives were willing to make the move, and now he's here."

Grimacing, Ella Mae said, "I disliked that man from the moment we met. When I heard about Eira's death, I immediately assumed Morgan was responsible. He treated his wife like she was a doll in a music box—something to be owned and admired, something to be wound up and made to perform on a whim. I never sensed an ounce of love or respect in him, even after she was gone."

"I had my suspicions about him as well," Hardy said. "Especially considering his interest in winning the affection of another man's wife. But Mr. Morgan is innocent of any wrongdoing, at least in the eyes of the law, and I've been told that he plans to donate funds to have a ballet studio built in his wife's honor at the Havenwood School of the Arts." He shrugged. "Let's just hope there's more to him than what we see."

Ella Mae made a noncommittal noise and shot at glance at the oven timer. The pies were almost finished baking.

Hardy got to his feet. "As for you, Ms. LeFaye, you remain a bit of a mystery to me. I'm usually adept at reading people, but I believe there's more to you than what meets the eye."

Ella Mae glanced down at her flour-covered apron and laughed. "I should hope so!" The pair chatted about other things for a few minutes while Ella Mae removed the pies from the oven and set them on the cooling racks. When they were ready, she boxed up two of the heart-shaped pies and walked Hardy to the door. "As for me being a bit of a mystery, don't you think all of us are more than we seem? The hidden selves are capable of betrayal and heartbreak. Even murder. But they're also capable of great acts of altruism and love." She handed him the pink bakery box. "These are for your wife."

"Thank you. She'll love them." Hardy opened the door and paused at the threshold. "You're an intriguing woman, Ms. LeFaye. I just hope that you can manage to keep yourself extricated from future police investigations."

"I'd much rather see you here in the pie shop than in that gloomy conference room at the station." She laughed.

Hardy smiled in return and then left.

Ella Mae took his vacant stool and finished her coffee. As she sipped the hot, rich brew, she resolved to be more guarded around Hardy. If he watched her too often or too closely, he might discover just how unique she was.

Finishing her coffee, Ella Mae loaded the dishwasher and tidied the rest of the kitchen. She then transferred the remaining heart-shaped pies into a pair of bakery boxes and headed to Canine to Five.

At the reception desk, she proffered one of the boxes to the woman on duty.

"This is my lucky day!" the woman exclaimed, opening the lid and grabbing one of the bite-sized pies. "Oh, they're still warm. Thank you, darling. I skipped lunch and my stomach is rumbling like a freight train. Hugh's in his office. Go on back."

Ella Mae suddenly felt so nervous at the thought of finally being alone with Hugh that she could barely hold the other bakery box steady. She walked down the empty hall, moving farther away from the rumbling barks and shrill yips of the dogs playing in the agility area or swimming in the pool, and tried not to think about how Hugh had looked at her under the water. She focused on more pleasant memories instead, like the way his cheeks dimpled when he smiled or how he pinched the bridge of his nose when he was deep in thought. She pictured him pouring too much syrup on his pancakes or how he could make a quarter roll back and forth over his knuckles. She heard his deep laugh, saw his strong hands gripping a fire hose, and thought of how he always got down on all fours to greet an unfamiliar dog entering the daycare for the first time.

Holding these images at the forefront of her mind, she knocked on his office door and grinned when he called out, "Enter if you dare," in what the receptionist referred to as his ogre voice.

"I come bearing gifts," she said with a smile.

He glanced up from a pile of paperwork and returned her smile. For a second, he was the man she loved, but then a veil fell over his eyes. Ella Mae ached to go back to the way things used to be, though she realized she hadn't been happy then either. She'd always hated lying to Hugh. They would either go forward from this moment knowing everything there was to know about each other, or they'd have to say good-bye. And although Ella Mae couldn't live with deceit any longer, she was frightened to be standing here, at the center of the crossroad.

"I brought you my heart," she said, setting the box on his desk. She'd meant to sound breezy and cool, but her throat tightened and the words came out as a hoarse whisper.

Hugh opened the lid and peered inside. "Hmmm, they smell good." He started to reach into the box and then abruptly withdrew his hand. "What are they made of?"

Ella Mae didn't like the distrust in his expression. She moved closer to him, fearing that he was slipping away too fast. She knew that if she didn't catch hold of him now, she'd lose him forever. "Sugar and spice and everything nice."

"The last time I ate one of your pies, I felt like I'd been drugged."

And there it was. The opening she'd been waiting for. Ella Mae pulled a chair next to his, close enough so that their knees almost touched. "I saw you in the lake Sunday night."

He didn't answer. Averting his gaze, he started shifting paperwork around. Ella Mae waited for him to say something, but he kept his lips clamped shut, pivoting his body away from hers. The silence stretched on, filling the room like a dark, heavy fog. Ella Mae knew that she had to choose her next words with extreme care. Everything hung in the balance.

"Did you see me?" she asked softly. "Did you recognize me?"

His hands stopped their fidgeting. She feared he wouldn't answer, that he'd ignore her until she was forced to leave. He stared down at his desk, and then picked up the string that had fallen from the bakery box and wound it between his index fingers. "Why did you take it? Why you?"

The grief in his voice nearly flattened her. "I needed to save my mother. I would have lost her forever. I never expected that you . . ." She paused, confused. "Did my taking the flower hurt you in some way?" She reached for his arm. "Hugh?"

He sighed heavily, and then slowly, haltingly, moved to cover her hand with his. "I've always been different, Ella Mae. The things I could do—they set me apart. It sounds great to be special, but it's a lonely existence. I could never tell anyone or I'd be locked up." He let out a dry laugh. "Then, I got to know Loralyn and I thought she was a little like me. I felt comfortable around her. It was only after you came back that I began to sense she'd been tricking me somehow. All along, she'd been making me feel things I wouldn't have felt voluntarily."

"She—"

"And then I fell for you." He fixed his eyes on her and Ella Mae saw pain swimming in those twin pools of brilliant blue. "A woman like no other woman. I got the same vibe I'd gotten with Loralyn, but with you, I thought I'd finally found a person who wouldn't use or deceive me. I trusted you, even though I knew there was more to you than you revealed. But you fed me a spiked pie, Ella Mae. You put me to sleep. You're no different than Loralyn."

The accusation made her flinch. "I started to suspect you were a water elemental, and I was afraid that you were the flower's guardian. I didn't want to fight you, to choose between you and my mother, but I had to do everything I could to save her. Can you understand that?"

His eyes kept boring into her. "How did you learn about me? About the flower?"

"In books," Ella Mae said, relieved that Hugh hadn't pulled away from her touch. "Old books that few have ever seen."

He stared at her, unblinking. "Who are you, Ella Mae LeFaye? *What* are you?"

She smiled at him, willing the love she felt to wash over him like a wave. "I can't talk about it here. I'm bound by rules and I'll be punished if I don't abide by them." She squeezed his hand. "But I can show you. I can take you to a special place. If you're able to enter, I can tell you everything. There won't be any secrets left between us. I hate secrets. They destroy people. And I never want to keep anything from you again."

The tension in his face abated slightly. "You would do that? Put it all in the open for me?"

"Gladly. I love you, Hugh. If I had known you weren't like other people, I would have done this at the very beginning." She could feel hope blooming in her heart. "I've hated having to tell half-truths or omit entire parts of my life to the *one* person I want to share everything with. You deserve more than that. And I've been burned by lies, Hugh. That's what Sloane did to me. I don't want you and me to end up that way. I want us to strip down to our bare souls in front of each other."

He nodded. "Call me an idiot, but I believe you. And I'll go wherever you want, but not right away. I'd like some time to process everything that's happened so I'm ready to handle our next chapter."

Ella Mae's smile grew wider. "Take all the time you need. And you're no idiot. You're the man I've loved before I even knew what love was."

Standing, he pulled Ella Mae to her feet and slid his arms around her back. "So you're not planning on seducing me with the pies in that box?"

She ran her fingers down the line of his jaw. "On my life, I will never do something like that to you again. Besides, why would I take a shortcut when doing it this way is so much sweeter?"

And then she kissed him. He hesitated at first, but then pressed her closer to him. The kiss was long and deep, and though Ella Mae waited for the feel of sparks against her lips, the burning sensation never began.

Breaking off the kiss, she whispered, "Is it possible? Could we be cured?"

Hugh didn't speak, he just held her tightly to him. They stood there for a long time in the warm haven of each other's arms. Hugh stroked Ella Mae's hair from root to tip, his fingers lingering on the skin of her neck before starting at the top again. She pressed her ear against the soft cotton of his shirt, feeling his chest rise and fall as he breathed. Closing her eyes, she listened to his heartbeat. The rhythm reminded her of waves curling onto the shore, beautiful in its predictability. For there, in the cadence of Hugh's beating heart, Ella Mae heard the sound of eternity.

February arrived and Havenwood began to show signs of an early spring. The sun burned off winter's gray pall and the chilly wind that had nipped at everyone's ears and noses moved north. Articles on Jarvis Gaynor and the murders of

Eira Morgan and Barric Young moved from the front page of the newspapers to be tucked among pieces on car theft and domestic abuse, and Havenwood began to feel tranquil again.

Ella Mae made raspberry and white chocolate heart-shaped pies for every customer that visited The Charmed Pie Shoppe on Valentine's Day and she was so flushed with love—for Hugh, her family, and her friends—that she didn't need to use magic to make her patrons feel special. Following the murders and the departure of the tourists after the winter carnival, she'd expected February to be a slow month, but the pie shop continued to draw new customers from around the region.

After a particularly busy Saturday, Ella Mae hung the closed sign and turned to stare at the empty dining room. She was exhausted but content. This was the life she wanted to lead. She wanted to bake the most wondrous food she could, bring joy to others, and spend her free time with the people who made her world a warmer, more colorful and wondrous place. Ella Mae was ready to take a breather from the stress of living and working among magical people, so when her mother and three aunts entered the kitchen carrying a garment bag, a hairbrush, and enigmatic expressions, she felt a stirring of alarm.

"What's in there?" She gestured at the garment bag.

"It's one of my vintage treasures. I added a few embellishments and I think it'll fit like a glove." Dee smiled.

Ella Mae's mother nodded. "There's no time to do anything but slip it on and give your hair a quick brush."

Ella Mae held up the garment and moaned in admiration. The strapless emerald green satin evening dress had a sweetheart neckline and a cascade of moss green satin falling from the left hip to the bottom hem. Clusters of beads shaped into tiny clovers had been stitched into the moss-colored fabric. "It looks like springtime. What's the occasion?"

Verena pointed toward the restroom. "You've been summoned by the Elders. Hurry, hurry!"

Now Ella Mae was genuinely nervous. "Why?"

Sissy made a shooing motion. "You'll find out soon enough. *Go!*"

Casting a brief, questioning glance at her mother, Ella Mae hustled to the restroom, shucked off her work clothes, washed her face and hands, and shimmied into the dress. Dee was right. It fit perfectly. She brushed her hair, touched up her lipstick, and then turned this way and that in the small mirror above the sink. Even in the dim light, she had never felt so beautiful, and when she reappeared in the kitchen, her mother and aunts were momentarily speechless.

"She certainly looks the part now, doesn't she, Adelaide?"

Ella Mae's mother nodded and helped her daughter into her coat.

"You're not going to tell me what this is about, are you?"

"If I knew, I would. Only Verena knows and she won't say a word."

They drove to the grove in silence, Ella Mae sitting as close to the air vent as possible. She wore her tennis shoes on the trail, but as soon as she entered the grove, she left her coat and shoes in a pile near the rock wall.

She and her mother and aunts walked quickly through the orchard, across the clearing, to where a small cluster of people waited near the silver ash tree. Ella Mae recognized a town librarian, physician, attorney, and the high school principal. One woman and three men.

When they drew close, her mother stopped walking and Ella Mae followed her lead. Only Verena kept going. She took her place next to the female doctor and turned to face Ella Mae and her two sisters.

"We are the Elders of Havenwood," the male librarian intoned. "We have asked you here today to thank you for your service to our community, and to extend an invitation to join us." He gestured at his fellow Elders. "Never has one so young been offered this honor, but we believe that you might be the key to our future."

Ella Mae shook her head. "That's kind of you to say, but—"

"We are not being kind," the attorney stated in a deep baritone. "Please come forward and hold out your right hand."

Ella Mae glanced at her mother, who nodded soberly.

Moving over the velvety grass, Ella Mae did as she was told. The attorney took her hand and turned it, palm facing up. He examined her clover-shaped burn scar and then stepped back and bowed. It was a formal act, such as a courtier might perform for a sovereign. Each of the Elders did the same. One by one, they looked at her burn and bowed. Even Verena.

"You have been marked," said the principal. "You have freed us from being reliant on a Lady of the Ash. Now, we ask you to take up the mantle of Elder. A new danger is coming from across the sea and we will need everything you have to offer, my lady."

"Please. Call me Ella Mae." She was discomfited and embarrassed to be addressed this way, especially on the heels of all the bows. These were Havenwood's Elders, for crying out loud. They were the most important people she'd ever met. "What is this new threat?"

"Principal Strong misspoke," the librarian said. "It is a very old danger, though newly awakened. A woman named Nimue. Centuries ago, Morgan le Fay was able to place her under a sleeping spell, but the spell has been broken and she is bent on revenge. Our people in Wales and Scotland are already suffering her wrath. Should she come here, which she is certain to do, we will face the fight of our lives."

Ella Mae glanced back at her mother and aunts. They looked frightened. "I will do anything I can to protect us." She hesitated. "But I must ask something of you as well."

Verena signaled for her to continue. "Go on."

"I'd like Opal Gaynor to become an Elder. Tonight."

The librarian shook her head. "No. Her husband—"

"She and her husband are separate people," Ella Mae said quickly, thinking that she needed to convince Hugh to enter the grove soon or the Elders might question the wisdom of her having a relationship with a water elemental. "And if the descendants of Morgan le Fay and Guinevere do not unite, we'll eventually disappear from the earth. If this terrible threat is imminent, then this is the perfect time to join forces. I believe we can break Merlin's curse for good if we work together. Merlin cursed both of our lines, so it's about time we united to put an end to centuries of misery. Just think of it! We can marry and have children without risk. We can grow strong and live in safety. As Merlin's descendants fade and die, ours will grow more powerful and more numerous."

"Seven Elders," the attorney mused aloud. "The prophecy is being fulfilled."

Again, they all bowed and then Sissy was dispatched to collect Opal Gaynor and Reba. Ella Mae couldn't go ahead with the ceremony unless Reba was present. After all, she'd been at Ella Mae's side for most of her life. She wasn't about to become an Elder without her.

The ceremony itself wasn't much to speak of. Opal was uncharacteristically subdued and kept staring at Ella Mae in wonder. But when her turn came to recite the creed to accept her role as an Elder, she stood, back straight and chin raised, and vowed to protect the grove and its people with her life.

When it was over, the Elders drank sweet wine out of gossamer-thin glass goblets and made plans to meet again soon. And then they dispersed.

Ella Mae's mother was the last to leave. She lingered by the ash tree, standing as close as she could to the trunk without coming into contact with the silver bark.

"Are you all right?" Ella Mae asked.

Her mother smiled. "Of course. After all, I'm mother to the Clover Queen."

Ella Mae waved off the title. "I have more Herculean tasks to check off my list before anyone starts calling me 'Your Highness.'" She gave a self-effacing shrug of her shoulders. "Actually, I hope that never happens. I don't know many queens who wear aprons and perpetually have flour in their hair." She held out her arm. "Come on, let's go home."

Together, the two women returned to the other side of the rock wall. After Ella Mae crossed into the cold February night, she stood still for a moment, taking in the high moon and a sky dotted with brilliant stars.

"Look!" she cried and squatted by the side of the path. There, in a patch of unyielding dirt, was a cluster of snowdrops. "Aren't they lovely?"

Her mother bent down to see. "Is this where Eira died?"

Ella Mae nodded.

"Legend has it that very long ago, an angel kissed a snowflake," her mother said. "When the snowflake fell to the ground, the first snowdrop bloomed. It was also the birth of hope."

Ella Mae liked the sound of that. "Can we bring it with us? Plant a whole garden bed of snowdrops as a memorial to Eira and Barric?"

Her mother already had her hands in the soil. "Absolutely."

She transplanted the flower that night, and by morning, there were dozens upon dozens of snowdrops sharing a garden bed with slumbering rosebushes. The bell-shaped blossoms glistened with a diamond frost in the February sunlight, and to Ella Mae's surprise and delight, a pair of butterflies with pale white wings danced over the delicate petals.

She watched their graceful ballet for a long time, until her fingers and toes were numb from cold. Finally, the butterflies lifted off. They flitted upward and hovered above her palm for a moment, circling around each other like two dancers waltzing on air, before rising higher and higher.

Ella Mae thought of angels and snowflakes. Of loss and of hope. It was only after the butterflies flew into the heart of a diaphanous cloud and vanished from sight that she finally turned and went inside.

Recipes

Charmed Piecrust

2 ½ cups all-purpose flour, plus extra for rolling (place in
    freezer for 15 minutes before use)
1 teaspoon salt
1 teaspoon sugar
1 cup (2 sticks) unsalted butter, very cold, cut into ½-inch
    cubes
6 to 8 tablespoons very cold water

Combine the flour, salt, and sugar in a food processor; pulse
to mix. Add the butter and pulse until mixture resembles
coarse meal and you have pea-sized pieces of butter. Add
the water 1 tablespoon at a time, pulsing until the mixture
begins to clump together. Put some dough between your
fingers. If it holds together, it's ready. If it falls apart, you
need a little more water. You'll see bits of butter in the
dough. This is a good thing, as it will give you a nice, flaky
crust.

Mound the dough and place it on a clean surface. Gently shape it into 2 disks of equal size. Do not overknead. Sprinkle a little flour around the disks. Wrap each disk in plastic wrap and refrigerate at least 1 hour.

Remove the first crust disk from the refrigerator. Let it sit at room temperature for 5 minutes or until soft enough to roll. Roll it out with a rolling pin on a lightly floured surface to a 12-inch circle (Ella Mae uses a pie mat to help with measurements). Gently transfer it into a 9-inch pie plate. Carefully press the pie dough down so that it lines the bottom and sides of the pie plate. Use kitchen scissors to trim the dough to within ½ inch of the edge of the pie plate.

Roll out the second disk of dough and place it on top of the pie filling. Pinch the top and bottom of dough firmly together. Trim excess dough with kitchen shears, leaving about 1 inch of overhang. Fold the edge of the top piece of dough over and under the edge of the bottom piece of dough, pressing together. Flute edges by pinching with thumb and forefinger. Remember to score the center of the top crust with a few small cuts so that steam can escape.

Charmed Egg Wash

To achieve a golden brown color for your crust, brush the surface with this egg wash before placing the pie in the oven.

  1 tablespoon half-and-half
  1 large egg yolk

Note—if you're short on time and decide to use the pre-made piecrusts found in your grocery store's dairy section, then use the egg wash on the crusts to give them a homemade flavor.

Charmed Red Hot Apple Pie

Charmed Piecrust
1 tablespoon lemon juice
¼ cup cinnamon Red Hots candies
1 teaspoon ground cinnamon
⅓ cup honey
4 large Granny Smith apples, peeled, cored, and chopped
1 tablespoon cold butter, cut into pieces
Charmed Egg Wash
Cinnamon sugar (½ cup sugar and 1 tablespoon cinnamon)

Preheat oven to 350 degrees. Place half of the rolled-out piecrust dough into pie plate. Trim the pastry edges with a knife or kitchen shears. In small saucepan, cook the lemon juice and cinnamon Red Hots over low heat until the candies melt, approximately 10 minutes. Remove the pan from the heat and stir in the ground cinnamon and honey. Arrange apples in bottom crust and pour the Red Hots mixture over the apples. Dot with pieces of butter.

Cut decorative shapes in the remainder of the piecrust dough with small cookie cutters (Ella Mae prefers hearts). Moisten the edges of the bottom crust with water and then lift the top crust over filling. Trim any extra dough with a knife or kitchen shears and then flute the edges or press them together using the tines of a fork. Brush with Charmed Egg Wash and sprinkle with cinnamon sugar. Bake for 15 minutes. Then cover the edge of the crust with a pie shield or aluminum foil and bake for another 45 minutes or until the crust is golden brown. Cool and serve with vanilla ice cream, if desired.

Charmed Meat Pies with Paprika Aioli

DOUGH

2 ½ cups flour
2 teaspoons salt
½ cup vegetable oil
½ cup ice water

FILLING

2 tablespoons butter
1 pound ground beef chuck
2 large garlic cloves, finely minced
1 onion, finely diced
3 tablespoons tomato paste
¼ teaspoon cayenne pepper
¼ teaspoon ground cloves
¼ teaspoon allspice
½ teaspoon chopped fresh thyme
3 splashes of Tabasco sauce (add more if desired)

PAPRIKA AIOLI

¼ cup fresh lemon juice
5 garlic cloves, finely minced
¼ teaspoon cayenne pepper
1 ½ teaspoons paprika (sweet or Spanish)
2 tablespoons sugar
1 ½ tablespoons tomato paste
1 ½ cups mayonnaise

In a large skillet, melt the butter. Add the ground beef and cook until no pink is showing. Add the garlic and onion and cook over medium heat, stirring occasionally, until the onion is translucent, about 8 minutes. Stir in the tomato paste, cayenne, cloves, allspice, and thyme, and cook for 3 minutes.

Season with hot sauce and let cool. Transfer the filling to a food processor and pulse until chopped.

Preheat the oven to 350 degrees and line a large baking sheet with parchment paper. On a floured work surface, roll out each disk of dough to a 12-inch round. (If you don't want to make the dough by hand, pre-made piecrusts will work just as well). Using a 4-inch biscuit cutter, stamp out 6 rounds from each piece of dough. Brush the edges of the rounds with some of the egg wash and place a rounded tablespoon of filling to one side of each circle. Fold the other half of the dough over the filling and press to seal. Crimp the edges with a fork. Transfer the pies to the baking sheet and brush with the egg wash. Bake for 25 minutes, until golden brown.

While pies are baking, blend together all the ingredients for the paprika aioli. Serve in individual bowls for dipping.

Charmed Mini Maple Pecan Pies

Charmed Piecrust
1 cup pure Grade A maple syrup
¾ cup packed brown sugar
3 large eggs
¼ cup sugar
3 tablespoons salted butter, melted
1 tablespoon all-purpose flour
1 teaspoon pure vanilla extract
2 cups chopped pecans

Preheat oven to 350 degrees. After your dough is rolled out, use a 4-inch round cookie cutter to cut out circles. Put each circle in a pre-greased muffin pan. In medium bowl, blend all the ingredients except the pecans. Sprinkle the nuts over crust. Pour the filling over until it nearly reaches the top of each tin. Bake until the filling is set, about 45 minutes. Cool completely and serve with maple whipped cream.

Maple Whipped Cream

    1 cup whipping cream
    ¼ cup pure Grade A maple syrup
    ¼ teaspoon ground cinnamon

Place a metal bowl and electric mixer beaters in the freezer for 10 minutes. Remove them from the freezer and add the whipping cream to the bowl. Beat until the cream starts to thicken. Now add the maple syrup and ground cinnamon, and whip until stiff peaks form.

Charmed Bacon Lattice Breakfast Pie

    10 strips black pepper bacon
    1 unbaked deep-dish piecrust
    4 large eggs, beaten
    1 ½ cups half-and-half
    1 ½ cups shredded Colby and Monterey Jack cheese (can
        substitute shredded Cheddar or Swiss)
    1 cup breakfast sausage, cooked and crumbled

Preheat oven to 400 degrees. Line a tray with parchment paper and create bacon lattice by lining up 5 strips of bacon from top to bottom and then weaving in 5 more strips from side to side (follow same method as making a lattice piecrust). Bake until crisp, approximately 25 minutes. Drain the grease from tray and set aside. Reduce oven to 350 degrees. In a large bowl, blend the eggs and half-and-half. Add the cheese and sausage crumbles. Pour into the unbaked piecrust. Bake until the eggs are set and a toothpick inserted into the center comes out clean, approximately 1 hour. Remove the breakfast pie from the oven, carefully transfer the bacon lattice from tray to the top of pie, return the pie to oven, and bake for 5 more minutes. Serve warm.

Charmed Apple Pear Cherry Crisp

2 Granny Smith apples, peeled, cored, and chopped
2 Anjou pears, peeled, cored, and chopped
¾ cup frozen cherries (you can substitute fresh cranberries or raisins)
¼ cup white sugar
3 teaspoons ground cinnamon
1 teaspoon ground nutmeg
⅓ cup quick-cooking oats
⅓ cup all-purpose flour
½ cup packed light brown sugar
¼ cup butter, cut into pieces
½ cup chopped pecans

Preheat oven to 375 degrees. Butter an 8-inch square pan. In a large bowl, mix together the apples, pears, cherries, white sugar, cinnamon, and nutmeg. Spread the mixture evenly in the baking dish. In the same bowl or in a food processor, combine the oats, flour, and brown sugar. Mix in the butter until crumbly. (If using food processor, use the pulse button to crumble.) Stir in the pecans. Sprinkle the mixture over the apples. Bake for approximately 45 minutes or until the topping is golden brown.

Charmed Heart-Shaped White Chocolate Raspberry Cream Two-Bite Pies

Charmed Piecrust
Charmed Egg Wash
Finishing sugar

FILLING

8 ounces cream cheese, softened
1 cup fresh raspberries
1 tablespoon pure vanilla extract
2 tablespoons granulated sugar
½ cup white chocolate chips

Add all the filling ingredients to a food processor and pulse until smooth. Refrigerate until ready to use. Preheat oven to 400 degrees. Line a cookie sheet with parchment paper. Roll out the Charmed Piecrust dough and cut it with a heart cookie cutter. Transfer the piecrust hearts to the cookie sheet. Add a dollop of filling (amount will depend on size of cookie cutter). Wet the edges of the bottom heart and press another heart gently on top. Seal the edges with the tines of a fork. Brush the hearts with Charmed Egg Wash and add a sprinkle of finishing sugar. For fun, use different-colored sugars like pink, white, and red. Bake for approximately 12 minutes or until the crust turns golden brown.

Dear Reader,

Thank you for spending time with Ella Mae LeFaye and the charmed characters of Havenwood, Georgia. In the next installment of the Charmed Pie Shoppe Mysteries, the magical baker will face another treacherous villain, solve complex puzzles, and, of course, whip up more enchantingly delicious pies.

In the meantime, I'd like to introduce you to my newest series: the Book Resort Mysteries. These books take place at an exclusive resort called Storyton Hall. What's Storyton Hall, you ask? Picture a stately English manor house—a sprawling behemoth of a building—and then move it, stone by stone, to the Virginia countryside. Next, fill each room with books. Hundreds of books. Thousands of books. And then decorate each room so that it reminds you of a famous author. You'll end up with places like the Jane Austen Drawing Room, the Ian Fleming Lounge, and Shakespeare's Theater. Next, fill the many bedrooms with comfy chairs, soft bedding, fresh flowers, and boxes of complimentary chocolates. When all is ready, throw open the massive front doors, offer the guests a glass of champagne, and join them as they enter this reader's Utopia.

But be warned. You're stepping into this haven for book lovers—this place of meandering garden paths, decadent afternoon teas, and secret passageways—at your own risk. For you see, a murderer has checked in along with you.

My friends, I invite you to take a brief sojourn into the delightful and occasionally deadly world of the Book Resort Mysteries by offering the first chapter of *Murder in the Mystery Suite*. A word of caution, however. Once you visit Storyton Hall, you might be so captivated by the resort's beauty and charismatic staff that you may never want to leave.

Yours,
Ellery Adams

There were books everywhere. Hundreds of books. Thousands of books. There were books of every size, shape, and color. They lined the walls from floor to ceiling, standing straight and rigid as soldiers on the polished mahogany shelves, the gilt lettering on their worn spines glinting in the soft light, the scent of supple leather and aging paper filling the air.

To Jane Steward, there was no sweeter perfume on earth. Of all the libraries in Storyton Hall, this was her favorite. Unlike the other libraries, which were open to the hotel's paying guests, this was the personal reading room of her great uncle Aloysius and great aunt Octavia.

"Are you ready, Sinclair?" Jane mounted the rolling book ladder and looked back over her shoulder.

A small, portly man with a cloud of white hair and ruddy cheeks wrung his hands together. "Oh, Miss Jane. I wish you wouldn't ask me to do this. It doesn't seem prudent."

Jane shrugged. "You heard what Gavin said at our last staff meeting. The greenhouse is in disrepair, the orchard needs pruning, the hedge maze is overgrown, the folly is hidden in brambles, and the roof above the staff quarters is rotting away. I have to come up with funds somehow. Lots of funds. What I need, Sinclair, is inspiration." She held out her arms as if she could embrace every book in the room. "What better place to find it than here?"

"Can't you just shut your eyes, reach out your hand, and choose a volume from the closest shelf?" Sinclair stuck a finger under his collar, loosening his bowtie. Unlike Storyton's other staff members, he didn't wear the hotel's royal blue and gold livery. As the resort's head librarian, he distinguished himself by dressing in tweed suits every day of the year. The only spot of color that appeared on his person came in the form of a striped, spotted, floral, or checkered bowtie. Today's was canary yellow with prim little brown dots.

Jane shook her head at the older gentleman she'd known since childhood. "You know that doesn't work, Sinclair. I have to lose all sense of where I am in the room. The book must choose me, not me, it." She smiled down at him. "Ms. Pimpernel tells me that the rails have recently been oiled, so you should be able to push me around in circles with ease."

"In squares, you mean." Sinclair sighed in defeat. "Very well, Miss Jane. Kindly hold on."

Grinning like a little girl, Jane gripped the sides of the ladder and closed her eyes. Sinclair pushed on the ladder, hesitantly at first, until Jane encouraged him to go faster, faster.

"Are you quite muddled yet?" he asked after a minute or so.

Jane descended by two rungs but didn't open her eyes. "I think I'm still in the Twentieth Century American Authors section. If I'm right, we need to keep going."

Sinclair grunted. "It's getting harder and harder to confuse you, Miss Jane. You know where every book in this library is shelved."

"Just a few more spins around the room. Please?"

The ladder began to move once more. This time, however, Sinclair stopped and started without warning and changed direction more than once. Eventually, he succeeded in disorientating her.

"Excellent!" Jane exclaimed and reached out her right hand. Her fingertips touched cloth and leather. They traced the embossed letters marching up and down the spines for a few brief seconds before traveling to the next book. "Inspire me," she whispered.

But nothing spoke to her, so she shifted to the left side of the ladder, stretching her arm overhead until her hand brushed against a book that was smaller and shorter than its neighbors. "I choose you," she said and pulled it from the shelf.

Sinclair craned his neck as if he might be able to read the title from his vantage point on the ground. "Which one did you pick, Miss Jane?"

"A British mystery," she said, frowning. "But I don't see how—"

At that moment, two boys burst into the room, infusing the air with screams, scuffles, and shouts. The first, who had transformed himself into a knight using a stainless steel salad bowl helm and a gray T-shirt covered with silver duct tape, brandished a wooden yardstick. The second boy, who was identical to the first in every way except for his costume, wore a green raincoat. He had the hood pulled up and tied under his chin and he carried two hand rakes. His lips were closed around a New Year's Eve party favor and every time he exhaled, its multi-colored paper tongue would uncurl with a shrill squeak.

"Boys!" Jane called out to no effect. Her sons dashed around chairs and side tables, nearly overturning the coffee table and its collection of paperweights and framed family photos.

Sinclair tried to get between the knight and the dragon. "Saint George," he said in a voice that rang with authority, though it was no more than a whisper. "Might I suggest that you conquer this terrifying serpent outdoors? Things are likely to get broken in the fierce struggle between man and beast."

The first boy bowed gallantly and pointed his sword at Jane. "Fair maid, I've come to rescue you from your tower."

Jane giggled. "Thank you, Sir Fitz, but I am quite happy up here."

Refusing to be upstaged by his twin brother, the other boy growled and circled around a leather chair and ottoman, a writing desk, and a globe on a stand in order to position himself directly under the ladder. "If you don't give me all of your gold, then I'll eat you!" he snarled and held out his hand rakes.

Doing her best to appear frightened, Jane clutched at her chest. "Please, oh fearsome and powerful dragon. I have no gold. In fact, my castle is falling apart around me. I was just wishing for a fairy godmother to float down and—"

"There aren't any fairies in this story!" the dragon interrupted crossly. "Fairies are for *girls*."

"Yeah," the knight echoed indignantly.

Jane knew she had offended her six-year-old sons, but before she could make amends, her eye fell on the ruler in Fitz's hands and an idea struck her.

"Fitz, Hem, you are my heroes!" she cried, hurrying down the ladder.

The boys exchanged befuddled glances. "We are?" They spoke in unison, as they so often did.

"But I'm supposed to be a monster," Hem objected.

Jane touched his cheek. "And you've both been so convincing that you can go straight to the kitchen and tell Mrs. Hubbard that I've given my permission for each of you to have an extra piece of chocolate-dipped shortbread at tea this afternoon."

Their gray eyes grew round with delight, but then Fitz whispered something in Hem's ear. Pushing back his salad bowl helm, he gave his mother a mournful look. "Mrs.

Hubbard won't believe us. She'll tell us that story about the boy who cried wolf again."

"I'll write a note," Jane said. The boys exchanged high fives as she scribbled a few lines on an index card.

"Shall I tuck this under one of your scales, Mr. Dragon?" She shoved the note into the pocket of Hem's raincoat. "Now run along. Sinclair and I have a party to plan."

Sinclair waited for the boys to leave before seating himself at his desk chair. He uncapped a fountain pen and held it over a clean notepad. "A party, Miss Jane?"

Jane flounced in the chair across from him and rubbed her palm over the cover of the small book in her hands. "This is Agatha Christie's *Death on the Nile*."

"Are we having a Halloween party then?" Sinclair asked. "With pharaohs and mummies and such?" He furrowed his shaggy brows. "Did the boys' getups influence your decision?"

"Not just a costume party. Think bigger." Jane hugged the book to her chest with one hand and gestured theatrically with the other. "An entire week of murder and mayhem. We'll have a fancy dress ball and award prizes to those who most emulate their fictional detectives. Just think," she continued, warming to her idea. "We'll have Hercule Poirot, Sherlock Holmes, Sam Spade, Lord Peter Wimsey, Nick and Nora Charles, Brother Cadfael, Miss Marple, and so on. We'll have readings and skits and teas and banquets. We'll have mystery scavenger hunts and trivia games! Imagine it, Sinclair."

He grimaced. "I'm trying, Miss Jane, but it sounds like an awful lot of hubbub and work. And for what purpose?"

"Money," Jane said simply. "Storyton Hall will be bursting at the seams with paying guests. They'll have the time of their lives and will go home and tell all of their friends how wonderful it was to stay at the nation's only resort catering specifically to readers. We need to let the world know that while we're a place of peace and tranquility, we also offer excitement and adventure."

Sinclair fidgeted with his bowtie again. "Miss Jane, forgive me for saying so, but I believe our guests are interested in three things: comfort, quiet, and good food. I'm not certain they're interested in adventure."

"Our readers aren't sedentary," Jane argued. "I've seen them playing croquet and lawn tennis. I've met them on the hiking and horseback riding trails. I've watched them row across the lake in our little skiffs and walk into Storyton Village. Why wouldn't they enjoy a weekend filled with mystery, glamour, and entertainment?"

The carriage clock on Sinclair's desk chimed three times. "Perhaps you should mention the proposal to your great aunt and uncle over tea?"

Jane nodded in agreement. "Brilliant idea. Aunt Octavia is most malleable when she has a plate piled high with scones and lemon cakes. Thank you, Sinclair!" She stood up, walked around the desk, and kissed him lightly on the cheek.

He touched the spot where his skin had turned a rosy shade of pink. "You're welcome, Miss Jane, though I don't think I was of much help."

"You're a librarian," she said on her way out. "To me, that makes you a bigger hero than Saint George, Sir William Wallace, and all of the Knights of the Round Table put together."

"I love my job," Jane heard Sinclair say before she closed the door.

Jane turned in the opposite direction of the main elevator and headed for the staircase at the other end of a long corridor carpeted in a lush crimson. She was accustomed to traveling a different route than the paying guests of Storyton Hall. Like the rest of the staff, Jane moved noiselessly through a maze of narrow passageways, underground tunnels, dim stairways, attic accesses, and hidden doors to keep herself as unobtrusive as possible.

Storyton had fifty bedrooms, eleven of which were on

the main floor. And even though Jane's great aunt and uncle were in their late seventies, they preferred to remain in their third-story suite of apartments, which included their private library and cozy sitting room where her aunt liked to spend her evenings reading.

Trotting down a flight of stairs, Jane paused to straighten her skirt before entering the main hallway. Along the wood-paneled walls hung with gilt-framed mirrors, gilt sconces, and massive oil paintings in ornate gilt frames massive oak doors stood open, inviting guests to wile away the hours reading in the Jane Austen Drawing Room, the Ian Fleming Lounge, the Isak Dinesen Safari Study, the Daphne du Maurier Parlor, and so on. There was also a Beatrix Potter play-room for children, but that was located on the basement level as most of the guests preferred not to hear the shrieks and squeals of children when they were trying to lose themselves in a riveting story.

Jane greeted every guest with a "hello" and a smile though her mind was focused on other things. She made a mental checklist as she walked. *The door handles need polishing. A light bulb's gone out by the entrance to Shakespeare's Theater. Eliza needs to stop putting goldenrod in the flower vases; there's pollen on all the tables and the guests are sneezing.*

She'd almost reached the sun porch when the tiny speakers mounted along the crown molding in the main hallway began to play a recording of bells chiming. Jane glanced at her watch. It was exactly three o'clock.

"Oh, it's teatime!" a woman examining a painting of cherry blossoms exclaimed. Taking the book from a man sitting in one of the dozens of wing chairs lining the hall, she gestured for him to get to his feet. "Come on, Bernard! I want to be get there first today."

Jane knew there was slim chance of that happening. Guests began congregating at the door of the Agatha Christie Tea Room at half past two. Bobbing her head at the eager pair, she walked past the chattering men, women, and children heading to tea and arrived at the back terrace to find her great aunt and uncle seated at a round table with the twins. The table was covered with a snowy white cloth, a vase stuffed with fuchsia peonies, and her aunt's Wedgwood tea set.

"There you are, dear!" Aunt Octavia lifted one of her massive arms and waved regally. Octavia was a very large, very formidable woman. She adored food and loathed exercise. As a result, she'd steadily grown in circumference over the decades and showed no predisposition toward changing her habits, much to her doctor's consternation.

"Hello, everyone," Jane said as she took a seat. This was the only time during the day in which she would sit in view of the guests. Very few people noticed the Steward family gathering for tea, being far too busy filling their plates with sandwiches, scones, cookies, and cakes inside the main house.

Fitz plucked her sleeve. "Mom, can I have another lemon cake?" He glanced at his brother. "Hem too?"

"Fitzgerald Steward," Aunt Octavia said in a low growl. "You've already had enough for six boys. So has Hemingway. Let your mother pour herself some tea before you start demanding seconds. And you should say 'may I' not 'can I.'"

Nodding solemnly, Fitz sat up straight in his chair and cleared his throat. Doing his best to sound like an English aristocrat, he said, "Madam, may we please have another cake?"

This time, the question was directed at Aunt Octavia. Before she could answer, Hem piped up in a Cockney accent. "Please, mum. We're ever so 'ungry."

Aunt Octavia burst out laughing and passed the platter of sweets. "Incorrigible," she said and put a wrinkled hand over Jane's. "Are you going to the village after tea? Mabel called to say that my new dress is ready, and I can't wait to see it. Hot pink with sequins and brown leopard spots. Can you imagine?"

Jane could. Her aunt wore voluminous housedresses fashioned from the most exotic prints and the boldest colors available. She ordered bolts of cloth from an assortment of catalogues and had Mabel Wimberly, a talented seamstress who lived in Storyton Village, sew the fabric into a garment she could slip over her head. Each dress had to come complete with several pockets as Aunt Octavia walked with the aid of a rhinestone studded cane and liked to load her pockets with gum, hard candy, pens, a notepad, bookmarks, and nail clippers. Today, she wore a black and lime zebra-striped dress and a black sunhat decorated with ostrich feathers.

And while Aunt Octavia's attire was flamboyant, Uncle Aloysius dressed like the country gentleman he was. His slacks and shirt were perfectly pressed and he always had a handkerchief peeking from the pocket of his suit. The only deviation from this conservative ensemble was his hat. Aloysius wore his fishing hat, complete with hooks, baits, and flies, all day long. He even wore it to church and Aunt Octavia had to remind him to remove it once the service got under way. Some of the staff whispered that he wore it to bed as well, but Jane didn't believe it. After all, several of the hooks looked rather sharp.

"What sandwiches did Mrs. Hubbard make today?" she asked her great uncle.

He patted his flat stomach. Uncle Aloysius was as tall and slender as his wife was squat and round. He was all points and angles to her curves and rolls. Despite their contrasting physical appearances and the passage of multiple decades, the two were still very much in love. Jane's great uncle liked to tell people that he was on a fifty-five-year honeymoon. "My darling wife will tell you that the egg salad and chive is the best," he said. "I started with the brie, watercress, and walnut." He handed Jane the plate of sandwiches and a pair of silver tongs. "That was lovely, but not as good as the fig and goat cheese."

"In that case, I'll have one of each." Jane helped herself

to the diminutive sandwiches. "And a raisin scone." Her gaze alighted on the jar of preserves near Aunt Octavia's elbow. "Is that Mrs. Hubbard's blackberry jam?"

"Yes and it's magnificent. But don't go looking for the Devonshire cream. The boys and I ate every last dollop." Her great aunt sat back in her chair, rested her tiny hands on her great belly, and studied Jane's face. "You've got a spark about you, my girl. Care to enlighten us as to why you have a skip in your step and a twinkle in your eye?"

Jane told her great aunt and uncle about her Murder and Mayhem Week idea.

Uncle Aloysius leaned forward and listened without interruption, nodding from time to time. Instantly bored by the topic, Fitz and Hem scooted their chairs back and resumed their knight and dragon personas by skirmishing a few feet from the table until Aunt Octavia shooed them off.

"Go paint some seashells green," she told Hem. "You can't be a decent dragon without scales. We have an entire bucket of shells in the craft closet."

"What about me?" Fitz asked. "What else do I need to be a knight?"

Aunt Octavia examined him closely. "A proper knight needs a horse. Get a mop and paint a pair of eyes on the handle."

Without another word, the twins sprinted for the basement stairs. Jane saw their sandy heads disappear and grinned. Her aunt had encouraged her to play similar games when she was a child and it gave her a great deal of satisfaction to see her sons doing the same.

"'Imagination is more important than knowledge,'" was Aunt Octavia's favorite quote and she repeated it often. She said it again now and then waved for Jane to continue.

Throughout the interruption, Uncle Aloysius hadn't taken his eyes off Jane once. When she finished outlining her plan, he rubbed the white whiskers on his chin and gazed out across the wide lawn. "I like your idea, my dear. I like it very much. We can charge our guests a special weekly rate. And by special, I mean higher. We'd have to ask a pretty penny for the additional events. I expect we'll need to hire extra help."

"But you think it will work?"

"I do indeed. It's splendid," he said, smiling at her. "It could be the start of a new tradition. Mystery buffs in October, Western readers in July, fantasy fans for May Day."

"A celebration of romance novels for Valentine's!" Aunt Octavia finished with a sweep of her arm.

Uncle Aloysius grabbed hold of his wife's hand and planted a kiss on her palm. "It's Valentine's Day all year long with you, my love."

Jane felt a familiar stab of pain. It was during moments like these that she missed her husband the most. She'd been a widow for six years and had never been able to think of William Elliot without a pang of sorrow and agony. Watching her great uncle and aunt murmur endearments to each other, she wondered if ten years would be enough time to completely heal the hole in her heart left by her husband's passing.

"Jane? Are you gathering wool?" Aunt Octavia asked.

Shaking off her melancholy, Jane reached for the teapot and poured herself a nice cup of Earl Grey. "I'm afraid I was. Sorry."

"No time for drifting off," Uncle Aloysius said. "There's much to be done to prepare for this Murder and Mayhem Week of yours. And might I say." He paused to collect himself and Jane knew that he was about to pay her a compliment. Her uncle was always very deliberate when it came to words of praise or criticism. "Your dedication to Storyton Hall does the Steward name proud. I couldn't have asked for a more devoted heir."

Jane thanked him, drank the rest of her tea, and went into the manor house through the kitchen. She tarried for a moment to tell the staff how delicious the tea service was and then walked down the former servants' passage to her small, windowless office.

Sitting behind her desk, Jane flexed her fingers over her computer keyboard and began to type a list of possible events, meals, and decorating ideas for the Murder and Mayhem Week. Satisfied that Storyton Hall's future guests would have a wide range of activities and dining choices during the mystery week, she set about composing a newsletter announcing the dates and room rates. She made the special events appear even more enticing by inserting colorful stock photos of bubbling champagne glasses, people laughing, and couples dancing at a costume ball. She also included the book covers of some of Christie's best known works as well as tantalizing photographs of Storyton's most impressive dinner and dessert buffets.

"They'll come in droves," she said to herself, absurdly pleased by the end result of the newsletter. "Uncle Aloysius is right. If this event is a resounding success, we can add on more and more over the course of the year. Then, we'll be able to fix this old pile of stones until it's just like it was when crazy Walter Egerton Steward had it dismantled, brick by brick, and shipped across the Atlantic. We'll restore the folly and the hedge maze and the orchards." Her eyes grew glassy and she gazed off into the middle distance. "It'll be as he dreamed it would be. An English estate hidden away in the wilds of the Virginia mountains. An oasis for book lovers. A reader's paradise amid the pines."

She reread the newsletter once more, searching for typos or grammatical errors, and, finding none, saved the document. She then opened a new email message and typed *newsletter recipients* in the address line. It gave her a little thrill to know that thousands of people would soon read about Storyton Hall's first annual Murder and Mayhem Week.

After composing a short email, Jane hit send, releasing her invitation into the world. Within seconds, former guests, future guests, and her newspaper and magazine contacts would catch a glimpse of what promised to be an unforgettable seven days. Tomorrow, she'd order print brochures to be mailed to the people on her contact list who preferred a more old-fashioned communication.

I'll have contacted thousands of people by the end of the week, Jane thought happily. *Thousands of potential guests. Thousands of lovely readers.*

But the lovely readers weren't the only ones who'd be receiving Jane Steward's invitation.

A murderer would get one too.